BORROW THE NIGHT

Judge Ralph Addison has been receiving threatening letters for the past six days, but he hasn't taken them seriously. Until now. The seventh letter is followed up by a phone call. He is being watched. Perhaps this isn't just a prank. The letter states that "you will die when Messick dies," and is signed "Mr. Justice." The judge had sentenced young Walter Messick to death for the murder of Faye Harper. But when he goes to the D.A. with his fears, he finds that Patrolman Matt Coleman, also involved in the case, has received the same threatening letters. And now that Messick's execution is upon them, together they only have one day to find out the truth…or die at the hands of Mr. Justice.

THE FIFTH CALLER

Dr. Lillian Whitehall has been brutally murdered. DA Inspector Doug Marchall knows that the crime occurred at 5:20pm because she was bludgeoned to death with a clock. Everyone assumes that the murderer is her Hungarian nurse, Anna Bardossy, who is lying in a hospital bed, the victim of a suicide attempt and now suffering amnesia. But there were other callers that day: her high-strung patient, her exacting lawyer, her unemployed brother. They all paint a picture of poor put-upon Dr. Whitehall, badgered by her unfaithful nurse. But could there have been another caller, someone who knew what had happened to An~ caused the doctor's all-too-timel~

HELEN NIELSEN BIBLIOGRAPHY
(1918-2002)

SIMON DRAKE SERIES
Gold Coast Nocturne (1951; reprinted in pb
  as Dead on the Level, 1954; UK as Murder by Proxy, 1952)
After Midnight (1966)
A Killer in the Street (1967)
The Darkest Hour (1969)
The Severed Key (1973)
The Brink of Murder (1976)

NOVELS
The Kind Man (1951)
Obit Delayed (1952)
Detour (1953; reprinted in pb as Detour to Death, 1955)
The Woman on the Roof (1954)
Stranger in the Dark (1955)
Borrow the Night (1956; reprinted in pb
  as Seven Days Before Dying, 1958)
The Crime is Murder (1956)
False Witness (1959)
The Fifth Caller (1959)
Sing Me a Murder (1960)
Woman Missing and Other Stories (1961)
Verdict Suspended (1964)
Shot on Location (1971)

Borrow the Night

— — — — — —

The Fifth Caller

TWO NOVELS BY

Helen Nielsen

Introduction by Nicholas Litchfield

STARK
HOUSE

Stark House Press • Eureka California

BORROW THE NIGHT / THE FIFTH CALLER

Published by Stark House Press
1315 H Street
Eureka, CA 95501, USA
griffinskye3@sbcglobal.net
www.starkhousepress.com

ISBN-13: 978-1-944520-72-4

Book design by Mark Shepard, SHEPGRAPHICS.COM
Proofreading by Bill Kelly

First Stark House Press Edition: May 2019

FIRST EDITION

7
Helen Nielsen's Ticking Clock
Suspense Novels
by Nicholas Litchfield

13
Borrow the Night
By Helen Nielsen

147
The Fifth Caller
By Helen Nielsen

Helen Nielsen's Ticking Clock Suspense Novels
by Nicholas Litchfield

Born in Roseville, Illinois, Helen Bernice Nielsen, who died in 2002 aged 83, was a prolific writer of mysteries and scripts for such television dramas as *Perry Mason*, *Alfred Hitchcock Presents*, *Alcoa Theatre* and *87th Precinct*. Prior to becoming a writer, she studied journalism, art and aeronautical drafting at the Chicago Art Institute, among other schools, and was a draftsman during World War II, working in a California airplane factory assisting in the designs of B-36 and P-80 aircraft.

She remained in California after the war, spending the best part of her life in Orange County and Oceanside, and turned to fiction writing in the late 1940s, penning nearly fifty short stories for *Manhunt*, *Alfred Hitchcock's Mystery Magazine*, and *Ellery Queen's Mystery Magazine*. Her debut novel, a mystery titled *The Kind Man*, was released in 1951 by Ives Washburn and reprinted by Victor Gollancz and Dell Publishing.

Nielsen went on to write at least eighteen novels, many of which received very favorable reviews in *The New York Times*, the *San Francisco Chronicle*, *New York Herald Tribune*, and other major periodicals. The jacket of *The Crime is Murder* (1956) quotes Mystery Writers of America Grand Master Dorothy B. Hughes as saying, "Helen Nielsen is one of the truly genuine talents of the past five years."

Perhaps her most significant success was her second novel, *Gold Coast Nocturne*, which was made into the 1954 movie *Blackout* (released as *Murder by Proxy* in the UK), directed by acclaimed British film director Terence Fisher who is best remembered for his many Hammer Horror films, including the classics *The Curse of Frankenstein* and *Dracula*. This wasn't Nielsen's only work to be adapted to screen. Several of her other stories were made into teleplays. She typically adapted them herself, as was the case with *The Fifth Caller*, a lean but well-developed murder mystery, published in January 1959 by William Morrow and Company, that she turned into an episode of *The Dick Powell Show* in 1961.

The plot concerns an elderly female psychotherapist—the testy, imperious Dr. Lillian Whitehall—who is found murdered in her study, with the chief suspect being the doctor's beautiful and intelligent assistant, Anna Bardossy, a Hungarian refugee with an interesting past and a delicate employer-employee relationship. Dr. Whitehall, whom we are told looked on Bardossy as her "spiritual daughter," sponsored her immigration from a refugee camp in Switzerland, and Bardossy, like it or not, was beholden to her.

The novel deviates somewhat from the traditional whodunit in that the suspect, discovered unconscious on a beach in Santa Monica with her wrists slashed, wakes in a nearby hospital suffering from amnesia. The following twenty-four hours consists of Douglas Marshall, an investigator from the district attorney's office, trying to determine the motive and encourage a confession. In an effort to get to the truth quickly, he invites into the hospital the people who visited the murder victim in the hours leading up to her death, and then he questions them in Bardossy's presence, while she recovers in her hospital bed. It's an unusual tactic that results in xenophobic outbursts, bickering, and candid disclosures.

As with the other novel in this Stark House combined edition, time is a crucial element. Conveniently, the thoughtful murderer used as their weapon a heavy desk clock, set in a wedge of thick crystal, and gave vent to fury, crushing the victim's skull with it. The stopped hands signal Dr. Whitehall's time of death.

Marshall, "a thorough man" with "a mechanical brain, an iron constitution, and an indomitable will" who "probes and probes and probes," hears each of the caller's statements, while at the same time gauging Bardossy's response, and attempts to establish the events leading up to the murder. Ultimately, his investigation hinges on the identity of the mysterious fifth and final caller.

Nielsen delights in throwing suspicion on each of the people in Dr. Whitehall's immediate circle of acquaintances, none of whom are likable. In fact, the more you learn about the victim, the more objectionable she seems, and the more you wonder about her relationship with Bardossy. Was there violent hostility between the two, and is the patient hiding her memory from Marshall or is she genuinely devoid of it?

The novel proved popular, despite mixed reviews upon its release, and while writers like Francis Iles, pseudonym of English crime writer Anthony Berkeley Cox, weren't overly complimentary toward the book in *The Guardian*, other critics expressed praise. In particular, mystery fiction critic Drexel Drake (aka Charles H. Huff) had positive things to say in the *Chicago Tribune*, and the acclaimed British crime writer Julian Symons, an Edgar Award winner and MWA Grand Master, described the novel in

The Sunday Times as "absorbingly and deliciously readable."

The other novel in this collection, *Borrow the Night*, published in January 1956, again by Morrow, is a highly suspenseful and unpredictable mystery that keeps you guessing until the final page. The strength of the novel lies in the exceptionally well-sketched principle characters and the skillful way Nielsen drops hints and revelations and introduces unexpected plot twists to cast doubt on just about everybody.

Discussing her fiction, Nielsen has been quoted as saying: "I am old-fashioned enough to believe that characters still make a story, and that every story, especially a mystery, must have a beginning, a middle and an ending." In the case of *Borrow the Night*, it is as much a character study as it is a story.

It begins with Judge Ralph G. Addison, an expectant father, receiving in the mail a typewritten death threat that is "as polite and direct as a form letter due bill." (There are echoes of *The Fifth Caller* here, where Dr. Whitehall received anonymous typewritten letters of complaint against her psychotherapy diagnoses.) Addison's letter, signed by a mysterious person calling himself "Mr. Justice," proclaims Addison guilty of sentencing an innocent youth to death and vows the judge "will die when Messick dies."

The "innocent youth" is Walter Messick, a poor boy from the slums who was tried, convicted, and sentenced to death for the murder of a young woman on Christmas Eve, fourteen years earlier. Labeled "the Christmas Eve Slayer" in newspapers, Merrick is due to be put to death in a matter of days.

Addison burns this and subsequent letters which is a strange act for a man in his profession, but there are circumstances that can make even the most illogical act seem rational. His justification is that he believes the threats to be a hoax and fears his wife may discover the letters and that the "great emotional upset could cause her to lose this child." He isn't the only recipient of such letters. Patrolman Matthew Coleman returns home from a vacation to find six letters from Mr. Justice holding him accountable for Merrick's arrest and accusing him of "withholding evidence and conspiring to obstruct justice." The final message has the added postscript: "It may interest you to know that you will not die alone, as Messick must, but will be accompanied into the hereafter by Judge Ralph Addison."

By the time Coleman approaches District Attorney Halam Mills with the letters, there is only one day remaining before Merrick's execution. As Mills won't reopen the case, and with their lives in jeopardy, Coleman proposes that he and Addison play detective for the next twenty-four hours and re-examine the case using police methods.

What follows is an utterly fascinating, desperate search for the truth, with the meticulous and conscientious Addison and the calm, methodical, tenacious Coleman attempting to achieve overnight what two months of investigation prior to Messick's arrest failed to do. Focusing on the pieces of the investigation that were overlooked the first time around, including a beige silk headscarf and an unidentified late-night visitor to the dead victim's apartment, their investigation leads to more clues and a growing list of suspects.

Adding to the tension is the ticking clock scenario. It was a stopped clock in *The Fifth Caller*, with Marshall piecing together the minute-by-minute events of the day right up until the murder. Here, Addison and Coleman have to beat the clock to establish the truth.

The characters also have to contend with the stifling summer heat, which grips the back of their necks and acts like "a barbed-wire coronet" around their temples, and over their eyes. This overwhelmingly warm weather provides everyone with a guilty-looking, sweaty sheen to their face, from the defendant's shady lawyer, who seems to be everywhere, and Addison's snooping best friend, who seems strangely out of place, to the troubled, altruistic Coleman, who appears to carry the world on his shoulders. On top of this, Addison is in a perpetual panic about his wife, who is due to give birth at any moment, losing the son he's always wanted.

All of these ingredients help make *Borrow the Night* an intense, slick thriller that shakes and stirs and teases the reader until the novel's powerful climax. Intelligent and provocative, with a clear anti-death penalty message, it's a memorable whodunit that plays out in sharp contrast to one of those edge-of-your-seat courtroom dramas where the audience cheers at the judge's verdict.

Unlike a jury, not every reader has to agree. Mystery author Anthony Boucher, who wrote numerous favorable reviews of Nielsen's books in his long-running crime fiction column for *The New York Times*, was evidently an admirer of the author. The many shocks and surprises and veiled motives in this novel made him yearn for more clarity.

By and large, though, the book received very positive reviews. Australian writer Ray Mathew of *The Sydney Morning Herald* called it engrossing, convincing, earnest, and exciting, and focused on Nielsen's enormous talent for characterization, considering Addison so fully-fleshed that he seemed like "a real man with a real history of character-formation and pain." Huff of the *Chicago Tribune* also liked it, selecting it as one of the best mystery novels of 1956 and calling it "a novel that sparkles with originality and accomplishes tremendous suspense." Richardson of *The Observer* declared it a "very tense superior mystery thriller" and a return to "pristine form" for Nielsen.

Reasoned and satisfying rather than contrived, my verdict is that the eloquent, philosophical, jaw-dropping conclusion to Nielsen's gripping tale provides a smart, impactful closing statement.

As with many mystery writers whose star shone brightest in the 1950s, Nielsen's once-popular fiction is not well-known today and is due for rediscovery. Fortunately, she left behind a vast canon of work, including these two exemplary mystery novels that are sure to leave you on edge and breathless and in search of more of her thrilling, intricate, and astutely written tales.

—December 2018
Rochester, NY

Nicholas Litchfield is the founding editor of the literary magazine *Lowestoft Chronicle*, author of the suspense novel *Swampjack Virus*, and editor of eight literary anthologies. He has worked in various countries as a tabloid journalist, librarian, and media researcher. He writes regularly for the *Colorado Review*, and his weekly book reviews for the *Lancashire Post* are syndicated to twenty newspapers across the UK.

Borrow the Night

Helen Nielsen

Dedication: FOR PAT AND ED.

I must become a borrower of the night
For a dark hour or twain.
—*Macbeth*, Act III, Scene 1.

CHAPTER ONE

It came by regular mail in a cheap white envelope that could have been purchased at any dime store. It bore a local postmark and no return, except a printed notation in the upper left-hand corner: After Five-Days Return to—, followed by two blank lines and one more printed line: Los Angeles, California. The address was typewritten: Judge Ralph G. Addison, 2704 Terrace View Drive, L. A. 39, and the single sheet of unruled tablet paper contained in the envelope carried a message, also typewritten, that was as polite and direct as a form letter due bill. It read:

Hon. Ralph G. Addison
Judge, Superior Court
County of Los Angeles

Dear Sir:
I regret to inform you that you have but one week to live. At ten o'clock Friday morning, July 29, an innocent youth will pay with his life for the murder of Faye Harper. Because you sentenced Walter Messick to death, I sentence you. "For with what judgment ye judge, ye shall be judged; and with what measure ye mete, it shall be measured to you again." (Matt. 7:2)
You will die when Messick dies. Until that hour, I will be watching you.
                                                              Mr. Justice.

The message was dated, Thursday, July 21. It was delivered the following morning and read by Judge Addison in his study just prior to leaving for court, read, studied, examined, and then crumpled and tossed into the wastebasket. A few seconds later, it was retrieved from the wastebasket and carefully burned in the fireplace until nothing remained but a fine, black ash.

That had been the morning of July 22.

It was the hottest July anyone could remember. It was so hot, and had been so hot for so many weeks, there was no longer any means of measuring the heat. A thermometer was inadequate. What was needed was some kind of scale that would register the relentless pressure steadily reducing an entire city to a state of nervous exhaustion. Residents who had complained all winter of the unusual cold were threatening to sell out and go back East, and tourists were muttering unkind remarks about know-it-alls who insisted they must pack a heavy coat for the chilly evenings. There were no chilly evenings, and the mornings were like the foyer of hell.

Ralph Addison swam in to meet the morning through a pool of his own sweat. There was always a time, between unconsciousness and awareness, when he had to remember where he was. This morning the shore seemed unfamiliar; it wasn't yellow. Yellow was the color of the bedroom walls, or had been when last he noticed. Prior to that, they had been pink, aqua, antique ivory, and at least half-a-dozen other shades he couldn't recall even when fully awake. Abbie was a habitual changer. She changed color schemes, draperies, and furniture arrangements perpetually, as if the constant changing and rearranging might make something old seem new again, or something lost seem found. Ralph never protested. It was Abbie's house, a wedding gift from her father, and in more than fourteen years of marriage just about everything in it had changed—especially the two people who shared it.

Just about everything, but not quite. Now that his eyes were opening wider, Ralph knew where he was. The study never changed. Paint had never touched these pine-paneled walls, his desk still stood on the spot he'd chosen the day it came from the furniture store, and the old leather chair by the fireplace was a homely survivor of his first law office. It was good, Ralph Addison thought, for a house to have one room that never changed, and his morning eyes took reassuring inventory as he separated his six-foot-long body from the five-foot-short couch. Everything was the same: the long bookcases where the lives and deeds of great men—Jefferson, Holmes, Brandeis—stood back to back (there was an unfinished manuscript of his own somewhere in the desk that had been meant to stand with them one day), the framed parchment replica of the Bill of Rights hanging on the wall, the old clock on the mantelpiece ...

Particularly the old clock on the mantelpiece. It was an ugly clock. Its hand-carved wooden case was chipped and scarred, and its face was a dirty yellow; but it had belonged to Ralph's father, who was a carpenter; his grandfather, who was a farmer; and his great-grandfather, who had made the clock with his own hands in a small European village where everything was made for the generations to come. Now it belonged to a man who was a lawyer and a judge, and this seemed significant. On his feet now, slipperless and with his pajama legs screwed high above his bony ankles, Ralph stumbled across the room to perform a daily ritual. Beside the old clock on the mantel was a big brass key. He took the key in one hand and was reaching out with the other to open the glass door over the yellow face when that time between unconsciousness and awareness suddenly ended. It ended with all the subtlety of a scream.

Why weren't the walls yellow? Why had he slept in the study? There were answers and answers. There was the one he would give Abbie: the heat.

The convenient heat, catchall excuse for a million sets of ragged nerves. God bless the heat wave and let it last! There was the unspoken reason: the seven months' imprisonment of two people confined to solitary in the same room. The long tension, the long denial.

"A serene state of mind," Stu had said, "that's the important thing. There's a better than even chance that Abbie can have this child if she maintains a serene state of mind. No exertion, no excitement, no anxiety. But if she loses this baby, too ..."

If you hadn't known Stu since your college days, or as in Abbie's case, since childhood, you spelled his name Stuart Wilder, M.D. and paid a stiff fee just to hear those words from one of the city's leading obstetricians. But if you had watched something dying for fourteen years, and then saw it bloom again, you remembered the words as if they were engraved on a bronze plate riveted to your brain. *A serene state of mind ... no excitement ... no anxiety.*

And no terror. That was the answer; that's why the walls weren't yellow. The pillow and the twisted sheet on the couch meant that he'd fled downstairs in the night again. How many times this week—three, four? No matter. As long as the heat held, no matter. He was safe in the study. He could shout down a dream without being heard, and he could meet the stifling dawn with a sudden chill of remembrance that Abbie wouldn't see. That was the important thing. That was the only thing now.

When his mind was quite clear, Ralph put the brass key back on the mantel. Then he gathered up the pillow and the sheet and went out to the front steps to pick up the paper. It was still too early for the mail, and that was a good thing. It was hard enough to face Abbie as it was, and now he must go upstairs.

The fact that Abbie was his wife had never ceased to amaze Ralph Addison. She wasn't the most beautiful woman in the world and never had been. Her features were too regular, her figure was the kind that looks best in tweeds or something with a little ruffling to fill out the bosom, and he'd often wished she would find some new way of doing that pale-yellow pageboy bob. But Abbie was a Braidwell; she belonged in the world and never let it tell her otherwise. The Braidwells were a fine people, proud, strong, and competent. If they lacked genius, they possessed intellect; if they lacked fire, they possessed fidelity. They were the people who had coaxed, goaded, and sometimes tricked the race into civilization; and if it all blew up tomorrow, they would gather up the pieces and start over again. They were the natural leaders of the earth, and they terrified Ralph Addison— sometimes even Abbie.

But Abbie couldn't terrify anyone this morning. She was awake when Ralph entered the bedroom. She was sitting up in bed, her yellow hair spilled out against the pillows and her blue eyes wide and watching. She must have heard him coming up the stairs, because the smile she had ready when he opened the door looked as if it had been overrehearsed. It was the kind of smile a natural leader wears when the band plays "Nearer My God to Thee" and the ship goes down.

Ralph crossed over and tossed the sheet and pillow onto his own empty bed, and then sat down on the edge of Abbie's, careful of that precious hugeness under the sheet. He planted a quick kiss on her forehead and laid the newspaper beside her.

"Going to be another scorcher," he said. "Eighty-six on the front steps now. If this keeps up, we'll have to install a cooler."

The words meant nothing, of course. They filled up the space left empty by the things he couldn't say, and got the jump on the worried frown that had superseded her smile. He understood about the frown. No man looks judicial in his pajamas, particularly when his long frame has acquired so little flesh in forty years, and Abbie had a mothering look in her eyes. She reached up and pushed a damp spray of hair off his forehead—dark hair seeded lightly with gray.

"Couldn't you sleep any better downstairs?" she asked.

"The heat—" Ralph began, but it wasn't easy to fool Abbie.

"And the other things?"

Ralph drew back, and the sudden movement told her what she already knew.

"The waiting. The anxiety," she said. "Oh, I've had bad dreams, too."

"Abbie, you mustn't!"

"But not anymore. That's what I want to tell you, Ralph. For weeks now I've had such a strange and wonderful feeling, as if everything was all over and everything was all right. And it is, darling. This time it really is all right. I *know!*"

There was such sureness in Abbie's voice that it seemed her words were already true. Ralph leaned close and kissed her again, warmly and not on the forehead, and for that moment it was just as he wanted it to be. What had been lost could be found, and fourteen years were nothing measured against forever. But forever was a long time. As he drew away, his hand brushed against the folded newspaper and it fell open across the bed. It had been a dull night for the world. With no new crime, crisis, or calamity to enliven the headlines, there was room for an old sensation warmed over: CHRISTMAS EVE SLAYER DIES TOMORROW. Tomorrow. *At ten o'- clock, Friday morning, July 29.*

Ralph came quickly to his feet.

"It's late," he said. "I'd better get dressed."

Abbie wasn't supposed to have noticed anything. She was supposed to just lie there against the pillow and not look so troubled when she said, "The dark-blue suit, darling. Remember?"

"The dark-blue—?"

It was much too hot for the dark-blue suit unless there was something special. And there was something special, of course. Abbie remembered.

"Your speech, Ralph. The luncheon—it's today."

"Oh, no!"

"You didn't forget!"

"But I did! I've had so much on my mind—"

He didn't want to leave it like that. He wanted to explain. He wanted to drop down on the bed again and make it clear, some way, somehow, why it was that today, of all the days of the calendar, he couldn't make a speech. But he couldn't explain. *A serene state of mind.* He couldn't explain anything, and Abbie couldn't understand.

"But you promised," she coaxed. "It's Father's committee, Ralph—you can't disappoint Father. He's done so much for us!"

Abbie shouldn't have said that. She should have known better than to say anything so flagrantly true. So much! Abbie's house, Abbie's name. It didn't hurt a man in public life to be the son-in-law of Dr. Braidwell, dean of political science, friend of the Governor, master of better government organization since his retirement from the university.

"What is it this time?" Ralph asked bitterly. "Peace, tax reform, or slum clearance in Outer Mongolia?"

"Ralph!"

"Or juvenile delinquency? And if so, why doesn't he start with his own daughter? Do you know what time it was when that girl got in last night?"

"I do," Abbie said calmly. "It was ten minutes past one by my illuminated clock. They can't start a drive-in movie until after dark, you know."

"A drive-in movie!"

It wasn't important. It wasn't important at all, but once he'd started, Ralph couldn't stop until he'd found some place to put his anger.

"All right!" he cried. "If you don't mind your sister staying out to all hours with boys you don't even know, all right! But she's supposed to be down here to look after you. If she doesn't want to do it, let her say so. She can go back to Ojai and I'll hire a girl. I can at least afford to hire a girl!"

But he couldn't afford to go on betraying himself that way. The naked silence made that outburst ridiculous. A serene state of mind! Stu had prescribed for the wrong patient. It was his own nerves that were cracking up.

And now Abbie, who had said almost nothing, was looking at him strangely. So strangely that he was frightened even before she spoke.

"Ralph," she said, "don't!"

That was all. For two or three seconds, that was all. And then, "You've got to stop borrowing grief."

"Borrowing?" Ralph echoed.

"You always have, you know. Always."

Abbie's gaze dropped to the bed, and her fingers picked nervously at the edge of the newspaper. She was like a budget-minded housewife shopping for words, and then she looked up again.

"There's nothing to worry about," she said. "I'm fine, Ralph—honestly. Midge is fine, too, much more reliable than she seems, *and the world isn't going to end tomorrow morning at ten o'clock.*"

She said it deliberately. She sat there in her bed, staring at him over the great hulk of Abbie Addison, and said it so deliberately that he couldn't deny, or protest, or do anything at all but ask foolishly, "What do you mean?"

And she answered,

"Walter Messick. I've heard his name mentioned a few times in the night."

"You heard? What did I say?"

Her fingers were shredding the edge of the newspaper now.

"You can't, Ralph. You can't borrow that grief, too. It was the jury that condemned Walter Messick. You had to sentence him to die!"

That was all Abbie answered. Ralph waited, but that was all, and so there was only one thing he could do. He went to the closet and took out the dark-blue suit.

"Forget it," he said. "It's the heat. I'm liable to dream anything in this heat."

When Ralph came downstairs again, showered, shaved, and dressed for a speech, or a funeral, he didn't know whether or not Abbie had accepted his explanation. Abbie was a Braidwell, and Braidwells didn't tell. It was almost an hour before he knew the answer—a very long hour for a man with his eyes on the clock. The post came at nine. Give a little, take a little, the post came at nine. It was about a quarter to when the front-door chimes broke the tension with a happy little melody. He raced to the door, but it wasn't the post. It was Stu. There was nothing unusual about that—no excuse for the surprise and dismay on his face. Stu came every day. This morning he was early because of a tournament—golf, something like that. Ralph hardly heard Stu's explanation because his eyes were already busy with the street. It was empty. Except for Stu's long convertible at the curb, the street was completely empty as far as eye could see. He glanced at his watch and smiled grimly. Maybe the carrier was delayed because of the heat.

He was still waiting in the doorway when Stu came back downstairs and called him into the study.

Stuart Wilder was a handsome man; Ralph had always known that. Tall, rugged, sun-bronzed and blond, he might have been a dozen years his junior instead of a mere dozen months. And Stu had a certain manner, a real Prince Charming, the kind of man most women can't resist—but not the one woman. She, for some inconceivable reason, had preferred Ralph Addison. There were times when Ralph couldn't look at Stu without thinking of that; but this morning, in the face of that unexpected summons, he could think of but one thing.

"Abbie?" he began.

"No, not Abbie," Stu said quickly. "Not for a couple of weeks if all goes well."

"If—?"

This time Stu didn't answer so quickly; in fact, he didn't answer at all. He leaned up against one corner of the desk, half-sitting, half-standing, with one leg dangling and his bare arms folded across his chest. He had the casual air of a man who had lived all of his life in a house where nobody but the servants ever took meals in the kitchen, but there was nothing casual about his eyes. His eyes made Ralph feel like a specimen on a microscopic slide.

"Ralph," he said at last, "what the devil are you doing to yourself?"

There was nothing subtle about Stu Wilder. His bedside manner was like a linesman breaking from scrimmage.

"Look at you," he added, before Ralph could recover his speech. "If I hadn't known Ralph Addison since his very dull college days, I'd say he was suffering from an acute hangover! Now, what's this Abbie tells me about you having nightmares?"

Ralph had his answer then, and he didn't like it.

"Nightmares?" he echoed. "She's exaggerating."

"Abbie doesn't exaggerate," Stu said tersely. "Abbie's a level-headed, conservative woman who doesn't exaggerate or imagine troubles. She's worried, Ralph. She's worried about you, and I won't have that."

"But there's no reason!" Ralph protested.

"Exactly," Stu said. "No reason whatsoever. You've had the luckiest break a man ever had. When Abbie left you last November—"

"Abbie didn't leave me!"

It was a foolish thing to say, a wild thing. But the words had erupted from Ralph's tongue, and he could do nothing then but defend them.

"She went home for the holidays," he said. "Abbie's always gone home for the holidays. You know that!"

Stu didn't argue. Stu merely stared at him with analytical eyes, the diagnostician studying an interesting set of symptoms. "Was it really that bad?" he asked at last. "So bad that you have to lie to yourself and pretend it never happened?"

Some other day, if there were to be another day, Ralph might face Stu's eyes; not today. He walked over to the fireplace. He stared at the yellow face of the old clock and tried not to listen to the voice behind him.

"Lying to yourself won't change anything," Stu was saying, "but the mere fact that you try makes me certain that I'm right. Shall I tell you what's wrong, Ralph? You'll never tell me, that I know. You'll bottle up everything inside until you crack wide open—but I won't let you. For Abbie's sake, we're going to have this out right now."

"There's nothing to have out!" Ralph insisted, but only the old clock seemed to hear. Stu's voice kept right on talking behind him.

"I read you, Ralph. I read you down to the finest print. It's a great thing that's happened, isn't it—this child coming just when it seemed that everything between you and Abbie was finished? It's a miracle. It's a gift from God, and a man like Ralph Addison, who's never allowed himself a margin of error, begins to wonder if he's worthy of such a blessing. He begins to search his conscience, to judge, and condemn himself; and if it so happens that he was appointed to a new court just in time to pass the first death sentence of his career on a boy almost young enough to be the son he'd always wanted, then the sentence he passes on himself may well result in nightmares.

"That's the terrible injustice of self-condemnation, Ralph. A conscientious man makes no recommendation for clemency."

The voice stopped and Ralph listened to the echo of the words. It was quite an argument Stu had made, but he'd omitted one important detail, and Ralph was a meticulous man.

"And for what crime am I supposed to have sentenced myself?" he asked.

"A first-class worrier can always think of something," Stu said.

"What crime, Stu?"

Ralph turned back from the fireplace. There was an awkward moment, but once their eyes had met it was too late for evasion.

"I'm not passing judgment," Stu said, "you are. I only know that Abbie did leave you last November. Something had to be wrong for her to come to that decision after fourteen years."

"*Something?*"

Something was an indefinite word, but not the way Stu pronounced it, and not the way Ralph gave it back. "So you think there was another woman?"

"I didn't say that."

"But you inferred it plainly enough. You didn't get that from Abbie!"

"No, I didn't get that from Abbie," Stu admitted. "I didn't get anything from Abbie, and I don't think anyone else did. She simply arrived at her father's house in Ojai one day, bag and baggage, and that was it. Oh, I won't say that I was surprised. I'd have had to be blind not to know there was something wrong with this marriage. And I can't say I was sorry, except for Abbie, of course. I hated to see her hurt. But you did marry my girl, Ralph. I'd been waiting a long time to get her back."

Calmly and deliberately, Stu spoke the words. It was a bit direct, even for him, but this seemed to be the morning for frank and honest statements. First Abbie, with a name she must have kept to herself all week, and now this.

"Waiting?" Ralph echoed. "You *admit* that?"

And because it was the morning for frank and honest statements, Stu made no denial.

"Why not?" He shrugged. "I'm not waiting anymore. I gave that up when Abbie became ill and I was called up to Ojai to attend her. As soon as I knew she was pregnant, I knew that I had nothing to wait for. All Abbie wanted, all she'd ever wanted, was to be Ralph Addison's wife and bear his child."

A dry finality crept into Stu's voice, dry as the dead leaves that clutter late November's gutters. There was a memory in his words—for two men.

"I determined one thing that night," he said. "I swore by whatever gods I acknowledge that this time Abbie would keep her baby and her happiness. Afterwards, when I'd made sure she was safe and resting easily, I went out to call you. It was late, nearly 3:00 A.M., but I didn't think you'd mind being called out of bed to hear the news I had for you. But I didn't call you out of bed. I didn't raise you at all."

"I told you where I was that night," Ralph said quickly.

"You told me that you'd gone on a fishing trip."

"Well?"

"On a stormy night in December?"

There was no humor in the smile that touched Stu's lips. He paused significantly, but Ralph was too stunned to do any more than wait for whatever frank and honest statement was coming next. He hadn't long to wait.

"Oh, I'm not calling you a liar for one night," Stu added, "but the fact remains that Abbie did leave you, Ralph, and now you're torturing yourself with some problem you won't confide even to your oldest friend. Can't you see, I'm not trying to pry out the details of your break with Abbie from any morbid sense of curiosity! I care for only one thing: the happiness Abbie can have if you'll just forget whatever it was that tore you apart and remember what holds you together."

Stu waited for an answer. This was the moment he'd been building up to, the moment of the great confessional; but an old clock was wearing out time at Ralph's shoulder, and fear was a needle that injected strange thoughts into the mind. Stu came every day. Like the postman, Stu came every day. That's all Ralph could remember when he asked, "Are you finished now?"

"Then you won't tell me what's troubling you?" Stu persisted.

"There's nothing to tell!"

It was such an obvious lie that he had to shout it to make the words come at all. Stu unfolded his arms and got down off the desk. Ralph thought he was leaving at last, but then he paused and fixed him once more with those calculating eyes.

"Of course, I may be on the wrong track," he said. "If the trouble is money—?"

The words were unexpected. "What do you mean?" Ralph gasped, and that was a mistake because Stu had an answer.

"I play golf with your banker," he said. "Some time ago he asked if you'd ever decided to go ahead with your plans to remodel this house. Then he explained that you'd been in to see him about getting a loan on the property when Abbie was gone last winter. It's community property, of course, so he told you to get her signature. You never came back about the loan, but you did close out your savings account."

"I closed out—?"

So unexpected, Stu's words, and so revealing! Until now he'd been only an annoyance, a nagging competition for that yellow-faced timepiece on the mantel; but suddenly everything added up. Everything Stu thought, and had been thinking these long months, added up to an ugly, untidy sum.

"What are you trying to say?" Ralph demanded. "That I've been withdrawing money to keep another woman—is that it?"

"Ralph, for God's sake—" Stu protested.

"All right, I'll tell you! I'll tell you about that loan!"

Ralph swung about and faced the clock again. Words were what he needed now, and words weren't easy to come by on a morning when time was running out and Stu stood watching him with careful eyes.

"It was all for Abbie!" he blurted out at last. "It was a crazy idea, but it was for Abbie. When I learned of her condition—when I went up there after getting your wire and learned what she was in for being confined all these months in that bedroom upstairs, I wanted to have it fixed up. You know, new paint, new furniture, everything. You know how Abbie likes to have things fixed up. I wanted it for a surprise when she came home."

It was harder to face the clock than it was to face Stu. Ralph turned around again. Stu hadn't moved from his place beside the desk.

"It was a crazy idea," Ralph repeated. "We needed the money for the baby. As soon as I realized that, I put it back in the bank. Didn't your golfing friend tell you that? Didn't he tell you that I put all the money back in the bank?"

Stu might at least have answered. The words were going badly. "Lying to yourself won't change anything," Stu had said. Stu was right, and Ralph hated him for that.

"All right, Abbie did leave me," he cried out suddenly, "but not for the filthy reason you think! And she came back. That's what bothers you, isn't it? Abbie came back, and that's why you're tormenting me now."

Torment was the only word for the thing on Ralph's face, but it was all wrong. It was the scene in the bedroom all over again, and with every careless word Stu was becoming more curious. It was time to shut off the flow of words and retreat into silence again; but silence was a rare commodity in Abbie's house this morning. When the words stopped, the chimes began.

The chimes. Ralph struggled back to awareness. The chimes meant that the postman had come at last, but now it meant even more. Now it meant an excuse to break up this third degree and let Stu think whatever his wild imagination let him think. "Tormenting?" Stu echoed. "What do you mean?" but his question was for Ralph's back as he moved toward the hall. The chimes. And then there was another sound. Running footsteps were pounding down the stairs, and then a lean, lithe figure in a boyish shirt and blue jeans flashed past the doorway. Ralph quickened his pace, but he was no competition for an eager teen-ager who wasn't expected downstairs this side of noon. Midge reached the door ahead of him. She was just turning about, her close-cropped, tawny head bent over an assortment of letters, when he reached her. Without ceremony, he snatched the mail from her hands.

"Well, I like that!" the girl howled. "There's nothing for you anyway. Your love letter didn't come this morning."

Midge. A face like a slightly cynical angel with a poked-up nose that could find its way into everything. Love letter, she said! And they had an audience, of course. Stu hadn't stayed in the study alone.

"Love letter?" he echoed, coming toward the doorway. "What's all this about? Who's been getting love letters?"

"They must be love letters to get old sourpuss so hot and bothered," Midge muttered. "They've been coming every day—"

"I think you'd better see about getting breakfast for your sister," Ralph broke in sharply.

There must have been a very special anger in his voice. Ordinarily, Midge would have put up an argument. Maybe her feelings were hurt, or maybe she just recognized a situation when she saw one. She shrugged indifferently and drifted off down the hall. That left only Stu waiting for the explanation he wasn't going to get.

"That girl," Ralph muttered, "always teasing!"

That's all he said, and all he would say if Stu glared at him until doomsday.

When Stu had gone, reluctantly accepting the inevitable, Ralph went back into the study and closed the door. He went through the mail again, but Midge was still right: there was no letter today. He went to the desk and opened the top drawer. Out of it he took a handful of letters, each in the same cheap envelope, each with the same typewritten message. "I regret to inform you that you have but six days to live ... five days ... four ... three ... two." But no letter today!

For a long time Ralph stood beside the desk weighing the paper evidence in his hands. Last Friday he'd known what to do with a crank's letter—dispose of it quickly before it chanced to meet Abbie's eyes. But five days of repetition had taken its toll. Six threats, and now it was the last day before the execution and there was no letter at all.

It wasn't until he noticed how his hand was shaking that Ralph realized what a fool he'd been. A crank, of course! Who else would write such fantastic letters and then drop the threat when there was nothing left to be done but put it in action? Stu had been right about one thing anyway. A worried man could borrow a lot of trouble with practically no collateral—and how stupid to think it wouldn't show! Abbie, dear Abbie, who mustn't be worried at all costs, watching with troubled eyes, and Midge making no secret of what she'd seen come each morning in the mail. And Stu. Ralph shuddered when he thought of what he'd almost said to Stu. It wasn't within the realm of reason that a man who loved Abbie as Stu did would resort to trickery like this.

The evidence weighed, Ralph rendered a swift decision. He crossed to the fireplace once more, knelt down and touched the little messages from "Mr. Justice" with flame. It was over. It was as easy as that. He stood up and faced the old clock again. Time could run out now. Tomorrow some men would die, Walter Messick among them, but others would be born. That was the important thing. All that needed to be done now was to take up the brass key and wind the clock as if it were any other morning of any other week.

His hand was reaching for the key when the desk phone rang. The study phone was for professional calls—that's why it had an unlisted number—and a professional call could be urgent. He left the clock still unwound and returned to the desk. It was a man's voice that answered, muffled and strange.

"Good morning, Judge Addison. Lovely morning, isn't it? I just wanted to remind you to enjoy it while you can because, like Walter Messick, this is your last day."

CHAPTER TWO

At about the same moment Ralph was replacing the study phone in its cradle, a dazed and incredulous expression on his face, District Attorney Halam Mills was experiencing a similar reaction. It was hot on Temple Street. By half-past nine it was hot everywhere in the city, but in the district attorney's office heat came in two varieties: Fahrenheit and centigrade. On his desk was a small, key-shaped thermometer with a dual reading, a souvenir of some European nation (he couldn't recall which) that Mrs. Mills had visited last year. This year Mrs. Mills was doing Honolulu, but Mr. Mills was just doing time behind a desk that held, at the moment, a strange assortment of correspondence.

Across the desk from the silver-haired D.A. with the college-boy build sat a man of some fifty-odd years whose thinning hair was lightly etched with silver, but whose build had long since ceased to resemble a college boy's. There was a definite thickness about his waist and a slight drooping of his broad shoulders, as if life was beginning to catch up a bit and no great effort was being made to outdistance it. He would have been a tall man standing, but sitting there, his knees spread apart and his large feet pointed out like the flippers of a performing seal, he just looked bulky, tired, and hot. He was wearing a neat but inexpensive light-blue tropical-worsted suit, a wilted collar, and a troubled expression. The expression was the one thing he had in common with the district attorney.

"I don't understand," Mills said, frowning at the letters on his desk. "If you've been getting these threats all week, why have you waited until today to report them?"

The man in the light-blue suit patted his neck with a folded white handkerchief.

"I can explain that," he said. "I've been away all week, up to the Monterey Peninsula on a little vacation. Just got back last night and found these letters on the living-room floor. There's a mail slot on my front door. Everything comes right into the house."

The man stopped patting his neck and stuffed the folded handkerchief back into his breast pocket.

"When I opened the first one," he continued, "I thought it was a gag. Then I read all the others and it began to sound serious, especially this last one." He leaned closer to the desk and tapped one sheet of paper with a stubby forefinger. "This one involves somebody else. Crank or no crank, I figured you should know."

Six white envelopes, six typewritten messages. Halam Mills took the first one—he'd already arranged them in chronological order—and read the message through again. It was addressed to Patrolman Matthew Coleman, 1034 N. Citrus Grove Avenue, Hollywood 28. The message was brief but impressive:

Patrolman Coleman
Dear Sir:
I regret to inform you that you have but one week to live. At ten o'clock Friday morning, July 29, an innocent youth will pay with his life for the murder of Faye Harper. Because you arrested Walter Messick for this crime, I arrest you on the charge of withholding evidence and conspiring to obstruct justice. "For with what measure ye mete, it shall be measured unto you again." (Matt. 7:2)
You will die when Messick dies. Until that hour I will be watching you.
Mr. Justice.

The other messages were identical, except for the diminishing number of days, but the last letter, postmarked in time to have been delivered the previous day, had an added postscript: "It may interest you to know that you will not die alone, as Messick must, but will be accompanied into the hereafter by Judge Ralph Addison." Mills read this last letter a second time. Still frowning, he nudged the intercom alive.

"Miss Burgess," he said, "have you been able to reach Judge Addison?"

From the outer office a feminine voice answered, "Judge Addison's secretary says he hasn't come in yet, but she'll send him over the instant he does."

The intercom was snapped off and Mills leaned back in his chair. "This is fantastic!" he said. "It must be the work of a crank. Someone has a grudge against you, Coleman. You've been on the force long enough to know how a grudge can be worked up against a policeman."

"That I have," Coleman sighed, "but it's not just a policeman who's being threatened. According to this last letter, it's also the judge who sentenced Messick."

"And whose name has been mentioned in every newspaper rehash of the case ever since Messick was denied a reprieve," Mills interjected. "You know how these things start. Some crackpot follows a front-page murder trial until he thinks he knows more about it than judge, jury, or the entire legal structure. How about it, Coleman? Do you know anyone in your neighborhood who seems a little peculiar?"

"Any one?" Coleman echoed. "Do you want them alphabetically?"

The district attorney laughed softly. He was looking less troubled now. "I know what you mean," he murmured, "but that's about all it takes to set off one of these letter campaigns. You're right to report it, of course, but I'll lay odds it's just the work of a neighborhood crank with a gripe against anyone in a police uniform. You did say that you're uniformed, didn't you?"

The man in the light-blue suit frowned at the toes of his out-pointed shoes. "When I'm on duty," he answered, "but I haven't been feeling too well lately. I took a leave of absence—" He paused and looked up at Mills again. "It couldn't be one of my neighbors," he added thoughtfully. "These letters came while I was away. My neighbors knew I was gone."

"Then it's someone who knows your address."

"And the fact that I arrested Messick. That was last February, Mr. Mills. This crackpot must have a good memory."

Coleman's words seemed to annoy Mills. He fingered the key-shaped thermometer and indulged in a wistful thought of Waikiki. Then he brightened. "As I recall," he said, "you gave testimony at the trial."

"I did," Coleman said.

"All of which was duly reported by the press. No, our crackpot doesn't need a memory. All he needs is a set of clippings. And I still think this postscript was added just to give you a scare, which it apparently has. If Mr. Justice has some, dark fate in store for Judge Addison, why tell you? Why not tell Addison?"

"Maybe he has," Coleman suggested.

"Without my knowledge?" Mills leaned back in his chair and broke the tension with a hearty laugh. "I *know* Ralph Addison," he said. "I can assure you that any threat made against his life would have been reported immediately. He's just that kind of a conscientious—"

The intercom buzzed again and Mills flipped the switch. "Judge Addison is here now," Miss Burgess reported.

"Fine! Send him right in," Mills ordered. He leaned back in his chair again, smiling.

"Now we'll hear what the judge thinks of our melodramatic Mr. Justice," he said.

And then he heard.

Ralph hadn't counted on an audience when he told his story to the district attorney because he hadn't received Miss Burgess' message. One message in a morning was enough. The letters he could burn. He could convince himself they were nothing but a vicious prank. It was easy to be convinced of what one wanted to believe. But the voice of "Mr. Justice" was something alive and ominous—and near. If a threatening voice could come into his home, so could the threatener. There was reason, good reason, for making that call at Mills's office, but it wasn't reason that brought him there. It was pure panic.

And so he walked into a room where two men were waiting. One man was Halam Mills with an eager, expectant look in his eyes; but the other was a stranger, a tired man in a light-blue suit who stared at him and said unexpectedly, "Good morning, Judge Addison."

And Ralph paused halfway between the door and Mills's desk until Mills explained.

"You remember Officer Coleman, Ralph. He testified at the Messick trial."

Ralph didn't remember, at first, but when he saw, and read, the letters on Mills's desk he began to understand.

No, he hadn't expected an audience, and he hadn't expected an appreciative district attorney when he told his own story, and on that score he was absolutely right.

For a few moments after Ralph finished talking, Mills just stared at him. "Good Lord," he said at last, "you have been threatened, too!"

Whether the incredulous wonder in his voice was for Mr. Justice, who made the threats, or for Judge Addison, who had failed to be as conscientious as had been expected, was problematical, but Ralph felt that he had the edge.

"How long?" Mills sputtered. "How long have you been getting these letters?"

"Six days," Ralph admitted.

"The same as Coleman?"

"The same."

Mills had half-risen to his feet. He sat down again, a confused and worried man.

"In heaven's name," he said, "why didn't you tell me? Where are the letters now? Do you have them with you?"

"I burned them," Ralph said.

"You *what?*"

Ralph couldn't blame Mills for looking so distraught. A man in Ralph Addison's profession should know better than to burn evidence, but there were circumstances that could make even the most illogical act seem rational. A man in Ralph Addison's profession knew that, too. That's why Walter Messick was going to die in the morning.

"My wife—" he began. "She's expecting a baby."

"I know that," Mills snapped.

"But what you don't know is that she's in a very delicate condition. She's lost every other child—"

Ralph's voice trailed off in a kind of helpless silence. He glanced at Matt Coleman and the man looked sympathetic. Perhaps he was a family man himself. He looked the part.

"I didn't dare risk the possibility of the letters falling into her hands," he added. "Any great emotional upset could cause her to lose this child, too."

"You could have brought the letters to me," Mills said.

"And had my house overrun with policemen!" Ralph protested. "My wife's no fool. She'd have known something was wrong. And that sister of hers, a teen-ager who doesn't miss a trick, she'd have known, too. Besides, until I got that call this morning I thought the whole thing was just the work of a crank."

"You *thought* it was the work of a crank?" Coleman echoed anxiously. "What do you think now, Judge?"

Ralph hesitated. What did he think now? There was half an answer in his mind, something wild and worrisome left over from that verbal bout in the study this morning, but why Coleman? Why involve this policeman, too?

"I don't know what to think," he said at last. "This—I never dreamed of a thing like this!" The top letter was in his hand. "Because you arrested Walter Messick for this crime," he read aloud. "The letters I received read, 'Because you sentenced Walter Messick ...' It's beginning to sound like a vendetta against anyone who helped place Messick in the death cell."

"Nonsense!" Mills protested. "Coleman arrested Messick and you sentenced him, but I prosecuted the case and won it. Why haven't I been threatened?"

"Then you still think it's the work of a crank?" Coleman asked.

"What else is there to think? It's a fine time to be starting an investigation if it isn't!" Mills picked up one of the envelopes and scrutinized the postmark. Nothing. Nothing to start with and no place to go. "You've been on vacation," he muttered, "and the judge, apparently, has been on a mental vacation. If we'd got started on this thing sooner there might be some chance, but now—"

As if by signal, each man in that office looked at his watch. It was almost ten o'clock, just twenty-four hours and nothing to go on but a pile of dime-store stationery decorated by a typewriter that would be as easy to find as free parking space in Civic Center.

"Messick's a tough cookie," Mills added grudgingly, "but these letters don't read like the work of a bunch of punks. They read like the work of the typical crank. The wording, the quotation from the Bible, this is old-lady stuff."

"Old lady?" Coleman echoed. "Because of the Bible quote? Are only old ladies supposed to read the Bible?"

It was a question that went unanswered. Halam Mills had another matter on his mind now. "Of course," he mused, a candle of interest lighting his eyes, "there is the matter of that phone call the judge received this morning. What about the voice, Ralph? What was it like?"

Ralph hesitated. "It was muffled," he said at last, "as if something had been placed over the mouthpiece. But it was a man's voice. I'm sure of that."

The district attorney pondered this answer while the candles in his eyes grew brighter. Two men ... six threatening letters apiece ... but only one telephone call. It was almost possible to hear the thoughts as they filed into his mind.

"I don't suppose you've received your daily reminder," he remarked, glancing at Matt Coleman.

"No, sir, not yet anyway," Coleman answered. "I waited around for the postman before coming down here, but there was no letter today."

Mills grew silent again. Minutes ago he was ready to laugh off that stack of letters on his desk. Now he was a long way from laughter. "An unlisted number," he reflected. "Now that's an interesting item. Can you give me a list of the people who have been given that number, Ralph?"

"Yes, I guess I can," Ralph said, "but I don't know how far it might have got beyond them, and I have this teen-ager in my home, remember."

"All right, ask her if she's given it out. So far, that's our only lead."

Mills pushed back his chair and came to his feet. He rounded the desk and walked over to the windows. Far below the city was coming alive, protestingly under the blazing sun of what looked like another temperature-record-breaking day. A big, sprawling city that spread out like a huge labyrinth just made for the hiding place of some demented crank with homicidal tendencies. But for the clue of that unlisted number— He turned about again, frowning.

"Crazy!" he muttered. "This whole thing is just plain crazy! But we've got to proceed on the assumption that our Mr. Justice, whoever or whatever he is, means business. I wish you'd go home, Ralph, and stay there for the next twenty-four hours. I'll contact the police and have a guard set up."

"No!"

The force of Ralph's protest made him the focal point for two pairs of questioning eyes. Mills's eyes he could see; Coleman's he could feel.

"I told you, I don't want the police hanging around my place and upsetting Abbie," he said.

Mills frowned over the thought. "Do you have a lawn?" he asked.

"Why, yes."

"Good. I recommend a gardener—a couple of gardeners, in fact. You can't be too careful of a lawn in this hot weather. The point is, Ralph, that Mr. Justice may try to contact you again. He's already changed his tactics. The mails aren't good enough; he's taken to telephoning." Mills walked back to the desk and took up one of the letters at random. Each one had the identical last line: "Until that hour I will be watching you." He read the words aloud. "I suppose this bit was in your letters, too," he said.

"It was," Ralph answered.

"Then, if we're to assume that the threat is legitimate, we'll also have to assume that Mr. Justice will be doing that very thing—watching you."

"And so you want me to go home and wait like a sitting duck!"

"Exactly. You and the gardeners. I'll arrange for the gardeners, of course."

"And what about Officer Coleman and his threat? What's he supposed to do?"

Matt Coleman, who had been watching the exchange with quietly alerted eyes, brightened at Ralph's question. He looked to Halam Mills for the answer, and Halam Mills gave the answer.

"We won't neglect Coleman," he promised, "but I have a hunch one set of these letters really is a hoax even if—and I'm not conceding this, mind you—the other set isn't."

"I take it you mean my set is the hoax," Coleman said.

"It looks that way now. Oh, I know that I had just the opposite idea before Judge Addison arrived, but that phone call has changed my mind. The judge has actually been contacted by Mr. Justice, who, mind you, knew just how and when to reach him. Presumably, then, this threat of being watched is being carried out in his case; whereas—" Mills was beginning to sound more like a district attorney now. More confident and less bewildered.—"he certainly hasn't been watching you, Coleman, or he would have known what you told me your neighbors knew—that you couldn't receive these daily threats because you were out of town. These letters on my desk may be nothing but a red herring to divert our attention and leave the judge open to attack."

Attack. Ralph heard the word, but he didn't understand it. He'd stopped understanding anything over an hour ago.

"Oh, I wouldn't lose weight worrying about it," Mills added quickly, noting his grave face. "As you say, your private number may have been passed around to any number of people, and a judge does come in for this sort of thing, you know."

"Cranks, you mean," Coleman muttered.

It was his tone that disagreed with the district attorney, not his words. But Halam Mills caught the intonation. He waited, and the man in the light-blue suit, who sat humbly in the presence of his superiors, gradually realized that the wait was for him. He cleared his throat noisily and came to his feet.

"That's what you mean, isn't it?" he repeated. "That the Messick case is just an excuse being used by some crank to hit at the judge and me?"

"Have you a better idea?" Mills challenged.

The perspiration was rolling down onto Coleman's collar again, but he didn't bother to wipe his neck with the handkerchief. He'd picked up one of the letters and a dark scowl was deepening the creases in his large face. Large, but not flabby. Nothing about the man was flabby.

"It's what it says here about me," he said at last. "This part, I mean: 'I arrest you on the charge of withholding evidence and conspiring to obstruct justice.'"

"Well?" Mills prodded.

"I was thinking about that scarf."

"Scarf?" Ralph echoed. "What scarf?"

He hadn't spoken for a few moments. Matt Coleman raised his head and stared at him in a way that made it seem he'd been forgotten; but then, for a little while, it was as if he and Coleman were the only ones in the room.

"You wouldn't know about the scarf, Judge," the policeman mused. "It never came up at the trial. Never came out in the newspapers, either. That's a peculiar thing, isn't it? It never came up in public at all, and yet this Mr. Justice, the crank, seems to know all about it. At least, I can't see what else he could have in mind."

"What are you getting at?" Mills demanded, but Matt Coleman continued to drive at his own rate of speed.

"Like it says here," he went on, "I did arrest Messick. I guess you remember the details. This young woman, Faye Harper, had been murdered Christmas Eve. Her body was found in a parked car way out on Mulholland Drive. She'd been shot—shot through the heart with a .38. The gun was never found. She was alone. The car was hers and she was found on the driver's side draped over the steering wheel. She'd been drinking. The medics said she was full of alcohol."

Ralph unbuttoned his jacket. The heat was becoming unbearable and the story had an old, monotonous ring. Mills seemed to share his discomfort. "Get to the point," he ordered, but Coleman didn't seem to hear.

"She hadn't been attacked," he continued, "but she had been robbed. Her purse was gone and there was no jewelry on the body. We started a city-wide check of known fences and pawnshops, but it was nearly two months before anything showed up. When it happened, it was in my territory. That's how I came to be the one to arrest Messick. I was in the pawnshop when he came in. He had a lot of stuff—rings, bracelets, a wrist watch—and it was all tied up in this scarf. That's what the kid called it, a scarf. It was more like a large handkerchief—silk and all figured, like the things young girls wear over their hair sometimes. I took him in and he was eventually booked on suspicion of murder. He couldn't account for his actions between eight and ten Christmas Eve when, according to the medics, Faye Harper died."

"I remember the trial," Mills remarked dryly. "As you may recall, I did the prosecuting."

Coleman seemed an amiable man. He took no offense at the district attorney's tone.

"That's right," he said, "so you must know that Messick stuck with his 'not guilty' plea even when his lawyer begged him to change it and throw himself on the mercy of the court. All along he claimed there was a girl with him when he drove up on Mulholland that night and came across Faye Harper's parked car, a girl who could back up his story that he thought Faye Harper was sleeping off a drunk when he took her purse and jewelry."

"A girl who could neither be identified nor produced," Mills broke in. "A pick-up called 'Pat' who never appeared to back up his unlikely story!"

Coleman nodded gravely. "But according to Messick—only this never got beyond Central Station—this girl left her scarf in his hot-rod, the same scarf he had wrapped around that jewelry when I arrested him. But nobody could check his story, or even try to trace that girl, because somehow between the time Messick was booked and the time he came to trial the scarf disappeared. He didn't even mention it on the stand. I guess his lawyer was afraid of being laughed out of court."

Matt Coleman's eyes were very troubled now. He still had that letter in his hand, and a line of it seemed to have stuck in his mind.

"'Withholding evidence,'" he murmured. "I don't know what happened to that scarf, or where it came from before Messick got it, but I do know there was a scarf. I saw it with my own eyes."

The policeman's words left a big hole in the conversation. He didn't seem to know how to fill it. He looked at Ralph and saw the stricken face of a man just beginning to struggle with a new and terrible thought. He looked at Mills and saw a man struggling only with his own disbelief.

"You don't *believe* Messick's story!" he gasped. "A hoodlum with his record!"

"Petty larceny, a few drunk charges, suspicion of the use of narcotics—" Coleman seemed to be talking to himself—"no, I don't say that I believe his story. But it might be that somebody else does. Somebody not so crazy as you think."

Ralph stirred uneasily. "What do you think we should do?" he asked.

It was the two of them again, just the two of them with Halam Mills shut out of their common trouble.

"I'm not sure," Coleman said, "but I don't like this idea of holing in and waiting for Mr. Justice to make the first move. Maybe it's because I'm a cop and think like a cop, but I'd rather go out looking for this character, even if it means screening every principal in the Messick case."

"Screening!" Mills cried. "What are you thinking of, man? We can't re-open the case now! Messick's been tried, convicted, sentenced, and to-morrow he dies!"

"I know," Coleman said dully. "That's what worries me."

He didn't have to say any more. Twenty-four hours, that's all they had left. Twenty-four hours to hole in and wait and call a crank's bluff. But Matt Coleman didn't think this letter writer was a common crank, and Matt Coleman didn't appear to be a nervous man. Ralph couldn't take his eyes from the man. What was there about this uninspiring figure that made his words sound so much more important than the terse, confident direc-tives of the district attorney? It was a question his mind had no time to an-swer, for the heavy silence in that stuffy room was suddenly shattered by the shrill ring of the telephone.

Halam Mills took the call. "Who? ... Why, yes. He's here." With bewil-dered eyes, he held out the instrument. "Miss Burgess says there's a call for you, Coleman. You can take it right here."

Matt Coleman took the phone, listened, and then held it out so they could all hear. "Lovely morning, isn't it? I just wanted to remind you to enjoy it while you can, because, like Walter Messick, this is your last day."

Coleman replaced the phone in its cradle and looked at Halam Mills with bland eyes.

"See what I mean?" he asked.

CHAPTER THREE

There might have been an answer to Matt Coleman's question—Ralph was never quite sure. There was a reaction, certainly, as Halam Mills be-gan to play a fast staccato on the intercom; and there were questions, rapid-fire questions, aimed at the man in the light-blue suit. Had he told anyone he was coming to the district attorney's office? Had he been followed? Did he recognize that voice on the phone? Ralph heard the denials, saw the be-wilderment and the shaking of heads, observed, rather than shared, the un-leashed activity the call aroused, because now the numbness that had be-gun an hour earlier when he answered his own phone was taking on identity. It's name was danger.

Danger. It was minutes before any other thought could find lodging in his mind, minutes before he realized that Matt Coleman was gone. All the questions that could be asked had been asked, and all the answers that could be given were given. Mills was on the phone again and the wheels were beginning to turn, but Matt Coleman, who must not get away, was gone. Ralph moved toward the door.

"Where are you off to?" Mills called after him, but Mills no longer mattered. Ralph didn't even look around. "I'll be back," he said.

In the outer office Miss Burgess was busy with the phones and the buttons, and the corridor was suffering from the regular morning coffee-break lull. There was no sign of Coleman, but one elevator had just started down and so Ralph rang for the next one. Still no sign of the man downstairs; but outside the building the morning sun was making the sidewalk an unpopular promenade, and it was an easy matter to recognize those wide, sagging shoulders in the distance. Ralph quickened his gait.

"Coleman!" he called. "Wait, I want to talk to you!"

Matt Coleman turned about easy—that was the only word for it, easy—almost as if he'd been expecting something like this. He was wearing a hat now, a wilted Panama straw with a wide blue band, and his eyes were like a pair of polished aquamarines underneath the brim.

"I thought maybe you would," he said, as Ralph joined him. "Did Mills send you after me?"

"No," Ralph answered. "He's busy right now."

A faint smile curved Matt Coleman's lips. "Hiring gardeners?" he queried. "Oh, the D.A.'s a smart man in a courtroom, all right, but I don't think he knows how to handle a situation like this one. Sure is hot out here on the sidewalk, isn't it? There's a drugstore down the street a ways. Maybe we could have our talk over a cold drink."

When Coleman started walking again, Ralph had no choice but to follow. A few blocks down the street they found the drugstore—one of those old-fashioned, hole-in-the-wall places that hadn't changed hands in thirty years and probably wouldn't until the old man behind the prescription counter cashed in on his burial insurance. The boy at the fountain drew a couple of Cokes and went back to work on some research he was doing in the comic-book section of the magazine rack. There wasn't another customer in the place.

"I guess you want to know more about that scarf," Coleman said, as soon as the fountain boy had gone.

There were quite a few things Ralph wanted to know more about, but the scarf was the logical place to begin.

"I remember it particularly because it was a peculiar-looking thing," Coleman added, "sort of a tan background, beige I guess they call it, with a kind of oriental design in all different colors. And it was real silk. I know because a young soldier sent one like it to my wife once. He was stationed in Japan at the time."

Coleman used his straw to stir up the chipped ice in his drink, but he drank from the glass.

"A souvenir," he added, and the aquamarine eyes were far away.

"I'd never even heard of the scarf until this morning," Ralph said.

Coleman nodded. "I didn't think you had. That's why I knew you'd be interested. I remember you from the other court, Judge. I remember you were always a fair man. If you'd suspected there was any kind of evidence—"

"Evidence!" Ralph broke in. "Do you really think it's as important as all that?"

"Apparently Mr. Justice does."

"But you don't know that. You can't be sure the reference in your letters concerns a missing scarf."

"Then what does it concern, Judge?"

It was a question without an answer, a calm, deliberate question posed by a calm and deliberate man. The quiet moved in. The drugstore had been a cool oasis from the sun, but now the contrast from the street was wearing off, and so the quiet and the heat moved in together. Ralph wrapped his fingers around the cold glass, but he had no time to drink.

"Then you think Walter Messick told the truth?" he said.

"About the scarf," Coleman answered. "That much I know."

"And the girl in his car?"

"It's possible. A young fellow doesn't usually go riding up on Mulholland alone."

"A young fellow bent on holding up the occupants of any parked car he could find would go alone."

It seemed—Ralph wasn't sure of this, but it seemed that Matt Coleman's big face hovered on the brink of a smile. "Lover's lane bandit," he murmured, poking at the crushed ice with his straw again. "One of the newspapers used that one on Messick. Not very original, but I suppose it helped a lot of people reach a decision before the jury did. But that brings up another thing that's puzzled me all this time. Why was Faye Harper parked up on Mulholland alone? She was quite a woman, Judge. Remember?"

"Remember?" Ralph echoed. "How—why should I?"

"Her record, I mean. Maybe you've forgotten, but she'd been in and out of the courts a few times herself. 'Party girl,' the papers called her. She just wasn't the kind of woman to be alone any night, least of all Christmas Eve, unless—" Coleman stopped poking the crushed ice and finished off his drink with one swallow—"unless she really was sleeping off a drunk," he concluded.

Ralph heard the words with a dull dread nagging at his mind. It had started back in Mills's office when Coleman came off that chair and began to reread the letters. It was something more than a threat of death, something much more. He tried to fathom what he wanted to know from Matt Coleman's troubled face, but suddenly the policeman's attitude changed. He swung about on the stool.

"But that's just woolgathering," he said abruptly, "and our problem is more urgent. Maybe I'm just a jittery old man, but there's something about the thought of a death threat hanging over my head that makes me want to get off the dime and do something about it. I just don't like feeling like a fish in a barrel!"

"I'm with you there," Ralph agreed, "but do what? Where do we start?"

"With that scarf."

"What?"

"The missing scarf. I've been thinking." Coleman looked the part. A whole series of frown lines were giving his forehead a corrugated look. "Did you ever have a problem," he went on, "that you just couldn't make any sense of at all, and then you start explaining it to someone—just talk to get it off your mind—and while you're talking it begins to work itself out? Now, suppose that scarf is what Mr. Justice has in mind when he accuses me of withholding evidence. That means Mr. Justice has to know there was such a scarf, but, aside from some of the men at the station who heard the kid's squawk when it turned up missing, I can think of only one man who could have known about it—Messick's lawyer."

"Leo Cox!" Ralph exclaimed.

"Then you remember him."

"I should. He's appeared before me often enough. He seems to make a career out of representing prostitutes and petty hoodlums."

"Young petty hoodlums," Coleman said. "Cox never seemed to make the big time. I guess Messick was the first accused murderer he ever defended. What do you say, Judge, seeing that it's our neck at stake and not the D.A.'s, what do you say we take a crack at this thing in the old-fashioned police method of doing a little leg work? Even if we come up with nothing, it won't be any less than what we have now."

Leo Cox. It was amazing how quickly a man's mood could change in the midst of a dilemma. Minutes ago Ralph had almost hated Matt Coleman for the thoughts he was insinuating into his mind. But Leo Cox was an interesting possibility. A man without morals, a man without respect for his own profession. Was there a chance he would go this far in a wild effort to save his client from the gas chamber?

"As I remember," Coleman was saying, "Cox's office is out in the West

Adams district. I can get the address out of a phone book."

He didn't wait for acquiescence. He unbuttoned his coat and raked up a couple of dimes from his trouser pocket, and Ralph couldn't help seeing the snub-nosed revolver on his hip. A policeman, he remembered, never really goes off duty. It was a comforting thought—and an ominous one. But the dimes were for the top of the counter, and then Coleman was on his way back to the phone booths in the rear of the store. Ralph watched him thumb through the directory until he seemed to find what he was looking for. He scribbled an address on a scrap of paper and walked back toward the fountain, a puzzled expression darkening his face.

"I guess I'll have to take back what I just said about Cox never making the big time," he murmured. "That's the latest directory back there, and it's got Leo listed at one of those expensive Sunset Strip addresses."

In the old days it would have taken an hour, maybe more, to get from a parking lot in Civic Center to an address out on the Strip that was a lot more scenic than the neighborhood where Leo Cox had formerly hung his shingle, but on the freeway travel time was cut in half, and time was beginning to seem important to Ralph Addison on this troubled morning. They took his car, a light sedan about half as long and half as expensive as Stu's current convertible; and all the way out Ralph had the uneasy sensation of heading for a rendezvous he wasn't going to like but couldn't afford to miss.

It was out among the antiques and the foreign cars. It was an old building with a flashy face-lifting job on the front and the stucco all cracked and crumbling around at the rear. Ralph parked the sedan a couple of doors down, and they walked back past a small parking area reserved for tenants and clients only. A few cars were nosed against the side of the building and one of them—a bright-red imported speedster with the top down—caught Coleman's eye. He stepped off the sidewalk long enough to read the registration slip on the steering post.

"Leo seems to be doing fine," he murmured. "The lad must have more talent than I thought."

Inside, a receptionist directed them up a short flight of stairs where they found a heavy plate-glass door with Cox's name in gold letters, and behind it a lovely brunette who didn't seem to have much to do but announce callers to the boss.

"Judge Addison to see Mr. Cox," Coleman said. He turned to Ralph with a word of explanation. "Your name will make a better impression than mine," he said. He seemed be right. Cox was on his feet when the brunette ushered them into the adjoining office—a well-polished, overdressed little man with a sparse growth of hair on his sun-tanned head but quite an impressive sprig on his upper lip. One hand was extended in greeting.

"Judge Addison!" he cried. "This is an unexpected pleasure! Come in, come in."

But all of that expansive enthusiasm faded as Cox caught sight of the big man behind Ralph's shoulders. The lights went out in his eyes as if a cold draught had hit a candle.

"Coleman," he said. "What are you doing here? What do you want?"

Obviously, these men weren't strangers. Ralph did a little quick calculation in the few seconds of silence following Cox's abrupt change of attitude. Coleman was an old-line police officer—he'd have had long experience running his arrests up against the Leo Cox variety of legal opposition. That would probably account for the sudden chill in the atmosphere. But a question had been asked, and Ralph Addison was accustomed to doing his own talking.

"A client of yours is giving us trouble, Cox," he said.

"A client of mine?" Cox echoed, his eyes still on Coleman.

"Walter Messick," Ralph said.

"Messick?"

Now Cox was confused. He sank back in the nice new beige-leather chair behind his desk and struggled with Ralph's words. Then he laughed sharply.

"Ex-client, you mean," he corrected. "I'm all through with that kind of practice, Judge. From now on I'm strictly a corporation lawyer." Cox paused and reconsidered Ralph's words. "But I don't understand," he said. "How can Messick be giving anybody trouble? He's in the death cell. He's—" Suddenly Cox turned pale. "He hasn't escaped?"

"That worries you?" Coleman asked.

Matt Coleman didn't seem to miss a thing. Cox was the kind of man who worried easily. He probably went through life glancing back over one shoulder.

"He hasn't escaped," Ralph said, and the little man behind the desk looked relieved.

"I'm glad to hear that," he said. "A crazy kid like that—no telling what he might do. But if he hasn't escaped, what's this all about?"

Cox's bewilderment sounded genuine, if that meant anything, and there was nothing to do but tell him the story of two sets of threatening letters and watch for any betraying signs of foreknowledge in that raptly attentive face. Either they had been giving the Academy Award to the wrong people, or Leo Cox had never heard of such an outrageous thing before.

"Death threats!" he gasped, once Ralph had told the story. "But why? Who would do such a thing?"

"We thought maybe you could tell us that," Coleman said.

"Me? How could I? I'm not even associated with the case anymore. Messick dismissed me right after the trial."

Leo Cox was excited now, and an excited man could easily say too much. With Matt Coleman monitoring his every word, too much was inevitable.

"So Messick fired you?" the policeman echoed. "Was there a special reason for that?"

"Special?" Cox reddened underneath his tan. "What do you expect from a crazy kid like that? I told him he'd get the gas chamber if he didn't change his plea. He's young. He'd have got off with life probably. But no, cocky Walter knew best! All right, he's over eighteen—let him settle the score! He got a fair shake, I know that. Any defendant in Judge Addison's court gets a fair shake, Coleman, everybody in my profession knows that. If I'd let the kid down in any way, the judge would have fired me off the case so fast my head would still be spinning. Isn't that right, Judge? Isn't that right?"

Ralph didn't answer. He stood frowning at the nice, new broadloom carpet on the floor and listened to the silence a few seconds. The silence was a relief after Leo Cox.

"What about that scarf Messick said he had on him when he was arrested?" he asked at last.

"Scarf?"

Cox's habit of repeating every question put to him was getting a little irritating. Perhaps it gave him time to dream up an answer.

"Oh, so you've heard that story, too," he said, casting a meaningful glance at Matt Coleman. "Frankly, I don't know much about it, Judge. I never saw the scarf myself."

"I did," Coleman muttered.

"Oh, I'm sure you did," Cox responded. "It was probably something Messick picked up along with the other stuff he took from Faye Harper. But if you check on this, Judge, you'll learn that no such item was taken from Messick when he was booked. He'd either got rid of it by that time, or had it hidden somewhere on his person and got rid of it later. I certainly never saw a scarf, and I think there's a damn good reason why. As Messick's lawyer, I'd have made every attempt to trace it to its owner; and whether that owner was Faye Harper, or one of Messick's girls, it's obvious to me that she couldn't have backed up his story."

"Then you think Messick disposed of the scarf himself?" Ralph asked.

"What else is there to think—unless there's a dishonest cop in the woodpile? The whole story was preposterous! A pick-up, a girl he knew only by the very common nickname 'Pat.' I ask you, Judge Addison, what kind of defense could I build on a yarn like that? I knew Messick was lying. I'd never have taken the case at all, but I felt sorry for the kid. I'd helped him out of scrapes before."

"For a fee," Coleman reminded.

Leo Cox glared at the policeman. "Sure, for a fee," he muttered, "and you can imagine what kind of a fee. That's why I quit the old practice. Messick was the last straw. When you try to save some fool hop-head's life, only to have him turn on you—" Cox was talking too much again, but this time he knew it. "Anyway, I'm out of it now," he added. "All the way out. I don't know anything about the scarf, and I know even less about these letters. Written by some crank, probably. Some people just can't resist writing letters."

The sound of his own words had a solemnizing effect on Cox. He might have had the same expression if he'd just remembered that that expensive red speedster was parked on the hill without the brakes set. When the secretary broke in, via the intercom, with a terse announcement that a certain Mr. Dorritt was on the telephone, he looked as if the speedster had just started rolling with nobody at the wheel. "Tell him to call back later," he ordered.

"But he's leaving for the airport," the secretary insisted.

"Later!" Cox shouted, and snapped off the instrument. "It must be a crank," he repeated, but this time it was as if he were talking to himself.

"Then you can think of nothing that might help us?" Ralph persisted.

Moisture had formed on Cox's neatly trimmed mustache. The heat was approaching noon-day ferocity, and even an expensive office hung on a hillside wasn't much cooler than a cubicle on Temple Street.

"I'm afraid not," the lawyer murmured. "This whole thing sounds fantastic, unless—" Suddenly Cox's eyes lighted up again. "Unless it's Messick himself! He's a weird one, Judge. He might have set up this whole thing thinking he could scare up a reprieve."

"But Messick's in the death house," Coleman protested.

"Sure, but he has friends. Pals, girl friends, a family. If I were you, I'd try that angle, Judge. Messick must have palmed off that scarf on someone. Find that someone and I'll lay odds you find your mysterious Mr. Justice."

If Leo Cox could convince a jury as easily as he seemed to convince himself, he'd have a great future. The intercom buzzed again. Mr. Dorritt still wanted to speak to Mr. Cox, and this time Mr. Cox was anxious to comply.

"You understand, gentlemen," he said, volunteering as an escort to the door, "important phone calls, clients due to drop in. Sorry I can't give you any more time, but keep in touch. Let me know how you make out with Messick's friends."

All the way to the door Leo Cox was extremely solicitous.

"Well," Coleman said, "I don't know how you feel about it, Judge, but I'd say we just had a very fast brush-off."

They were back at the sedan, which had turned, meanwhile, into a four-wheeled oven. Ralph had already slid in behind the wheel, but Matt Coleman lingered on the sidewalk and frowned at the recently vacated building.

"I don't know," Ralph protested. "There may be some merit in what Cox suggested, particularly the family angle. Messick does have a mother."

"Have you ever seen her?" Coleman queried.

Now that he considered the matter, Ralph realized that he hadn't seen Messick's mother. It was strange. Messick was twenty-one; the court couldn't command parental attendance at his trial. But it was strange.

Yet, so was Mr. Justice.

And then an incident occurred that gave Ralph and Matt Coleman something else to puzzle over on a troubled morning. A man came out of the building they'd just left, a well-polished, overdressed little man who seemed to be in a great hurry. He made straight for the red speedster in the parking area, and seconds later Leo Cox was roaring off down the hillside to somewhere.

"Now, isn't that a shame," Coleman said, watching the scene with careful eyes. "All those important clients Leo was expecting won't find him in."

Then Coleman crawled into the front seat of the sedan next to Ralph and shoved the wilted Panama off his forehead in a gesture of submission.

"All right, Judge, we'll do it your way," he said. "Now we'll remember Mama."

CHAPTER FOUR

At twelve o'clock the factory whistles blew all over the city and everybody broke for lunch, everybody except men like Halam Mills, who was still busy with the phones and the intercom trying to locate two men the police were going to keep an eye on when, and if, they could be found; and men like Ralph Addison and Matt Coleman, who were just walking away from a small sedan parked in front of a cheap café that was located quite a way down the hill from Leo Cox's hastily vacated office. Down the hill in more ways than one. This was Walter Messick's world they'd come to, a cheap, overcrowded world cluttered with run-down bungalows, red-brick factory buildings and warehouses, and this one particular café where the noon-hour trade gave a fleeting impression of high prosperity. It was Coleman, of course, who knew where to find Mrs. Messick. He explained that on the drive from Cox's office.

"I had to check up after Messick's arrest," he said. "You know, look to see what else he might have had stashed away. I looked for that gun, too, that .38 that killed Faye Harper; but it never was found."

"He probably threw it in the ocean," Ralph said.

"The ocean? What makes you say that?"

Coleman could wander off on the strangest byways if nobody stopped him. "I don't know," Ralph said. "It just seems a logical thing to do. Mulholland runs out that way."

"Yes," Coleman admitted, after a moment of serious thought, "it does that, doesn't it? Now if only Walter Messick was the logical type—"

They'd gone first to a run-down bungalow, where a week's accumulation of advertising throwaways and a crate of empty beer bottles provided the exterior decoration on the sway-backed porch, only to find the house empty except for a dirty-faced boy of some ten years. Reluctantly, the boy tore himself away from the television set long enough to answer Coleman's questions. No, his mother wasn't at home. Yes, he guessed she still worked at the café down the street. Why all the questions anyway? What were they—cops? This younger Messick evinced no more respect for the police than his brother; in fact, there was a certain bravado about him, as if having a brother in the death cell was an honor comparable to winning the Congressional Medal of Honor.

"He'll be cock o' the walk after tomorrow morning," Coleman said bitterly, as they turned back to the sedan. "Values have a way of getting turned upside down in a neighborhood like this. I don't know—" and here Coleman paused to kick a broken roller skate off the weed-infested walk—"maybe I'm wrong, but I can almost understand a kid like Walter Messick giving himself a joy pop to get out of a world like this."

"That's no excuse!" Ralph insisted. "There's nothing original about poverty. I came from a bad neighborhood too. My people were poor, dirt poor!"

"So were mine," Coleman murmured, "but only on the outside."

Ralph was getting a headache, a sharp, shooting headache that seemed to start at the back of his neck and clamp like a barbed-wire coronet around his temples and over his eyes. Blame it on the heat. That's what hot days were for—to provide a dumping ground for everybody's grief. Blame it on the heat and the stuffy interior of the café where, eventually, they did find Mrs. Messick. Every stool and booth in the place was filled when they came in, but Coleman pointed out a thin, nervous-eyed woman with bottled blond hair who was trying to keep the customers happy without causing herself any undue exertion. She wore a checked waitress' uniform; tight about the hips and damp about the armpits, and had an air of irritated boredom that wasn't likely to titillate the patrons.

"Marie Messick," Coleman explained. "Walter's mother."

Ralph stared at the woman, but for a moment it wasn't she whom he saw at all. He saw a boy—old enough to be a man in the eyes of the law—but a boy in face and figure. He saw the hollow eyes and belligerent mouth; he saw Walter Messick on trial for his life, and then, finally, through the heat and confusion, he saw the woman who was this boy's mother. She didn't look like anybody's mother, and it wasn't because the peroxide took away the years. It didn't.

A party crawled out of a booth at the far end of the room, and Matt Coleman led the way back. A good man at leading, Ralph thought, as he followed down the narrow aisle. The rear booth was next to the kitchen, where the smell of grease and frying food could help that barbed-wire crown draw tighter. What am I doing here? he wondered. Why am I tagging along with this man like a lost sheep? He leaned his head back against the wooden booth and tried to avoid meeting Coleman's penetrating eyes. That was when he noticed the pay phone hanging on the wall up front next to the cashier's booth and remembered what he never should have forgotten.

"I've got to call home," he announced suddenly. "Mills may have the grounds overrun with gardeners by this time. Abbie's sure to notice."

"Abbie?" Coleman looked interested. "Your wife?"

Ralph nodded.

"Is it almost time—for the baby, I mean?"

"Two weeks," Ralph said. "At least, that's what our doctor says."

Coleman's eyes were very grave, and his fingers began to play with the salt shaker. "It's tough—everything coming at once this way," he said. "I sure hope it goes well with your wife. I know what this baby must mean to both of you. A marriage without kids can get to be a pretty drab affair after ten or fifteen years. You get to wondering what all the struggle's for. You get restless and sick of trying."

The man sounded as if he knew what he was talking about. Sick of trying. Was that Matt Coleman's story, too? It suddenly seemed very important to have an answer.

"Married, aren't you?" Ralph asked.

"Thirty years," Coleman said. "Thirty years, two months, and five days."

"It must be quite a marriage if you're still counting the days."

"Yes, quite a marriage."

Coleman might have said more, and Ralph would have listened, but this wasn't the place for playing detective with a stranger's character. Just when the conversation was getting interesting, the woman in the checked uniform appeared at the booth and started piling up the dishes left by the last occupants. Mrs. Messick. Now Ralph could get a good, close look at the objective of this journey into squalor. He could look and he could listen.

A piece of silver showed up where a saucer had been. "Ten cents!" the woman muttered. "How do you like that? The cheapskate eats three bucks' worth of food and leaves a lousy dime tip! You gents want to order now?"

"How are you, Mrs. Messick?" Matt Coleman asked.

It wasn't until he spoke that she looked up from the stack of dishes on the table. She stared at him. She stared hard.

"Oh, it's you," she said at last. "Coleman, ain't it? Didn't recognize you out of uniform. What brings you here?"

"What always brings me here," Coleman said, "trouble. Can you spare a minute?"

"You want to order?"

It sounded like an ultimatum. "Sure, in a minute," Coleman agreed, "but first we'd like to ask a few questions. Have you met the judge, Mrs. Messick? Judge Addison?"

Ralph hated to meet the woman's eyes. The name seemed to burn a little niche in her memory. She looked at him with almost empty eyes.

"What does he want?" she asked. "He's done his dirty work."

"Mrs. Messick," Ralph began, "I merely did what my office requires. I'm sorry about your son, but I had to do my duty."

The eyes seemed emptier the longer she stared at him.

"You want to order now, or don't you?" she asked.

"But you don't understand— Walter dies in the morning!"

It was his own incredulity that spilled out in Ralph's exclamation. Whatever else he was not, Walter Messick was this woman's son. There should have been some emotion, some regret. But the exclamation accomplished one thing: it filled those empty eyes with quick anger, and loosed a reluctant tongue.

"Do you think I don't know that?" the woman cried. "Sure, Walter dies tomorrow, but I don't and my other kids don't. We go right on getting hungry at mealtimes, and needing clothes and money for the rent. God knows I don't make much in this cheap hashhouse, what with dime tips and all, but I got to make what I can. So if you two got anything to say, say it quick and then order or get out. I got other customers waiting."

So they said it quick, with Matt Coleman doing the talking this time and Ralph trying to convince himself that the nausea he felt came only from the heat and that blinding pain in his head. They put the story to the woman as straight as it had been put to Leo Cox, and she listened with the disbelief and surprise on her perspiring face gradually giving way to understanding and indignation.

"And so you come to me thinking I'd do a thing like that!" she exclaimed, the instant Coleman finished his story. "You think I'm crazy? Haven't I had enough trouble without writing threatening letters to a judge and a cop?"

"We haven't accused you of writing the letters, Mrs. Messick," Coleman said. "The judge just thought you might have an idea who did. A friend of Walter's, maybe."

"A friend!" Marie Messick tossed her bleached head derisively. "If Walter'd ever had a decent friend he might not be in this mess! Trouble, nothing but trouble all my life, and most of it with that boy! Never was any good, you know that, officer. In trouble with the police since he was ten years old. Me carrying Dougie, the war going on, and that boy getting mixed up with hoodlums even then.

"All right, so he dies in the morning. You want to know how I feel, Judge? I feel like he's already dead. The day he was booked for murder I said to myself, this is it ... this is the end. The fighting, the stealing, the drinking and the marijuana I could take, but not murder! I didn't go to the trial, didn't even go to the jail. Walter's dead, I told myself. Accept it. Bury the dead and feed the living. I done all I could."

The speech was over. The emptiness came back to the woman's eyes. Her fingers fidgeted with the order book that was stuck under her belt.

"All right, you want to order now?" she asked.

This time Ralph didn't try to avoid Coleman's eyes. He was right—Walter Messick's mother wasn't writing threatening letters in a desperate attempt to save her son's life. It seemed to Ralph, suddenly, that this whole attempt to find Mr. Justice was madness. Halam Mills was right—it was the work of a crank. It had nothing to do with Walter Messick *because nobody cared if Walter Messick lived or died.*

The thought stuck in his mind like an uneasy awareness of something important, something not quite remembered that he really should know; but now this woman with the too blond hair, the too tight uniform, and the too damp armpits was hovering over him with an order book and a pencil in her hand. "How about a beer?" she was saying. "Nothing like a cold beer in all this heat. I'll be glad when these factory stiffs clear out so I can get a beer for myself." He had an insane urge to shove her aside and run for the door, to break away from Matt Coleman and his big curiosity and get back to Abbie, dear Abbie, who mustn't be hurt.

But even as his eyes sought the doorway, something happened that drove the thought from his mind. The door opened and a new customer came into view. A conspicuous customer, because this seemed a peculiar place for Leo Cox to be taking lunch.

Cox spotted the occupants of the rear booth at the same instant Ralph spotted him. He look startled for a moment, ducked his head as if he didn't want to be recognized, and then changed his mind and walked back to greet them.

"Well, gentlemen, we meet again," he said. "And Mrs. Messick. How are you these days?"

"Dancing on a cloud," she muttered. "What are you doing here? You got all Walter's money already."

"Money!" Cox dropped down, uninvited, on the seat alongside Matt Coleman. He looked as cool as a man could look with the temperature in the high nineties and the wind coming furnace-hot off the desert. "That sure didn't make me rich!" he declared.

"What did make you rich, Leo?" Coleman queried. "I didn't know you had any gilt-edged uncles."

"Not uncles—clients," Cox said. "I told you this morning, I got smart. Fifteen years I played legal nursemaid to punks like Walter Messick." He could say that now. Mrs. Messick had gone back to the kitchen. She didn't seem to care for the company any more. "So, finally I got smart. Let the punks cry on somebody else's shoulder. I've had it!"

"I never heard that you took charity cases," Coleman said, but Leo Cox, now that he was seated opposite Ralph Addison, took no notice of any small annoyance at his shoulder. "Any luck?" he asked, and the question was obviously for Ralph.

Ralph looked across the room where Marie Messick was now exchanging small talk with a couple of shirt-sleeved customers. Somebody must have told a joke because her laughter came loud and full. Yes, Walter Messick was already a long time dead. Ralph could see that now.

"I don't think so," he said. "Not yet."

Cox pulled out a box of cigarettes—an expensive brand with a fancy mouthpiece—and left it open on the table. "I thought you might be having trouble," he said, getting himself a light. "That's why I dropped in. Thought I might find you here."

"Are you sure that's why you dropped in?" Coleman asked.

Cox ignored the question. "Mrs. Messick is out," he said flatly. "She gave up on Walter years ago. He's been in trouble before, you know."

"I'm familiar with Messick's record," Ralph said.

"Oh, it's not just his record. Kids like Messick get in plenty of jams a judge never hears about. Petty stuff, but it adds up. Then there's this narcotics business. The law had nothing on Messick in that line until he was booked for murder, but he was hooked long ago. I think that's why Mrs. Messick takes what's happened as well as she does. She knows it would be only a matter of time anyway. Isn't that right, Judge?"

Ralph didn't answer. No matter how much he might agree, he didn't like to have a man like Leo Cox doing his thinking for him. But Cox wasn't finished.

"Gets them all, sooner or later," he said. "Why do you suppose the kid did such a fool thing as holding up Faye Harper if he wasn't desperate for money to buy the stuff? Of course, he probably never intended to shoot her—that only made the stuff he took too hot to move. But it was only a matter of time until his craving overcame his sense of danger."

"The judge knows all about that," Coleman interrupted. "He was at the trial when the D.A. made the speech the first time."

Cox smiled crookedly. "So I recall," he said, "but I also recall other trials when Judge Addison wasn't presiding. A couple of years ago I defended a pal of Messick's, a crazy kid who'd gone on a drunk and smashed his jalopy into a liquor store trying to get more of the dog that bit him. 'The Poet,' he was called. Crazy kid. Wrote poetry, quoted Shakespeare."

Cox took two quick puffs on his cigarette and then snuffed it out in the ash tray on the table.

"I just happened to think of him after you left my office this morning, Judge. It might not mean a thing, but I was trying to think of someone Messick knew who would be capable of writing a letter such as you described. I thought you should know."

"Is that why you took off in such a big wind after we left the office?" Coleman asked.

Leo Cox turned around and glared at the inquisitive policeman. "Took off?" he repeated. "What do you mean?"

"Just what I said. You left in an awful hurry for a man who was supposed to be expecting a lot of important clients."

It was a small booth. There was hardly room for a big man like Matt Coleman and an angry man like Leo Cox on the same side of the table, and that was a good thing. With more room, somebody might have started swinging.

"If you must know, I had a telephone call," Cox said. "A client was leaving the city and wanted to see me before he left. I'm only trying to be helpful, Judge, but Officer Coleman seems to have it in for me. I guess a man like Coleman just has it in for the world. Some people can't live down their own mistakes."

Coleman's face darkened. It was the first time Ralph had seen the man angry, and it wasn't a soothing sight.

"Watch it, Cox," he muttered. But Cox, who didn't seem to frighten easy, only grinned. "Then lay off," he said. "If there's anything you want to know about me, go ahead and check. I've got a legitimate practice with legitimate clients. I told you before, I just got fed up playing nursemaid to a bunch of punks. Messick was the last straw."

Cox didn't say any more for a few moments, and Ralph would just have to wonder about the meaning of the innuendo he'd tossed out like a bombshell in his private war with Matt Coleman. Mrs. Messick reappeared at the booth with a couple of hamburgers and beers he couldn't remember anyone ordering, and Cox groped his way back to the subject of this unscheduled conference.

"I don't know," he murmured, as the woman laid out the food, "the whole idea's just a stab in the dark. But it might be worth your trouble to look up the kid I told you about. Carlos, I think that was his name. Carlos Chavez—something like that. Do you remember, Mrs. Messick? Do you remember the Mexican boy Walter used to pal around with, the one they called 'The Poet'?"

The woman eyed Cox suspiciously. "He went to Preston," she said.

"Sure, he did, but that was two years ago. He's back by now."

"Maybe. Maybe he's in trouble again."

The woman continued to stare at Cox, then at Ralph, finally at Coleman. "Why?" she asked. "Why all the questions? You think Carlos wrote those crazy letters?"

"It's possible," Cox said.

Mrs. Messick pondered the problem. "I suppose so," she admitted grudgingly. "With somebody like Carlos anything's possible. But why? Why would he do a thing like that?"

"To stir up trouble. Create confusion and doubt."

"Doubt?"

Cox's suggestion seemed a brand-new idea to Mrs. Messick. A new and troubling idea. While she was thinking about it, Matt Coleman, who seemed to have been waiting for an opening, came in with a question about that pet subject of his—the long-missing scarf. He had to go into a little detail, because Mrs. Messick appeared not to have heard of the item before.

"A girl's silk scarf? No, I don't remember nothing like that," she said. "But then, I didn't know Walter had that dead woman's jewelry and watch, either. He never told me anything."

"And he never mentioned the scarf to you after he was arrested?" Ralph asked.

Mrs. Messick seemed to have trouble meeting his eyes.

"After Walter was arrested—after Officer Coleman, here, brought him back to the house to look for the gun, I never saw him again," she explained. "I told him, months before I told him, 'Get into trouble with the police once more, just once more, and I'm through with you. Finished. It's trouble enough taking care of the other two without worrying about a boy old enough to look after himself.' That's what I told Walter, and that's what I did!"

The words were firm enough, but that defiance in her eyes wasn't quite what it had been before Matt Coleman started talking about a girl's scarf. "What does this all mean, anyway?" she demanded. "A scarf. Was it true what Walter said at the trial? Was there really a girl with him that night?"

"Now, how could anyone know that?" Cox scoffed, but the question wasn't for Leo Cox.

"It might be true," Coleman said. "I know there was such a scarf, and there might have been such a girl."

"But why didn't she come forward then? Why didn't she speak up when Walter was on trial?"

"There's an obvious answer to that," Cox began. He got no further.

"Obvious answers sometimes have a way of being wrong," Coleman said. "Just like obvious people. There's a reason, Mrs. Messick, and, in my simple mind, a very good reason why the girl—assuming there was a girl—didn't come forward. Let's face it, Walter isn't a fine, upstanding young man, and that murder charge did nothing to enhance his character. Any girl from a respectable home would hesitate to admit she'd spent an evening with him even under ordinary circumstances."

"A respectable home?" Ralph repeated. "Are you suggesting that a girl from a respectable home was Walter's Christmas Eve pick-up?"

The pale-blue eyes didn't falter. "Why not?" Coleman asked. "You've been on the bench a few years, Judge. Haven't you ever heard of a girl from a good home getting into trouble? Maybe on a dare, maybe because she's unhappy at home, or just craves excitement. I've done a lot of work with juveniles through the years, and most of the time the trouble comes from the parents not knowing, or not even caring, where the child finds company.

"Then there's another thing to think about. Walter admitted taking Faye Harper's jewelry. Any girl who might have been with him at the time was automatically implicated in robbery. It seems to me this girl couldn't open her mouth without getting into trouble, even if she wanted to."

There was a lot of logic in what Matt Coleman was saying. Disturbing logic that would scuttle Ralph's determination to pull out of this free-lance manhunt if he listened too long. Midge. Only this morning he'd complained to Abbie about Midge's companions. Did they really know any more about them than the father of the girl Walter Messick could have met Christmas Eve? The girl. How easy it was to accept suggestion as fact when fact was so elusive!

But it wasn't quite so easy for Leo Cox. "Remember," he protested, "this was a case of life and death for Walter."

"I remember," Coleman said dryly, "but I don't underestimate the urge for self-preservation. I'll be frank with you. I checked up on Walter Messick's known girl friends when I first heard this scarf story. None of them fit his description of 'Pat,' and all of them had an alibi for Christmas Eve. Apparently this girl wasn't from his set at all. She must have been just what he said she was, a pick-up."

"'She must have been!'" Cox howled. "It seems to me you're assuming an awful lot, man. You're admitting the existence of someone of whom there's not a shred of evidence."

"Because the evidence disappeared," Coleman insisted. "And I don't buy your idea that Messick got rid of that scarf himself. He had it when I arrested him. He had it when I took him to jail, and he didn't have any visitors, not even from those cell-shy friends of his."

Ralph followed Coleman's words with interest. Whether he realized it or not, one thing was becoming obvious. "You must have taken quite an interest in this case," he suggested.

"Officer Coleman would," Cox remarked. "You might say he has a fixation, Judge. He's paying a debt to society."

"I told you to watch it!" Coleman snapped.

"Sure, sure, you told me. But I'm telling you that I think it's a dirty shame to come in here and get Mrs. Messick all stirred up over nothing. Look at her. Don't you think what she's going through is tough enough without some stubborn cop, who never even got a stripe on his sleeve, running a post-mortem of Walter's trial right under her nose?"

The woman did look troubled, almost frightened. "You didn't say anything to me about a girl's scarf," she said.

"I didn't know anything about it," Cox answered.

"You said Walter didn't have a leg to stand on."

"He didn't. The trial proved that! Believe me Mrs. Messick, this whole affair is just some wild plot to stir up trouble at the last minute. Carlos Chavez, that's the name, Judge. Take my advice and look him up. He's just the type to pull a hare-brained stunt like this!"

Cox came to his feet. He apparently wasn't hungry after all, or perhaps the greasy cuisine wasn't in his class any more. His eyes lingered on Mrs. Messick for a moment, and then he turned on his heel and walked back to the door and out to the street. Mrs. Messick stared after him with an indefinable expression bothering her eyes. She seemed troubled, frightened, and then angry.

"My son's dead," she said suddenly, "already dead. I don't want to talk about him anymore, you hear? I don't want to listen!"

The words were for anyone interested, and they were her last. There were other customers who might want to order.

Ralph had no idea how long he sat staring at the hamburger and beer in front of him. He couldn't eat—that was a certainty. Before Leo Cox's arrival he had the answer, all safe and sure and sensible. There was no girl with Walter Messick Christmas Eve; there was no sinister significance in that missing scarf, and Mr. Justice was just a crank having a bit of ghastly fun. But Leo Cox was too anxious. He should have known his insistence that Coleman was on the wrong track would convince Ralph Addison the way a Moscow peace offensive convinced the Free World.

And so they were nowhere again—two men with a narrow table between them, and what had been advertised as the last day of their lives more than half-spent getting there. What now, Matt Coleman? Where next? Ralph waited, knowing there would be an answer sooner or later, but in the meantime he still had a telephone call to make.

The café was almost empty now. The pay phone wasn't in a booth, but he had no trouble hearing Midge's voice when she came on the wire. He'd called the unlisted number so the call would be confidential. Abbie had a bedroom extension for the other phone.

Midge sounded excited from her first word. "Say, the D.A.'s office has been trying to get in touch with you for hours," she said breathlessly. "They sound real upset. What's wrong?"

Midge Braidwell was the last person on earth Ralph intended to let know what was wrong, but he did have to make some explanation for those gardeners Mills had promised to send over.

"Oh, you mean the cops," Midge said. "They've been here for a long time."

"Cops?" Ralph echoed weakly. "Did they tell you they were policemen?"

From the sound of her voice, Midge must have been eating again. He'd probably find chocolate icing all over the mouthpiece. "They didn't have to tell me," she said, between bites. "You should see what they're doing to the hedge. Wait until Abbie sees the scallops!"

"No, she mustn't!" Ralph cried. "She mustn't see the hedge or the gardeners! Remember, she's not to get excited. Promise, now. Promise!"

Midge promised. She sounded bored about the whole thing, but she did promise. "New fathers!" she muttered. "I sure hope you live through this. And don't forget to call the D.A. He's having fits, too."

Midge wasn't sure if Ralph heard the latter admonition or not. He hung up so suddenly—he sounded so strange. She frowned over the thought while finishing off the last of the chocolate cake; but there was no use trying to make sense of her brother-in-law. He took life too seriously, was all wound up inside. Probably had some kind of a complex that went back to his childhood, or maybe even earlier.

When the cake was eaten, Midge wiped her fingers on the hips of her tight blue jeans and started to leave the study—and then she stopped and sniffed the air. Was something burning in this room? The smell seemed to come from the fireplace. Surely poor old Father Addison wasn't so mixed up he'd started a fire on such a hot day!

Nothing was burning, but something had been burned. There were a few charred ashes in the grate and a few strips of something white. Midge knelt down and examined them closer. Envelopes. Only the top one was badly charred; the others had hardly been touched by fire. Carefully, Midge picked up the letters.

CHAPTER FIVE

Halam Mills was an angry man.

Midge's admonition wasn't wasted. Checking back with the district attorney seemed a very good idea to a man more than anxious to terminate a pointless journey through Walter Messick's past. Coleman didn't agree. There was something about a malt shop he wanted to visit, a teen-age hangout where Messick claimed to have picked up his Christmas Eve date; but Ralph was adamant. The district attorney had wasted no time getting that guard posted at the house. He was either more concerned about Mr. Justice than he'd appeared earlier, or had picked up some additional information that stimulated his fear. And so, over Matt Coleman's protests, they returned to the office on Temple Street and heard a lecture on what not to do until the assassin arrives.

"Are you two crazy, going off *together?*" Mills demanded. "Suppose this lunatic means business? What could be sweeter than being able to pick off both of you at one attempt?"

It was a sobering thought, but Coleman shrugged it off.

"There's no danger yet," he reminded. "The fireworks don't start until ten o'clock in the morning."

Matt Coleman seemed a little bored, annoyed might be more to the point. He resumed his previous perch on the straight-backed chair and allowed Ralph to tell the story of the morning's search without embellishment. His mind seemed on other matters. But Halam Mills was alert enough. He followed the recital closely: the visit to Cox's office on the quest of a missing scarf (a tolerant smile over this), the trek to Walter Messick's home, the interview with his mother, and, finally, the unexpected appearance of Cox again. It was the latter incident that drew his first response.

"Was he following you?" he asked.

"Until that hour I will be watching you." Ralph knew what Mills had in mind, but the recollection of Cox's entrance at the café didn't bear out the suspicion.

"I don't think so," Ralph said. "I had the impression he was rather surprised to find us there. No. Wait. He did say he'd hoped to find us. Then he mentioned this friend of Messick's. Carlos Chavez."

He had to explain, then, about Carlos Chavez, and Mills listened, his eyes alert and his silvered head cocked a little off center. "It's a possibility," he murmured. "Far-fetched, perhaps, but so is Mr. Justice. Yes, it might be something at that."

Matt Coleman stirred out of his mood of preoccupation. "Vendetta?" he queried, almost smiling.

"I doubt that," Mills answered, "but it might be a trick to stir up new interest in the case and smoke out a last-minute reprieve. That could account for the accusation against you. A charge of withheld evidence would be certain to create doubt and confusion."

"And the judge?"

"Prestige. Threaten a police officer and create small confusion; threaten a judge and manufacture the large family-size. Of course, the whole idea is theoretical, but any possibility is worth looking into. But we haven't been sitting on our hands in this office, either. It may interest you to know, Coleman, that the call you received here this morning was traced to a booth in the Hollywood area. Same exchange as your own, in fact."

Coleman sighed heavily. "Exit suspect Chavez," he muttered. "Re-enter the neighborhood crank."

Maybe Coleman was just tired. He should have known better than to use that tone on a man who was already angry. Ralph saw the red rush up on Halam Mills's neck, and his voice, when it came again, was taut.

"Not necessarily," he snapped, "but, now that you mention it, I have been a little puzzled over that call. You told me this morning that you'd mentioned to no one that you were coming to this office, and that you weren't followed. How, then, did Mr. Justice know where to reach you at that hour?"

"Common sense," Coleman replied.

"Common sense?"

"Exactly. Mr. Justice says he'll be watching the judge and me. All right, let's suppose he's doing just that and has been doing it all week. He must have known, as you pointed out this morning, that I wasn't at home to get his letters. He also must have known, if he knows anything about me, just what I'd do when I got back and found all that mail waiting for me. That was last night late. Anyone driving past the house could have seen the lights. But I couldn't do anything about those letters until this morning, and chances were I'd wait until the postman came just to see if the seventh letter arrived. How about that, Judge Addison? Were you waiting for the postman this morning?"

The query caught Ralph off guard. Had he waited? The question had a memory in it, and he answered quickly so too much of the memory wouldn't show.

"As a matter of fact, I did wait for the postman," he said. "It was after he came, and I received no letter, that I finally decided this whole thing was a hoax."

Coleman nodded knowingly. "So, you see, the time element works out simple enough," he said. "The postman comes to my house about nine o'-clock. Allowing driving time down here, this office is the logical place for a man with a death threat to report to be at ten o'clock this morning. I see no big mystery, and no need for a neighborhood spy parked on my doorway. But then, I'm assuming that Mr. Justice is perfectly sane, and can reason something like that out for himself."

"Perfectly sane!" Mills exclaimed. "How can a man be perfectly sane when he goes about making threats of this sort?"

Coleman hesitated only an instant. "That," he said, "depends on his motives."

Ralph was beginning to be very sensitive about this man, Matt Coleman. In a little more than three hours, he'd learned to measure every change in that tired, rather cynical face, and to notice every signal in a voice that pronounced this casual phrase, or that undramatic statement, in a way that meant something important was either implied or on the way. Motives, the man said, and it had to mean something. Mills caught it, too. He demanded an explanation, and Coleman, who couldn't have been very comfortable perched on the edge of that hard chair, complied with troubled eyes.

"Call it a hunch," he said. "Call it a cop's instinct. What I've been thinking is that maybe we've been going at this problem from the wrong angle—all of us, I mean. You, Mr. Mills, are trying to trace a crank—someone not interested in Messick at all, but merely using his execution as a convenient outlet for a little home-brewed venom. All right, maybe you're right, but you know as well as I do that we'll never locate that kind of a crackpot between now and ten o'clock tomorrow morning, and if you're not right, and those 'gardeners' you've given the judge aren't successful in intercepting Mr. Justice—"

Coleman let his words trail off in a very effective silence. Before Mills could object, he was talking again.

"Now the judge and I, on the other hand, have been looking for someone who did have an interest in Messick. From this angle, our Mr. Justice is more than a crank; he's a crank with a purpose. He's trying, somehow, to stop Messick's execution.

"But maybe there's another side of the case to consider. There's a side for Mr. X, the disinterested crank; there's side for Walter Messick's unknown friend; but a triangle has three sides."

"A triangle?" Mills echoed. "What are you driving at? What other side is there?"

"The victim's," Coleman said.

"What?"

"The victim, Faye Harper. Maybe it's her friends we should be looking for instead of Messick's."

Matt Coleman dropped the thought quietly and let it lie in a nest of silence. It was Halam Mills who finally found the tongue for his question; it was Ralph who waited for the answer.

"Faye Harper's friends!" the district attorney exclaimed. "Why, in heaven's name, would a friend of Faye Harper be interested in saving Walter Messick's life? That's getting a bit far afield!"

But Halam Mills had missed the point. It wasn't Messick's life at all. The glance Coleman sent in Ralph's direction seemed to be searching for affirmation. When it failed to come, he had to explain.

"The reason is spelled out plain enough in those letters," he said. "'At ten o'clock Friday morning, July 29, an innocent youth will pay with his life for the murder of Faye Harper.' *Innocent*, Mr. Mills, that's what I'm driving at."

"You don't believe that!" Ralph gasped.

It was his first comment in some time. The force of it surprised even himself. Coleman paused only a fraction of a minute.

"What I believe isn't important," he said. "It's what Mr. Justice believes that concerns us now. It just strikes me that anyone so positive Messick is innocent might have an alternate suspect in mind. That's what I meant about the motive for these threats. It may not be one of saving Messick so much as of stirring up an investigation that might condemn someone else. A friend of Faye Harper's wouldn't be happy about tomorrow's execution if he thought her killer was still walking the streets."

Ralph turned away and walked over to the windows. Coleman was still explaining his latest idea, but he didn't need to hear the words. Hadn't he known all morning? Hadn't he, somewhere in the back of his mind, known why he had to follow Matt Coleman on this desperate search? The traffic noises drifted up from the open window, hot, angry sounds of a city at nerve's edge. This was life, the struggle, the pressure, the never ending doubt. Why was it so precious that any price was worth paying just to grasp a little more of it? An innocent youth. Was that the truth about Walter Messick? Could it ever have been the truth about that human wreck? And Faye Harper. What was the price of such a woman for the dubious privilege of inhaling and exhaling?

Like the response to a telepathic cue, Matt Coleman's voice rose above the street sounds. "We all know what kind of woman she was," he was saying. "She knew plenty of men, and the worst kind. Look up her record. She was in court on a charge of offering just a month or two before her death."

Still at the window, Ralph spoke. "I'm aware of that," he said coldly. "It was my court."

"I know," Coleman answered.

"You?" Ralph turned about and stared hard at the policeman.

"I was in court that day myself," Coleman said. "I remember the case."

"Then you must remember that the charge was dismissed."

"I remember. You threw the case out of court because the arresting officers had resorted to entrapment. You made quite a speech on the dignity of the law and the responsibilities of its defenders."

"I remember hearing something about that," Mills interrupted.

"What about it?" Ralph snapped.

"The officers involved drew a stiff reprimand. They might have resented it and you."

"Enough to risk their jobs trying to get even with these threats?" Coleman queried. "Now who's getting far afield?"

"I'm only trying to be thorough," Mills replied. "We want to consider every possibility."

"Then consider the possibility of a police officer, two police officers to be exact, with a grudge against Judge Addison threatening my life as well. It just doesn't make sense, does it? No, I may be just a stubborn cop, but I still think Mr. Justice has a stronger motive for what he's doing than just to make a couple of men miserable. If he knows, or thinks he knows, something we don't—"

"Officer Coleman!"

There was an edge of anger in Ralph's voice that cut a neat hole in the conversation. Coleman didn't finish his argument. He shifted his weight on the little chair and looked toward the windows.

"Walter Messick did have a trial, you know. He wasn't convicted by a kangaroo court!"

Coleman said nothing.

"Or do you think it's easy to condemn a man to death?"

"Now, just a minute, Judge—" Coleman began.

But this wasn't the minute. Ralph had listened long enough; now it was his turn to do the talking.

"You get a lot of ideas, don't you, Coleman? That missing scarf, for instance. When a man's upset and confused he'll go along with almost anything; but I've been thinking, too, and the story of a missing scarf is a pretty flimsy excuse to go chasing about the way we've been doing. And that visit to Messick's home neighborhood, that was really touching! The poor boy from the slums, the kid who never had advantages—"

"But, Judge," Coleman broke in. "You're the one who insisted on interviewing Marie Messick. I knew it was a waste of time."

It didn't seem possible to ruffle Matt Coleman. Only one man had been able to do that—Leo Cox, with a veiled accusation Ralph didn't understand and had no right to question. No, the tempers could rise like the temperature, but Matt Coleman still squatted on the edge of a straight-backed chair, with the sweat rolling down his thick neck and his eyes as quiet as the hands that dangled motionless between his wide-spread knees.

Ralph glanced at Halam Mills for reassurance, and Mills responded with an immediate endorsement.

"The judge is right," he said. "This idea of yours is nonsense, Coleman. Faye Harper's friends and contacts were all checked out at the time of her death."

"Not all of them," Coleman corrected. "I seem to recall that quite a search was going on before I picked up Messick with the dead woman's jewelry—a search for an unidentified man she'd been keeping company with. There wasn't much to go on—the statement of a bartender at one of the places she frequented, and a match folder from some motel that was found in her car. Never did find the man. After Messick was booked, nobody seemed to care."

"And you, I suppose, propose to find this man!" Mills thundered. "What two months of investigation prior to Messick's arrest failed to do, you propose to achieve overnight!"

Ralph felt better knowing that Halam Mills, with all his dignity, could lose his self-control too; but Matt Coleman had an answer for everything.

"As you say, Mr. Mills, we must consider every possibility."

At times there didn't seem to be any air at all. At times it was like drowning, when the pressure built up inside you and you knew your lungs were going to burst if you couldn't have air, just one gasp of pure, clear air. The mountains. They would go away to the mountains where everything was the way God had made it, and not cluttered up with hot, crowded buildings and noisy, crowded streets. They would forget about yesterdays and tomorrows, and try to find one moment of time when they knew who—and why—they were.

Down in the street, below the window Ralph's eyes had sought again, a small boy was selling newspapers. He was a poor boy, and he would grow up to be President, of course. He'd study while the other boys played; he'd work while the other boys hung around poolrooms and whistled at girls; he'd dream while the other boys wrote on latrine walls and snickered over dirty stories—and so he'd grow up to be President, of course, or Attorney

General, or Chief Justice of the Supreme Court—or maybe just Judge Addison of the Superior Court, County of Los Angeles, who worried too much over too many things.

Back on the other side of the room, Halam Mills was asking a question. "You're up for retirement soon, aren't you, Coleman?" he queried.

"Eight months," Coleman answered, "two weeks, and six days."

A man with a careful sense of time, Matt Coleman. Ralph remembered another conversation in the rear booth of a cheap café. "Thirty years, two months, five days." Was he always so exact, or were these things especially important? Interested, Ralph turned about.

"Eight months," Mills repeated. "Fine record, too. I've heard about you, Coleman. Done a lot of work with juveniles, haven't you?"

"You can't be a cop as long as I've been a cop and not work with juveniles," Coleman answered quietly.

"Yes, I suppose so. Sorry about your illness. I guess it was quite a blow losing your wife last year."

Mills was busy stirring up some papers on his desk. He might have been making casual conversation, but Ralph knew better than that. He was getting at something.

"A terrible blow," he murmured, "particularly when there are no children."

"Look here, Halam," Ralph interrupted. "There's no need stirring up that sort of thing."

But Matt Coleman didn't seem to mind the personal direction the conversation had taken. He looked at the source of this unexpected succor with something almost like a smile lighting his pale-blue eyes.

"That's all right, Judge," he said. "The D.A.'s just trying to reassure you, and himself, that I'm not to be taken seriously. It's true that I lost my wife last year, and it was a terrible blow, as Mr. Mills says; but I didn't take this leave of absence because I cracked up. It's also true that we never had children of our own, and maybe that's one reason why I've been interested in other people's kids all these years; but that doesn't make me a sloppy sentimentalist over every young punk who gets into trouble. I just like to make sure everybody pays for his own trouble—no more. I've known boys younger than Messick who had to die for next to nothing."

Coleman spoke slowly and deliberately. He looked older, somehow. He must be tired,

"Then, too," he added, "I know what the both of you know and won't admit even to yourselves. I know Walter Messick was convicted before he even walked into that courtroom."

There would be no answer to that statement. Ralph caught Halam Mills's eyes, and the district attorney shook his head as if to say, "See what

I mean? A stubborn cop is a stubborn cop. Forget it!" Ralph was more interested in Coleman's eyes.

But if Mills failed in his attempt to discredit Coleman's third-angle theory, he didn't allow the setback to silence him for long.

"We're getting nowhere!" he exclaimed abruptly. "Sorry if I got out of line, Coleman, but you two did give me quite a scare chasing off that way this morning, and I can't see what we're going to accomplish if we continue to work at cross-purposes. How can this office protect a citizen threatened with death if we can't even find the citizen?

"Now, let's get back in the scope of reason for a while. It may not be so exciting, but it might be more fruitful. What about that list of names you were going to give me this morning before you rushed off so fast, Ralph? The names of persons who are known to have your private telephone number."

It was something to do, that was the main thing. Halam Mills could grab a pencil and look busy, and it would seem that tracking down Mr. Justice was just a matter of conscientious, routine checks. And Ralph, who wanted Coleman to be wrong, tried to pretend Mills was right.

"Well, there's Stu," he reflected, because Stu, oddly enough, hovered at the wings of his mind. "Stuart Wilder, my wife's physician."

Mills dutifully jotted down the name on a little pad. "I think I've met the doctor once or twice," he said.

"Everybody's met the doctor once or twice," Ralph muttered. "He's a very popular man. And then, of course, there's my father-in-law, Dr. Braidwell. Oh, God! What time is it?"

Mills looked up, startled. "Something wrong?" he queried.

"The luncheon," Ralph said. "The speech!"

"I was wondering when you were going to remember that," Matt Coleman observed.

It was a surprising comment, considering the source. Ralph knew he hadn't mentioned the speech. How did Coleman know? Before he could ask, Coleman answered. As he answered, he came to his feet.

"I read about it in the papers," he explained. "Your father-in-law's quite a speaker himself, Judge. I remember being on duty in a hall one time when he spoke about politics. Interesting talk, too. He claimed that all candidates for public office should be psychoanalyzed and certified mentally fit before their names could be placed on a ballot."

It may have been mere coincidence that Coleman looked at the district attorney when he spoke the words, but Mills didn't seem to think so.

"Nonsense!" he protested. "No man really mentally fit would allow his name on a ballot! I never had this kind of trouble in private practice!"

"I didn't think much of the idea myself," Coleman admitted. "Dr. Braidwell forgot to tell us who was going to certify the psychoanalysts. But I guess that only shows how little difference there really is between a smart man like the doctor and a lot of others who aren't so smart. There's no such thing as too much authority, as long as it's in the hands of the people *they* think know best."

And then the big policeman smiled in a way that seemed to say he would do his own thinking, no matter what the powers that be decreed, and got in one parting shot before he walked out on Halam Mills for the second time.

"You take good care of the judge, Mr. Mills," he added, "but don't worry about me. I'll do my own worrying—at ten o'clock in the morning."

The office seemed empty without Matt Coleman, and Ralph felt a little lost. He had to race across the city and deliver some unfelt words to people who had heard too many words already; and if there was any doubt as to what Matt Coleman intended to do, it was dispelled when he took the same exit route a few minutes later. Coleman hadn't gone far. He was still in the outer office where he'd appropriated one of Miss Burgess' telephones. It must have been a departmental call, because he seemed to be getting a refresher on some old information.

He didn't look up as Ralph came out of the office, but his voice was louder than it need be.

"... north of Topanga Canyon," he was saying. "Yeah, I've got it straight about the motel. Now, what's the name of that bar again?"

It was almost two o'clock when Ralph reached the luncheon hall. Dr. Braidwell sat at the head of the table, an empty chair beside him and an anxious expression on his aging but handsome face. He was a distinguished gentleman so he even managed anxiety with casual good taste. It eased perceptibly as Ralph slipped surreptitiously down the length of the hall and into the waiting chair.

"My boy," he said, "where have you been? It's almost time for your speech."

Ralph barely heard the words. He stared down the length of the long table that was lined with straight-backed chairs. Seated in the chairs were twin rows of straight-backed people, all of whom had handsome faces, male and female, young and old. Intelligent faces. Proud faces. Above all, clean faces. Ralph looked at them all, up and down the two rows, and it was inconceivable to think of any of these people as ever being dirty or diseased, or even hungry—in spite of the remains of creamed chicken on their plates. They were too intelligent for that. They had read books, written books, made charts, and knew all the statistics by heart. They could have told Ralph exactly why Walter Messick was a murderer and they were not.

But Dr. Braidwell was still murmuring at his shoulder.

"I trust Abbie is well," he was saying.

"Too much trust is a dangerous thing," Ralph said thinly. "If you really want to know how Abbie is, why don't you stop by the house and find out for yourself?"

This wasn't the way Ralph usually spoke to his father-in-law. He could see the long white hand on the tabletop tighten and feel the eyes that were examining him from behind those distinguished spectacles.

"I shall, of course, if there's time," the doctor said, "but I must drive up to Sacramento after this meeting." Then he paused, struck by a sudden thought. "Is anything wrong?"

Ralph wanted to laugh. Wrong! What could possibly be wrong in the midst of all these right people? It was wrong, of course, to stir up apprehension in the mind of Abbie's father. It was wrong to resent a man just because he had money and was generous. But other things were wrong, too, and even the omnipotent wisdom of Dr. Braidwell couldn't set them right.

"Why, Judge Addison! How nice! It's been such a long time!"

It was a shrill, feminine voice that interrupted Ralph's troubled thoughts and removed the necessity of finding an answer for Dr. Braidwell's question. Seated at his left was one of those indomitable females without whom no civic function could be complete—a handsome woman, of course. It was impossible to think of her sleeping with a stranger for the price of a meal or a few dollars to put toward the rent.

"I was thinking of you just the other day," the woman added eagerly. "I saw your name in the paper—"

"My name?" Ralph echoed.

"But of course! It was something about that murderer who's being executed tomorrow. You were the presiding judge at his trial, weren't you?"

Ralph tried to turn away. His father-in-law was better company on such a day, but he was too late.

"I really must visit your court one day," the woman persisted. "I'd love to watch an important trial."

"Certainly," Ralph answered coldly. "Just be patient. There's sure to be another murder."

"The other court was much more interesting," Dr. Braidwell volunteered, over the woman's brittle laughter. "I visited Ralph one day when he had some very colorful ladies appearing before him. Much more interesting, really."

The laughter came again. This was just luncheon conversation, Ralph reminded himself. The words weren't supposed to be significant. Only the speeches were meant to be profound. But now the woman on his left had tired of Dr. Braidwell's humor. She was getting serious, and that was even worse.

"I think it's ghastly," she said. "In this day and age—the death penalty! And he's only a child!"

Ralph tried not to listen. He wanted to tell her that he didn't make the laws; he merely tried to interpret them. He wanted to remind her that Messick wasn't a child. He was of legal age. But he couldn't tell her anything. Matt Coleman was out at this very moment driving toward a beach motel; but Judge Addison had to sit among the handsome people and try to think of something to say in his speech.

"As long as we submit to barbaric codes of justice," the woman insisted, "I can see no hope for the world. Can you, Judge Addison?"

Ralph didn't answer.

"I remember a speech you once gave on the adverse effect of capital punishment on the crime rate. It must be a terrible thing for a man of your convictions to be placed in the position of virtual executioner."

Ralph shoved back his chair. "You'll have to excuse me," he said. "I just remembered another appointment."

"But Ralph," Dr. Braidwell protested, "your speech."

By this time Ralph was on his feet and nothing his father-in-law might say or do could make any difference. He stared about him. It seemed that all of the handsome faces were watching him now. They looked a bit embarrassed, as if they were afraid they'd missed hearing the introduction and weren't sure whether or not it was time to applaud. They did so want to do everything right and proper, these people, even as they did so want to save the world from destruction. They might succeed, too, if they could ever find the world that needed saving.

"You make it!" Ralph said. "You shouldn't have any trouble. You do everything else for me so very well!"

Ralph left the hall quickly before Dr. Braidwell could recover from his surprise and put up an argument. He almost ran to the parking lot. Behind him was a torture chamber; ahead of him was a road that led to the sea, and on it, somewhere, a plodding policeman who didn't trust easy answers. Matt Coleman. With no mind for anything else, it was no wonder Ralph narrowly missed running headlong into the big convertible that swung into the parking lot just as he was coming out. There was a screaming of brakes, and then the face behind the wheel of the open car took on a surprising familiarity.

"Hey, Ralph! Hold it!" Stu called. "I want to talk to you!"

Stu should have been playing a golf tournament. It would be moments before that thought, and all its implications, crystallized in Ralph's mind. Now he could only ask, "Is it Abbie?"

Stu shook his head. "No, confound it, it's not Abbie!" he shouted. "It's you."

Ralph didn't wait to hear any more. That road was still waiting, and on it, somewhere, Matt Coleman.

CHAPTER SIX

North of Topanga Canyon. It was cooler on the Coast Highway. The ocean was a silver-blue sheet with white-lace edges, and the sky a vaulted container for a sun only slightly insulated by a thin skein of coastal fog; but Ralph had no time to admire the scenery. He drove slowly, much to the chagrin of the sun-worshippers in their red and yellow convertibles. A few miles up the coast, he signaled and made a left-hand turn into the driveway of an imposing spread of plate glass and pink stucco with a huge neon sign raised like a mast above the manager's office. Motels came very fancy on the seashore, but this was an off-hour for business. Only one other car was parked near that door, a faded green coupé about five years old. Ralph cut the motor and prepared to go into the office, but before he could leave the sedan a familiar figure in a light-blue suit sauntered around the rear of the green coupé and stuck a sweaty face in at the open window.

Matt Coleman didn't seem surprised at Ralph's change of plans. He seemed to take his arrival as a matter of course.

"Did you see him?" he asked, squinting on past the opposite window and out toward the highway Ralph had just quitted.

"See him?" Ralph echoed. "What do you mean? See who?"

"Cox," Coleman said. "At least, I'm pretty sure it was Cox. There was a red speedster pulled up on the shoulder when I stepped out of the manager's office just a couple of minutes ago. I started toward it and it took off like a fighting-mad hornet. He must have passed you coming in."

A red speedster. The highway was full of sports cars, all colors of the spectrum. Ralph hadn't paid any attention to any of them.

"What would Cox be doing here?" he challenged.

"I don't know," Coleman admitted. "What was he doing at that café this noon?" And then, apparently abandoning a question no one could answer, Matt Coleman withdrew his attention from the highway and regarded Ralph with a good-natured grin. "Short speech," he suggested.

"I walked out," Ralph said.

"I don't blame you. It's too hot for speech-making today." As if to illustrate his sentiment, Coleman brought out that folded handkerchief again and did a quick mop-up job on his sweating neck. "It's also too hot for wild-goose chases," he muttered. "I didn't get much out of the manager.

Some officers from homicide were out asking the same questions last December, he said. He told me what he'd told them. Faye Harper used to come here, all right, but he never got a good look at the man who came with her. He never came into the office. The Harper woman handled the renting herself."

"If the man was never seen," Ralph commented, "how do you know it was always the same one? We may be on the trail of a dozen men."

But Coleman shook his head. "The manager thinks it was the same one," he said, "and he did see him from a distance. It was at night, of course, so he couldn't give much of a description. A tall man, he said, and a shy one."

"Probably married," Ralph said.

"That might account for it," Coleman admitted, replacing the handkerchief in his breast pocket again. "That and other things. But I'll tell you what I'm going to do now, Judge. I'm going back to the city and look up the bartender who first mentioned Faye Harper's mysterious boy friend and see how his description stacks up with the motel manager's." The big policeman poked about in his pocket until he came up with an address scribbled on a scrap of memo paper from Miss Burgess' desk. "Probably should have gone there first," he added. "Still, I wouldn't call this trip a complete waste of time. The location of the motel suggests something, doesn't it?"

There was something fascinating about Matt Coleman—his calm, his stubborn calm and methodical persistence. There wasn't a shred of evidence in anything he'd reported the motel manager as having told him, but he looked as pleased as a cop who'd just found an eyewitness.

"Mulholland Drive," he said, answering the question in Ralph's eyes. "I told you this morning that I've been puzzled all this time about what Faye Harper was doing parked up there alone. Now I've got a possible answer. If this friend of hers was too shy to show his face to a motel manager, he must have been just as careful about where he met the woman. Mulholland Drive is a lonely road, and, if you follow it far enough, it runs into Topanga."

Coleman turned his back on the motel. He stared at the ragged hills across the highway, burned brown by the summer's sun. He stared at everything and nothing and waited for the inevitable protest.

"That's pure conjecture," Ralph objected. "You can't prove—"

"I don't have to prove anything," Coleman cut in. "I'm a policeman, not a lawyer."

"But this bar you want to visit. Surely the men from Homicide have been there, too."

"Christmas Eve," Coleman murmured, "that's when the woman was murdered, and it's a bad season for getting information from a bartender.

There's no telling what might have come to his mind since. How about it, Judge? Are you still with me?"

It was foolishness, of course. Nothing but foolishness. The legal mind of Ralph Addison knew that, but, as Coleman turned away and ambled back to that faded green coupe, his hand was already putting the sedan in driving gear.

For a dollar sixty-five (drinks extra) you could get a steak dinner, a one-armed piano player, and a brassy female soloist who made a career of shouting down the melody of every number in her repertoire. This was the charm of a small, dark bar situated at the foot of the hills on which Leo Cox had a shiny new office and the inspirational benefit of a panoramic view. There was nothing inspirational about the view at the foot of the hills. It was as if everything had slipped moorings and finally slid to a stop a few blocks below the high-rent district. The same seemed to apply to the clientele which, at four o'clock in the afternoon when there was no piano player and no shouting, was meager. Coming in out of the sunlight Ralph couldn't see a thing but Coleman's broad back ahead of him, but he could hear voices.

"Antifeminist!" an unhappy soprano was complaining. "That's what you are—antifeminist!"

The words seemed to be directed to a shadow in a white shirt who stood behind the bar. Coleman moved forward and Ralph followed. It wasn't much of a place. Too narrow for dancing, but not too narrow for a felt-topped table where nobody, of course, ever placed a side bet on the games that kept the customers busy while running up a bill at the bar. The table was quiet now, too. Only the one-sided conversation at the bar brightened the gloom.

"It's always the same," the woman said. "Every time you guys come back from a war with your little short haircuts, it's the same. Somebody shot at you, so you got to take it out on women!"

"Look," the white shirt answered, "all I said was that you should go home before your husband comes in and raises hell again."

"My husband! You know what he can do, don't you?"

It seemed a shame to break up this philosophical discussion, but when Coleman moved up to the bar the man in the white shirt didn't seem to mind. By this time the shadow above his collar had become a face, and the face looked relieved at the prospect of a diversion. "Something for you gents?" he asked brightly. Then he leaned forward and looked at Coleman again. "Oh, it's you," he added. "Didn't recognize you out of uniform."

"I've been here before," Coleman murmured in Ralph's ear. "I'm not the only cop who's been here before." But to the man behind the bar he said,

"Nothing to drink, thanks. We just came in for a little information."

"Faye Harper again?"

"Faye Harper," Coleman said.

"I knew it. All day I've been getting questions about Faye just because that kid goes to the chamber in the morning. But what can I tell you that I haven't told a dozen times before? Faye used to come in here a lot, sure. She got into trouble one night, but that's none of my affair. I can't be responsible for everything that goes on in the place. She was picked up and hauled into court, but she got out of it. Case dismissed. That same night she came back in—to celebrate, she said, but I told her to clear out. Trouble, that's all I get from women!"

The bartender paused to glare at the woman at the bar.

"Antifeminist!" she muttered.

"Trouble," he repeated. "Nothing but trouble."

"And so she cleared out?" Coleman asked.

"Not right away. Faye wasn't a girl to be pushed around, I'll say that for her. She had guts, that kid. Guts, among a few other things."

"That's all you men ever think about," the barfly protested. "A woman's just a body, nothing else."

"Well, did she or didn't she leave?"

The bartender considered Coleman's question with upraised eyebrows. Then he sighed. "A dozen times," he answered, under his breath. "Sure, sure she left—eventually. Long about midnight some guy came in and sat at the booth back by the door. Faye seemed to recognize him. She went back and they talked a while, and then they went out together. And that, so help me God, is the last time I saw Faye Harper, dead or alive! Now, have you got it straight?"

A nervous bartender could be a very unhappy man. He would have run his fingers through his hair, but it was cut too short for that. He started to move away, but then he noticed Ralph standing quietly behind Coleman's shoulder. He stopped and stared at him quizzically.

"You wanted something?" he asked.

"I'm with Officer Coleman," Ralph said.

"You don't look like a cop."

The air was dead and heavy in this place. Ralph's headache was coming back. He shielded his eyes from the little glow of light behind the bar. "What about the man who came for Faye Harper?" he asked. "How did he look?"

It was a foolish question. That was a long, dark walk back to the doorway. The bartender shrugged. "We were pretty busy that night," he said. "I wouldn't have noticed the man at all if I hadn't been watching for Faye to clear out. He was tall, that's all I know for sure."

"Well dressed?" Coleman queried.

"Dressed? How should I know? You think I pay any attention to clothes on a man? What is all this, anyway? Faye was killed and the guy that killed her dies tomorrow. Why the questions? What's to talk about?"

"Poor Faye," the woman at the bar said dolefully. "There's the proof for you. Antifeminist, just like I said. Push 'em around, treat 'em rough, fill 'em full of lead."

Until this moment, the woman had been just an annoyance, a nameless, faceless annoyance. Suddenly she was more. Ralph saw Matt Coleman's sagging shoulders straighten as his mind leapt to attention. He turned around and stared at the woman. She might have been thirty, give or take a few. She wore a cotton blouse that hung low on her shoulders, and a pair of tight velvet trousers that came just below the knees. She was a little drunk but not too much not to know what she was saying.

"Did you know Faye Harper?" Coleman demanded.

"Like a sister," the woman said. "Sweet kid."

"Do you know the man she kept company with just before her death?"

"I guess you mean 'the high and mighty,'" the woman said.

"The what?"

"'The high and mighty'—that's what Gigi called him. Real exclusive, you know. I never saw the guy myself. Faye knew better than to parade a good catch around a man-trap like this. I can tell you one thing though—he was no damn good!"

"How do you know that?" Ralph asked.

The woman peered around Coleman's shoulder and fixed him with an accusing glare.

"He was a man," she said.

It was a moment of anticlimax. Ralph didn't realize how hard his heart had been beating until it started to slow down. It was foolish to put any stock in what this woman said. It was just another false alarm, another trek to nowhere. He started to pull away from the bar, but Matt Coleman, who didn't miss much at any time, had caught sound of something that needed further explanation.

"Gigi," he repeated. "Who's Gigi?"

It took a little time to get a straight answer. It took the woman and the bartender working in relays.

"Gigi Fontaine," the man said first. "She means Gigi Fontaine. She and Faye used to pal around together."

"Like sisters," the woman said. "Sweet kids."

"Gigi Fontaine," Coleman repeated the name slowly and then turned to Ralph. "Does that name mean anything to you?" he asked.

The question didn't seem to make sense at first. "Why should it?"

Ralph countered.

"It didn't come up at the trial, I mean."

"No, I've never heard it before."

Coleman looked puzzled. Even in the dim light his eyes were clouded. "Neither have I," he said, "and that seems a peculiar thing. Any close friend of the victim should at least have been questioned by the police, if not the D.A." Coleman turned back toward the bartender again. "Any idea where we could find this woman?" he asked.

The bartender shrugged.

"Flotsam and jetsam," the woman murmured. "That's all a woman is to a man. A pretty face, a pretty body. Who cares where they end up?"

"Your husband's going to care plenty if he comes in here and finds you plastered again," the bartender remarked.

"That weasel!" Along with her gripe, the woman was nursing what had been a tall, cool drink until she'd done such a good job of shortening it. She clutched the glass defiantly. "Why do you think a woman drinks?" she challenged. "Men, that's why! Poor Gigi. They ruined her life, and now they condemn her if she gets a little drunk once in a while. Sixty days the last time! What a lousy rap—sixty days for a Christmas present!"

There was nothing left of that tall, cool drink when the woman placed her glass back on the bar again, and that was about as much as was left of Matt Coleman's characteristic calm. Ralph was no better off. Christmas—sixty days. If what the woman said was true, there might be a reason why Gigi Fontaine had been overlooked by all of the parties interested in Faye Harper's murder.

Excitement was contagious. He could hear the anxiety in Coleman's voice when he swung back to the bartender gain.

"What's the woman talking about?" he demanded.

"A lush," the bartender said. "Gigi's a lush, like this one, only worse. Got more than she could handle Christmas Eve and was salted away for sixty days. Say, there's an idea for you. You might find her back in the drunk tank. She's been out long enough to be about due."

That pointed observation wasn't going to endear the man behind the bar to his most vociferous customer, but he didn't seem to mind. He turned away, looking for a little trade that might make music on the cash register, and the woman glared at the back of his close-cropped head.

"Antifeminist!" she muttered. "That's what's wrong with this goddam world. No respect for women!"

Gigi Fontaine. It was a name as phony as the imitation leather on the upholstered booth where Ralph waited while Matt Coleman did the telephoning. Gigi Fontaine wasn't in the directory, but she was recorded downtown in that extensive who's who of the police department. It took a little time to get the full report. The sixty-day Christmas present wasn't Gigi's first sojourn as a guest of the taxpayer, but it was her most recent. The address she'd been booked in at did have a telephone listing, but the second call Coleman made was even less illuminating. Five months was a long-term lease to a girl like Gigi, and she didn't live there anymore.

"No forwarding address," Coleman reported, joining Ralph at the booth. "That's a bad break."

"She may have left the city," Ralph suggested.

Coleman scowled at his own dim reflection in the tabletop. "That's always a possibility with a gal like Gigi. Still, if I know the breed, and I've dealt with a few, she'll never stay away from this neighborhood long. I'd sure like a chance to ask what she meant about that 'high and mighty' crack."

Ralph was getting restless. They'd been a long time in this dark hole and his headache was getting worse all the time. But business was picking up. A few working men had stopped by for a quick one before going home to dinner, and a few others with no home to go to and no place to spend the evening. They wouldn't be lonesome. This was the neighborhood of the Hollywood hopefuls with the part-time jobs and the full-time appetites, and for a dollar sixty-five a girl could eat steak for dinner—if she could find someone to pick up the tab. Ralph knew those things because he sat on a bench. Matt Coleman knew them because he didn't.

"Somebody must know where the girl is," he said. "She couldn't just disappear! Think I'll stick around until the trade gets heavy and ask a few questions. Can I buy you a drink, Judge?"

Hopeless. It had to be hopeless. Two months of investigation hadn't turned up a thing. What could Matt Coleman hope to learn in one night? And that's all there was now—one night. Ralph glanced at his watch. It was almost five. That left only seventeen hours.

But Matt Coleman was waiting for an answer to an invitation that meant a lot more than a drink.

"I'm butting out," Ralph said, sliding toward the aisle. "I know when I'm licked. Even if you find this girl—and that's a long, long chance—what makes you think she can identify Faye Harper's friend? A man as careful as he seems to have been wouldn't have gone about handing out calling cards."

"But women talk," Coleman murmured, "especially to other women."

"And even if she could identify him, what would it prove? A man who had reason to keep his association with Faye Harper a secret wouldn't be likely to come forward when she was killed. The mere fact that he didn't doesn't make Messick innocent!"

Ralph wasn't arguing with Matt Coleman; there was no object in that. Coleman wasn't a man to change his mind. But a kid in tight blue jeans had come in and was having a beer at the bar. Just a kid, so full of life and energy he couldn't keep his feet still even if it was too early for the music. He tapped out a couple of fancy steps and swung about, grinning. Walter Messick's face might have looked the same way if he'd ever smiled.

"Sometimes they look like angels," Coleman murmured.

Angel didn't seem quite the right word until Ralph pulled his eyes away from the bar and saw what Coleman was staring at. The street door had opened and a girl was poised against the sunlight. She had short, dark hair rimmed with a halo of fire, and a proud young body no dress designer could ever make mannish. She stood against the door for a moment, and then the door closed and she walked toward the bar with a kind of defiant swagger. Coleman's eyes followed her all the way.

"Remember Faye Harper that day in court?" he murmured. "She was like that—young, alive. Like a beautiful animal it would be a crime to lock up."

Coleman might have been talking to himself. His voice was low and his eyes were still fixed on that girl at the bar. Ralph's eyes were fixed on Matt Coleman.

"That was nearly nine months ago," he said. "You must have a good memory."

"Was it really that long?" Coleman whipped out that handkerchief again and tried to wipe off some of the sweat that was making rivers of the deep wrinkles in his face. "Hot as Hades in that phone booth," he said. "Peculiar thing about Faye, though. I was just thinking, if she'd come up before any judge but you she might still be alive."

"She might still be—?"

Ralph was on his feet by this time, but he couldn't walk away from a statement like that.

"What do you mean?" he demanded.

Coleman looked up with those bland, aquamarine eyes. "I've heard you called 'the conscience of the court,' Judge. A man with less regard for justice might have overlooked a little police indiscretion and put Faye behind bars. If she'd been locked up Christmas Eve, instead of sitting in that car on Mulholland, we wouldn't be sweating out Messick's execution, would we?"

It was a question that didn't need an answer, but Matt Coleman was waiting. He was sitting there with his eyes again fixed on that growing congregation at the bar, and he would go on sitting there even if the odds were one in ten thousand that Gigi Fontaine would join the congregation tonight, or any night. A man who could wonder seven months why a party girl had parked on Mulholland alone, and worry five months over what might have happened to a scrap of silk, wouldn't be dismayed by a thing like odds. But why? For the time Ralph thought of that, he hesitated.

And then the anger rose up inside him and fought back, because Matt Coleman was waiting for more than Gigi Fontaine. He was waiting for Judge Addison, the very conscientious Judge Addison, to take on another burden and sit back down in the imitation-leather booth and sweat out the wait with him. Maybe he'd think up more games to play—more scenic rides to nowhere, and more careful speeches calculated to make a man's mind itch with curiosity. But this time the speech was a failure, because Faye Harper was dead and there was only one thing to be done for the dead—bury them.

"It's your party from now on," Ralph said. "Go ahead and waste your time if you can afford it. I've got a wife who'll worry if I'm late getting home, and she means more to me than any of this nonsense! Mr. Justice be damned!"

And then, before Matt Coleman could put any more disturbing ideas in his mind, Ralph spun on his heel and strode out into the sunlight.

It was settled. A man who couldn't make a decision, and stand by it, was a man without a mind. It was settled, once and for all. Ralph didn't loiter on the sidewalk outside the bar, nervously smoking a cigarette, because he might reconsider and go back inside. He had to compose himself. He had to grope his way out of a fantastic day and come up with a story for Abbie—something rational, some few inconsequential lies to cover the time he'd been away from her. Some few nothings to talk about. Abbie, that was the important thing. Concentrate on Abbie, because a man who couldn't make a decision was a man without a mind.

It was time to go home. Drop the cigarette to the sidewalk. Grind it out with the heel. Always careful, always law-abiding. Go to the sedan and drive back to that small house on the hillside, because it was five o'clock and all things go home at eventide. In a couple of hours the sun would drop into the ocean, and then it would get dark, and the people who could sleep nights would go to bed. And then, after a few millenniums of waiting, it would be ten o'clock and everything would be over.

"Until that hour, I will be watching you."

The sun was still furnace-hot, but Ralph shivered. Crazy, it was just plain crazy for an adult, sober-minded man to be so panicked by a wild threat. Watching? Who was watching? That old lady coming across the street with a bag of groceries on her arm? The kid on the corner selling newspapers? The Japanese gardener driving home with his equipment on his truck? And then Ralph saw it—a small, red, foreign-made speedster sniffing along the curb like a dog hunting light poles. Leo Cox! It took a few seconds for the idea to register, and that was a few seconds too many. The man behind the wheel must have recognized him. There was a sudden roar of the exhaust as the small car nosed out into the stream of traffic and sped away. Ralph kicked the sedan into motion, but it was merely a reflex action. He hadn't covered half a block before that little red hornet had buzzed out of sight.

And so that was the way Ralph composed himself to go home to Abbie. Maybe it was nothing. Cox's office was somewhere in those hills above the street he'd been driving—perhaps he came that way every day; but it had been a long time since Ralph argued a case and he wasn't very convincing. It was the second time the little lawyer with the sudden prosperity had appeared at Matt Coleman's heels—the third time if he'd really been parked in front of the beachside motel. Coleman should know of this, but Ralph couldn't turn back now. If he did, he might never get home for dinner.

Leo Cox, Matt Coleman, and a lady of the night named Gigi Fontaine, all fled from Ralph's mind the instant he came in sight of his own drive. The gardener's truck parked down the street didn't matter—he had expected that. What did matter was Stu's long convertible and most of all— the long, black sedan parked behind it. The sedan didn't belong in his drive. It belonged on the road to Sacramento unless something was wrong with Abbie.

He took the long flight of cement steps two and three at a time. The key was in his hand before he reached the door. Inside, all was strangely quiet. Ralph didn't know what he expected—some kind of confusion, surely, but not quiet. He glanced toward the stairway. There was no sound coming from above. The only sound—and a most peculiar one—was coming from his own study down the hall. He moved forward.

They didn't see him come into the room. Dr. Braidwell stood beside the desk with his back toward the door. Stu was seated at the desk, too busy with the typewriter—Ralph's typewriter—to hear anything above that measured, one-finger treatment he was giving the keyboard. They didn't see, and they didn't hear. It must be something interesting to hold two men at such rapt attention. Ralph came closer until he could see for himself.

Stu was writing a letter—a letter addressed to The Hon. Ralph G. Addison, Judge, Superior Court, County of Los Angeles.

Dear Sir:
I regret to inform you that you have but six days to live ...

CHAPTER SEVEN

For a few moments there was no sound but the slow and groping pecking at the keyboard—a few incredible moments, during which Ralph struggled vainly to understand the scene before him. It was a study in concentration: Stu's, Dr. Braidwell's, and his own. Stu was writing one of those death threats—that's all he could grasp at first. And then he became aware of something else on the desk—the letters! Some were black and burned half away, but one had hardly been touched by fire. The familiar sheet of unruled tablet paper was spread out at Stu's left hand. Painfully, he was copying its message on Ralph's machine.

"I don't know," he murmured, pausing to compare the two messages. "The *e* blurs the same way, but the *g* doesn't drop out of line as it does on the original. It may be that my stroke makes the difference."

Dr. Braidwell leaned forward. The late-afternoon sunlight glinted off his spectacles, making his patrician face seem weirdly eyeless. A deep frown corrugated his forehead.

"It's a fantastic notion, anyway!" he protested. "Ralph's a rational man—he'd never do such a thing!"

"What wouldn't I do, Dr. Braidwell?" Ralph asked at his shoulder.

The evening was full of surprises. Dr. Braidwell looked up, startled, and out of the sunlight his face had eyes. Blue eyes—as blue as Abbie's and as troubled. Stu sat motionless, one hand poised above the keyboard. Then he turned around and looked at Ralph without flinching.

"How long has this been going on?" he asked.

No need to ask what he meant. The letters were in plain view on the desk. They shouldn't have been, of course. They should have been in the fireplace—burned.

"Where did you get these?" Ralph demanded. "What do you think you're doing?"

"I asked a question," Stu said.

"And I've asked several questions! Damn it, Stu, what are you up to? What's going on here?"

Ralph grabbed for the sheet of paper in the typewriter and ripped it out of the machine. It was a violent gesture, but not half so violent as the anger welling up inside him. The message on the paper—the message in the letters. There must be some connection.

"Ralph! Stuart!" Dr. Braidwell scolded. "We can be civil about this. There's no cause to get so upset!"

No cause! Ralph stared at his father-in-law with a look of total incomprehension. No cause! A week of anxiety, a day like a walking nightmare, and now the omniscient Dr. Braidwell, who seemed to think he had two small boys in a classroom, insisting there was no cause to be upset! Somewhere there had to be a limit to what even a civilized man could take without cracking under the strain, and Stu seemed to recognize that even if the older man didn't.

"All right, calm down and I'll tell you what's going on," he said. "Early this afternoon I received a call from Midge. She was scared and excited. She told me a wild tale about a set of letters she'd found half-burned in the fireplace in this room. Letters she'd read."

"She would!" Ralph said grimly.

"Yes, she would. So would you, or Dr. Braidwell, or myself. Anyone who found half-burned letters in a fireplace would be curious enough to read them, and Midge was worried. There were policemen posing as gardeners, she said, and you had just made a very strange phone call. I thought it was just the kid's imagination until I got over here and had a look for myself. It looked serious, but I didn't know where to reach you until Abbie mentioned you were lunching with Dr. Braidwell."

"Abbie!" Ralph exclaimed. "You didn't tell Abbie!"

Stu's eyes were steady. If there was anything more than puzzled anxiety in that searching stare, he was an expert at deception.

"Tell Abbie?" he echoed. "Do you think I'm mad? A thing like this would—" He didn't finish the thought; it wasn't necessary. "I made a quick exit and raced out to that luncheon in the hope of catching you," he added. "You know how close I came."

So that was it! A man with the threat of an unknown shadow at his heels could get wild ideas, but now Ralph was beginning to get another idea. The message on the paper—the message on the letters. Yes, there was a connection.

"I picked up Dr. Braidwell," Stu continued, "and we came back here together."

"And set out to prove that I'd written these letters to myself," Ralph said. There was only an instant of silence, but an instant was enough.

"We've decided nothing!" Dr. Braidwell protested, but a quiet voice had no chance now.

"Oh, haven't you?" Ralph taunted. "Well, Stu has. What's the diagnosis, Stu? Some ingenious kind of self-torture—a variation of masochism? This guilt complex of mine is really getting out of hand, isn't it? Here I am, writing myself death threats because a boy who might have been my son has to die in the morning!"

"Ralph, for God's sake, sit down and stop talking nonsense!" Stu said.

Nonsense! He couldn't even pronounce the word with conviction! It was the truth Ralph had spoken, the naked truth, and it was written all over that handsome, sun-browned face. So proud, so confident, so patient with poor, old-fashioned Ralph Addison, who made such a big thing over anything so trivial as marital indiscretion! Ralph looked at his father-in-law. Dr. Braidwell was more experienced in the art of feigning composure, but even his all-knowing visage betrayed the truth.

"Surely, Stu's told you about my trouble," he added, in an acid voice. "You two have had all afternoon to discuss me. Am I really in such bad shape that you have to call in my father-in-law for consultation, Stu? What's the professional verdict? Do you plan to have me committed?"

"Good Lord," Stu gasped, "you really are upset!"

"Of course, I'm upset! I'm on the verge of a breakdown, remember? That's what you were trying to tell me this morning. I'm going to crack up because I won't fall on my knees and confess my sins. Oh, you must have heard about that, too, Dr. Braidwell—about my great infidelity, about why Abbie left me last year!"

But Dr. Braidwell didn't look all-knowing any more. He looked startled and bewildered. "Ralph, what are you talking about?" he demanded.

"Then he didn't tell you! Maybe that's why he wanted this talk with you, hoping you could tell him why Abbie left. It's a good question, isn't it? One that takes nearly fourteen years to answer—and there's not that much time! There's only a few hours left!"

He was talking too much. Too much, too loud, and using all the wrong words. He strode over to the fireplace in order to escape the searching stares of two pairs of eyes; but the yellow face of the old clock was waiting for him, and the time had a memory in it. It was twenty-two minutes past five.

Abbie met him at the door. She was wearing hat, coat, and gloves, and her bag stood waiting in the hall. "I'm leaving you, Ralph," she said. "It's not such a change, really. We haven't been together for a long time. You don't need me." When she was gone, he came into the study and stared at the yellow face of the old clock. It was twenty-two minutes past five on a lonely day in November.

Ralph whirled about suddenly, and faced those searching stares.

"All right," he cried, "I'll confess! I'll say anything you want me to say! What is it you're waiting to hear—that I'm not good enough for Abbie Braidwell, that I never was? That I failed her for fourteen years, and went back to my own element the moment she was gone?"

"Ralph!" Stu exclaimed. "I think you've said enough!"

"Enough?" Ralph tried to laugh, but the sound caught in his throat. "You're too easily satisfied. Why don't you go in for the kill while you've got me on the ropes? Poor Stu, standing by all these years, waiting for Abbie to come to her senses and return to her own kind! And maybe you weren't the only one waiting. Maybe *you* were waiting, too!"

These words were for Dr. Braidwell. Angry words that would have aroused any mortal man. But Dr. Braidwell wasn't quite mortal. He was a serene intelligence with a body, and he took the accusation with tolerant eyes.

"It's the strain," he murmured. "It's all this worry about Abbie, and the pressure of that boy's conviction. It's a pity the new appointment had to come at such an inopportune time."

"Then why did it?" Ralph snapped. "Why didn't you telephone your dear friend, the Governor, and call it off? Oh, don't think I don't know about that appointment! That poor fool Abbie married is in a rut—lend the boy a hand! Too bad you aren't so close to the President. I might have made the Supreme Court!"

The shouting had to end sometime. Ralph knew that even before he saw Stu get up from the chair and come toward him. He didn't move. He stood there with his back to the old clock while Stu's strong hands grasped his shoulders and shook him as if he were some bad-tempered child.

"Shut up!" Stu said. "Shut up this instant! What are you trying to do?"

Stu didn't shout. The words were soft, almost whispered; and his eyes were filled with a strange comprehension that made it impossible for Ralph to meet them with his own.

And Ralph's words, when he found them, sounded rather foolish in a suddenly quiet room.

"Abbie," he said. "Abbie mustn't worry!"

"Abbie's all right," Stu said. "Abbie's fine."

"I didn't write those letters."

This time Stu didn't answer. It was Dr. Braidwell's voice that came quietly across the room. "I never thought you did, son," he said.

After that, it was easier to tell the story.

When Halam Mills heard of six threatening letters that had gone into a fireplace, instead of to his office, he was understandably angry. Matt Coleman—well, Ralph wasn't sure how he had reacted. He'd made no comment. He must have just sat there on the edge of a straight-backed chair and frowned at the toes of his shoes. But now Ralph had two other listeners—listeners who should understand why he'd kept his silence and not gone running to the police until a muffled voice on the telephone breathed life into the words on that cheap tablet paper. He waited for reassurance of that understanding, but the story had become more important than the teller.

"Do you mean that the man called here?" Dr. Braidwell queried. "On your private wire?"

Ralph nodded. "That's not all," he said. "There's someone else who's been getting these same threats—a policeman, Matt Coleman. He received a call this morning, too, at the district attorney's office."

Somewhere out in the city, Matt Coleman was asking questions at this very moment. Maybe he was still sitting at that booth in a bar at the foot of the Strip, watching with careful eyes and listening to the gossip of the regulars. Maybe he was scouring the neighborhood, moving from bar to bar at that slow, ponderous gait—steady, persistent, stubborn Matt Coleman. Ralph didn't tell that story. It was question-and-answer time again.

"It's fantastic!" Dr. Braidwell gasped. "Who would do such a thing?"

"And why?" Stu added.

And how? Ralph thought. Aloud, he said, "That's what the district attorney said—fantastic. That was just before he ordered a watch put on this house. The gardener pose was at my request that nothing be done to disturb or arouse Abbie."

"Then the district attorney thinks this Mr. Justice may try to strike at you here," Dr. Braidwell observed. "Really, this is too much!"

The sunlight glinted on Dr. Braidwell's spectacles, and his eyes were gone again. But Stu had eyes—puzzled, thoughtful eyes. He took that half-copied message from Ralph's hand and read one line aloud. "Because you sentenced Walter Messick to death ..." He stopped reading and sought Ralph's eyes. "What about this police officer, Matt Coleman?" he asked. "Why does Mr. Justice threaten him?"

"He arrested Messick," Ralph said.

"Is that all? It sounds like an awfully weak reason."

"Reason?" Dr. Braidwell echoed. "Does a lunatic have reason?"

"Motivation, then. Is that all Mr. Justice has to say to Coleman?"

"He accuses him of withholding evidence," Ralph said.

"What kind of evidence?"

Stu was beginning to sound like a prosecuting attorney, and Ralph was tired of questions. He wanted to get out of this room. He wanted to go upstairs to Abbie and forget an agonizing, futile day, but Stu was waiting for an answer, and he had to tell another story. He had to relive that day—the search for the missing scarf, the visit to Leo Cox's office, the depressing journey into Walter Messick's world. Something of the horror of it must have crept into his voice. Dr. Braidwell interrupted with a fatherly admonition.

"You mustn't let the boy's environment upset you, Ralph," he said. "It's a tragic situation, but you can't take the burden on yourself."

He was trying to be helpful, but that patronizing tone brought up Ralph's anger again.

"I'm not burdening myself," he insisted. "Walter Messick dug his own grave. He always had a choice, every step of the way!"

"Of course he did."

"Every step! Just because a boy's born without material advantages—"

Ralph broke off suddenly. He was talking too much again, and Stu was still watching him with those busy eyes.

"We learned nothing," he said. "For all our chasing around, we learned nothing at all."

"But there actually was a scarf," Stu reflected.

"What do you mean?"

Stu met Ralph's question with a steady stare. "I'm not sure," he murmured. "I was just thinking as you told us about this man, Coleman, and the places he took you this morning, that he must consider that scarf an important bit of evidence. It is an intriguing item at that. Why should a scarf disappear unless it has some importance?"

"To whom?" Ralph challenged. "Halam Mills doesn't think it's important, and we have only Coleman's word for it that such a scarf was ever seen on Messick's person."

"Can't Coleman be trusted?"

Ralph hesitated. What Stu asked was a difficult question to answer. "He's an old man," he said. "He's nearly ready for retirement—and he's been ill."

"Is he senile?"

"Damn it, Stu, what are you driving at? Do you think Messick's innocent, too?"

It was Stu's fault. He should have known—he should have understood this was no time to ask questions of a troubled man. But now the words were out, and not until he heard them himself did Ralph realize how true they were. Matt Coleman did believe Messick was innocent. He wasn't looking for Mr. Justice—he was looking for a killer.

"I sentence you, Walter Messick, to die ..."

Ralph was all alone. There were two shop-window dummies with him in the study—a tall one with a sun-browned face and blond, wavy hair, and another tall one with a white wax face and that distinguished gray at the temples. Shop-window dummies in a shop-window room. It was all imitation. It was all pasteboard and wax.

But the telephone wasn't pasteboard or wax. The telephone was reality screaming at his ear. The third time it screamed, Ralph walked to the desk and lifted the instrument from its cradle.

There was a sound of music—a piano with a crazy beat—and then the voice came through.

"Judge Addison? Coleman, here."

"Coleman," Ralph repeated dully. "Yes, what do you want?"

"I think I've got a lead on Gigi Fontaine."

"Gigi Fontaine?"

Gigi Fontaine wasn't pasteboard and wax either. She was real, then.

"Faye Harper's girl friend," Coleman said. "I just bought a beer for a man who saw her last week. He gave me her new address, unless she's moved again. I'm going home for a bite to eat and then run out there. I thought maybe you'd like to come along."

Matt Coleman waited for an answer. The dummies in the shop window were waiting, too, and all Ralph could do was hang onto the phone and try to understand what was happening. He needed time. He needed a quiet place where he could weigh the evidence and reach a decision. "Ridiculous," said Halam Mills, "the work of a crank!" ... "Fantastic!" said Dr. Braidwell. "Who would do such a thing?" ... "And why?" echoed Stu. There were too many voices and too much chasing around. How could a man think? How could he be sure?

"I told you before," Ralph shouted at the telephone, "from here on it's your party! So far as I'm concerned, the Messick case is closed!"

He slammed the phone back on the cradle before it could give him an argument. Abbie was waiting upstairs. It was twenty-two minutes past five, and Abbie hadn't left him after all.

Spring lingered long in the mountains. It was almost June before they could get away, but the snow was still deep at the higher levels, and the wind was cooled by the breath of it all the way down to the cabin. But in those days you took whatever you could grasp from a wild calendar of time without season. There were only two things in the world then—the war and Abbie.

For some men the war was a paper headache—a desk in hell where the only uniform was a rationed suit with a shiny seat on the pants. For other men the war was adventure in a custom-tailored tunic with bright bars on the shoulders. Stu was very handsome the day he said good-by. "Take good care of my girl," he said, "and, for heaven's sake, do something to cheer her up. The world didn't end when she lost that baby. You're both young. There's plenty of time."

And so they had gone to the mountains, where everything was cool and quiet, and there was only one thing in the world—Abbie.

"I've been thinking," Ralph said, "when it's all over, let's go back to that cabin. Let's have a real vacation for a change."

It was after the small talk, the unimportant lies that were meant to dispose of a too important day. Abbie sat propped up against the pillows. She'd changed to a fresh bedjacket, something frilly and white that made her look like an angel with yellow hair. She'd been having a dinner tray, the remnants of which Ralph nibbled as he sat on the edge of her bed.

"I'd sure like to drop a line in that lake again," he added. "It's been a long time."

Abbie didn't seem to hear. The late light cast a shadow across her eyes, and there were times when Ralph didn't know Abbie unless he could read her eyes.

"I thought I heard the typewriter when Midge brought up my tray," she said.

He needed a fresh lie now. "It was your father," he said. "He changed his mind. He's not going back tonight, after all."

"I know. He told me." Abbie's fingers worked restlessly at the hem of her bedjacket. "I'm glad," she added quickly. "His eyes bother him when he drives against the lights. He's not as young as he used to be."

Nothing was as young as it used to be. You just hung on tight and pretended.

"Do you know what I thought?" she asked suddenly. "I'd been napping, and then Midge came in with the tray. I heard the typewriter and I thought it was you. I thought you were working on your book."

"My book?" Ralph echoed.

"Don't you remember? It's been years, oh, so many years. You were going to write an outline of history on human rights. It was right after the war when everybody was so excited about that brave, new world. It was to be a birthday present for our child."

"Abbie!"

The light was failing. Ralph reached over to the night stand and switched on the lamp. He still couldn't read her eyes. They were closed tight.

"I had a talk with Stu this morning," he said. "He told me you were worried about some bad dreams I've been having. You mustn't be, you know. It's just the strain."

"I know," Abbie answered, but her eyes were still closed.

"And you know Stu. He has some wild theory that my past sins are coming back to haunt me on the eve of the birth of our child."

"What a horrible thought! No wonder you've had bad dreams!"

She was teasing him, but Ralph couldn't be sure, not while her eyes were still closed. He had to say the rest of it.

"Abbie, I want you to know this."

Her lids were tight now, as if she had to strain to keep them closed.

"There's never been anyone in my heart but you, not in all these years."

There were moments, like this one, when the world was good again; when nothing was wrong, or ever could be wrong, as long as they were together. Abbie's arms drew him close. There was no danger anywhere.

"When you left me I nearly went mad," he murmured. "I didn't care what happened. I wanted to destroy myself."

"Don't talk about it," she said.

"What went wrong, Abbie? What happened to us?"

"Time," she said. "Time and life."

And that was the answer. Stu wouldn't believe it, and Dr. Braidwell couldn't understand it; but that was the answer just the same. And the way Abbie said it, with her arms holding him close to the warmth of her, it was good. It was all in the past, which was dead, and there was nothing to remember but the time—and the life—to come. The new life, the miraculous beginning again—a son, perhaps, with immortality in his eyes. This was the important thing. There was nothing else to remember.

Ralph closed his eyes, as Abbie had done, and for a little while the terror of the day was just a bad dream that would soon be over. There was no danger and no doubt. It was all in the mind of a sick and weary policeman, who jumped at shadows and chased after one taste of glory before he retired without even "a stripe on his sleeve." Ralph had to think hard to recall where he'd picked up that phrase—Cox, Leo Cox in the rear booth of that hot, crowded café. Poor old Matt Coleman, who had no tomorrows.

Suddenly, Ralph sat up stiffly on the edge of the bed.

"What is it?" Abbie asked.

"The telephone," he said.

She smiled at him. "You must have been dreaming. The telephone didn't ring."

Abbie was wrong. The telephone had rung a long time ago. Ralph glanced at the windows. It was almost dark. How could that be? He might have dozed a few minutes, but it was early when he left the study. He looked at the small clock on the night stand and couldn't believe his eyes. Almost eight o'clock. And then he understood.

"I didn't finish winding the old clock this morning," he said. "It must have stopped."

He was on his feet by this time, and Abbie's eyes were puzzled. "Must you wind it now?" she asked.

"It's not that. It's an appointment. I have to go out for a while."

"Tonight?"

"Tonight."

Ralph left the room quickly before Abbie could ask any more questions. He passed Midge on the stairway coming up for the tray. She'd washed her hair. He could see the neat pincurls peeking out from under the silk kerchief tied on her head. "I'm sorry dinner's so late," she said, "but you can eat now."

Midge was wrong, too. It wasn't five twenty-two at all. It was much, much later.

After Midge went downstairs with the tray, Abbie was all alone for a time, and then the door opened and Dr. Braidwell came into the room. He was a quiet-moving man. He'd almost reached the bedside before she heard him coming and turned her head aside. But the light was still on. He could see her face and the way her fingers twisted on the sheet.

"Abbie, honey, is everything all right?" he asked.

She had to get a senseless smile on her face before she could look at him. "Of course," she said. "Where's Stu?"

"Are you in pain?"

Even a quiet man could be startled. Even a wise man could look helpless and afraid.

"I'm fine," she lied. "I just wanted to see Stu to tell him something."

"Oh, I'm sorry, baby, but you can't. Stu's gone out."

"With Ralph?"

"No, he left before Ralph. But I think I know where I can reach him if it's important. He mentioned that he was going to the district attorney's office—"

If Dr. Braidwell hadn't broken off his speech in such an obvious attempt to swallow his words, Abbie might not have looked at him so strangely. She might even have seemed more convinced when he added, hurriedly, that the call had something to do with an impending golf tournament. But then, Abbie wasn't listening too closely anymore. Ralph was gone and Stu was gone, and the time was running out.

A tight line of pain laced around her mouth. Her fingers found the sheet again and twisted it tighter and tighter.

CHAPTER EIGHT

An appointment. It wasn't as if Ralph had lied to Abbie when he left her so abruptly; he had an appointment, and no amount of shouting at Stu and Dr. Braidwell, or of burying his head in Abbie's breast and closing his ears to everything but the warm beat of her heart, could cancel that appointment now. Twice he'd tried to break away from Matt Coleman. He would try just once more.

It was nearly eight-thirty when he reached the house. Coleman was in the telephone directory—a Hollywood number, Halam Mills had said. It made things easier knowing that. The city had grown too large for one directory. They came in sets now. He had thought of that as he wrote down

Matt Coleman's address. He had thought of that and several other things. It was a house in one of the older sections of Hollywood, a small, frame bungalow with a wide front porch and a low picket fence lining off the neat, green lawn. There were fat green hedges in pots at either side of the steps, and a pair of painted metal chairs where Matt and his missus must have spent the warm summer evenings in years gone by. Similar porches along the quiet street were already so occupied as he mounted the front steps. If there was to be any relief from the heat of the day it would come now.

A light was showing at the rear of the house, and the old green coupé still sat in the driveway. Coleman hadn't left, then, on his promised visit to Gigi Fontaine. Ralph rang the bell. In a few moments, the door swung open on a shirt-sleeved Matt Coleman with a percale apron tied about his thick waist and a limp dishtowel in one hand.

"Why, Judge Addison!" he exclaimed. "What a nice surprise. Come in, come in."

All that was missing was the red carpet, and Ralph couldn't help feeling that Coleman might have arranged that, too, if he'd stayed away just a little longer. He stepped into an old-fashioned living room that sprang to meet him as the light snapped on. It wasn't much of a room: small, somewhat cluttered with bric-a-brac, and furnished in the style of the five-room bargain specials that have a set of kitchenware thrown in as a buying incentive. Someone had put a lot of time and patience into the hand-crocheted arm runners and head rests on the parlor suite, and there was an obvious do-it-yourself look to the greenery shelf under the front windows. At the far end of the room was a gas-log fireplace, and on the mantelshelf stood a row of photographs—young men, mostly, with self-conscious smiles and conspicuously new uniforms, but in the very center of the row was a large portrait of Matt Coleman and a woman with unconcealed years in her pleasant face.

"Celia, my wife," Matt Coleman said, noting Ralph's interest. "That was taken on our twenty-fifth anniversary. The others are a few of our boys."

"*Your* boys?" Ralph echoed. "But I thought—"

The unfinished question brought a smile to Coleman's eyes. "That's right," he said, "I have no children of my own. These are just a few of the boys my wife and I befriended through the years. Boys in trouble, mostly. Some of them are gone now. It's a sad thing to work with a boy, trying to get him straightened out to meet life, and then all he gets is a chance to meet death." As he spoke, Matt Coleman moved closer to the mantel. Folded in a neat square beside one of the photos was a piece of silk that became, as he took it down and shook it out, a scarf printed in an oriental design. "One of the boys sent this to my wife when he was stationed in Japan," he added. "A couple of months later he was dead. But I guess I told you about the scarf, didn't I? It was one just about like it that Walter Messick had wrapped about the Harper woman's jewelry when I arrested him. A little different color, maybe, but the same silk and the same design. I guess a lot of the boys overseas must have sent home scarves like this."

Ralph barely glanced at the scarf. It wasn't important. What was important was the way Coleman had brought it up again, so casually one might almost think this scrap of silk was always kept on the mantel for convenient display to callers. A couple of hours ago, he had accused this man of sharing Mr. Justice's faith in Messick's innocence. Sometimes a man spoke truth in an outburst of nerves. It was time to find out one way or the other.

"I'm glad you changed your mind about coming with me tonight," Coleman added, carefully refolding the scarf. "There's an interesting thing about Gigi Fontaine—"

"I didn't say that I was coming with you," Ralph interrupted.

Coleman replaced the scarf on the mantel and turned about, slowly. "But you're here."

"And you're waiting."

There was no mistaking the implication of Ralph's words. That big surprise act at the door had been too much of an act; Coleman wasn't the type to carry it off. But he was the type to recognize a situation when he saw one. He grinned sheepishly. "Well, I was hoping you might reconsider," he admitted. "Just sitting around with an ax hanging over your head can get awfully nerve-wracking. The Fontaine woman may be no help at all, but talking to her gives us something to do. Isn't that right, Judge?"

"That's right," Ralph said, "but I'm getting a little confused, Coleman. What is it we're trying to do? Do you remember?"

Now Matt Coleman looked surprised and it wasn't an act. "Do I remember?" he echoed. "What do you mean?"

"What it is we're trying to do," Ralph .repeated. "Oh, I knew this morning. I followed you out of Halam Mills's office for one reason. You were going out to track down Mr. Justice, and I liked the idea. I have a long-standing disapproval of anonymous letter writers, particularly when the letters threaten my life. I want to meet such a man. I want to ask him why he does such a thing."

"So?" Coleman queried.

"So I think we've wandered off the track. Frankly, I don't think you're half so concerned with finding Mr. Justice as you are with the possibility that he may be right about Messick's alleged innocence."

Some men could be nailed down with nothing less than six-inch spikes, but Coleman didn't wince. Instead, he reached for his own hammer.

"Aren't you?" he asked.

"What?" Ralph gasped.

"Aren't you concerned with the possibility that Messick may be innocent? I should think you would be. It worries me and I merely arrested the boy. You sentenced him."

"But I had to sentence him! The jury found him guilty!"

For just an instant, Ralph hated Matt Coleman. This wasn't turning out right; Coleman wasn't telling him what he wanted to know. He was just standing there, his back to the cold fireplace and that silly little apron tied about his thick waist, calmly studying out the grave matters on his mind.

"Yes, I guess there's always that for a judge to fall back on," he mused, "the jury. A cop, now, holds death in his hands every time he draws his gun and no one but himself to blame if he makes a mistake."

He might have been talking to himself, but he wasn't. Ralph was listening. In spite of all that fine determination, he was listening! But who was this man to drag, drive, and lead him about on the very unscenic tour of the life and death of miserable Walter Messick? A sick man, a lonely man, with a father complex for every delinquent boy he came across. He could see that now that he could see Matt Coleman in his home surroundings. And wasn't that what Halam Mills had been trying to get across in his office this afternoon? Just a sick and aging man with a one-track mind—that was Matt Coleman!

But the doubt in Ralph's mind wasn't so easily appeased. He still had to know.

"I'm not aware that a mistake has been made," he declared, "but if you are, Coleman, and if you have evidence to that effect—*evidence*, not just hunches or hearsay—then I think you'd better tell me about it while there's still time to act. Unless you do have evidence, I see no reason to change my mind. The Messick case is still closed."

If six-inch spikes weren't long enough, you got them longer. Ralph drove them in hard and waited for an answer, waited an eternity while Matt Coleman scowled at the floor.

"That's what I'm looking for," he said at last, "evidence."

"Isn't it a bit late for that?"

"Late?" Coleman's head came up. He glanced at the windows where the late twilight was still hanging onto the coattails of darkness, and donned a wry smile. "Why, we have a whole night!" he said brightly. "That's practically a lifetime, Judge—Walter Messick's lifetime. As I recall, it only took the jury forty-five minutes to find him guilty. That doesn't seem much thought to give a life, does it?"

It was the smile that got under Ralph's skin. "It was probably forty-five minutes more than Messick ever gave it!" he snapped.

"I'm not so sure, Judge. I'm not so sure."

Now the smile faded as quickly as it had come. Coleman turned about and faced the row of photos on the mantelshelf. He studied them for a few quiet moments, looking both grave and ridiculous with his apron, his dish-towel, and his problem.

"Sometimes I think the kids, the wild ones, I mean, like Messick and my boys here, give life more thought than most of us," he mused. "The wrong kind of thought. The negative, 'what's the use?—you can't beat the odds' kind of thought. They have a case, too. That's the pity of it. Every big Caddy driven by some smart operator whose manicured hands have never lifted anything heavier than a marked deck, every bleached chippie in mink getting the front-page glory treatment, is just another star witness for their case. But that's nothing compared to the witnesses they get at home. Nothing at all."

Suddenly Coleman looked away from the faces on the mantelshelf. He looked at Ralph's face, and he looked hard.

"So you're going to be a father soon," he said.

For a moment Ralph was thrown off guard by what he mistook for a change of subject.

"God willing," he murmured.

"God willing," Coleman repeated after him. "Oh, the worry and pain that goes to bringing them into the world, and then the carelessness af-terwards. I can't help being curious about what a judge thinks when he sen-tences a human wreck like Walter Messick. Does he think about his own child? Does he think, 'This might be my son'?"

There was no resemblance between Matt Coleman and Stu Wilder, physical or otherwise, and yet the words were strangely familiar by im-plication. "That's ridiculous!" Ralph bristled. "Preposterous!"

"And sentimental nonsense," Coleman added. "Don't forget that one, Judge. It's the capital crime of our age to be sentimental. And yet, it does happen that children from good homes and fine families come to stand where Messick stood, and to hear the words he heard. Have you ever thought about that, Judge? Have you ever wondered how that could be?"

This wasn't what Ralph had come to hear: a sermon preached to a con-gregation of paper faces and a man who needed no reminder of his parental obligations! But he had to listen. That was the terrible thing—he had to listen until Matt Coleman told him what he must know.

"I've thought about it for more than a quarter of a century," he contin-ued. "A kid like Messick, with the start he's had—well, you can almost un-derstand when he takes to the needle for a quick dream. But what about the others? What about the boy, or the girl, maybe, from that good home who does the same thing? What kind of a world do we have when youth has to get its dreams from a hypo? What are they running from? What is it they don't want to face?"

All of these questions had to mean something. Ralph was beginning to learn that whatever Matt Coleman said had to mean something.

"I suppose you know the answer," he challenged.

The man in the percale apron was much too serious now to trade barbs. "I know at least a part of it," he answered. "A big part. It's the lies. You can't lie to kids, Judge. They're too smart. They see right through a lie, and what they see is more hideous than if the world never pretended to be civilized and decent. There's no uglier sight than the face of hypocrisy.

"But we do lie to kids. We do it deliberately, as if it were a patriotic duty. We start when they're toddlers with those cute storybooks where the evil ogre is always destroyed and nobody wins his heart's desire unless he's pure in heart; but while Mother reads the story, Father's out pulling off a deal that makes Jesse James look like a Sunday school teacher, except that Jesse got shot and all Father gets is the reputation of a dynamic go-getter. But that's only the beginning of the lies. Later, we send the little fellows off to school where they learn to stand up tall and recite, '... one nation, indivisible, with liberty and justice for all.' But Junior can't play with a certain little boy in the schoolyard because his skin's a different color, and he can't invite a certain little girl to his birthday party because she's been taught different words in her prayers. That's the most terrible lie of all, the lie we make of faith. We pray in the name of a Man who commanded us to love our enemies, and all the while we're reaching for a gun! Is it any wonder the kids get confused? Is it any wonder they hate us for the lies?"

There was a big quiet after Matt Coleman's sermon, a big hush that lasted all the time it took Ralph to grope for a rebuttal. And he had to make one, because whatever Coleman said meant something.

"That's life," he protested. "That's what life is—compromise and adjustment! A mature mind—"

"Mature!"

The one word cut through Ralph's argument like the blade of a guillotine. Coleman stared at him with tragic eyes.

"That's fine," he said. "That's a sensible attitude, and I'm sure my boys here would have got around to it, if they'd just had the chance to mature! But it seems something's always happening to boys I know. They get bombed, or torpedoed, or blasted down by a trigger-happy cop with a brand-new badge on his chest!"

It was no accident, what Matt Coleman said. Ralph had time to realize that in the silence that came after. In the silence and in the old man's eyes. And now, for the first time, they were an old man's eyes. Then he screwed up a twisted smile that Ralph could feel in the pit of his stomach.

"That's what you wanted to know, isn't it, Judge?" he asked. "You came here to learn why this stubborn cop, Matt Coleman, is so concerned over a boy who's no good to anybody, especially himself. Well, maybe that's it. The beginning of it, anyway. Murder isn't an easy thing to forget."

"Murder!"

The word Ralph whispered was like a shout against the silence.

Coleman nodded gravely. "Oh, it was legal," he said. "A burglar alarm was ringing, and I yelled at the kid to halt, but he was scared. He was just fifteen years old and scared. I was scared, too, but I had a gun." Coleman wiped one big hand across his face, as if to wipe away a memory. The gesture wasn't successful. "Oh, I tried to justify myself, the way every man does when he knows he's in the wrong. The kid was a lawbreaker at fifteen. He'd probably have grown up to be a criminal, a killer even. I was doing society a favor by getting rid of him. That's some of the line I'd tell myself when I couldn't sleep nights. But it never helped. I knew why that boy died. It wasn't to protect society, or that shopkeeper, or anybody else. It was because I was just as scared as he was, and I had a gun and a badge on my shirt."

It was terrible how a man could go bankrupt for words. Ralph wanted to answer, more than anything else in the world, he wanted to answer and deny Matt Coleman's guilt, but he couldn't remember so much as one word of his own. All he could remember was the insinuating voice of Leo Cox in a cheap café: "... a man like Coleman just has it in for the world. Some people can't live down their own mistakes."

And Matt Coleman, who never stopped watching Ralph's face, seemed to know exactly what he was thinking.

"I haven't told you this out of any morbid pleasure of confession," he said. "I'm just trying to explain why it is that I'm going out tonight and hunt Gigi Fontaine, or that unknown friend of Faye Harper's, or that missing scarf, or anything else that might possibly clear up some of the doubt in my mind about Walter Messick's guilt. And I'll keep right on hunting until ten o'clock in the morning, because I know something you don't know, Judge Addison. I know what it is to live with a big mistake.

"I may be crazy as hell. There may be no chance for Messick, or for any of us. The lie may win out over the dream that doesn't come off the end of a needle, and I may be just an old fool who never grew up. But I have to make the effort. That's how I learned to sleep nights."

Matt Coleman untied the strings of the percale apron and laid it across the arm of the divan. He put the dish-towel beside it. Then he walked over to the greenery shelf and prodded the dirt in one of the pots with a stubby finger.

"I'll have to remember to water these when I get back," he mused. "Miss

a day or two in this hot weather and plants just wither up and die." And
then he turned around expectantly. "Are you coming with me, Judge?" he
asked.

And Ralph, now that he had the answer he'd come after, could do only
one thing.

CHAPTER NINE

There was an interesting thing about Gigi Fontaine. Matt Coleman got
back to his interrupted disclosure as they drove off in Ralph's sedan toward
an address wangled from one of the girl's drinking companions. The address, he explained, had a familiar sound, and a check with headquarters
explained why. Gigi was living at Faye Harper's old apartment. There was
nothing particularly unusual about someone taking over a friend's vacated
quarters—Gigi wasn't likely to be bothered by more than one kind of
spirit—but there was a note of excitement in Coleman's voice as he told
the story.

"There's a possibility that the landlady might have seen the man we're
after," he explained. "Landladies are supposed to be adept at that sort of
thing."

But Coleman was forgetting his own theory. "I thought it was already
decided that our mystery man never met the Harper woman anywhere but
on Mulholland Drive," Ralph reminded.

"I said it was a possibility," Coleman retorted. "It won't hurt to ask."

A couple of miles west of that frame bungalow with fat, green hedges on
the front porch was an area a few notches up the income bracket. Most
of the frame bungalows had long since been taken on long night rides and
replaced with ultramodern apartment courts constructed of chicken wire,
stucco, and loans nobody had got around to investigating; but there were
still a few blocks of stubborn duplexes and one conspicuous two-story
frame that must have been built by someone who was homesick for Cape
Cod. It was a homy place, too homy for the likes of Faye Harper and Gigi
Fontaine, but the landlady soon explained that incongruity.

She was an odd-looking landlady. She wore levis, a red plaid shirt, and
dark circles under her eyes. She was about halfway between a teen-ager and
an applicant for Social Security, and looked no friendlier, at first contact,
than the huge brown-and-white dog that peered out, growling, between
her legs. Coleman asked for Gigi Fontaine and the woman's frown deepened. For a moment it seemed they had come to the wrong house.

"Oh, Fontaine," she said at last. "She's in the rear apartment. Just take
the walk around to your left."

But they had already taken the walk around to the left.

"There's no light showing and nobody seems to be home," Coleman explained. "We wondered if you might know where she's gone or when she might return. It's important that we see her tonight."

"What are you, bill collectors?" the woman asked.

"Not exactly," Coleman said.

The woman looked relieved. "That's good," she said. "Every time a bill collector comes asking for one of the tenants I know I'm going to have trouble collecting the rent." Then the landlady paused and a look of apprehension came into her eyes. "You're not the police?" she asked.

Coleman looked confused. He glanced at Ralph, but the glance he received in return said that this was his idea and he could work it out himself. "No, we're not the police," he said finally. "Why do you ask?"

"Gigi Fontaine," the woman said.

"Does that mean Gigi isn't a nice girl?"

The woman scrutinized Coleman's face with careful eyes. An overhead light caught her frown that gradually eased into a kind of secret amusement. The dog seemed to share the change of mood and stopped growling.

"Well, as long as you *aren't* the police," she answered, "I guess I can speak freely. Let's just say that it isn't likely she'll ever appear on 'What's My Line?' That's the penalty of having a nice, private little rental on the back of your property. Privacy has so many uses."

"I suppose it has," Coleman murmured. "Isn't that the place where Faye Harper lived?"

That careful look came back to the landlady's eyes. For a few seconds there was a period of comparative silence—comparative because someone with the volume of Ezio Pinza was vocalizing in the upstairs apartment and a loudspeaker was blaring out heavy drama from somewhere behind the woman's back. "Excuse me a minute," she said, and stepped away from the door long enough to close off the hall that led to the rear of the house. With the doorway temporarily unobstructed, Ralph and Matt Coleman could get a good look at the room beyond. It was a long room, dining and living area combined, and at one end of it, spread out over the top of a large table, was a marvelous array of paperwork surrounding a typewriter. There was no opportunity to get near the typewriter, of course; not with an uncooperative dog blocking the doorway. In a moment the woman returned from her chore. The noise of the loudspeaker had lessened somewhat, but the vocalizing continued at full voice.

"Now, where were we?" she murmured. "Oh, yes. Faye Harper. Are you sure you aren't from the police?"

"Positive," Ralph said, when Coleman hesitated.

"That's good," the woman answered. "I haven't had much use for them ever since one of the tenants went crazy and started tearing the place apart. Here I was, barricaded inside the house with a lunatic overhead, and the police weren't even interested. No act of violence, they said."

"There's a legal technicality," Coleman tried to explain.

"Sure," the landlady said, "no death certificate. Still, it was my own fault in a way. I should have known the old girl was off her rocker. She always paid the rent when it was due."

"But about Faye Harper," Coleman said.

"That's what I'm getting at. Just another example of police bungling. No wonder they never found the killer."

It was time for that silence to come back—that quiet disturbed only by the basso profundo, the loudspeaker, and the added ingredient of an exploding hot-rod backing out of the next-door driveway. The landlady had dropped a small bombshell and was enjoying it. She hitched up her levis and waited for these men who so emphatically were not policemen to make comment.

Ralph heard his own hollow voice asking the first question. "Never found the killer?" he echoed. "What do you mean? There's an execution set for tomorrow."

"Legal murder!" the landlady said. "Walter Messick was a dead man when he walked into the courtroom."

Ralph shot a quick glance at Matt Coleman. The woman's words sounded familiar in sentiment. Had she been coached? Was this meeting a put-up job? But there seemed no sign of recognition between the landlady and the policeman, and certainly none between the policeman and the dog.

"What makes you say that?" Coleman asked, as if the thought were completely new to him.

"No motive," the woman answered. "Walter Messick had no motive at all."

"But the stolen jewelry," Ralph protested.

"He didn't have to kill her to get that. Faye wasn't the kind to put up an argument with a gun in her face."

"She'd been drinking."

"That's right, and Messick was probably high on a joy-pop. I know the story. I followed it in the newspapers. Always do with a case like that. It's part of my work." The woman glanced back over her shoulder at the cluttered table across the room and sighed. "I write," she said sadly. "Amid the din and confusion, between the housework, the tenants, and the family, I write. Mysteries, whodunits. Got one coming out next month based on the Harper case. One thing about it always bothered me. I wondered about that man who went back to her apartment the night she was killed."

"Man?" Ralph exclaimed. "What man? Did you see him?"

He shouldn't have sounded so eager. The woman in the doorway was already suspicious of her callers. For this demand he drew the full attention of those tired but searching eyes.

"No, I didn't see him," she said. "I never saw Faye's men friends. I made it clear to her that I wouldn't have this place used that way. But I heard him. My room is on the south side of the house next to the passageway to the rear apartment. I only work here in hot weather. Gets like a hot-box in my room. But this was on Christmas Eve. I was working all night to meet a deadline, and I distinctly remember hearing a man walk back to her apartment. I remember thinking that he would be disappointed because she'd gone out earlier in the evening."

"Alone?" Coleman asked.

"She drove off alone. I know because I was trying to get the evening paper untangled from the rose bushes when she left."

The conversation was getting a long way from the purpose of finding Gigi Fontaine, but there was nothing to do now but hear out the landlady's story. The Christmas Eve caller had come late, she explained. "I was taking a break for coffee. I'm pretty regular with that break. It must have been about three o'clock."

"And how long did the man stay?" Coleman asked.

The landlady frowned over the thought. "That's another thing that's bothered me. Not at the time, of course, because I didn't know then that Faye was dead; but it must have been twenty minutes or more before I heard the man come back through the passageway. That's a long time for a man to hang around an empty apartment unless he has a reason. Now in my book—"

"Just a minute," Ralph broke in. "If you didn't see this caller, how can you be sure it was a man?"

His answer came in two parts. The first part was visual—an expression of magnificent disgust. The second part left nothing to the imagination.

"This may come as news to you," she said bluntly, "but there's a distinct difference between the sound of a man's shoe on a cement walk and that of a woman's heeled pump. What I started to explain was the way I've worked it out in my book. The man who returned to Faye Harper's apartment that night was her murderer."

"This is in a work of fiction," Ralph reminded. He was masterfully ignored.

"A murderer," the landlady repeated, "who did have a motive for killing Faye. A respectable man, a family man, who'd fallen under her spell and was trying to break loose. But Faye knew a good thing when she found it. Realizing he couldn't get rid of her in any other way, this man made a date to meet her at their usual rendezvous on Mulholland Drive."

"If you ever need a collaborator, I know just the man," Ralph muttered.

"And there, in a fit of panic, shot her. But later, hours later, he began to worry about her diary."

"Diary?" Coleman repeated. "Did Faye Harper keep a diary?"

The landlady shrugged. "How should I know? I never pry into my tenants' private affairs. Wouldn't have time for anything else if I did. But in my book she keeps a diary. That's how the detective solves the case. The murderer, you see, had been very careful to keep his relationship with this woman on a 'back street' basis, but he forgot about that diary until it was too late. That, of course, was what brought him back to her apartment hours after her death."

"It sounds like a fascinating book," Ralph said dryly. "I'm sure it will be very successful."

"It won't," the woman said bitterly. "Every time I do one of these things I determine to put in all the gore the public seems to want, but my heart isn't in it. I'm out of step with the times. I don't think murder is heroic, even when it's done by some avenging crusader who prays to God daily for guidance. I think it takes a lot more courage not to kill what you fear. I guess that shows how old-fashioned I am."

The woman sighed and leaned back against the door frame. For a moment she seemed to forget all about the callers on the porch.

"'Whereunto shall I liken this generation?'" she murmured. "'It is like unto children sitting in the markets and calling unto their fellows, and saying, we have piped unto you and ye have not danced; we have mourned unto you, and ye have not lamented.'"

"What's that?" Ralph demanded. "What's that you just quoted?"

"The Bible," she said. "There are still a few of us about who think of it as more than a cheap excuse for another wide-screen extravaganza with technicolor belly dancers."

"Then I suppose you're familiar with this passage: 'For whatsoever judgment ye mete, it shall be meted unto you again.'"

"The Sermon on the Mount," she answered. "Matthew 7." And then the woman's mood changed abruptly. She cocked one eyebrow at him and smiled a crooked smile. "You must think I'm a mental case," she said. "Sorry, I didn't mean to mount my soapbox. It's just that I have so few opportunities to talk to anyone. Now, what was it you two wanted? Where to find Gigi Fontaine? Heaven only knows, but you might try the local pubs along the boulevard. Like a lot of other people, Gigi gets lonely after dark. And you're right. Who am I to judge?"

She started to back away from the doorway, and the dog, having stood stubborn sentry all this time, made a move to follow. This particular Bible verse meant nothing significant to the woman, or else she was taking advantage of an easy way to end an annoying inquisition. But not yet. Not just yet.

"But the story you've just told us about the man who came to Miss Harper's apartment the night she was murdered," Ralph protested. "Why didn't you tell it to the police?"

"Oh, but I did!" she said.

"They weren't interested, then?"

"For a time, yes. Then Walter Messick came along with the stolen jewelry, and you know the old saying about the bird in the hand. Now, if you don't mind, I have a chapter to finish."

The door was closing, but there was one other question Ralph had to ask.

"In your book," he said, "who *did* commit the murder?"

The volume of the loudspeaker down the hall must have been increased. A theme came up strong, adding to the general din, and the woman glared back over her shoulder.

"The arresting officer," she said. "To hell with *Dragnet!*"

Back at the sedan, it was Coleman who broke up the moody silence. "Well, I guess that tells me!" he said. "It's a good thing the D.A. wasn't with us on that call. He'd have found his crank letter writer for sure!"

Ralph didn't comment. He was too busy thinking about the three o'clock caller at Faye Harper's apartment Christmas Eve. It was foolish to let the landlady's story prey on his mind. Foolish to give it a moment's thought. But this was a night for frivolity, a very grim frivolity. This was a night for hunting phantoms by the clock, and the story of an imaginative landlady was no more to be shrugged off than a match folder or an elusive lush who went by the name of Gigi Fontaine. Try the local pubs along the boulevard, the landlady had said, and so that's what they must do, going from bistro to bistro with the same crazy questions. Do you know Gigi Fontaine? Has she been around lately? Do you expect her in tonight? Crazy questions because a girl like Gigi never made reservations or planned her actions as much as ten minutes in advance. But once a thing was started, there was no turning back.

And then, somewhere just short of midnight, it happened.

"Sure, I saw Gigi just a few minutes ago. She was with some guy at the bar. I think they went back to a booth."

Ask a crazy question long enough and you got an answer. It was a dark, narrow hole-in-the-wall exactly like the dozens of other dark, narrow holes-in-the-wall they'd been crawling through for hours. No different to the eye,

the ear, or the nose; different only in the answer. Ralph tagged along behind Coleman's drooping shoulders while a little tattoo of excitement began to make a liar of logic. Phantoms couldn't be found by the clock, and
yet, the bartender was right. A man and a woman were sitting at a booth
in the back. The woman was a silver-bleached blonde of about twenty-five
who had seen better days and much better nights. She was having difficulty
keeping her face out of the refreshments, but the man, a rugged shadow
with some very expensive cuff links glittering in the dim table light, was
lending attentive assistance.

Coleman reached them first. "Miss Fontaine?" he began, but he got no
further. The sound of his voice brought up the man's head, and it was
Ralph's gasp of recognition that put a sudden end to Coleman's introduction.

"Stu!" he cried. "Stu Wilder! What are you doing here?"

CHAPTER TEN

The cry was involuntary. For a moment Ralph thought he was having
hallucinations, a victim of his own excitement; but the moment passed, and
that well-groomed escort at the wilted blonde's side didn't change identity.
It was still Stu, where he didn't belong, and with a woman he wasn't supposed to know! It was Stu, with a blasé smile on his lips and one eyebrow
upraised.

"Gentlemen, be seated," he said. "You look tired. In fact, you, Ralph,
look completely bushed! And this, I take it, is Officer Coleman."

Stu leaned forward and extended his right hand in a greeting that was
never acknowledged, whereupon the blonde toppled forward into her drink
again. By this time, she was beyond caring anyway, so Stu let her stay there.

"What'll you have?" he asked brightly, as Ralph and Coleman, suffering from a sudden epidemic of knee trouble, eased into the opposite side
of the booth.

"An explanation," Ralph suggested weakly. "Who is that woman?"

"Gigi Fontaine," Stu answered. "Isn't she the one you're looking for?"

"Who told you that?"

"You did. I distinctly heard the name when you spoke to Officer Coleman on the study phone this evening. That was you calling, wasn't it, Coleman? I know it wasn't Halam Mills because I dropped by his office on my
way out here. Just wanted to be brought up to date on what else is going
on that nobody tells me about."

The meaning glance was for Ralph's benefit, but now there was a bit going on that Stu hadn't told. "But this woman," Ralph protested, "how did

you know where to find her?"

"And what have you done with her?" Coleman wailed.

"What have *I* done." Abject dismay washed away the last of Stu's smile. "Look here, officer," he said, "I'm not responsible for this young lady's condition. She's been working on that thirst of hers for a long time to get this far along the road to oblivion. I only arrived ten or fifteen minutes ago!"

"But how did you know where to come?" Ralph persisted.

"Process of elimination," Stu murmured. "But wait, I'll give you a recap. Officer Coleman seems a bit confused."

Matt Coleman wasn't the only occupant of that well-filled booth who was confused. Six hours ago Stu Wilder had been a grim-faced man at a typewriter; now he was a gay man-about-town with a glib tongue and a too friendly manner. It had to mean something.

"I'm Stuart Wilder," he explained. "Dr. Stuart Wilder. Long-time family friend and Mrs. Addison's physician."

"I know," Coleman said. "I've heard of you."

"You have?" The confusion lapped over on Stu's face for a moment, but only a moment. "I've been concerned about Ralph," he added. "He's been nervous and depressed all week—more than normal, I mean. This afternoon some half-burned letters were found in his fireplace which threw a great deal of light on the situation. It's my understanding that you've been the recipient of similar letters, Mr. Coleman."

"I have," Coleman said.

"And it's also my understanding that you and the judge have joined forces today in an effort to track down this Mr. Justice, an effort that has embraced, among other things, a search for a missing scarf, a missing suitor of the late Faye Harper, and a young lady named Gigi Fontaine."

At the sound of her name, the silver-blond head lifted up from the table and a rather indistinct face stared at the two newcomers.

"Pleased to meetcha," Gigi said. "Whatcha drinkin', boys?"

"Not now," Stu urged at her ear. "Take a little breather, okay? Take a little nap."

"Can I put my head on your shoulder?"

Stu made a wry face. "Anything for the cause," he murmured, "but breathe toward the aisle, honey. That's a good girl." With a shrug of resignation, he resumed his recitation. "As I was saying—a lady named Gigi Fontaine. The scarf story I got from Ralph this evening; the story of Faye Harper's mysterious friend was wangled out of the district attorney, who, incidentally, sends a message to you, Coleman."

"A message?" Coleman echoed. "What is it?"

Gigi hadn't been drinking alone. Stu had a glass of his own and sampled it before answering. Over the rim of the glass he said, "I quote, 'What the hell are you up to now?' unquote." The words were for Matt Coleman, but Stu's eyes never left Ralph's face. "I don't think Mr. Mills is very happy," he added. "He seems to think that you two are taking unnecessary risks."

"Is that all?" Coleman asked coldly.

Stu sampled the drink again. "I said I'd deliver the message if I ran into you, and I have," he said. "As for my thirsty friend here, I had to get her package—is that what you fellows call it?—her history, that is, elsewhere. Mills had never heard of her. I, on the other hand, had. Gigi and I are old friends."

"You?" Ralph exclaimed.

Nothing Stu might have said could have been more surprising or unbelievable. Stu Wilder. Everything Ralph thought at that moment must have crossed his face, because the smile that eased over Stu's came like an answer.

"You'd be absolutely appalled at some of the company a bachelor keeps," he observed. "You really would. But the truth of this matter goes back to an old golfing companion—horrible fellow, but one has to put up with all sorts in my profession. He's a bachelor, too, of the confirmed variety and an enthusiast for more than one kind of sport. Has a big house above the Strip and loves to give parties. Sure you won't have a drink, Ralph? You look as if you could use one."

"I could use an explanation," Ralph muttered.

Stu sighed. "All right, but it's dull. Several weeks ago I dropped in on my friend when one of these parties was under way—they're not the kind reported in the social columns, understand. Our little Gigi was present, among others of the sisterhood, and she made an indelible impression. I've never in my life seen anyone, male or female, with such a thirst!"

"And so you knew exactly where to find her tonight," Coleman said.

Matt Coleman looked unhappy and Ralph didn't need a lecture to know why. In her present condition, Gigi wasn't going to be any help at all. Whatever she might know about Faye Harper's careful companion was a secret well preserved in alcohol.

Stu reflected on Coleman's sarcasm. "No," he said thoughtfully, "I didn't know *exactly* where to look, but I did know where to begin looking. I went to see my friend, and he's a man of magnificent resourcefulness. What he doesn't know, he can find out just by making telephone calls. About half-an-hour ago he hit pay-dirt, and then I did know exactly where to find Miss Fontaine. I was only trying to be helpful."

"Thanks," Coleman said grimly. "Thanks a lot."

"And now that we've found her," Stu added, "what do we do with her?"

Coleman scowled at the sleeping Gigi. "You're a doctor," he said. "How long do you think it will take for her to sober up enough to answer a few questions?"

"What kind of questions?"

"She was a friend of Faye Harper."

"Really?"

"And girls sometimes exchange confidences about the men in their lives."

Add a few seconds for mental digestion, and Matt Coleman's words were self-explanatory. Stu drew back his head and stared at the blond heap on his shoulder. "And you think *this* might identify the mysterious suitor?" he marveled.

"That thought never occurred to you, I suppose."

"To me? How could it? I merely overheard a familiar name during Ralph's telephone conversation and tried to be helpful. Where have you two been all evening?"

All this time Ralph had been trying to make up his mind. Was Stu telling the truth? Was he really merely trying to be helpful? He didn't belong here—that was the only thing that seemed to stick in his mind; Stu didn't belong in this element at all.

But now Stu was asking the questions, and Ralph couldn't answer. He'd been to a little frame bungalow in search of the man who was Matt Coleman, and had found both more and less than he'd anticipated, but he couldn't tell Stu that story. He'd been to see Gigi Fontaine's imaginative landlady; he'd been to a dozen or so noisy, smelly bars with air so thick it could be packaged and sent as a gift to anyone you hated; he'd been so far up and so far down the emotional range of a man with, as Coleman put it, "an ax hanging over his head" that nothing was left of him now but eyes, ears, and an uneasy dread of whatever might happen next. But Matt Coleman had more than eyes and ears; he had a tongue. It was Coleman who answered Stu's question, and in such detail that Ralph began to wonder if he was really taking Stu into his confidence or merely laying a trap.

And Stu, innocent-eyed and fascinated, listened to every word.

"Now, if only the mystery-writing landlady were conducting this probe, we might get somewhere," he said when Coleman concluded. "I imagine she'd consider us all as suspects and demand an accounting for our individual whereabouts at three o'clock Christmas Eve. Where were you at that hour, my pet?"

The question was for Gigi. She opened one eye and smiled. Apparently, she'd caught only the last word of Stu's question.

"Sure, honey," she murmured, "but let's have a li'l drink first. Okay?"

"Sweet child," Stu murmured. "She was probably waiting for Santa. If Faye Harper was anything like this one, I fail to see what Mr. Justice is so concerned about. The world's suffered no great loss."

"No greater than the loss it suffers tomorrow when Messick's executed," Coleman suggested.

Stu hesitated. That trouble had crept into his eyes again. He was beginning to look more like the man Ralph had discovered at his typewriter.
"The conversation is getting philosophical," he protested, "and I hate
philosophers. Where was I? Oh, yes—Christmas Eve. Where was I Christmas Eve?"

"Stu, be serious!" Ralph broke in.

"But I am serious! Never more serious in my life. Officer Coleman already regards me as a highly suspicious interloper who's spoiled your interview with Gigi by getting her too drunk to talk. He very likely thinks I
deliberately liquored her up for that very purpose."

"It's an idea," Coleman admitted.

"And such an interesting one," Stu agreed. "Think how well I fit in as
the landlady's suspect. A prominent doctor with a valuable reputation to
protect, and a woman of Faye Harper's ilk threatening me with a fate worse
than death—her death, that is."

"Stu, for God's sake," Ralph protested.

"The high and mighty," Coleman murmured.

He had to explain, of course, and the phrase that had set off this search
for Gigi Fontaine seemed to intrigue Stu. "The high and mighty," he repeated. "Yes, I do make an excellent suspect, don't I? Except for one thing.
You see, Coleman, on Christmas Eve I went to a week-end party, a rather
touching family reunion affair at Dr. Braidwell's home in Ojai. You can
vouch for me, Ralph, because you were there, too. Remember? You drove
up about—what? Ten, ten-thirty? I know we were all waiting for you, especially Abbie."

"Abbie?" Coleman echoed.

"The judge's lovely wife," Stu explained. "He's not half good enough for
her—at least, that's what he's been telling himself for almost fifteen years.
Did a good job of it, too. Finally convinced just about everybody—even
Abbie."

"Look here," Ralph broke in, "I know I've given you a rough time today, Stu, but let's leave Abbie out of this!"

"Leave Abbie out?" Stu frowned over the rim of his glass, and the glass
was almost empty when he set it down again. "But we can't leave Abbie
out," he insisted. "She's our Abbie, yours and mine, and we were all re-
united like one big, happy family at Ojai on Christmas Eve. I got very
drunk, Coleman. Very drunk. The party broke up about one o'clock because Abbie couldn't stand too much excitement, but I stayed down at the
bar all night having my own private celebration. I must admit that I can't
remember much until morning when that repulsive housekeeper of Dr.
Braidwell's woke me up with a tray of horrible-tasting coffee, but I certainly

wasn't in any condition to drive back to Los Angeles and go looking for
Faye Harper's diary."

Stu paused to chuckle over the thought. "Although it might have been
worth the trip at that," he reflected. "Such an item, if such an item existed,
must have been quite fascinating reading."

Stu was talking too much. It was a habit of Stu's that got out of control
whenever he was too excited or too drunk. Ralph, crouched on the edge
of the padded bench, tried to determine which cause had brought on this
recitation. With Stu it was hard to tell.

"All right, now that you've had your little joke," he said, "let's get back
to the subject."

"But I'm on the subject," Stu insisted, "and I'm not joking. Officer Coleman has offered the interesting theory that someone else may have had a
better motive for killing Faye Harper than the man the court's convicted.
Now, unless we're going to be sensible and accept the decision of our established legal system, we've got to dig up this mystery man. There are
about five million people in this county, we have—" Stu paused to consult the watch on his wrist— "slightly over nine and one-half hours, and
I'm trying to eliminate one of those five million by establishing my whereabouts on the night in question. And yours, Ralph, since, so far as I know,
you remained at the house all night, too. At least, you were there the next
day. I actually sobered up enough to put the bags in the car when you drove
Abbie home."

Stu wasn't drunk. Ralph realized that now. He had a purpose in everything he said, and Matt Coleman, who didn't seem to mind how much he
was ridiculed, entered into the spirit of it.

"Maybe you'd like to know how I spent Christmas Eve," he suggested.

Stu drained his glass. "That's a good idea," he said. "After all, you are
the landlady's choice."

"And truth is stranger than fiction," Coleman added. "I went to church
Christmas Eve—candlelight service. You'll have to admit that's a highly suspicious act."

"'... and with what measure ye mete, it shall be measured to you again,'"
Stu murmured. "Yes, under the circumstances, it's highly suspicious. Now,
let's see how that would work out. If you had killed Faye Harper—and you
did know of her and the place she could usually be found—you could have
gone straight from your crime to your church."

"I'd have had time to drive on out to the beach and toss the gun into the
ocean," Coleman said. "According to Messick's testimony, it wasn't much
after eleven when he found Faye's parked car, and the coroner figured she'd
been dead several hours before that."

"The ocean?" Stu repeated.

"That's Judge Addison's contribution. He suggested it this morning."

Ralph had almost forgotten. He caught Stu's eye for an instant, but it was a hard eye to hold. "The ocean," Stu said again. "Yes, I like that touch. It has a certain mood quality. I had no idea you were so imaginative, Ralph, but then you do encourage people to underestimate you. All right, then, after disposing of the gun, Coleman, you drive back to your church to ease your troubled soul. But later, much later, you remember Faye's diary. By the way, how did you know where to find Gigi's apartment tonight?"

The question went unanswered. Stu's story needed an ending.

"And now," Coleman mused, "I'm tortured by my conscience, but can't find the courage to admit my guilt, so I've been writing threatening letters to Judge Addison, and myself, in order to stir up an investigation that will bring about my own apprehension in time to save Messick's life."

"Excellent!" Stu cried. "I really like that solution. It has originality and sheer pathos!"

Pathos it might have, but not originality. "What's so original about a guilt complex?" Ralph demanded. Perhaps he was mistaken about the reaction on Stu's face. Perhaps he didn't actually look startled, as if Ralph had spoken out of turn. In the dimly lighted booth it was difficult to be sure of anything as brief and changing as Stu's expressions.

"Now, who shall we eliminate next?" he asked brightly, as if this nightmare had become an amusing game. "'The high and mighty.'"

"How about the D.A.?" Coleman suggested. "He doesn't seem to approve of my nosing around."

Stu nodded encouragingly. "Then, of course, there's always Dr. Braidwell. He may have walked out on that party for all I know. He does get around for an old boy."

An amusing game, but Ralph wasn't amused. Surprise, amazement, curiosity, all of these things he'd experienced since he stumbled out of the darkness to find Stu Wilder helping Gigi Fontaine with her drinking—but not amusement. Something had to be behind this easy banter. If he could only get Stu alone, if he could just clear out of this stinking hole!

"Let's get out of here," he said, easing toward the aisle. "All this talk is getting us nowhere, and I've crawled through enough gutters for one day!"

"Eagle Scout!" Stu taunted. "That's your trouble, son. You've never learned to relax."

"Which is one thing you can't say for Gigi," Coleman observed. "But I'm with the judge this time. If we all lend a hand, maybe we can walk the lady around the block."

It was going to take a lot more than a walk around the block to put the roses back in Gigi's cheeks, but Coleman was already emulating Ralph's movement toward the aisle when he had a sudden change of heart. The first Ralph knew about it was when a restraining arm pulled him back and held him down.

"Wait a minute," Coleman said. "Unless my eyes are giving out, we have a little friend watching us from the bar."

It took a few seconds to be sure. The room was dark and crowded, and the smoke hung like smog on a councilman's bad day. But one of the shadows that crouched on a barstool was a bit shorter than the others—and much more interested in what was going on in a certain rear booth.

"Leo Cox!" Ralph exclaimed.

"The same," said Coleman.

"But why?"

"That's what I'm wondering—why? And now that we're on the subject, why do you suppose Leo made that trip out to see Mrs. Messick this noon?"

"I must have missed something," Stu hinted.

Stu had missed quite a lot—Cox's trip to the café, the glimpse of a red speedster nosing around a beachside motel.

"And I saw him again," Ralph recalled, "just as I drove away from that bar Faye Harper frequented."

"You what?" Coleman demanded. "Why didn't you tell me?"

Why? It was a stupid question, and Matt Coleman must have known it the moment he asked. He'd preached a sermon in his living room—he'd told a reluctant follower the story of his life. There had been no time for anything so trivial as Leo Cox.

But suddenly Leo wasn't trivial anymore.

"So that's Messick's attorney," Stu mused. "Shouldn't he be spending these last hours with the condemned man, or is that done only in fiction?"

"He should," Coleman answered, "except that he's not Messick's attorney anymore. That makes his curiosity all the more interesting, doesn't it? Why should Leo Cox be tailing the judge and me when he's no longer connected with the case, unless—"

The amusing game was over. Matt Coleman was turning bloodhound again. He was getting excited, and Ralph, sitting so close beside him, was caught in the swell of it even if he didn't know what it was all about.

"Dr. Wilder," Coleman said suddenly, "are you serious about wanting to be helpful?"

"Serious?" Stu echoed. "Do you think I'm holding up this female sponge for pleasure?"

"All right, then, I have an idea. If I'm right about Cox, and he is tailing us, he'll leave the bar right after we go out with Gigi. But I'd like you to stay behind, Doctor, and let the judge and me manage our sleepy friend. It occurs to me that she's well enough preserved to keep for a while. We'll just pile her into a cab and send her home."

"And what do I do?" Stu asked.

"How are you at entertaining old friends—old college chums, let's say, who can't even remember your face?"

Now Stu was getting the swell of the excitement. "The greatest!" he said. "I'm just the greatest host in the world. I take it that I'm about to acquire a new fraternity brother. How long do you want him entertained?"

By this time Ralph was on his feet and Coleman was rapidly attaining that position. The next move was to do the same for Gigi.

"As long as possible," Coleman answered. "Once we get rid of the girl, the judge and I have to go on a treasure hunt. Something I should have thought of long ago."

It was Matt Coleman's show. It had been his show all day, and Ralph was getting rather good at tagging along. They left Stu to take care of Cox, and made as quick an exit as possible with a rubber-legged Gigi propped up between them. Gigi didn't seem to mind. Outside, a couple of cabs waited at the curb for just such emergencies as this. It was getting about that time of the night.

Coleman gave the driver his instructions. "Remember, I want her home. I'm checking back later to make sure that's where she is. It's a rear apartment. The key's probably in her handbag."

The badge Coleman flashed gave his words authority, but the cab driver was unimpressed.

"I know the place," he said wearily. "This one's a regular customer. And I don't need a key. The door's never locked."

"Never locked? That's an interesting thought," Coleman reflected. "I don't like it."

"Why?" leered the cabbie. "What's this one got to lose?"

Matt Coleman had turned awfully grim since those last few minutes in a crowded booth near the bar. Scowling, he sent the driver on his way with a thought Ralph found even more interesting than that unlocked door.

"Just one thing," he said, "her life."

CHAPTER ELEVEN

No explanation followed Matt Coleman's words. The cab pulled away with a faintly smiling Gigi piled in the back seat, and for a moment the midnight street was silent and empty. The big policeman glanced over his shoulder. Stu must be doing his job, all right, because there was no sign of Leo Cox coming through that leather-studded door.

"Do you remember the location of Cox's office?" he asked Ralph. "It can't be far from here."

Cox's office. Ralph groped his way back from Gigi's unlocked door to find a reason for the question.

"Is that where we stage the treasure hunt?" he queried.

Coleman's grunt must have been affirmation. "It may not be ethical," he admitted, "but when a man gets as curious as Cox seems to be about what I've been doing, I get a little curious myself. Let's get started."

Coleman was right—it wasn't far. They'd done a lot of chasing in the past twelve-odd hours only to return, like a new species of homing nighthawks, to within a few blocks of where the search had begun. Ralph nosed the sedan north at the first cross-street and climbed up to where the bright boulevard held back the hills with a neon rope. It was the rush hour on the Strip. Inside the squatty stucco night clubs with the fancy tariffs, high-priced bands were making a lot of noise for tourists who thought this was the way to see celebrities, and outside on the street the Cadillacs were rolling by like a state funeral in Texas. But the parking area outside Cox's office was empty—until a snub-nosed sedan took over the space previously held by an imported red speedster.

"There must be a service entrance around back," Coleman said. "Let's have a crack at it."

"Won't it be locked?" Ralph asked.

The policeman's smile was almost diabolical in the glow of the instrument lights.

"In my profession you learn to overcome such little inconveniences," he said. "And if anybody objects, I'll just let them tell it to the judge."

But nobody objected. There wasn't a soul on the premises—guard, janitor, or night watchman. "It's not the Bank of America," Coleman muttered, when Ralph made mild remonstration, "and we don't have time to get a search warrant." Time. Matt Coleman acted as if time were going out of production and he had to lay in a supply before the stock ran out. The door opened easily. That was the way with these reconstructed showcases. Plate glass and flagstone for the front, and cut-rate hardware on the back door.

"Come on," Coleman said. "This way."

At first it was too dark to do anything but stumble along behind the echo of Coleman's footsteps, and then the darkness washed out a little and a stairway loomed up like a reaching shadow. At the top of the stairs was the door to that little office where a neat brunette held down the reception desk on Cox's trade, but nobody could announce or forestall this visit. When Coleman threw open the second door, that expensive view sprang up before them like a valley full of stars.

There was no darkness now. They could see everything—the chairs, the desk, the filing cabinets. If they'd known where to look they might even have seen beyond the window to that cocktail bar at the bottom of the hill where Stu was entertaining a doubtless reluctant guest. *Stu, who shouldn't have been there at all.*

There were times when Matt Coleman seemed telepathic. "Do you think we can trust the doctor?" he asked.

It was unnerving to have his mind rifled that way. Ralph turned away from the window with a self-conscious start.

"Oh, you mean to hold Cox," he said.

Coleman snapped on the lights. His face was still grim.

"What else?" he asked.

"Nothing, nothing else," Ralph said quickly. "I'm just a little jumpy. I've never broken into an office before."

"I guess you've done a lot of things today that you haven't done before."

"I guess I have."

"And the night's still young."

Coleman didn't make the future sound rosy, and he didn't waste time elaborating. He went directly to the filing cabinet, which was locked, and took care of that slight annoyance in short order.

"One thing that puzzles me," he remarked, pulling open the top drawer, "is what kind of clientele Cox has acquired so quickly. Maybe I'm just an old, evil-minded busybody, but—"

The broken sentence was like an alarm. Ralph swung away from the window to find Coleman poised over that open drawer with an expression of bewilderment on his face.

"What is it?" he asked. "What have you found?"

"Nothing," Coleman said.

"What?"

"Nothing. Look for yourself—nothing—nothing—nothing!"

With each additional "nothing" Coleman jerked open another drawer until the tall filing cabinet stood open from top to bottom. Inside were a lot of folders arranged alphabetically but completely empty.

"Nothing," the big man repeated, in a hollow voice. "Now what do you suppose—?"

"Maybe he's just moved in," Ralph suggested. "It looks like new furniture."

"It looks," Coleman reflected, "like a fancy front. Wait, I'll have a look in the outer office. That cute little secretary must have something besides Cox to keep her busy."

This time Ralph didn't follow the leader. He hung onto the side of the tall metal cabinet and tried to understand what he was doing. This was a man's private office, a law office. It might have been his own.

But no, not with that expensive furniture and that high-bracket view. Not with the impressionistic oils where Jefferson should have hung, and the sports car digests where the legal monthlies should have lain. Coleman was right. Something was very wrong about this office.

"Now, this might be interesting—"

Coleman came back from the outer office. He carried an open folder in his hands. It seemed to be filled with papers.

"A jar of facial cream—with hormones—a hand mirror, and a box of stale doughnuts," he murmured, "plus one lonely correspondence file. That's the sum total of what I found in the secretarial department. D, for Dorritt. Say, isn't that the name the girl mentioned when we called on Cox this morning?"

Ralph heard all of the words. It just took a few seconds for them to compete with the other trouble in his mind.

"Dorritt," he repeated. "Yes, I think you're right. There was a telephone call—"

"An urgent telephone call," Coleman agreed. "I remember now—an urgent call Cox wouldn't take while we were present. I wonder."

He leaned up against Cox's expensive desk and calmly, and apparently without qualms, began to read through the correspondence in that confidential file. "Doesn't seem to amount to much," he murmured. "Maybe I just don't understand legal language. Have a look, Judge?"

Ralph could taste the salt of his sweat on his lips, and it couldn't be that warm at this hour. "This is all highly unethical," he protested.

"Isn't it?" Coleman said dryly. "You know, this set-up reminds me of those lies I talked about earlier this evening. I don't think there's anything lower than twisting the law into a big, fat privilege for those who can afford it—and a club for the poor devils who can't. Doesn't it seem peculiar that a man like Leo Cox, who's never seemed to have an extra dollar, should suddenly blossom into a big legal eagle *with only one client?* Dorritt, Paul, Air Futures, Incorporated. Wait a minute. Paul Dorritt! Of course!"

A lot of things seemed peculiar to Ralph, only one of which was Leo Cox and his sudden wealth. There were a couple of things within the last few minutes. But there was something contagious about the undertone of excitement in Matt Coleman's voice. It was still Coleman's show, and he'd play it out to the very last scene.

"You've heard of him?" he asked.

"I'm not very air-minded," Ralph said.

"He's quite a fellow. Prominent citizen department. I guess he made a pile on war contracts."

"Then he can probably use a lawyer," Ralph said, "a lot of lawyers."

"Sure, he can, and afford them, too. But why does he need a cheap shyster like Leo Cox?"

Why does he need a cheap shyster like Leo Cox? It was a riddle. This was an audience-participation show. Ralph ran the question over in his mind, competing, as it were, with all the other questions that boiled and bubbled like a witches' brew, and then, suddenly, he saw a light in the darkness. A bright, blinding light.

"The high and mighty!" he cried.

Matt Coleman put down the folder on Cox's desk and stroked his jaw with a restless hand.

"It's possible," he said.

"Of course it's possible!" Ralph insisted. "And that would explain everything!"

"Everything?"

"Cox's actions today—the way he's followed us wherever we went. Can't you see what must have happened? In the course of investigating Faye's murder in behalf of his client, Walter Messick, he must have stumbled across the identity of her unknown suitor. Don't ask me how. A man of Cox's questionable connections can probably ferret out anything. And in view of what we both know about the man, I don't think he'd hesitate to use that knowledge to better his own circumstances."

"Blackmail," Coleman reflected. "Yes, I guess that's what I've had in the back of my mind all day, but I still don't see how that explains everything."

"I don't know why not! It's very clear to me. When we called on Cox this morning, he was alerted to our suspicions. He'd naturally be curious to know just how much we might uncover."

"About Mr. Justice," Coleman reminded, "and that missing scarf. Nobody mentioned Faye Harper's mysterious friend in that conversation. I didn't mention him myself until hours later."

"All right, if you don't think Paul Dorritt is Faye Harper's 'high and mighty' friend, what *do* you think?"

Coleman gave his jaw another rubdown. An irritating man, Matt Coleman. Eager enough when an idea was his own, but a regular wet blanket when anyone else made a suggestion.

"I really don't know what to think," he admitted, "except that I'd like to have a heart-to-heart talk with Leo Cox right now."

"And what good do you think that would do?"

The question seemed to surprise Coleman. Ralph had to explain what he meant.

"We have, in our own minds, a case against Leo Cox and, possibly, his benevolent client, Paul Dorritt. But what evidence do we have? What proof that any crime, any malfeasance of any kind, has occurred? If Leo Cox chooses to change his practice, who can stop him? If Dorritt chooses to retain Cox, for any purpose whatsoever, he's certainly within his rights."

Coleman grinned wryly. "This is Judge Addison speaking?" he asked.

Judge Addison. It sounded good. Ralph had experienced a few bad moments this evening, but on his own ground he felt sure again. On his own ground those wild suspicions began to disappear—an imaginative landlady's uncorroborated memory, Stu Wilder's peculiar curiosity, Matt Coleman's little preachments. Without proof they were all figments of the mind.

"This is Judge Addison speaking," he repeated firmly, "and reminding you that even if our worst suspicions are true, even if Paul Dorritt was involved with the dead woman, it still doesn't make him a substitute for Walter Messick in that death cell. A man such as Dorritt would probably pay a great deal to Leo Cox just to keep his name out of the papers, even if he was nowhere near Mulholland Drive on Christmas Eve."

"Then you think our treasure hunt is just another wild-goose chase?" Coleman queried.

"I wouldn't say that. I think this tie-in between Cox and Paul Dorritt may have cleared up a few questions in your mind."

Ralph shouldn't have sounded so patronizing. Halam Mills had got nowhere using that attitude on this man, and Ralph would get no further. He knew that the instant Coleman stopped leaning on the desk. He was almost smiling, but it wasn't the kind of smile that would make anybody happy.

"In my mind, maybe," he said, "but not in the mind of Mr. Justice—and he's the one we have a date with in the morning. No, I can't buy it, Judge. I can't believe we've explained everything. There has to be something else! If Cox is blackmailing Dorritt, he must have some proof, some documentation!"

Coleman wasn't smiling any more. For an instant, he looked like nothing so much as a mad, tiring, and desperate bull making one last gigantic effort before the kill. He swung back to the filing case again, the gaping, empty filing case, and began to ransack it with an almost savage ferocity.

"Something!" he muttered. "A man doesn't pay out a fortune, even to keep his name out of the papers, on hearsay alone. There has to be something."

He came back to the desk again. The top drawer was unlocked. He tore through the contents unmercifully. A mild man he might be in his own living room, but now he was just a bulldog cop who didn't know when he was licked.

"I think we should get out of here," Ralph said. "Stu may not be able to hold Cox, and he's bound to be suspicious."

"Good!" Coleman roared. "Let him walk in on us. Let him tell us where he's got it hidden!"

The top drawer, the drawers on the right-hand side. Nothing, always nothing. It wasn't until he tried the left side of the desk that Coleman struck an obstacle, and he was in no mood to quibble with obstacles. Ralph winced as the lock broke, but Matt Coleman was too busy digging through the contents of this last drawer to feel any pangs of conscience.

"It has to be here! It has to be."

And then came the silence.

Quietly, quietly and gently, a now subdued Matt Coleman drew back his hand from the not-so-locked drawer. By the light of the overhead fixture Ralph saw the reason for this abrupt change—a shimmer of silk, a scrap of something soft and flowing that hung from Coleman's upraised hand like a captured battle flag. A scarf printed in an Oriental design.

And then Coleman turned about, slowly, with his face shining like the light on that shimmering silk.

"I think this is what you were asking for, Judge," he said. "Evidence."

Something. There had to be something. Matt Coleman had said it, and Matt Coleman knew. Long hours ago he had stood in Halam Mills's office and told two skeptics a tale of a missing scarf—and here it was, a scrap of flimsy silk that could bind tighter than straps of leather and steel. So there had been a scarf all the time. Messick hadn't lied. There had been a scarf that was stolen, and it must have been stolen for a reason. That bright light Ralph had glimpsed in the darkness was dying out, and there wasn't a thing he could do but stand there and let it die in silence. Matt Coleman had said it, and Matt Coleman knew.

But as the light died, so did the silence, and the death of the silence was violent. Violent footsteps in the corridor, the violent slamming of the outer door that tore Ralph's gaze away from that shimmering strip of evidence in time to face the last man he wanted to see now.

And violent words from a little man who stood about eight feet tall in his anger.

"What the hell's going on here? Damn you, Coleman!"

It was an impressive beginning for an outraged citizen who'd just walked in on a pair of uninvited guests, but Leo Cox didn't get any further. One look at the object in Coleman's hand and the conversation was over. One look and those pounding footsteps were going the other way.

"Stop him!" Coleman cried. "Don't let him get away!"

Ralph heard the command, but he couldn't move. He saw Cox run; he saw Coleman reach for the gun on his hip and waited for the shot—but no shot came. Instead, there was a loud grunt from the outer office, as if Cox had run into a brick wall, and then a voice only slightly strained with annoyance.

"Why, Leo, old chum, back in my arms so soon? I had no idea that you cared!"

CHAPTER TWELVE

"Say, this is fun," Stu added. "Let's play some more exciting games."

Leo Cox wasn't having much fun. He was trembling. All that heat, and the little man stood trembling in the presence of his captors. That scrap of cloth in Matt Coleman's hand meant a great deal to Leo. It meant this expensive office with the glittering view he couldn't see anymore; it meant that imported red sports car he'd left downstairs in the parking lot, and that hand-tailored suit, he was wearing with the lapels a little wrinkled where Stu Wilder had grabbed him and shoved him back into his own office. It was going to mean more, much more, and the fact that he knew it was written across his face in terror.

"What's the big idea?" he stammered. "Where do you get off breaking into my office without a warrant? I'll get you for this, Coleman! And Judge Addison! The righteous Judge Addison!"

Cox wasn't being smart but he could be forgiven a lapse of intelligence at a time like this. And nobody stopped him. A frightened man should be allowed to talk. It always saved time.

"And my files! What right have you got to go through my files? Don't you know a lawyer's business with his clients is strictly confidential?"

"With his one client, you mean," Coleman said dryly.

"What?"

"One client, Leo. That's all you seem to have. But I guess one is enough if you have enough on him."

"Enough on him?" Cox bawled. "What is this? What are you talking about?"

"Paul Dorritt," Coleman said. "What's the story, Leo? What's the connection between Dorritt and this piece of silk?"

"There's no connection!"

"What's the connection, Leo? I'm asking in a nice way."

Ralph couldn't blame Cox for cowering. The same Matt Coleman who'd torn through a desk and a filing cabinet a few minutes ago, now stood with his feet planted about eighteen inches apart and his big body leaned forward a little so that his arms hung down from those sagging shoulders like a couple of clubs with fists on the end of them. He'd put away his gun, but he was still mad, just plain, old-fashioned mad, and the expression in his eyes was enough to bring glistening sweat drops out on Cox's neat mustache. The little man glanced behind him, but Stu was still there with all those shoulders and a pair of hands of his own ready for emergency action. Then Cox turned to Ralph, who might have been wearing his judicial robes for all the solemnity of his attitude.

"Judge Addison, you're a fair man," he whined. "Tell him—tell this bloodhound I'm within my rights. He has no warrant!"

A few minutes earlier Ralph would have sided with Cox, but a sheer scrap of printed silk had changed everything now. Evidence he'd asked for, and evidence he'd got. The knowing glance from Matt Coleman wasn't necessary. Now they had to flush out the story all the way.

"I don't think you're in any position to complain of a violation of ethics, Mr. Cox," he said, "but it's your privilege if you wish to take action."

Cox glanced at the scarf again and gnawed on his lower lip. "Now, it's not as bad as it looks," he protested. "Just because Coleman found a scarf in my desk—"

"Messick's alibi scarf!" Coleman interrupted.

"Can you prove that?"

"I can identify it. It's the same scarf, or an exact duplicate, of the one Messick had Faye Harper's jewelry in the day I arrested him in the pawnshop. Finding it here in your desk sort of rules out that duplicate idea, doesn't it?"

"It rules out nothing! You can't prove a thing!"

Coleman shook his head sadly. "Leo," he said, "you're acting like a fool! Even you should know better! Don't you remember why the judge and I called on you this morning? We came to tell you about some threatening letters and to ask about this scarf. Nothing, that's what we got from you, Leo. Nothing! And this in your desk all the time!

"But we did get one thing from that visit, no thanks to you, Leo. You received a call while we were here, an urgent call, your secretary said, from a Mr. Dorritt. You didn't ask us to wait while you took the call. You were too nervous, or maybe too shy, and that's understandable now. What you did was to get rid of us and then, in spite of all those important clients you said were coming, you took out of here like a scared rabbit. We saw you drive away. What was the trouble, Leo? Did Dorritt get worried when you told him about the letters?"

"You can call me Mr. Cox," the little man muttered.

"Some other time, Leo. Some other time call you a lot of things, but right now I'm going to call Paul Dorritt. If you won't level with us, maybe he will."

Coleman wasn't bluffing. Cox made that quick, darting inspection of faces again: Stu behind him, cross-armed and waiting, Ralph in front of him with a face like gray stone. Nobody was going to stop Matt Coleman when he reached for the phone on the desk except a little man who had-n't been a defense lawyer fifteen years for nothing.

"Wait," he said, sliding between the policeman and the desk. "There's no need to disturb Dorritt at this hour. I can explain everything if you'll just calm down!"

"I'm perfectly calm," Stu remarked from his post at the doorway. "Let's hear what the man has to say, shall we?"

It was a life for Cox and he looked grateful. Although he was still a long way from the man who'd tossed barbs at Matt Coleman in a crowded café that long ago noon, he was getting back a little color and composure. He looked at Ralph when he spoke again. It was natural for a man accustomed to making his pleas to a judge.

"I'll admit it looks bad," he began, "that scarf being in my desk, I mean. Actually, I'd forgotten it was there."

"I'll bet you had!" Coleman said.

Cox took no note of the interruption. He was gaining confidence as he went along.

"What's more," he said in a louder voice, "I'll admit that it is what Cole-man has referred to so colorfully as Messick's 'alibi scarf.' Walter had it on him when he was jailed—slipped it inside his clothing so it wouldn't be taken from him. He's a smart kid in a warped sort of way. Even then he was figuring an angle. When I came to see him in the cell he passed it on to me along with that cock-and-bull story of the girl with him when he found Faye Harper up on Mulholland."

"Cock and bull?" Ralph interrupted. "Then there was no girl with Mes-sick Christmas Eve?"

Cox hesitated, glancing at Matt Coleman's dark scowl. "Yes, there was a girl with Walter Christmas Eve," he admitted, "a girl he picked up at a teen-age hangout near her home. They went out to his car and drove around a while, and then—well, I guess Walter got too far out of line, be-cause the girl jumped out of the car and left him. That's how she happened to leave her scarf behind."

"Who told you that story?" Coleman demanded.

Cox stared at the big man with bland eyes. He wasn't trembling at all now.

"That should be obvious," he said, "the girl."

"You found her then?" Ralph asked.

"I found her. It wasn't too difficult, considering that I knew the location of the place Walter said he'd picked her up. A decent little malt shop, too. Not Walter's style at all, but he'd do anything for a lark. Then too, I had the description he'd given me, that nickname 'Pat,' and the scarf."

Cox looked so hungrily at the last-named item that Matt Coleman, a careful man, backed up out of reach.

"A rather unusual scarf," Cox added. "I knew it was Japanese merchandise, so I asked around if any of the girls frequenting this place had a boy friend, or a brother, maybe, who was in that area. Had my field pretty well narrowed down before the girl I was after put in an appearance. I played a trick on her, one I regretted later. I watched until I could get her alone and then dropped the scarf on the floor. Did you drop this, miss?' I asked, and the poor kid fell for it. Before she realized what she was doing, she was claiming her property—a gift, incidentally, from the brother who had died in Korea defending his country."

Leo Cox should have been in a courtroom. A jury would have loved that throb in his voice.

"All right," he said, dropping his arms to his sides in a gesture of defeat, "I admit the charge! I'm guilty of withholding evidence, guilty of lying to my client when I told him the scarf had disappeared! I can be disbarred, but I'd do it again. Put me in that same position, Judge, and I swear I'd do the same thing again! That kid, that poor little kid! Can you imagine what they'd have done to her on a witness stand? Can you, Judge Addison? Maybe you have a daughter. Maybe you can understand."

Ralph could understand. He could understand that Cox was making a big pitch to save his own skin, but there was truth in what he said. A daughter. Suppose he did have a daughter.

"Just a kid, sixteen, seventeen, maybe," Cox pleaded. "She'd done a crazy thing, that's true, but it was Christmas Eve and she was lonely. Her brother was dead, her mother had been gone for years, and her father—well, he's one of those busy empire builders with important friends to entertain over the holidays. She did wrong to pick up with a boy like Messick, but she left him soon enough when she found that out. She told me the whole story, and I believed it. What else could I do? She begged me not to drag her into court and ruin her good name. If her testimony would have helped Messick it would have been different. She'd have testified then, and I don't think I'd have had to do much talking to persuade her. She's a decent kid, Judge. The kind of a kid you might have for a sister."

"The judge has a sister," Stu reflected soberly. "A sister-in-law, that is."

"Then he understands," Cox said eagerly. "How would you feel about having your sister-in-law pulled in by the heels through a mess like the Messick case? All I could possibly have achieved was the humiliation of a girl who could do nothing to save my client. The case was hopeless from the beginning. I told Walter that when I took the case. I begged him to plead guilty and save himself from the death sentence!"

Ralph didn't like Leo Cox. He didn't like Cox or any of his breed, but the picture he painted of that girl—it might have been Midge—had a memory in it. Hadn't he heard this story before? This story or one so very like it that everything Cox said seemed familiar.

But someone else had heard the story and didn't like the ending.

"But Walter refused to plead guilty," Matt Coleman reminded. "Why do you suppose he did that, Leo?"

"Why?" A gesture of despair, a shrug of incomprehension. "You tell me," Cox countered. "Tell me why Walter's done any of the things he has. Make sense of his crazy, mixed-up life. Go ahead, try and make sense of it."

"I am trying," Coleman said. "I'm also trying to make sense of what you've just told us. According to you, this girl couldn't have testified in Walter's defense because she was no longer with him when he drove up on Mulholland."

Cox blinked rapidly. "That's right."

"But it isn't what Messick said."

"Messick lied. He was desperate. He knew a story like that was his only chance. Some sentimental fool might believe it."

Cox's words were for Ralph again—Ralph Addison, judge and jury. But it was a mistake to call Coleman a fool. Cox had to be desperate himself to do that.

"But you never believed it, did you?" Coleman asked.

"Never! I believed that girl."

"Then why didn't you return her scarf?"

Leo Cox was suddenly an unhappy man again. A moment ago he'd had an out, a real good story and at least one responsive listener. Now all he had was a pasty-looking face and a tongue that had run out of words.

Coleman lifted the scarf and dangled it under his nose.

"A sentimental keepsake from her dead brother, and you wouldn't even give it back to the poor kid!" he taunted. "Leo, I'm ashamed of you! What was the matter? Afraid her father would stop paying off if you let go of the evidence?"

"I don't know what you're talking about!" Cox screamed.

"I'll tell you what I'm talking about. Dorritt, Paul, Air Futures, Incorporated. Your one and only client, Leo, and such a well-heeled client, too. Dorritt has a daughter, doesn't he? A nice, teen-aged daughter."

"How should I know?" Cox gasped.

"Because you just told us. Now, I think we've held out on the poor kid long enough. I think it's time we returned her pretty scarf."

"Now? You're going to Dorritt's house now?"

"Why not?"

"It's late. It's one o'clock."

Matt Coleman wadded up the scarf and stuffed it into his coat pocket. Then he looked at his wrist watch.

"So it is," he murmured. "That gives us just nine hours to find someone who can tell the truth."

It was still Matt Coleman's show, but now the cast was gaining characters. Two men started out for Leo Cox's office; four men came away. It wasn't much of a city for night life. Beyond those few bright blocks on the Strip the streets were as wide and empty as a boulevard in Tibet, and as quiet. Ralph did the driving. Coleman gave the directions. Leo Cox just sat in the back seat and scowled. Wide streets, deep lawns, sprawling stucco houses. Two pairs of headlamps cored the darkness: Ralph's and the bright beam of Stu's convertible trailing along behind.

"I played stooge at the bar and held your boy when he tried to run out on you at the office," Stu had insisted. "I'll be damned if I'm going to miss out on the kill."

For a man with an impressive vocabulary, Stu could be awfully careless in his choice of words—and yet, they were grimly apropos. Four troubled men didn't descend on a man's home in the middle of the night without a desperate purpose.

"... a decent kid, Judge. The kind of kid you might have for a sister."

Cox's words were pounding a tattoo on Ralph's brain as he gripped the steering wheel, but he couldn't do a thing about it now. There came a time when there was no turning back, no matter who had to be hurt. After a while they came to a white house with a curving drive and a row of beautifully clipped hedges that reminded him of a couple of apprentice gardeners a few miles away. Were they still mowing lawns in the starlight, or did Halam Mills have some other disguise for nocturnal duty? Poor Halam, still worrying about that demented crank! Still convinced Matt Coleman was a meddling old fool!

The lights were still on in the lower-floor rooms of that big white house, and it was Dorritt himself who opened the door. A tall, blustery man with a barrel chest, a ruddy face, and a few flecks of gray sprinkled through his military haircut. He was wearing a tuxedo with a white jacket. His tie was crooked, and he was mopping something off his face with a handkerchief that looked suspiciously like a lipstick smear. The drink in his hand needed freshening.

"Police?" he echoed vaguely, as Coleman flashed his credentials. "Judge Addison? I don't understand."

And then Dorritt caught a glimpse of Leo Cox cowering behind his three escorts, and in a few seconds of time he seemed to understand much more than he could possibly have understood if Cox hadn't got to him earlier with the tale of two men in search of an ominous letter writer.

"Cox!" he exclaimed. "What's the meaning of this? What have you been telling these men?"

Leo Cox stumbled forward and blinked at the brightness of the hall chandelier. It was a wide, spacious hall with a staircase curving up behind Dorritt's broad back and a pair of double doors opening into a room from which came the muffled strains of a mambo beat and the unmistakable rattle of someone poking about in an ice bucket.

"I told them the truth, Mr. Dorritt," he said. "I had to. They found your daughter's scarf in my desk."

"My daughter's scarf!"

"The one she left in Messick's car Christmas Eve. You remember—Messick. The boy Elaine met at the malt shop and went riding with *for just a few blocks.*"

Cox was trying hard, but he didn't seem to be getting through. Dorritt paled. He backed up a few steps and closed that door leading into the room where the mambo and the ice bucket were making so much noise.

"Out-of-town business associates," he said. "Office hours never close for an executive."

"Nor for Leo," Coleman said. "He's been a busy man tailing us around all day and night."

"I tailed you?" Cox cried.

"All the way," Coleman said, "with regular reports back to Dorritt, no doubt. Look here, Mr. Dorritt, we'd like to have a few words with your daughter."

"At this hour?" Dorritt protested.

"It'll never be any earlier."

"But Elaine's in bed asleep!"

"Of course she is," Cox broke in, "and she can't tell you anything anyway. I told all there was to tell."

"You shut up!" Dorritt exploded.

"But I was just trying to explain."

"What could you explain? You'd say anything to save your own skin! Now, what's all this nonsense about my daughter and—what's his name?—Messick? What would Elaine have to do with a hoodlum like that? What kind of a set-up is this? Blackmail?"

"Mr. Dorritt, I'm an officer of the law," Coleman said.

"What of it? That makes you a saint, I suppose!"

"And this man is Judge Addison of the Superior Court, the presiding judge at Messick's trial."

Dorritt barely glanced at Ralph. "I don't care if he's Chief Justice of the Supreme Court!" he raged. "I've heard enough of this slander. Now you clear out of here, all of you!"

Nobody moved toward the door. The only movement was Matt Coleman pulling that scarf from his pocket.

"I suppose you've never seen this before," he said.

"Never!"

"And you won't call your daughter?"

"I will not! I have a little influence in this city. If you think I'm going to stand for a thing like this—!"

Dorritt stopped shouting long enough to drain the glass in his hand. He set it down on a table that stood near the stairway. On the table was a framed photograph, the portrait of a good-looking young man in an army uniform. He picked up the photograph and stared at it for a moment of incredible silence.

"My son," he said softly. "My son—Paul Junior. Killed in action in Korea." Then he looked up again with the anger rising up behind the pain in his eyes. "A hero," he said. "Decorated posthumously. Gave his life for his country—and why? So some fool policeman with hallucinations can come around in the middle of the night and try to drag his name through the muck and mire!"

"I'm trying to find the truth," Coleman corrected.

"Truth! I'll give you some truth! You forget this whole thing or you'll never stay on the force long enough to collect a pension. That goes for you, too, Judge—whatever your name is. I've got a little influence. You can't prove a thing!"

All this time Ralph had remained silent, trying to decide whether Paul Dorritt was intoxicated or just frightened. He was a big man, in more ways than one, and shouting came natural to him. And there was truth in what he shouted, because without Elaine Dorritt's story that scrap of silk was just a scrap of silk and it wasn't going to do a thing for Walter Messick.

But sometimes a man shouted so much the thing he wanted to hide came up like silt rising to the surface of agitated waters; and sometimes he shouted so loud the words woke echoes and reached places that had better remained undisturbed. It was Stu who first saw the figure on the stairway. Ralph noticed his reaction and followed the direction of his gaze. It was a girl, a girl about the size and age of Midge. She wore a yellow robe pulled tight about her narrow waist, and her face, almost colorless under the bright light, was framed by an unpinned mane of soft brown hair. Her eyes were circled with shadows, and one small hand clutched at the railing for support. There was no telling how long she'd been there.

"Not a damned thing!" Dorritt repeated, his back still toward the stairway. "Now take your damned scarf and get out."

"My scarf!"

Two words. Two words hurled down from the staircase, and every eye turned toward the girl in the yellow robe. Paul Dorritt swung about, a look of incredible dismay canceling out that arrogance on his face. He tried to speak but no sound came. There was nothing but frozen silence until Matt Coleman, shaken but still dogged, stepped forward.

"Your scarf, Miss Dorritt?" he asked.

Soft was the answer. "Yes, of course it's mine. Paul sent it to me from Japan."

"And you'll make a statement to that effect, Miss Dorritt?"

"She will not!"

Dorritt could speak now. Ashen-faced and trembling, he could speak.

"The girl doesn't know what she's saying!" he cried. "She's been ill. She just doesn't know."

"I'm a doctor," Stu said, stepping forward. "Perhaps I can help."

"You leave her alone! Elaine, get back to bed."

But the furor her words had unleashed didn't seem to touch the girl at all. She still stood at that same place on the stairway, her eyes fixed on the scarf that dangled from Matt Coleman's big fist, and her voice was flat and lifeless.

"I'll make a statement," she said. "I wanted to all along. I wanted to tell—"

"Elaine!"

Dorritt took one step up the stairway. He looked wild with his tie askew and that photograph clutched in one hand. "You didn't," he choked, "you didn't write those letters!" Then he caught himself and drew up tall. "I'm your father, Elaine. I order you to go to your room!"

"I have no father," the girl said.

"What?"

"I have no father. If I had a father, my father would have a daughter. But he doesn't. He just has a son—a dead son."

"Elaine!"

"I don't exist anymore. I'm no more important than poor Walter Messick."

Walter Messick. Ralph felt the muscles of his stomach go tight. Cox had lied, then. The girl did know Walter Messick. She had been with him on Mulholland! Vaguely, he heard Coleman ask the questions. Vaguely, he heard the girl answering.

"I met him at the malt shop Christmas Eve. It was almost empty. All the other kids had parties at home. He asked me to go out with him and I did."

"Where did you go?"

"Driving, mostly. We stopped at a liquor store and Walter bought a bottle of whisky. Then we drove up on Mulholland."

"Then you didn't jump out of the car a few blocks after Messick picked you up?"

"No. Why should I do that?"

"Because he got out of line."

The girl raised up her head and looked straight at her father as she answered.

"I wanted him to," she said. "That's why I went with him. I wanted someone to notice me, to know I'm alive even if Paul is dead. I couldn't help it that he died. I loved him, too, but I'm alive. I'm alive and nobody cares!"

Ralph felt ill. Those muscles in his stomach were tied in knots now. He turned away from the staircase and tried not to think about the little lives that didn't matter. Walter Messick in that shabby bungalow, Elaine Dorritt in this white stucco mausoleum. What a sermon Matt Coleman could preach on that text! Someone should have drawn a curtain, or shut a door, because some griefs were too naked to be paraded before hungry eyes.

But death had a ten o'clock call in the morning. It was too late for decency.

"Then you were still with Messick when he found Faye Harper's parked car?" Coleman continued.

"Yes, I was there. He said he was going to pull a stick-up and get some money so we could have a real ball. I thought he was joking."

"Joking? Why did you think that?"

Paul Dorritt wasn't even trying any more. Sometime during the past few minutes he'd been struck dumb. Nobody did a thing to stop the girl's words.

"Because," she said, "he didn't have a gun."

CHAPTER THIRTEEN

Walter Messick didn't have a gun. It was as simple as that: he couldn't have shot Faye Harper because he didn't have a gun. The words were familiar. Messick had sat in the witness chair facing a jury of twelve men, tried and true, and sworn on his holy oath that he never had a gun. But Walter Messick had been a cowering caricature of a human being, a wasted body, a withered soul, and no one had believed him. He was a dead man when he walked into the courtroom.

But a white-faced girl spoke the words and a dead man rose up like a ghost from Paul Dorritt's staircase. Ralph was never quite sure what happened next. There was silence and shouting, there were protests and pleadings, and, finally, a grand exodus led by a triumphant Matt Coleman; but all Ralph really retained from the confusion was the irrelevant memory of Paul Dorritt staring at the photograph of his son as if he couldn't recall the face and then letting it slide from his fingers to fall forgotten to the floor.

Irrelevant because everything was irrelevant now except the awful knowledge that Walter Messick was innocent and Mr. Justice had known all the time.

It was later. Ralph couldn't even imagine how much later because time had stopped, like the old clock on the mantel, back in Dorritt's entry hall. Now he was in an office on Temple Street where the lights burned long and the tempers burned short, because it was later and a girl could change her mind.

"This is the damnedest situation I've ever come up against," Halam Mills declared. "Have we got a witness for Messick, or haven't we? Do we have a responsible statement for the Governor, or merely the ravings of a high-strung girl?"

Mills sat behind his desk, his face gray with weariness and his silver hair gleaming like frost under the bright ceiling light. His question was for no one in particular, although there were three listeners in the office. Matt Coleman was back on that straight-backed chair where Ralph had first seen him on a morning that seemed a lifetime ago, and Stu Wilder, who should-n't have been involved at all, leaned against a bookcase on the opposite wall. Somebody had sent out for coffee, and Stu was studying the contents of the paper carton in his hand as if he might read a fortune in that pool of steaming blackness. All of these things Ralph saw while his mind wandered elsewhere ...

"We all heard the girl's statement," Coleman insisted (Coleman's mind never wandered), "Judge Addison, Dr. Wilder, Cox, and Dorritt himself. What more do you want?"

"But Dorritt claims the girl was hysterical," Mills protested.

"Hysterical! That's ridiculous! Ask Dr. Wilder. He should know whether or not she was hysterical."

It was late, really late—two, maybe three o'clock. Ralph tried to focus his eyes on his watch to make sure. Focusing his eyes was easy; it was his mind that wouldn't come to bear. Now his mind was on Stu, a suddenly not so jaunty Stu, who heard his name and looked up from that carton of coffee with troubled eyes.

"Well," Mills demanded, "what do you think, Doctor?"

What did Stu think? Ralph waited for the answer knowing it wouldn't be the one he wanted.

"She was upset," Stu said. "Pale, tense—I think she must have been brooding about this execution for some time. Her father seemed to think so, too. If I recall correctly, he made some remark about the possibility of her having written the Mr. Justice letters."

"That's right, he did," Coleman agreed, "and that's another point to consider. Why would he say a thing like that if he didn't know the girl was sitting on a big secret?"

"Coleman, for God's sake shut up and let the doctor give an unbiased opinion! It's too late for conjecture. We've got to have proof!"

Halam Mills was running close to the end of his nerves, but there was truth in his outburst. It was too late for conjecture. Much too late. It was a quarter-past three—Ralph had finally figured that out—and nobody could save Walter Messick without proof. Matt Coleman knew that, but he didn't stop trying.

"What about Cox and his one client?" he persisted. "Doesn't that suggest something? Doesn't that prove there's dirty linen being hidden?"

Mills scowled at his own untouched coffee. "Don't worry, I'm going to take care of Mr. Cox," he said. "He's been a shrewd operator for a long time, but this time he's outsmarted himself. The scarf belongs to the Dorritt girl, no doubt of that, and whether or not it could have helped his client's case, it is evidence he withheld from the trial. It seems pretty obvious that he's been blackmailing Dorritt."

When Halam Mills spoke of Leo Cox he sounded grim and determined. Cox was something he could strike back at, and at a quarter-past three in the morning a tired man feels like striking back. But Leo Cox wasn't going to die in less than seven hours, and Matt Coleman wasn't tired of trying. "What about Messick?" he reminded, and Mills fell silent. Ralph knew what he was thinking. Paul Dorritt was a big man. He had other lawyers besides Leo Cox. He had a physician for his daughter. He had a vocabulary full of threats.

"Drag my daughter into this mess, Halam Mills, and I'll have your job before the month's out!"

The echo of his words still hung in the air, and in the adjoining office, beyond this temporary sanctuary, the battle still raged. Elaine Dorritt was a child, a minor. One moment she stood on a staircase calling down defiance of her father; the next she was stunned and silent as if all of her courage had gone into that one declaration and she couldn't find strength to make it again. These were the memories in Mills's eyes when he finally answered.

"I don't like Dorritt's attitude," he admitted, "but confound it, Coleman, I've got a daughter of my own. I understand how the man feels."

"And how do you think Messick feels?" Coleman asked.

Words, nothing but empty words. Ralph turned his back on the deskside debate and stared out at the blackness beyond the window. In a couple of hours it would be getting light, and then, in a few hours more, it would be too late. Words couldn't save Walter Messick or stop Mr. Justice. Only one thing could do that.

But in the dark window he could see the reflected images from across the room. He saw Stu come away from the bookcase. Saw him hesitate and then come close to Coleman's chair.

"There's no guarantee that the girl's statement could save Messick anyway," Stu said. "She told us he didn't have a gun, but how could she know?"

"How could she know?" Coleman echoed.

"Exactly, how could she know? She stayed in Messick's car when he went to pull his announced hold-up. How could she see what happened? The evidence still points to Messick."

Coleman looked surprised. He came to his feet, a little angered by an added complication. "Evidence!" he exclaimed. "Maybe we should go over the evidence, Doctor. Maybe we should review the facts."

They were still only words, but now Ralph listened. It was always a good thing for a man in doubt to listen. Sometimes he heard more than anyone intended to say.

"This morning we had nothing but a pair of death threats," Coleman was saying, "Judge Addison's and my own. Mr. Mills didn't think much of them. He advised us to hole in and count on police protection to ward off Mr. Justice, but I wanted to go out after him and the judge threw in with me. We went to see Leo Cox, as a starter, and right away I began to wonder where he'd found the fairy godmother. Cox must have wondered about a few things, too, because he raced off to see Dorritt the minute we were out of his office."

"Just a minute," Mills broke in. "How do you know that's where Cox went?"

Coleman looked down at the district attorney as if he were a not-so-bright student.

"There's Dorritt's remark about the letters, for one thing," he said. "How did he know about Mr. Justice if Cox didn't tell him? And another thing, Dorritt was leaving the city—on his way to the airport Cox's secretary said when that call came in. Obviously, he changed his plans and it should be easy to understand why. When Cox raced out and intercepted him with the Mr. Justice story, he didn't dare leave. Both he and Cox knew the girl's involvement. It was only natural to suspect she was responsible, in one way or another, for those letters."

"She might be at that," Mills murmured, but Coleman took no notice. He must have been thinking of that impending dawn, too.

"Later Cox went to see Mrs. Messick," he continued. "He must have known that would be our next stop when we left his office, and I imagine he intended to pump her about our line of questioning, just in case we knew more about Mr. Justice than we'd told him. But we were still in the café when Leo arrived, so he came up with a fast story about Walter's friend, 'The Poet,' just to throw us off the scent. I take it you've checked out Chavez?"

The image of Halam Mills shifted uneasily in the dark window. "We're working on it," he said. "You know how hard it is to pick up a punk like that, especially if word gets out on the grapevine that we're looking for him."

"As Leo Cox well knows," Coleman commented. "But even then he didn't get off our tail. Judge Addison saw him near that bar where Faye Harper used to hang out, and I'm sure I caught a glimpse of him at the beach this afternoon when I was checking out that match-cover motel. And there was a man, Mr. Mills. The motel manager remembers that Faye used to come there with a tall man."

Coleman's voice sounded just a little too smug. "I'm aware of that," Mills snapped back. "It's all a part of a seven-months-old investigation. It doesn't mean a thing!"

"It might—if Gigi Fontaine hadn't been so drunk when we found her."

Ralph turned away from the windows. Matt Coleman stood with his feet wide apart and his shoulders hunched forward like a very tired fighter moving into the last round. He was battling the dawn with nothing but words and the words didn't go unchallenged.

"Just a minute," Stu objected, "if you're still insinuating—"

"I'm insinuating nothing," Coleman protested, "except that it was no co-incidence that Leo Cox was in the same bar where you found Gigi."

"Gigi?" Mills repeated. "Gigi Fontaine?" There was a stage of exhaustion when a man looked almost sick. He rubbed a groping hand across his face, as if to wipe off the weariness, and looked up with puzzled eyes. "Oh, yes," he said. "The woman Dr. Wilder inquired about this evening. You found her, then?"

"Dr. Wilder found her," Coleman said, "and we found Dr. Wilder. Gigi was Faye Harper's closest friend, Mr. Mills, and she'd been known to refer to this mysterious tall man as 'the high and mighty.' I was in hopes she might be able to tell us more about him. But that's beside the point right now. Gigi was drunk, so drunk we had to pour her into a cab and send her home, and because of that the judge and I found the scarf in Leo Cox's office.

"Can't you see what's been going on, Mr. Mills? Cox had to stay on our tail today, not only because he was afraid for his own skin, but because he was under the orders of the man who's been paying all his bills lately. And why? Because of an innocent meeting such as the one Cox described when we had him squirming in his office? I think we all know better than that."

Only words, but Ralph was beginning to feel a kind of excitement itching through the numbness and the fear.

"What do you mean, Coleman?" he demanded. "What is Cox being paid for?"

And Matt Coleman, turning to face him, answered, "For Walter Messick's execution."

"What?"

The exclamation had three voices, but Coleman had only one pair of eyes. "Because it's easy that way," he added. "Easier and cleaner. Don't fool yourself, Judge Addison. Dorritt knows the story his daughter blurted out on the staircase is the truth, but he'd rather let Messick die, knowing he's innocent, than have his daughter exposed to public censure. A man like Dorritt thinks like this: Messick's no good anyway. Messick's a lost soul. Let him die and save the decent people."

It was Matt Coleman's living room all over again. It was the crocheted doilies on the divan; it was the potted plants on the window shelf and the row of photographs on the mantel. It was a man with the memory of a hasty gun trying to square the world all by himself.

"A man like Dorritt thinks that way?" It was Stu's voice that pulled Coleman's eyes away. "There may be many men who think that way," he said.

Coleman turned around slowly. "Including Dr. Wilder?" he asked.

Ralph wanted to warn Stu. This was no man to argue with; this was no man to fight with words. But Stu was being very deliberate about what he was doing, almost like a matador entering an arena.

"I'm not a moralist," he said. "I'm a scientist. I try to face facts."

"And what is the fact in this case?" Coleman asked.

"That Messick is, as you put it, a lost soul."

"And for that reason he should die, even if he's innocent of the crime for which he was convicted?"

"We don't know if he's innocent, Coleman."

"But what if we did know?"

It was too late to warn Stu then. He hesitated. It seemed he would never find an answer. And then he raised his head and looked beyond Coleman's slouching shoulders.

"Elaine Dorritt is innocent, too," he said, "and she isn't a lost soul."

Only words, and yet, now that Ralph had really listened, it seemed amazing what could be done with words. Coleman seemed to think so, too. He forgot the answer he should have given. He waited too long.

"This is ridiculous!" Mills protested. "Here we are debating abstractions when all I'm trying to do is get a few facts to put before the Governor."

"You've got your facts," Coleman said crossly. "Three confirming witnesses to Elaine Dorritt's statement."

"But I'm not sure it's enough."

"It's enough—if you're not afraid of Paul Dorritt!"

It had to happen sooner or later. The hour was too late and the nerves too ragged. It had to happen that someone said too much at the wrong moment; and it must have happened to Matt Coleman because he was upset at having his verbal duel with Stu so rudely interrupted. And now there would be no continuance, because Halam Mills had been shouted at once too often. He was on his feet in an instant.

"Afraid!" he screamed. "Look who's talking about fear! What about you, Coleman? Why have you been on your bicycle all day? Why have you dug up this mess if not because you're afraid for your very life? Save Walter Messick or Mr. Justice strikes at ten o'clock—that's it, isn't it? Save Messick, innocent or guilty, because a lunatic has been writing letters and making telephone calls! Since when are you a man without fear?"

All that anger, and only one man to catch it as it fell. Coleman looked stunned. He was a tired old man trying to do what he thought was right, and Ralph felt a little sick at the sight of him groping for words that wouldn't come. He turned away and that's when he noticed Paul Dorritt standing in the doorway of the other office. There was no telling how long he'd been there or how much he'd heard, but whatever new protest he'd come to register was forgotten now.

Because Matt Coleman did find some words. Not many, but enough.

"All right, I admit I'm afraid," he said. "I'm like any other man, Mr. Mills. I don't want to die. I particularly don't want to die for somebody else's mistake."

"Meaning mine, I suppose," Mills snapped, "if I don't persuade the Governor to stop Messick's execution."

Coleman didn't answer right away. He counted the house first. He looked at Stu with the container of forgotten coffee in his hands, at Ralph, the judge who no longer made decisions, at Paul Dorritt in the doorway. Then he looked at Halam Mills again and shook his head sadly.

"No," he said. "The mistake I have in mind is bigger than that, much bigger."

And then Matt Coleman walked over and sat down on the straight-backed chair again, and didn't speak another word.

All the rest was confusion.

It was a long time before Ralph got all of the words sorted out and straight in his mind. He stood in front of the dark window staring out at the fugitive night, no longer caring about those reflected images in the glass. They were such busy little men: Halam Mills with his buzzers and telephones, Paul Dorritt with his protests and threats. Once he caught sound of a decision. "I'm trying to get through to the Governor," Mills said. "It may not do any good, but I'm trying." The words didn't seem important. They were just a part of the noise time made as it ran out, because now Ralph knew what Matt Coleman meant by that big mistake and nothing else was important.

The first thing he noticed, when he returned from his long thoughts, was how empty the office looked. Dorritt was gone now, and someone else.

"Stu," he said. "Where's Dr. Wilder?"

Halam Mills looked up from his desk with harassed eyes.

"Gone home, probably," he sighed. "I used to do that myself before the world went mad. You look exhausted, Ralph. Why don't you go home and get some sleep? There's a guard on your house, and you certainly can't do any more here."

Home. The thought of it was like a sweet memory that had almost been forgotten. It was Abbie with her yellow hair spread out on the pillow, and her little bedjackets, and her hugeness underneath the sheet. It was Midge coming in late from an outdoor movie, and an old clock on the mantel that stopped unless it was wound every day. If only time could be stopped so easily.

But Halam Mills was right. He couldn't do any more here. It was about fifteen minutes later when the telephone rang. Mills answered eagerly, then frowned.

"Oh, hello, Dr. Braidwell," he said. "Who? No, Dr. Wilder isn't here now ... Ralph? Just a minute."

He looked up. A short time ago his office had been crowded. Now it was deserted.

"No, he's not here either. Must be on his way home.... What's that? ... Of course! Anything I can do."

Mills replaced the telephone in its cradle and stared at the empty room with troubled eyes. It was quiet. Too damn quiet. Somebody should be shouting.

It was even quieter in another part of the city.

Ralph had no trouble finding the place again even without Matt Coleman to guide him. The old frame Cape Cod was rather conspicuous amid the stucco, and the light that still burned in the dining room was the only light showing on the block. He found a parking space across the street and sat for a few minutes with just his thoughts and the silence. It was almost four o'clock by that round dial on the instrument panel and each additional tick was another piece chipped off the darkness. Six hours, that's all he had now. Six hours in which to find an answer that would have to last a lifetime. He was sweating. It wasn't hot at this hour of the morning, but his hands didn't know that. He pulled out a handkerchief and tried to wipe them dry, knowing all the time that this waiting was nonsense. If Gigi Fontaine had that answer, it was time to hear her story. And so he got out of the sedan and crossed the silent street.

It was easier than he'd hoped. The night-writing landlady was pecking away at a typewriter behind those bright windows, and no one could hear as he made the long trek back to the rear apartment. It was a house, actually. A small, secluded guest house, ideal for a lady who liked privacy when she entertained. It had a private yard with a white fence and a gate that sighed wearily as it opened. A tall avocado tree shaded the doorway, but the screen stood open and the door swung inward at the touch of his groping hand.

The cab driver must have left in a hurry. The door was not only unlocked, as advertised, it was ajar. Ralph listened. Ahead was nothing but darkness, and yet it seemed that he'd heard a muffled sound. Gigi, perhaps. Gigi sleeping off her great thirst behind the bedroom door. He moved forward, and then the sound came again and there was no mistaking it this time.

"What the hell y'tryin' to do, buster? Who asked you to spend the night?"

No mistaking at all. It was Gigi, the thick, well-liquored voice of Gigi Fontaine, and she wasn't muttering in her sleep. She wasn't alone.

"If I want company I'll invite company! Get outa here!"

It was the sound of breaking glass following this declaration that plunged Ralph into cold understanding. A thought Matt Coleman had expressed hours ago was running through his mind: *Gigi Fontaine had nothing to lose but her life!* Who else remembered those words? Who else was looking for an answer? He lunged forward, his hand reaching for the doorknob, when his knee struck a low table and sent something loud and ceramic crashing to the floor. There was a moment of dead silence, and then the door burst open in his face. Gigi screamed, but there was no time now for Gigi. A tall shadow brushed past him in the darkness and Ralph was compelled to follow.

Outside, the white gate swung crazily on its hinges and the night was alive with the sound of running footsteps. There was only one way to run. The dull glow of the street was like a trap at the end of a dark passage; in a moment he would know—and then, suddenly, there was no darkness anywhere. There was a bright, blinding light and a man pinned like a marionette against its brightness. Ralph stumbled and fell forward, and the man, turning, caught him in his arms.

"Stu!" Ralph gasped. "My God! Stu!"

It was madness. The blinding light was from the police car that had nosed into the driveway. A uniformed figure brushed past on his way to see what was making the screaming Gigi so unhappy, but Ralph hardly saw him. All he could see was the face of the man who had been in that bedroom—

and then something else—a bottle. A small bottle that flashed bright in Stu's hand before it slipped from his fingers and dropped to the grass. There was no time to retrieve it. Out from behind the blinding light came a huge, lumbering figure that stooped and then straightened again with the tiny glass bottle clutched in one clumsy fist. Matt Coleman hardly glanced at what his hand had found. His eyes were on Stu Wilder.

"It's all right, officer," Ralph heard Stu's voice saying. "I just dropped by to see how our little friend was making out with her hangover. She was frightened—"

But Matt Coleman seemed to be hearing something quite different from what Stu was trying to say. He stared at him as if they'd never met before.

"You?" he said numbly. "You, Dr. Wilder?"

This was the one thing Ralph retained in all that noise and confusion of the moment: the strange expression on Matt Coleman's face, and the hollow, unbelieving, "You, Dr. Wilder?" What might have been said then was never said at all, because someone else had heard Matt Coleman's words and responded in a way that put an end to explanations. A face appeared at the open window of the police car, an inquisitive face with an unexpected question.

"Dr. Wilder?" the police officer asked. "Is this man Dr. Stuart Wilder?"

This query made as much sense as anything else. It was all madness now. "That's right," Stu said. "I'm Dr. Wilder."

"There's an all-points call out for you, Doctor. You're wanted at the hospital. Emergency. Judge Addison's wife."

"Abbie!"

The cry that escaped Ralph's lips was like a prayer to a stoop-shouldered god who stood before him with a small bottle in his hand and a terrible knowledge in his eyes. Abbie. The nightmare had to end somewhere. It couldn't destroy Abbie, too!

And then, while Ralph groped for the words his tongue couldn't form, he saw Matt Coleman take one step backward and open the door of the police car.

"You'd better come with us, Doctor," he said. "With the siren going we can get you to the hospital a lot faster."

CHAPTER FOURTEEN

The heat had to break sometime. If it was going to break you could tell it in the morning, the first thing in the morning right after the birds started hollering and the sun nosed up out of the desert. If the sky was clear and the trees stood as motionless as a painted backdrop, the heat was still on; but if the light came filtered through a skein of ocean-borne fog, and there was a dampness over and through everything, then the heat had broken at last—and it had to break sometime.

Ralph watched the day emerge, misty and gray, beyond the tall windows of the hospital waiting room. The last day, really the last day now. But every day was the last day for someone, just as, a few hours ago, it had almost been the last day for Gigi Fontaine. The thought of that was like a horrible dream now. It didn't seem real, nothing of the past twenty-odd hours seemed real except a moment when the inquiring face of a police officer appeared at the window of the radio car and asked, "Dr. Wilder? Is this man Dr. Stuart Wilder?" That was when reality began again, and reality could be more terrible than any dream. He ground out another cigarette in the overfilled tray at his elbow and looked at his watch. Seven-fifteen. That gave Walter Messick—and Ralph Addison—just under three hours.

And so Ralph Addison prayed, not on his knees and not with his lips, but with every beat of his heart. Let it be all right, God. Let it go well with Abbie, my precious Abbie, and let it go well with our child. And let it be soon. Please, God, let it be soon enough!

Outside in the hall a big policeman with drooping shoulders and sleepless eyes stared at the clock over the reception desk and waited, too. Was he praying? Ralph thought he must be. Matt Coleman would do that. He hoped Matt Coleman was praying because it seemed that he must have had a lot more experience at it and stood a much better chance of getting through. Suddenly Ralph began to feel sorry about Matt Coleman, sorry because they had been so close to one another for so many years and hadn't met until this past day. It would have been nice to have known him years ago, and to have known Mrs. Coleman, who crocheted doilies and lined up photographs of the sons she never had on the mantelshelf. Poor, lonely Matt Coleman. Why did it have to be him?

Listen to him, God. If you can't hear me, listen to Matt Coleman. Give us time, just a little time. I can't go now with my Abbie in the operating room.

Seven-thirty. The sun was a pale spot of brightness rubbing through the fog. What kind of a day was it at San Quentin? How did the sun look to

Walter Messick this morning? Two and a half hours, Walter. Twenty-one years, a few months, and two and a half hours. This is your life, Walter Messick. Measured, set, all arranged even to the funeral. This is the life Judge Addison gave you—two and a half hours—two hours—one and a half.

At eight-thirty a nurse in a crisp white uniform came into the waiting room and told Ralph that he was the father of a fine, healthy, six-pound boy, and about ten minutes later, Stuart Wilder came out of the operating room and looked into Ralph's haggard face with deep, searching eyes, and said, "It's all right, Ralph. Abbie and the baby are both all right, just as I promised myself that night in Ojai. Everything is all right now."

It could happen then—anything. Death could happen any way and any time. Ralph knew he was crying and it didn't matter, because whatever gave fools the idea a man had no right to tears when the nightmare was over and his prayer had been heard?

"Everything," Stu repeated. "Do you hear me, Ralph? Everything is all right!"

Ralph looked at the doctor, gray-faced and weary in his white uniform, and it seemed they were meeting for the first time. Old friends and yet new, because a man could imagine such evil in his heart when he was afraid. Ralph wanted to say something great and ringing about the love of a man for his friend, and about the folly of a man eaten with jealousy and driven by fear; but the clock on the wall was still measuring out precious minutes and one thing still had to be done.

"I've got to see her, Stu," he said.

"Go home," Stu said. "Get some sleep. Everything's all right, I tell you."

"I've got to see her!"

He must know that. Matt Coleman, who had joined them in the waiting room, knew it. No matter what the clock said, he had to see Abbie before he left.

"She's still under the anesthetic."

"How long?"

Now Stu understood. He looked hard at Ralph and hard at Coleman, and then he understood.

"You'll have to wait a little while," he said. "The nurse will tell you when it's time. I have to change."

And so it was morning and the heat had broken. It was a cool, gray morning with the streets wet with dew so that the bicycle wheels left tracks and made a sucking sound along the paper route, and the grass so wet the subscribers would phone the circulation manager and raise cain if you missed the front porch with that folded pellet. But not with young Ralph Addison, fine lad, who never missed. Best newsboy on the staff, the subscribers said. Keep up the fine work, lad, and you'll go far. Backbone of America. Hope of the great tomorrows.

"I have a son," Ralph said. "Did you hear that, Coleman?"

"I heard," Coleman said.

"It's a fine thing to have a son."

"The very finest," Coleman said.

"What time is it now?"

The clock was still hanging on the wall, but Ralph couldn't read it anymore. His eyes couldn't focus on such faces as were on clocks.

"Almost nine," Coleman said. "Only one hour."

There was an echo in the place from the emptiness. The activity in the operating room was all over now and the corridor was cleared. An elevator whined somewhere down the hall, and there were faraway footsteps on the stairs. Only one hour. Coleman knew the answer then. He'd seen the little bottle and he knew.

"It doesn't matter," Ralph said in a loud voice. "I have to see Abbie, my wife."

The first time he saw Abbie he knew she would be his wife. He had no doubt at all. Some things were like that. You planned your life carefully, you laid it all out just the way it was going to be with so many years for this and so many years for that, and someday, when you could afford it, so much time for looking for the woman who would be your wife. I'll be a lawyer, you said. I'll work nights and study hard. I'll make something of myself, even if I have had a poor start, and one day, when I'm a great trial lawyer or a prominent jurist, there will be time for a girl. And then you saw Abbie and knew that nothing else mattered. It didn't matter that she'd come along too soon; it didn't matter that she was the daughter of Dr. Braidwell and accustomed to all the things you couldn't give her for a long time. She was your Abbie and that was everything. And that was the truth even if you had once forgotten.

So you abandoned the time for this and the time for that, and told yourself that it wouldn't matter because, with Abbie at your side, you could do anything and become anything you wished. You could be Judge Addison, Judge Ralph Addison of the Superior Court. The very superior court. Superior to Faye Harper, superior to Walter Messick, superior to the whole stinking, hypocritical world that couldn't be saved from destruction because it was nothing but a pyre of lies!

"Judge Addison!"

The nurse's voice spun Ralph about. She must have walked in on feathers.

"You may see your wife now," the nurse said.

Now. Ralph looked at Matt Coleman and it seemed the man must surely know everything that had been passing through his mind. "Coleman," he cried, "what kind of a world? What kind of a life for my son?"

But Matt Coleman didn't answer. He was staring at the clock.

Five minutes was all they had together. Five precious minutes to square the world, to hold soft white hands and speak of wonderful things, tenderly, with his eyes.

"We have a son," Ralph said, and Abbie smiled.

"I told you," she said. "I told you everything would be fine this time."

"A son," he repeated. "A man is born again in his son. He gets another chance."

"Ralph—"

She knew. It wasn't just the way she spoke his name; it was the troubled way she looked at him, all that dread mingled with new found happiness. He knew then that the secret he'd kept so long wasn't such a secret after all. The bad dreams hadn't started with the letters. Deep in her heart, Abbie must have known all this time what her mind refused to accept. But Abbie was a Braidwell, and Braidwells were built for crisis and loyalty.

"Don't be afraid," she said. "You were always afraid of such foolish things, always afraid that I wouldn't love you enough."

"You're not to talk," he said. "Stu told me you weren't to talk."

"But I do love you, Ralph. I always have, even when I walked out on you!"

"It was nothing," Ralph said. "You mustn't talk."

"But I shouldn't have walked out on you. I shouldn't—"

And then Abbie had to stop talking because Ralph Addison kissed his wife and that was when the nightmare really ended. The rest was nothing. There was only one death, the death of not being loved, and if you had love the rest was nothing at all.

When the five minutes were over, Ralph came back to the lobby and looked around. It was empty. There was no sign of a big policeman with drooping shoulders and sleepless eyes. He felt strange and lonely—and puzzled. He looked at the clock on the wall. Nine thirty-seven. Only twenty-three minutes left and Matt Coleman was gone. Then he heard the street door opening and felt a gust of wind.

The man who came toward him had a vaguely familiar face. Mills's office had been full of men with faces like that when they were all trying to break down the Dorritt girl's attack of silence. He came directly to Ralph and touched the brim of his hat with one finger.

"Judge Addison," he said brightly, "my orders are to stick with you. We don't expect any trouble now, but the D.A. says we've gone along with this crazy threat this far so we might as well play along to the finish."

Nothing the man said made any sense.

"Matt Coleman?" Ralph muttered.

"Oh, he's gone. I saw him leave just as I drove up with the news."

"Left? News?"

"It was on all the nine-thirty newscasts, but I guess you weren't listening in here. You can relax now, Judge. If this Mr. Justice is as watchful as he claims to be, he already knows that the show's been called off. Walter Messick got a stay of execution."

A stay of execution! The words had to filter through a wall of shock. A stay of execution! Ralph glanced at the clock again, but it wasn't important now. For the first time in almost twenty-four hours it wasn't important to know the time.

"Then the Dorritt girl—" he began.

But the man from the D.A.'s office shook his head. "Never budged," he said. "No, it wasn't the girl who stopped it. Faye Harper's killer confessed."

CHAPTER FIFTEEN

There wasn't a soul in Halam Mills's office when Ralph walked in. Miss Burgess, a bit disheveled for so early in the day, was busy with the buttons and the telephones and made no move to stop him, and the district attorney was nowhere in sight. He'd be a busy man this morning. Confessions were such complicated things.

Ralph walked over to the windows and looked down at the city. Another busy day was getting started—this time without the heat. Relief, that's what the newspapers would say in headlines right above the headlines about Walter Messick. Above, because a live man wasn't such good copy as a dead one and not half so important as the weather. But there would be other headlines soon enough. Vaguely, Ralph knew these things. Vaguely, he heard the noise and confusion in the hall, vaguely saw the street below. He was thinking of a day, one day, twenty-four hours. It must be just about that long since he'd walked into this room and found a tired man in a light-blue suit sitting in the straight-backed chair waiting for him. Now it seemed that he must have known, even then, how it would end. It had to be this way. From the very beginning there had to be a Matt Coleman waiting for him before it was too late.

Across the city came a sound Ralph did hear, not vaguely, but with every fiber of his being—eight, nine, ten. It was finished. The bells tolled the hour and it was ten o'clock. Ralph still listened. He heard the door to the outer office open and close again. He heard the footsteps behind him. He turned around.

"I've been expecting you, Mr. Justice," he said.

Yes, this was the way it had to end. The tired man in the light-blue suit was much more tired now, and there was no glint of victory in his haggard eyes. But he was on time, and he'd kept his promise. He'd been watching all the way.

"I thought you knew," Matt Coleman answered. "I was pretty sure of it when you changed your mind about coming with me last night to look for Gigi Fontaine. What gave me away—that call on your private wire? You'd be surprised how easy it is for a cop to get a judge's number."

There was nothing facetious in his words. Coleman looked grim. He'd aged visibly in twenty-four hours. Everything had aged.

"The call was the big thing," Ralph admitted, "but there were so many others. What you said, what you did—and those nice, green plants on your window shelf when you were supposed to have been away from home for a week."

"Careless of me," Coleman murmured.

"Careless?" Ralph smiled wearily. "I thought you called my attention to them deliberately. You wanted me to know, didn't you? You wanted me to follow along right to the end of the line."

Coleman didn't answer, and that was all right because Ralph knew. One man had been suspicious from the first. One man hadn't completely accepted a verdict. He remembered a scarf; he remembered a woman who didn't spend her night sitting alone in a parked car on Mulholland Drive. And he remembered, too, a row of paper faces on the mantelshelf.

"It didn't begin yesterday, did it?" Ralph asked. "All day and night I've followed your lead as clearly as if you'd taken me by the hand, but you knew the route we traveled too well for it to have been discovered only yesterday. How long, Matt Coleman? How long have you known the truth?"

Matt Coleman looked down at his feet and frowned.

"A long time," he said. "I started looking for it right after the trial was over. It was a farce, that trial. Cox should have been thrown out of court and a public defender appointed to represent Messick. A judge more experienced in a capital case would have done that, I thought."

Coleman's eyes came up for just an instant. They were still knowing eyes, as they had been all along, but they were different, too. They were troubled, as if more bothered them than a mere lack of sleep.

"I checked on Cox, first of all," he continued, "and I didn't have long to wait for the first development. Cox was a little too anxious to cash in on his luck. He prospered too fast."

The telephone books. Ralph understood about that now. Last night, looking up Coleman's address, he'd remembered how easily Leo Cox's new location had been found in that downtown drugstore. Coleman knew in which book he would find him, even if it was another section of the city. Of course he'd been there before!

And now Coleman was admitting it. "I had no trouble finding the scarf in Cox's office," he said. "It was in the filing cabinet the first time I found it. Cox must have noticed the files had been tampered with and transferred it to his desk. I was worried for a while last night. I had to have that scarf to get you to Dorritt's place. Naturally, once I'd identified the source of Cox's income, I had no trouble identifying Elaine Dorritt as Messick's Christmas Eve pickup; but that wasn't enough. The scarf might get Cox into trouble for withholding evidence, but it wouldn't do Messick any good unless I could depend on the girl to back up his story. That was too risky a chance to take, so I decided to sit tight on what I'd learned up to that point and try another angle. After what happened last night, I'm glad I did."

"And the other angle was Faye Harper's unidentified companion," Ralph reflected. "How did you find him, Coleman? How did you know?"

Coleman's head came up again. The aquamarine eyes were still troubled.

"It wasn't easy," he said. "You're right, Judge. The route we traveled yesterday took several months the first time around. The bar where Faye Harper hung out, that motel at the beach, the landlady's story of the Christmas Eve caller, which I got from the transcripts of statements made right after the crime was committed—all of it took a lot of time and trouble. That's why I had to take a leave of absence. Of course, I didn't do everything myself. Some of those boys I told you about do the old man an occasional favor."

"Such as making a certain telephone call to the district attorney's office at ten o'clock yesterday morning?" Ralph asked.

Coleman smiled wearily. "Just a joke," he said. "That's what I told the boy who made the call. Just a joke I was playing on the D.A. Nobody knows the real story but we two, Judge."

There was a strangeness in Matt Coleman's voice when he spoke those words. He let them nest in silence for a few seconds. Then he continued, "As time went on, I began to see things I hadn't seen at first, or, to be more exact, things I'd seen but not seen clearly. For example, there was the bartender's story of the night Faye Harper met this mysterious man—the coincidence of time, I mean. On the very day she'd been in court, Faye acquired a companion so afraid of having his identity discovered that he wouldn't even talk to a motel manager or call for the woman at her usual haunts. I asked myself what kind of man would be like that. A famous man? Maybe. But fame in this city has been pretty well kicked around. Nobody lifts an eyebrow at anything so trivial as adultery any more. A rich man? Hardly. Why should a rich man take so much trouble to hide what a checkbook can always cover? No, Judge, I began to think that I understood this man. He was hiding, you see, long before there was a murderer to hide from. Hiding afterwards, that I could understand. As you pointed out a couple of times yesterday, even an innocent man would be likely to keep quiet about an affair with a woman who had been murdered—but hiding *before*. Why would he do that? What I finally decided, Judge, was that this man was hiding from himself. He hated himself for what he was doing even more than he hated Faye Harper."

Coleman fell silent. He seemed to be waiting for a question that didn't come. Ralph saw him waiting, but only with his eyes. With his mind he saw a woman standing in a courtroom, a beautiful woman, a woman who should have been ashamed and wasn't; and she smiled defiantly at a man who should have been proud and wasn't. Then, with his eyes, Ralph saw Coleman's fingers work restlessly at the small thing in his coat pocket. Almost forgotten that small thing, but not quite. He withdrew the bottle Stu had dropped in the grass last night and began to turn it over and over in his hand.

"It was a terrible thing I did, leaving that girl unguarded last night," he reflected, "but it was my last hope of smoking out the truth in time to save Messick. If what I suspected was true, Faye Harper's mysterious 'tall man' couldn't risk even an outside possibility of an identifying witness, not after the Mr. Justice letters and the discovery of the long lost scarf. I knew he'd go back to that apartment."

Coleman unscrewed the top of the bottle and sniffed the contents. His half-closed eyes were inscrutable.

"And she didn't know a thing," he added ruefully. "Gigi Fontaine didn't know any more than what we heard at that bar yesterday—'the high and mighty.' So you see, Judge, there never was any proof, not any proof at all. Just a crazy, old cop nobody would listen to. Just a hunch and a hope."

He didn't have to explain; Ralph had worked that part out himself. What Matt Coleman knew, or thought he knew, was something he couldn't prove. What he'd uncovered couldn't be sold to a district attorney who would have laughed him out of the office just as he'd tried to laugh off Mr. Justice before the master stroke of that office phone call. But Judge Addison wouldn't laugh off Mr. Justice, and Matt Coleman, equipped with his own set of letters, would be on hand to conduct a tour. It must have been rough sweating out a week of waiting for the judge to make the first move. When he failed to do so, Coleman himself had to put the wheels in motion with six letters written to himself and a tall story of having been out of the city all week.

Yes, Ralph understood all about the letters now. There was only one thing he didn't understand. "Dr. Wilder—" he began, but Matt Coleman didn't let him finish. He knew what that one question had to be.

"You're wondering how Dr. Wilder identified Faye Harper's companion," he said. "All I can tell you, Judge, is what he told me. It started, he says, with an uncompleted telephone call he made from Ojai one night last December."

It started? This time Matt Coleman was wrong. It had started—when? Who could answer such a question? At what hour of what day does a man stop believing in himself? Then the cold comes over him like the breath of distant death, and an ugly rumor whispers at the brain: "It's finished, Ralph Addison. Your life is already finished, and it was nothing after all."

But there was a day he remembered. It had started like any other day— the same tedious quarrel that never really began, never ended, and was so vague in purpose that neither he nor Abbie could any longer remember what they were about. Just another day in a long, undistinguished line of days, until he looked down from his bench and saw what he'd never before seen in a woman such as Faye Harper. She was alive, young and alive. Who was Ralph Addison to deny her nature? Later, when he recalled his anger as he dismissed the charges against her, he felt a bit foolish—but not sorry. No, not sorry with that image of life burned in his brain.

And so he'd gone home at eventide and met Abbie at the door. Cold, stately Abbie pulling on her gloves. "I'm leaving you, Ralph," she said. Then she was gone. It was five twenty-two by the old clock on the mantel and Abbie was gone. There was nothing left but the cold ghosts of fourteen years, and the warm image of a woman who could be found for the asking at a dark bar where nobody had faces.

Stu was right about that uncompleted call one night in December, but it had started long before.

But Matt Coleman was still talking and Ralph tried to listen. He really wanted to hear.

"There were other things," he was saying. "The money you tried to borrow from the bank and that withdrawal."

"The withdrawal?" Ralph echoed. "You knew about that?"

A thorough man, Matt Coleman. He nodded soberly. "Once I'd got the crazy notion in my head, I couldn't rest until I knew the truth. I was in court the day Faye Harper's case was dismissed, as I've told you. What you did and what you said—well, it was all right, but I couldn't forget the way you looked at the woman. Then there was the thing about that Messick trial. The more I thought about it, the more it didn't seem the kind of trial Judge Addison would conduct."

"I didn't want the boy convicted!" Ralph protested. "I wanted to tell what I knew! Can you believe that, Coleman? I wanted to tell, but I couldn't. I had to think of Abbie."

He spoke the words loud and clear, as if trying to convince himself of their truth. But what was truth, after all? The words of the court oath whispered at his mind—"the truth, the whole truth, and nothing but the truth." What folly! What man could swear to tell the truth when truth was known only to God? Because this was the most important morning of his life, Ralph Addison thought these things and remembered, too, how Matt Coleman had looked in that old-fashioned living room, an apron around his waist and a dishtowel over his shoulder, when he told of having killed a boy, not because he wore a badge and was charged with protecting society, but because he was afraid. Was that the truth about Ralph Addison? I had to think of Abbie. And yet, how long since Stu had declared Abbie was out of danger?

The heat had broken, but Coleman had his handkerchief out again and was patting his neck. The handkerchief was rather soiled by this time. Nothing stayed white forever.

"I didn't know about your wife until yesterday," he said at last, "about her delicate condition, I mean. I knew that she'd left you—neighbors come in handy with information like that—and the day of her leaving figured right in with what I suspected. I knew she'd come back again right after Christmas, and that figured too; but I didn't know of the danger she'd been in."

Coleman's voice trailed off into an uncomfortable silence. He finished with the handkerchief and put it back into his pocket. He still had a story to tell, and a man shouldn't start a job he couldn't finish.

"About Dr. Wilder," he continued, "all the details haven't been explained yet, but I imagine that uncompleted call was enough to make him suspicious. He must have tailed you after that until he finally identified the woman you were mixed up with. It wouldn't take a man like Dr. Wilder more than one look to know that you were in real trouble. Blackmail can be nasty business for a man whose wife is in a dangerous condition and whose father-in-law is a comparatively wealthy man."

"Stu told you that?" Ralph asked incredulously.

It was astonishing how much Stu must know. Did he know the rest of it, too? Did he know how it was that night after Abbie had gone and the cold moved in like a slightly previous shroud? He'd tried not to think of her, or of the fourteen years. He'd gone into the study to do some work, but what was his work, after all? A few sterile speeches, an unfinished manuscript—this was the sum total of forty years of living, this and an empty house. Abbie's house. Dr. Braidwell's house. Even his own precious study

had been bought and paid for by another man, and the great words of the
great men standing back to back on the bookshelves mocked him with this
truth, and the simple men who'd handed down the old clock on the mantel made him ashamed until he could stand the silence of Abbie's house no
longer.

And so he'd gone out to find a bar where a lonely man could have a drink
and a little conversation. He'd sat in a rear booth and waited, knowing that
a woman like Faye Harper would come without asking, and when she did
come they had gone out together to drive along the ocean and talk of such
lofty things as rehabilitation, a decent job, and the kind of life a beautiful
young girl should be able to lead. And all the time she knew, and he knew,
where they were going and how the night would end. But not, certainly,
that last night of all.

"I'm the one who told Faye about Abbie," Ralph admitted bitterly. "Like
a fool, I told her as soon as I received Dr. Wilder's wire from Ojai. I wanted
to be fair. I wanted her to know why we wouldn't be seeing each other
again. I gave her some money, a hundred dollars, and thought that was the
end of it. After all, that's the way she lived.

"Then I went up to Ojai and saw Abbie. She wanted to come home right
away, but Dr. Wilder said she'd better not travel just then. Abbie still
wanted to come home, and so he finally gave his permission and agreed
that she could come back with me after Christmas. We always had Christmas at Dr. Braidwell's house. For fourteen years we'd had Christmas there."

Now it was beginning to come clear. Now Ralph could understand the
gay front Stu had put on last night—all that nonsensical banter with an
inebriated blonde on his shoulder and a guarded puzzle in his eyes. The
game he'd been playing wasn't meant to be humorous. It was a deadly serious business to learn how much Matt Coleman really knew.

"But when I came back from Ojai," Ralph added, "Faye started calling
me. She'd learned the identity of my father-in-law and wanted more
money. Once she actually came to my house. I couldn't have that, not with
Abbie due home after Christmas!"

"I guess that's the way Dr. Wilder saw it," Coleman observed. "You had
to be rid of Faye Harper before your wife came home."

"Yes, I had to be rid of her, but I don't have much money, Coleman. I
tried to raise some on the house and failed, so I drew out our savings, a
thousand dollars. I telephoned and told her about it, and she seemed satisfied. She said that she wanted to go to New York and that would give
her a start."

Ralph broke off abruptly in his story. For just a moment it seemed quite
fantastic that he should be standing here calmly reciting these things to Matt
Coleman. It was all so far away now. It was all a bad dream that had ended

at Abbie's bedside a short while ago. It had never been real at all.

"I finally got together the money and called her on Christmas Eve," he continued. "I asked her to meet me at our usual place. I was driving on to Ojai and Abbie afterwards. Faye was late arriving. She'd been drinking, I noticed that right away. She was too drunk to be wise or careful. She laughed when I offered her the thousand dollars and threw it back in my face. She said that she knew where to get more if I didn't."

Coleman nodded gravely. "Then Dr. Wilder was justified in his suspicion," he murmured. "He must have known all along that Faye Harper would never let go of a good thing, and he knew, even better than yourself, what the shock of a mess such as she was capable of creating would have done to your wife at that time. He also knew about that Christmas Eve rendezvous."

"But how?" Ralph protested. "How could he have known?"

It was a question that received no answer. Matt Coleman was telling a story. He seemed annoyed at the interruption.

"He followed you that night," he continued. "He parked his car and waited in the darkness until he saw your car pull away. Then be got to the Harper woman before she could do the same. He shot her immediately, drove down to the beach and got rid of the gun, and then beat you up to Ojai in his high-powered car. It wasn't until hours later that he began to worry that she might have some evidence in her apartment that could link her to you. After the party broke up and everybody had gone to bed, he drove back to the city and made a search of her apartment. That accounts for the man the landlady heard in the passageway."

The landlady. Matt Coleman might have been reciting the denouement of one of the landlady's books—a glib detective story with a twist ending. Ralph didn't interrupt any more, even though he wanted to, and the big policeman hardly paused for breath.

"When Walter Messick was arrested, Wilder probably had a bad time; but he couldn't save the boy without doing the very thing he'd killed Faye Harper to avoid: exposing your relationship with the dead woman and endangering the lives of your wife and her expected child. He sold himself on the idea that Messick's life was already lost, just the way he tried to sell the idea to me last night. By last night, you see, he knew about Mr. Justice and the call I'd made on your private wire. I think he had Mr. Justice identified even sooner than you did, Judge. I don't seem to be very good at fooling people, do I?"

Coleman smiled briefly and humorlessly. He still had that little bottle in his hand, and his eyes were everywhere but where Ralph could meet them.

"That's why Wilder had to reach the Fontaine girl before we did last night," he added, "but, as you recall, she was too drunk to answer any questions. When we came along and broke up that scene in the bar booth, Wilder decided to go along with us for a while. He could always get back to Gigi later. And that's just what he did—unmolested, too, because the only man who believed Walter Messick innocent was, as he well knew, busy watching you."

Now the trouble came up strong in Matt Coleman's eyes. His story was finished except for the thing he'd never counted on—the thing two men were just beginning to understand.

"I guess there's no limit to what a man will do for a woman he loves," he said.

It was awfully quiet when Matt Coleman finished telling his story. It was the kind of quiet that is for sorting out things and getting them straight in the mind. Stu had long known that something was wrong. He'd been wrong about the reason for Abbie's leaving, but not about the rest; not about the bank withdrawal, not about a telephone call at 3:00 A.M., or a man's troubled dreams. He was prepared for trouble. All he needed to alert him to danger was a set of partially burned letters and a phone call. But Abbie mustn't know. That was the thought that stuck like a knife in Ralph's mind. A man he'd never trusted, a man he'd actually suspected of writing the Mr. Justice letters, was, in truth, a man who'd gone out into the night to find Gigi Fontaine and commit the final act of folly.

Ralph turned and looked out of the window again. Some things his mind couldn't grasp, but one thing was coming clear. Somewhere out across the city, Abbie was resting now in a narrow hospital bed, and it was good to know that she was so much loved. So safe and so loved. Now he could do what he had come to do.

"May I see Dr. Wilder now?" he asked.

Coleman didn't answer. He stood there with a small bottle clutched in one hand and his eyes cast down toward the toes of his outspread feet. When he did raise his head, there was a question in his eyes; but the question was never phrased because, at that instant, the door to the outer office burst open making way for a man with much business on his mind.

"Addison!" Halam Mills cried. "What are you doing here? Oh, you heard the news, of course."

Ralph would have preferred being alone with Coleman, but Halam Mills was no man to be ordered out of his own office.

"I heard," Ralph answered. "That's why I'm here."

"Oh, God, what a night!" Mills rubbed his sleep-starved eyes with both hands and then came toward Ralph and Coleman. "And now it's morning," he sighed, "and I haven't had a wink of sleep. Still, all's well that ends well. We've got a confession. I don't know how straight it is, but I got Messick a stay of execution on the strength of it. What's that in your hand,

Coleman? What's in the bottle?"

Coleman made a gesture as if to step aside, but he was too late. Mills took the bottle from his hand, unscrewed the cap, sniffed the contents, and grinned wryly. "Well, I must say it's appropriate after what we've all been through," he remarked, "but I never suspected you were the type to go about carrying spirits of ammonia, Coleman. Now, about Chavez—"

"Chavez?" Ralph echoed.

Chavez. So it was all a lie. With one word Halam Mills had destroyed the last effort of "Mr. Justice." Stu hadn't confessed after all, and that story Coleman had been telling was just another lie. No wonder his eyes couldn't meet Ralph's.

But Mills was too tired to notice the sudden quiet his untimely revelation had brought to the room.

"Yes, Chavez," he repeated. "We finally caught up with him and he told us everything. More, much more than we expected."

"And why not?" Coleman protested. "It was all laid out for him, wasn't it? A crazy, half-sick kid like Chavez reads all the crime stories in the papers. It doesn't take much of a nudge to make his confused mind think he's guilty. Throw him a few more hints and he'll confess to every unsolved crime on the books ... and look real proud for the photographers."

Coleman was bitter, but only Ralph could understand why. Halam Mills was just happy to have something to show for a hard night's work. He hardly noticed the interruption.

"Oh, he played innocent at first," he added, "but once he did break, it was a deluge. He confessed to everything—the letters and the murder. Everything. It seems he used to hang out around the bar Faye worked and had quite a crush on her; but she couldn't see him at all until Christmas Eve, when she condescended to have a few drinks with him. She left finally, mentioning something about a date up on Mulholland, and Chavez thought it was an invitation. He got in his own car and drove up there, but when he found her she wasn't friendly and so he shot her."

Halam Mills spoke mechanically, like one of those recordings the telephone company makes for people who dial the wrong number. Ralph heard all the words he'd spoken, but they weren't important. The only important thing was knowing that it was Chavez and not Stu who was being held for murder, and that it wasn't some deadly poison in that bottle. Stu hadn't gone to the Fontaine woman's apartment with murder in his heart—for hours this thought had haunted Ralph—he'd merely gone in a desperate search for that elusive thing called truth.

"Spirits of ammonia," he said aloud. "Completely harmless."

Coleman knew what he was thinking. Now their eyes could meet.

"It has different uses," he said. "It's really not practical for reviving drunks, I'm afraid, but if it's all a man has on him—"

"Drunks?" Mills echoed. "Who's drunk. Show me and we'll make it a twosome. Sounds like a wonderful idea."

Halam Mills didn't understand. Only two men understood the different uses for a harmless bottle of spirits of ammonia. Stu Wilder could attempt to uncover and then conceal the truth; whereas Matt Coleman could use it as a lever or a wedge to pry for truth. But now Coleman was giving up at last. He slipped the bottle back into his coat pocket—Stu's well-intentioned attempt to obstruct justice needn't concern anyone so narrow-minded on the subject as the District Attorney. He shrugged wearily. It was just as he'd said: there was no proof, and a faked confession was less than no confession at all.

And so it was starting all over again. Walter Messick, Carlos Chavez—different names and different faces, but everything else the same. Coleman's eyes were still troubled, but not so troubled as when he'd first come into the office. He was just a cop—that's what his eyes were saying. Matt Coleman was a cop; not a judge and not an executioner. He could take a man on a tour of the truth and point out the scenic view along the way; but he couldn't pass judgment or make decisions for anyone but himself. "You will die when Messick dies." That was the promise of Mr. Justice, but all it meant, and all it had ever meant, was that some men walk with death inside them when they kill the truth.

"Give my best to your wife, Judge," he said, and then, remembering the bottle again, brought it back out of his pocket. "And give this back to your *friend* the doctor. You can't blame a cop for trying. I had hoped ..." He shrugged.

And then Matt Coleman was turning away for the last time. He walked toward the door, and Ralph knew that he'd never see this man again. He'd go back to his job for the few months remaining before his retirement, and then he'd have all the more time to work with his boys: the Messicks, the Chavezes, the little newsboy in the street below who was going to be President some day if Matt Coleman could fight off the lies that were trying to destroy the dream. And he'd try. One setback wouldn't stop a man who knew the big answer. What hope could there be for the world if a man couldn't make peace with himself?

But it was too big a fight for just one man alone.

"Coleman!"

Ralph's voice stopped him at the door.

"Ask Miss Burgess to come in, please, and ask her to bring her book."

"Miss Burgess?" Mills echoed. "What do you want with my secretary?"

Halam Mills didn't need an answer. Coleman knew what Ralph wanted, but Coleman didn't obey. He just stood there in the open doorway looking a little stunned while Miss Burgess, whose hearing was perfect, reported promptly, book in hand.

"I have a son, Miss Burgess," Ralph said.

"How wonderful!" Miss Burgess beamed.

"Yes—wonderful." Ralph stood tall because tall was how he felt this morning. "Years ago I thought I might have a son and so I started to write a book," he said, "a book that would tell him who he was and how he came by his great heritage of freedom; but I never finished it. I didn't know the words. I know them now."

Ralph paused. What was in a name, after all? Stu Wilder, Carlos Chavez, Walter Messick—justice knew no names. Matt Coleman should have remembered that. He hadn't really needed that lever. A false confession from a friend was no less a lie than a false confession from a stranger. The job Ralph had come from Abbie's bed to do still had to be done even if Stu was in the clear. His reassuring smile was for an honest cop who had to be right or the world wasn't worth saving; but his words were for a judge who had to make a decision.

"You may take this down, Miss Burgess. I killed Faye Harper."

THE END

The Fifth Caller

Helen Nielsen

DEDICATION:
For Judy

CHAPTER ONE

The single-bed hospital room was a bright cubicle on a floor otherwise dark except for the light on the nurse's desk in the corridor and the floor indicators above the elevators—dark and silent at an hour when nothing lawful or sober was abroad unless on official business. It was just before dawn, that time when life reached its lowest ebb and then began again or ended.

The woman on the bed looked so small; she could weigh little more than a hundred pounds. Delicate was the word that came to Douglas Marshall's mind—delicate in the sense of fineness of structure and balance. Her skin was exceptionally fair—some women never tanned even under the California sun; her hair was dark, almost black where it formed a close-cropped halo against the pillow; her lips were pale from the loss of blood, but they were full and generous. Her eyes were closed. They would be blue, he thought.

Douglas Marshall stood at the side of the narrow bed, towering a full six feet above the immaculate tile floor. He was a young forty—clean shaven and clear-eyed in spite of the hour. He wore the well-tailored clothes of a man who had an appointment with success—a disciplined man. He'd been waiting at the hospital for nearly six hours, but he didn't glance at his wrist watch or show any other sign of impatience. Some things couldn't be hurried. He stood quietly, hat and topcoat in hand, and waited for the woman's eyes to open.

Another man, still in professional white, stood beside him. Dr. Huntziger's face mirrored an additional twenty years of age and weariness. The lines about his eyes testified to many a dawn watch, and to him the faintest flicker of life was discernible. He leaned forward over the bed.

"She's coming around," he said. "When she does, you may talk with her, but I'm going to stand by. She's lost a great deal of blood. A little longer out on that beach and the transfusions wouldn't have made any difference."

As Huntziger straightened again, he removed a cigarette case from his trouser pocket. He extracted a cigarette from the case but made no move to light it. It was an automatic gesture; hands freed from duty had to find something to keep them busy. His eyes never left the woman on the bed.

"Beautiful woman, isn't she?" he remarked.

"Very beautiful," Marshall acknowledged.

"I always get a thrill out of saving a life," the doctor added. "You might think it didn't matter after all these years—just routine, mechanical, a way of providing for the family—but it does matter. Something alive is dying, the great mystery is about to end; and then the spark flares up again and takes hold and the thrill's as great as the first time I watched it happen. But tonight—" Huntziger slipped the cold cigarette, quite forgotten, into his white tunic pocket—"I almost wished for failure."

His gaze returned to the woman on the bed. Marshall's had never left her. Her breathing was stronger now. Respiration was visible under the sheet held tightly about her body by the weight of her arms stretched outside of it. Both wrists were heavily bandaged where they had been slashed.

"Anna Bardossy," Huntziger said. "Nationality—Hungarian. Age—thirty-two."

He reached down to check the pulse above one bandaged wrist. As he did so, he turned the arm over and whatever the imagination needed to fill in the nature of those thirty-two years was triggered by the sight of the number, that lifetime souvenir of the concentration camp, which showed vividly against the white flesh. She could have been little more than a child when it was put there.

Huntziger placed the arm back on the sheet, his point made.

"Is there such a thing as justice?" he asked.

"I think there is," Marshall said. "I wouldn't have waited here all this time if I didn't."

"I hope you're right. Still, I'm glad my part of this job is almost over.... Wait a minute, I think this is it? Here she comes. Your witness, Mr. Marshall."

A muscle twitched at the edge of the woman's mouth. A barely audible moan, which was more of a sigh, escaped her lips, and then her eyes opened. The first thing Marshall noticed was that they were blue—a deep, almost purple blue. They opened wide, but they didn't look at him. Consciousness was returning from a far, dark place, and the journey required time. Focusing her eyes came slowly. At last she found the ceiling—strange, unfamiliar; then walls, window, bed, herself lying on the bed, her body, her arms, her bandaged wrists. The first sign of recognition came then, but it was blurred with bewilderment.

"Miss Bardossy ..."

Marshall spoke the name distinctly. It seemed to bring her into a kind of dazed awareness.

"How do you feel, Miss Bardossy?"

She looked at him then. She seemed to listen to the words long after they were spoken, as if the language itself were strange.

"Do you think you can talk now?"

Again the listening. Finally, one word.

"Talk ..."

There wasn't enough inflection in her voice to make the word a question.

She had merely repeated, parrot-like.

"Do you know where you are?"

Her eyes went wandering again. This time they came to rest on Huntziger in his whites.

"Hospital," she said.

"Yes, that's right. This is a hospital in Santa Monica. That man you're looking at is Dr. Huntziger. He's just saved your life."

She made no effort to speak; but her eyes seemed to be memorizing every wrinkle in the doctor's face.

"And my name," Marshall continued, "is Douglas Marshall. I'm from the district attorney's office, and if you feel strong enough I'd like to ask a few questions."

He watched her face as the words brought her eyes back to his. This was the important moment—when adversaries met. She betrayed no emotion; but she was still just within the border of consciousness. A few routine questions might draw her the rest of the way.

He stepped closer to the bed.

"Anna Bardossy," he began. "You are Anna Bardossy, aren't you? Miss Anna Bardossy?"

Now there was a shadow of an emotion—fear.

"I am," she pronounced slowly, "Anna Bardossy."

"And you reside at 1947 North Hillmont Avenue, Los Angeles?"

"Yes ... I do."

"Which is also the residence and professional office of your employer, Lillian Whitehall?"

She didn't answer. Her eyes had begun their searching again.

"Lillian Whitehall," Marshall repeated, and then he corrected himself. Whatever his personal opinion, the woman did have a title. "Dr. White-hall has maintained a method of psychotherapeutical practice in her home, at which you have been employed in the capacity of nurse for the past four years—is that correct?"

The woman's eyes stopped searching when she located Dr. Huntziger again. Something seemed to be bothering her.

"Santa Monica?" she asked.

Marshall couldn't allow her attention to wander. This was the time to get at the truth—before the mental guards were up.

"Miss Bardossy," he said sharply, "please answer my question."

"Yes," she said. "Yes, it is correct. But please, I don't understand—"

"You will understand in a few minutes; we'll explain everything. But first, I must ask a few more questions. Now, Miss Bardossy, yesterday—Thursday—was your day off, I believe."

"Yesterday?"

The windows were lightening now. When she noticed that, Anna Bardossy seemed to understand that a day was gone.

"Thursday is my day off," she acknowledged.

"And I suppose you spent it away from the house—a shopping trip, errands, that sort of thing."

She looked at him now. Her gaze was intense and penetrating; but that cloud of bewilderment was still in her eyes.

"I don't know ..." she said.

"You don't know? Do you mean that you can't remember what you did yesterday?"

"I can't remember."

"But you did leave the house. Think now, was it in the morning—say, at ten o'clock?"

"I can't remember!"

The frown lines had appeared on her forehead, as if she were trying to force a memory. Marshall glanced at the doctor. An almost imperceptible nod gave him permission to continue.

"Miss Bardossy!"

She sighed. "If yesterday was Thursday, then—yes, I left the house."

"But you don't remember?"

"No, I have told you twice—I do not remember."

Marshall shifted his hat and topcoat from one arm to the other. This was becoming more difficult than he had anticipated; but he was still a patient man.

"Perhaps I can help you to remember," he said quietly. "Didn't you go on a shopping trip yesterday? Didn't you make several purchases at Bannock's Westwood?"

"Bannock's ... Westwood?"

It was impossible to be certain whether or not mention of the store had aroused memory. The bewilderment in her eyes was touched with apprehension, and yet it seemed genuine.

"That is a very expensive store," she said. "I earn little money."

"But don't you remember making several purchases—mostly lingerie?"

"Lingerie?"

"Three boxes bearing the Bannock's label were found in your car, Miss Bardossy. Do you remember that you own a car?"

"An automobile—yes."

"A dark-green Volkswagen, license number HGM 570?"

"Yes, that is my automobile."

"Then surely you can remember this ..."

Marshall stepped back quickly from the bed. Three store boxes of various sizes were stacked on a chest of drawers at the foot of the bed. He deposited his hat and coat on a side chair and returned with the top box, opened it and withdrew from within a soft, filmy article referred to in the better shops as intimate apparel. It was a negligee—pale-pink chiffon trimmed with ribbons and the finest lace. Anna Bardossy's eyes widened at the sight of it.

"There's a nightgown to match in one of the other boxes, and in the small one a pair of slippers," Marshall announced.

"And you found these things in my automobile?"

"In your automobile, Miss Bardossy. Now, don't you remember them at all?"

She couldn't conceal it. The response in her eyes at the sight of the negligee was more than admiration: it was recognition.

"I have seen this in the store—yes."

"And you were in the store yesterday?"

She closed her eyes. For a moment Marshall was afraid she'd lost consciousness; but before Huntziger could reach her the eyes reopened.

"Please, what I mean was that I have seen these things in the store and admired them. If you say they were found in my automobile, then I must have purchased them. But I don't remember doing so, and I can't afford them. Doctor ..."

She tried to raise up from the pillow. Huntziger's hand was pressed against her shoulder immediately.

"None of that!" he ordered. "You lie back quietly or this interview is over."

"But I must know! What is it? Why am I in a hospital in Santa Monica?"

"Don't you know?" Huntziger asked softly. "Look at your wrists."

Her eyes traveled down to the arms beside her body. She had seen them before on the way to consciousness; now she looked more carefully, raising each arm just a few degrees until the bandages were visible from her pillow.

"At nine-thirty last night," Dr. Huntziger said, "a man named Oscar Dunlap decided to take his German shepherd for a walk along the Santa Monica beach. About ten minutes later he stumbled across a body lying on the sand. At first he thought it was a dead body, and it very nearly was; but Dunlap knew enough first aid to apply a couple of quick tourniquets above the slashed wrists—you owe him a new shirt, by the way—and then left the dog on guard while he sprinted for the police. That's why you're in a hospital, and that's also why the hospital is in Santa Monica. You've had a rough night, Miss Bardossy, but you'll soon be good as new. As to the reason why you went to the beach and put the razor blade found beside your purse to such violent use—well, that's the reason Mr. Marshall is asking questions."

The woman listened to him with no change of expression. She looked once more at her bandaged wrists and then let them drop back on the mattress.

"So that's it," she said. "So small a thing."

"I'm afraid it isn't a small thing," Marshall insisted. "Why did you try to kill yourself?"

There was no answer.

"Is it because of something else you have forgotten—or is it something you remember?"

For an instant there was expression in her eyes—anger. She was fully conscious now and capable of hiding her emotion quickly; but the one glimpse was intense and revealing.

"Do you remember driving to the beach, Miss Bardossy?"

There was no answer.

"Do you remember what time it was when you returned to the house yesterday?"

"No, I don't remember."

"Was it five o'clock ... five fifteen ... five twenty?"

"If I were a judge," Huntziger interrupted, "and we were in a courtroom, I don't think I'd allow that question."

"I'm merely trying to prod Miss Bardossy's memory," Marshall said, "since she seems to be having so much trouble with it. If I were to tell you, Miss Bardossy, that you were seen approaching the Whitehall residence at a little past two yesterday afternoon, would that arouse your memory?"

She heard the question; her eyes were wide open and they never left his. A touch of color had come to her face as a result of the anger. Good. A person who could fight back was a person who could live. The thought, as it came, wrenched Marshall's mind. He was like Huntziger; it was impossible not to be on the side of life, and yet that made his job all the more cruel.

"Mr. District Attorney—" she began.

"I'm not the district attorney," Marshall corrected. "I'm merely an investigator from the district attorney's office."

"And you have been waiting here all night to ask me such questions?"

"Most of the night—yes."

"Is that how the law is?"

"That's how the law is under certain circumstances."

"I see. And what are the certain circumstances?"

It was impossible to know if she were hiding her memory, or was actually devoid of it. The doctor might have an opinion on that, but there was no time or place for consultation. Marshall had started this; he had to go on with it.

"I don't suppose there's any object in asking if you remember anything that happened yesterday," he said, "but you do remember your employer, Dr. Whitehall."

"Yes, of course."

"Unless I have been misinformed, she was instrumental in effecting your escape from communist Hungary four years ago."

"In effecting my escape, no; in my coming to the United States, yes," she said.

"In other words, she was your sponsor. You must have been very grateful."

"Very grateful, Mr. Marshall."

"And yet I understand that your relationship has become strained during the ensuing years; that you have been known to quarrel—sometimes violently; that you have gone so far as to threaten Dr. Whitehall's life."

This time emotion was instantaneous.

"Who told you that? Who spoke such a lie?"

"Just a minute," Huntziger broke in. "Even if this isn't a courtroom, I'm going to stop you, Marshall. This isn't the time or the place for that—"

"You're right," Marshall said. "I apologize, Miss Bardossy. You needn't comment on that statement or answer any more questions without benefit of counsel unless you so desire. There's something Dr. Huntziger left out of his story of why you're in a hospital in Santa Monica, and why I'm here. I'm afraid it's more than a matter of attempted suicide. Last night, about two hours before you were found on the beach with your wrists slashed, Dr. Whitehall was found in her study—dead. She had been murdered."

CHAPTER TWO

Douglas Marshall spoke the words quietly and without emotion. He'd given her time to become fully conscious and gain strength for the shock—if it really came as a shock. Now he watched her face for the clue. The windows had turned paler, and the eyes of Anna Bardossy seemed to grow more blue with the change of light. They continued to stare at him until the instant she spoke.

"No…"

It was barely a whisper. She closed her eyes and turned her head on the pillow, as if there were a place to hide. This was no fragile, spoiled woman who burst into tears at the hint of crisis; but she was fighting tears now. Her breathing seemed to stop for a moment, and then came again—deep and labored. Dr. Huntziger stepped forward, and Marshall was afraid he was about to be ordered out of the room; but it was Anna who interfered. As soon as she had control of her emotions, she faced him.

"Am I under arrest?" she asked.

Direct, disarming. With such a woman only straight answers would suffice.

"I can't tell you that until I hear your story," he said.

"But I have no story."

"Do you mean that you still can't remember anything that happened yesterday?"

"Anything that happened ... ?"

"Anything. Just to get a start somewhere, try early in the morning. When did you arise? What kind of a day was it? How did you feel?"

He fed the suggestions quickly. She seemed to be trying.

"Happy? Anxious? Did you have plans for the day?"

He seemed to touch on a nerve. Her eyes left his face and found the filmy negligee still in his hand.

"It is a beautiful thing, isn't it?" Marshall said. "When was the first time you admired it in the store?"

She frowned again—such an intense frown, the fate of nations might have rested on her answer.

"I'm not sure. Perhaps last week on my day off."

"Do you always go to Westwood on your day off?"

"No—sometimes. I like to see the lovely things in the shops. I don't remember when I saw the negligee—everything is so mixed up."

"Mixed up, Miss Bardossy?"

"Time, I mean. Days ... weeks. I only remember that at some time I did see it, and I said—"

Her voice stopped abruptly. The sentence hung conspicuously unfinished.

"What did you say, Miss Bardossy?"

"I said that it was lovely."

"And to whom did you say this?"

"To the clerk. Yes, the clerk. But it was so expensive."

"And yet, yesterday you purchased it and two other items as well. Did something happen to make it seem less expensive? Did you come into some money?"

"No!"

"You sound very positive. You do remember something, then."

"No! I remember nothing! Nothing!"

And then she broke, not just the turning of the head but a writhing and twisting that brought Huntziger to the bedside and drove Marshall from it. He'd seen this thing happen before: initial calm under the anesthetic of shock and then a delayed reaction. If he persisted in questioning her now she might go into hysteria and a night of waiting would be wasted. Anticipating Huntziger's signal, he retreated to the chest of drawers at the foot of the bed. The negligee was back in the box by the time the nurse who answered the doctor's buzzer opened the door. Retrieving his hat and coat, Marshall left the room.

The corridor was still silent but not quite so dark. He walked past the elevators and through a small waiting room—empty at this hour—into Dr. Huntziger's office. This room wasn't empty. A chunky, blunt-faced man wearing a felt hat and a wrinkled raincoat stood beside the desk sipping a cup of coffee from the electric pot that had been plugged in all night. He turned at the sound of Marshall's entrance, grimacing.

"I must have squeezed out the dregs this time," he said. "If this stuff doesn't wake me up, nothing will." Then he paused. "What about the Bardossy woman? Is she conscious?"

"She was when I left her," Marshall said.

"Did she confess?"

Marshall didn't answer the question. He walked across the room to the window and stood with his back to the man in the raincoat. The darkness had raveled loose at the horizon, and a dull, yellowish glow was working its way through the early morning fog of a drab December day. For a moment he seemed to forget where he was or why he was there.

"I don't suppose I'll ever watch a dawn again," he said, "without thinking of that field in England, the sky dripping like a dirty sponge and everybody's eyes tearing at the sockets for the first glimpse of whatever returned from the night mission over Germany."

"You must have been overseas a long time," the man in the raincoat said.

"Six years including the occupation. A lifetime ..." The door opened behind him. Marshall turned about as Dr. Huntziger entered the room. "What about Anna Bardossy?" he asked.

"I gave her a sedative," Huntziger answered. "She'll sleep it off in an hour or two." He walked over to his desk. Now he saw the second man in the room. "Well, if it isn't Sergeant Lansing back again. I think I'll have to put you on my staff, or else apply to the police department for a branch station. What's new?"

"That's what I'm here to find out," Lansing said, "but so far all I've heard is a page from the war memoirs of Mr. Marshall."

"Really? Well, at least somebody remembers something."

"That's what I meant when I asked about Anna Bardossy," Marshall cut in. "Is she telling the truth? Doesn't she really remember anything that happened yesterday?"

"What do you think?" Huntziger asked.

"I don't know. She had no time to build up a defense—I saw to that. She sounds genuine, but they learn to lie. It becomes almost a reflex action."

"They?"

Huntziger's fingers had gone prowling through his pockets for the cigarette previously abandoned. It was rather wilted by this time, but he didn't notice. Over the match flame his eyes were censuring Marshall.

"They," Marshall repeated deliberately. "The DPs, the victims, the refugees of society. I'm not being self-righteous, Huntziger, merely realistic. Prolonged deprivation and fear of punishment will make almost anyone dishonest. They have to learn to lie; it's their only chance of getting out alive."

"I suppose you know more about that than I do."

"I should. I've had experience."

Marshall's mouth went hard. He came away from the window and moved toward the desk.

"I'm asking again," he said. "Is Anna Bardossy telling the truth?"

"She may be."

"Is there a way of making certain?"

"I suppose there is—a drug, hypnosis."

"That's no good. I'll have to have evidence that will stand up in court."

"A confession, you mean?"

"If she's guilty—yes."

By this time Sgt. Lansing was finished with his bitter brew. He put the empty cup down on the desk with a slight shudder.

"I'm not sure that I follow this conversation," he said. "But from what I've heard it appears Dr. Whitehall's nurse has pulled a mental blackout alibi and you're not sure if it's genuine. I can see how that's frustrating after waiting most of the night to get her story, but I don't see what it has to do with evidence that will stand up in court. You've got that already, Marshall. Just listen—"

Lansing reached into his coat pocket and brought out a small notebook. He flicked open the pages and looked up, grinning.

"I stopped a bullet during a raid on the robbery detail last year," he said, "and took up shorthand to keep from going crazy while I was recuperating. Now let's see if I can read the stuff. 'Griswold, Naomi. Age 50.' That's approximate, you understand," he explained, looking up from the notebook. "I never ask a lady's age unless it's necessary. 'Patient and disciple'— I think that's what they call it—'of Dr. Whitehall. Discovered the body at approximately seven-thirty last night in the doctor's study, the room in a state of violent disorder—books and pamphlets written by Dr. Whitehall ripped and scattered over the floor and the murder weapon, a heavy desk clock set in a wedge of thick crystal, stained with blood and the hands stopped at five twenty-two.'"

"How very convenient," Huntziger observed. "It was thoughtful of the murderer to use a clock. Incidentally, how did this woman—Griswold—get into the house?"

"The front door was unlocked. It was kept unlocked from eight in the morning until eight at night, except Thursday night when Dr. Whitehall held a study class at a little hall down on Vermont. Last night was Thursday and Mrs. Griswold had come by to pick her up. She's a nervous woman—acts like a sheep who's lost her shepherd—but her testimony concerning the nurse, Anna Bardossy, was definite. She didn't get along with the doctor. Mrs. Griswold claims she overheard them quarreling many times, the last time being yesterday morning when she came for her ten o'-clock appointment. She met the nurse going out as she was coming in, and was nearly knocked down in the process. When the call came in from the Santa Monica police last night saying they'd picked up the nurse in an attempted suicide, Griswold didn't have a doubt. That's when she told me Bardossy had threatened Dr. Whitehall's life."

"Which she denies vehemently," Marshall interposed.

"She does?" Lansing frowned and then returned to his notebook. "Well, no matter. There's other testimony. 'Elrod, Harold. Dr. Whitehall's lawyer and member of her cult. Summoned from the meeting hall by Mrs. Griswold after her discovery of the body.' Both he and his wife were on the premises when I arrived last night; in fact, it was Elrod who called the police. Elrod corroborates the story that the nurse had a temper and didn't get along well with Dr. Whitehall. And then there's brother Byron—" Sgt. Lansing snapped the book shut and returned it to his pocket. "He's a cutie. Must be sixty if he's a day, but he didn't show up on the premises until after one of my men had found him getting home to his apartment at half-past three. You should have seen him, Marshall—wavy white hair, profile, plaid cummerbund, and reeking of whiskey. I have my doubts that brother Byron was ever a member of Dr. Whitehall's cult, but he has one thing in common with the others. The first thing he said after learning why he'd been summoned was 'Where's the nurse?' That seems to make the vote unanimous."

"Byron," Marshall repeated. "That would be the Byron Davies you reported as having seen Anna Bardossy near the Whitehall house shortly after two o'clock yesterday."

"The same. He had an appointment with his sister for two—apparently Dr. Whitehall was a very methodical woman; she saw nobody without an appointment. But Byron isn't so methodical—he was late. Just as he pulled into the driveway—it's one of those old houses below Los Feliz with a long, curving approach—he noticed the nurse's car turning the corner and coming toward the house. He thinks she must have recognized him and didn't want to come in while he was there, because she drove on past. We have one witness who saw Anna Bardossy leave the house in the morning, and another witness who saw her trying to return. We have three witnesses who know she didn't get along with Dr. Whitehall. We have a crime of violence and a study in a shambles, and we have a woman who attempted to kill herself within a few hours after the murder. What more do you want for an arrest, Marshall?"

Douglas Marshall didn't have a ready answer. Everything the sergeant said was true, and yet he wasn't ready to move. It had been too long a night to wait for nothing.

"I think Mr. Marshall is wise to hold off on making an arrest," the doctor remarked. "I'm not a criminologist, but I read the newspapers occasionally. The crime you just described, Sergeant—the rifled study, the violent death—doesn't that usually turn out to be the work of some degenerate prowler or an interrupted burglar? You just told us the house was unlocked."

"If it was a prowler or a burglar," Lansing said stubbornly, "why did the nurse slash her wrists?"

"It's possible the two events were unrelated. This just doesn't seem like woman's crime."

"Is that a professional opinion, Doctor?" Marshall asked.

Dr. Huntziger peered up at him through a haze of smoke and his face wrinkled into a smile.

"A layman's guess and a doctor's wishful thinking," he said. "Still, it does seem a little like shooting fish in a barrel—especially if she really can't remember. And what's the motive—what's the reason? She seems an intelligent young woman. Doesn't it make you wonder why a lovely, living thing who's survived hell to get free will decide death is the better way after all?"

Douglas Marshall's eyes were somber as he heard the question. It really didn't need phrasing; it had hung between them all night. It had hung heavier than Dr. Huntziger knew. He studied the old man's face for several moments before making a reply. Dr. Whitehall was dead now; there was no need for secrecy.

"There's something about this case that you don't know, Dr. Huntziger," he said. "It didn't begin tonight."

The statement drew a response. Interest instead of sad weariness in his eyes.

"Tell me, just what is your professional opinion of Dr. Whitehall?"

Dr. Huntziger mulled over the question in his mind. He took two quick puffs on his cigarette and then ground it out in an ash tray on his desk.

"I never knew the lady personally," he said, "but I've heard rumors. Some people thought she was an outright fraud; but fraud, to my mind, denotes deliberate deception. I believe Dr. Whitehall was sincere; she just wasn't qualified. She was one of those people who believe that if one method of healing works, a mixture of six or seven methods will work six or seven times as well. With all those methods she was bound to help some people— a lot of us just need our hand held occasionally."

"You think, then, she was harmless?"

"Harmless?" Dr. Huntziger chuckled. "Marshall, I don't even think that I'm harmless ..." And then he sobered and reconsidered the question. "Why do you ask?"

"Because someone didn't think she was."

There was a comfortable-looking leather chair near the desk. Marshall sat down in it. It was the first time he'd been off his feet in hours, but he didn't relax. He was still working.

"I told you a few moments ago that this case didn't start tonight," he continued. "Actually, it began—so far as my office is concerned—nearly a year ago. That's why I got on the case as soon as word reached me from homicide. It was nearly a year ago that we received the first complaint about Dr. Whitehall. It was in the form of an anonymous letter, and we might have passed it off as the work of a crank if it hadn't been for the language in which it was written. As you've just mentioned, Dr. Whitehall practiced a form of psychotherapy, mixed with a distillation of several religious viewpoints. She had a degree from a metaphysical college she'd founded herself, and a degree in psychology from one of those mail order colleges south of the border. She was allowed to practice within a limited scope; but she wasn't permitted to practice surgery, medicine, nor was she a qualified analyst. The anonymous complaints—there were five in all—named specific violations of her legally prescribed practice and did so in highly professional terms."

Dr. Huntziger was rapidly losing all trace of his sleepless night. "Professional terms," he repeated. "That's interesting. Were the complaints valid?"

"I don't know," Marshall answered. "No names were mentioned so no check could be made. The letters were typewritten and set down in detail the symptoms of each case, as well as Dr. Whitehall's diagnosis and treatment and the suggested diagnosis and treatment of the letter writer. None of the letters were malicious—purely informative. I consulted with specialists in the various fields indicated and learned that the letter writer's views were exceptionally accurate and advanced. According to our unknown informant, Dr. Whitehall had incorrectly treated both physical and mental cases.

"Three months ago the letters stopped coming."

"No more complaints?"

"No more complaints, and yet Dr. Whitehall continued her practice."

"Perhaps the informant moved away."

"I don't think so. As I told you, these letters were written in a highly professional language. My initial investigation was of Dr. Whitehall's staff and close associates. This was simple. Her practice was carried on in her home—a house shared only with the nurse, Anna Bardossy. She had no resident servants. The yard work was done by an independent gardener, the day work—once a week—by a free-lance cleaning woman. Dr. Whitehall, according to her own dietary book, subsisted on a meager diet. She employed no cook. She had only one living relative, her brother, Byron Davies, who didn't live on the premises and isn't a medical man. Harold Elrod, as Sergeant Lansing has already told us, is the legal and financial advisor of her enterprises as well as being a member of her sect. A disciple usually doesn't inform on his teacher."

Dr. Huntziger's mouth twisted toward a smile.

"It's been done," he reminded, "and for only thirty pieces of silver."

"That's true; but it was when I began to delve into the background of the nurse that my investigation proved interesting. This is no ordinary woman, Dr. Huntziger. There are gaps in her history that I haven't been able to fill in as yet; but I did learn that her father was one of the most prominent physicians in Budapest until his outspoken liberalism led to sudden and brutal death at the hands of the Nazis in 1940. It was then that Anna and her mother went into a concentration camp. Anna came out alive. After the war, she entered medical school and is a graduate physician specializing in diagnosis."

An expression of dismay crossed Huntziger's face.

"And she's been wasting her time working for Lillian Whitehall?"

"I'm afraid she had no alternative. According to information given the Immigration authorities when she entered the United States, Miss Bardossy escaped communist Hungary in 1954 with her life and nothing else. She has no certification of her medical status—nothing but her own sworn statement. She can't practice medicine on that. What's more, it was Lillian Whitehall who sponsored her immigration from a refugee camp in Switzerland."

Dr. Huntziger's face was gray in the early morning light. He reached out and switched off the electric coffee pot. The dregs were beginning to burn.

"A situation like that could create a schism," he said thoughtfully. "Loyalty to a savior, so to speak, opposed to professional integrity. You have the elements of a fine emotional upheaval, my friend, added to which you have a woman who's already endured more abuse than most people are asked to endure in a lifetime. I don't like to discourage you, but there's every reason to believe the nurse's mental block is genuine."

"Then we've got to get through to her."

Sgt. Lansing had waited patiently during Marshall's explanation of the letters. Now he shifted his weight with not quite so much patience.

"I still don't see why it's necessary to get a confession," he said. "Everything you told the doctor adds to the case against her. She was emotionally upset—the doctor just said so—and I can tell you that study wasn't torn up by anyone with a well balanced mind. And what about those slashed wrists? I don't call that a sign of mental stability! You're a fair man, Marshall, but I still say you've got your case without the nurse's memory. Let the others do her remembering for her. I'd like to get home and start explaining to my wife where I've been all night."

There wasn't a thing wrong with Lansing's viewpoint. They were three tired men who needed nothing more than to go home and catch up on their sleep. Sgt. Lansing had done his job well; Huntziger had saved the life he had to save even if it wasn't wanted by the possessor, and Douglas Marshall ...

He couldn't escape the feeling of frustration. If Anna Bardossy maintained her silence, she could be convicted. But her silence was an aggravation. He wanted to break it; he wanted to probe at it as the doctor might probe for a malignant condition. Questions had to have answers in Douglas Marshall's disciplined world.

And then he seemed to hear an echo of something Lansing had stated.

"Wait a minute," he said. "You've given me an idea."

"I hope so."

"No, not the one you wanted to give me. 'Let the others do her remembering for her,' you said. It's just possible we can do that.... Dr. Huntziger, when Anna Bardossy awakens will she be in a condition to receive visitors?"

It was an odd request. The doctor looked interested. He seemed incapable of surprise.

"I don't see why not," he answered. "She's lost a lot of blood, but we've pumped a lot more into her. It depends, naturally, on the number of visitors you have in mind and how long they stay."

Marshall reflected.

"Mrs. Griswold, the lawyer, the brother— Did you talk to anyone else, Lansing?"

"Isn't that enough?"

"I don't know. What about the patients Dr. Whitehall saw yesterday? Did she keep an appointment book where you could find the names?"

"I didn't see any."

"But she must have kept some record—for taxes if nothing else. I want you to go back and look for it, Sergeant. Every day has a beginning and an end, and in between a history written somewhere in some manner. Anna

Bardossy claims she can't recall anything that happened yesterday; but if we can reconstruct the day—if we can bring into her room, one by one, each caller who came to the Whitehall house between the time she left the house at ten o'clock until whatever time she returned, we may be able to draw her out. We might even locate someone who saw her return. I think it's worth the effort. What do you think?"

Sgt. Lansing sighed and began to button his coat.

"I think it must be great to be a bachelor," he said.

"I'm not a bachelor," Marshall answered. "I've been married."

"Then you know what it is to have a wife waiting and worrying all night."

"No, I'm afraid I don't. When I had night duty, I wasn't even missed. But that's ancient history. What I'm interested in right now is breakfast, a shave, and ..." Marshall paused to consult the watch on his wrist. The long night no longer seemed to have touched him. There was work to do, and he was as efficient as the timepiece—"The first caller, which will be Naomi Griswold, back here at ten o'clock. That will give Miss Bardossy time to recover from her sedative—providing Dr. Huntziger is willing to go along with the Marshall therapy."

"I wouldn't miss it," Huntziger said. "I'm fascinated already. Of course, you realize it may not work."

"I know," Marshall said. "In that case, I'll have to fall back on your more professional methods; but first we'll have a try at mine. I like to satisfy myself that I've made every effort to get at the truth before ordering an arrest. What I want is to hear the story of what happened yesterday directly from Anna Bardossy's lips."

He still remembered them, full and generous; but they could be deceiving. His face was a shadow against the window.

"They do learn to lie," he said, "all of them."

CHAPTER THREE

The death of Lillian Whitehall wasn't the quiet passing her followers would have desired. It was lurid and ugly, and sensationalized in the press. But because those who had been close to her in life wished to co-operate with those who had become close to her in death, the link between an attempted suicide on the beach and a missing nurse from the Whitehall household was withheld from the press. It was only a matter of time until they uncovered the truth; but when time stood at ten A.M. by the hands of the clock on the wall of the waiting room outside Dr. Huntziger's office, Anna Bardossy's presence in the building was still a secret only then being divulged to the woman who had been Dr. Whitehall's first caller on the last day of her life.

Naomi Griswold was afraid of hospitals. She was also afraid of Douglas Marshall, Sgt. Lansing, and Dr. Huntziger. She was a slightly built, graying widow whose narrow, gloved hands worked nervously at the clasp of her black fabric handbag. Her complete attire, from the small, unstylish hat to the sturdy arch-support shoes was black. Black was for death, and all life had gone out of her world.

"Of course, I know that Dr. Lillian isn't dead," she declared firmly. She never used the name without the title. "Death is an illusion—the 'final illusion,' as Dr. Lillian used to say, 'the end of nothingness.'"

The words would have sounded stronger if her lower lip hadn't trembled so much.

"That seems to be the consensus of philosophical opinion through the ages," Marshall observed.

"But the horrible way she passed on!"

The gloved hands working at the clasp of the handbag achieved their purpose. Naomi Griswold withdrew a small square of linen and dabbed at her eyes.

"Socrates told his friends, as he was dying of the poison he'd been forced to drink, 'nothing evil can happen to a good man in this life or the next.'"

The words had an immediate effect. Naomi Griswold looked up with quick gratitude in her tear-rimmed eyes. After that, she wasn't quite so afraid of Douglas Marshall. She allowed him to explain why Sgt. Lansing had brought her to the hospital with a minimum of interruptions and only one brief protest.

"Oh, but I couldn't go into the same room with that woman—not after what she did!"

"She doesn't remember what she did, Mrs. Griswold."

"Did she say that? She's probably lying. A woman who could commit murder wouldn't hesitate to lie in order to save herself."

"That's a very real possibility, Mrs. Griswold, but how are we to prove she's lying if we don't test her?"

The woman's eyes brightened. They were small, dark eyes —almost black. They were also penetrating once she became intrigued with an idea.

"Is that what you want me to do—prove that she's lying?"

"No, Mrs. Griswold, I don't want you to prove anything. All I want you to do is accompany me into Miss Bardossy's room. I'll ask certain questions, most of which you've already answered for Sergeant Lansing, and your answers will tell the nurse what happened when you arrived at Dr. Whitehall's home yesterday morning. If she's under shock, your story may stimulate recollection. If she's pretending shock, she may give herself away. Are you willing to do that?"

Naomi Griswold still hesitated.

"What is it, Mrs. Griswold?"

"It's the hospital, I think," she said weakly. "I have such a terrible dread of hospitals. I was sick for so many years before I found dear Dr. Lillian ..."

Her voice broke. The handkerchief returned to her eyes again, and then she squared her narrow shoulders defiantly.

"I'm sorry, Mr. Marshall. I'll find the strength somehow. Anything to bring that murderer to justice!"

The second time Douglas Marshall stood at the side of Anna Bardossy's bed, his feelings were exactly the same as the first time. She was so small and so beautiful. Four hours had wrought great changes. The sleep seemed to have done her good—the tears, too, perhaps. There was color in her face now, faint but quite distinct after the marble whiteness of his first visit. The hospital nurse had combed her hair, and she sat up in bed propped against the pillows with only the bandaged wrists to distinguish her from any recuperating patient awaiting dismissal. He found himself wondering how she would look in the pink negligee.

But there had been a murder. At the sight of him a little of the color left her face. At the sight of Mrs. Griswold some of it returned—a tinge of that swift anger he'd once seen in her eyes. There was a reaction from Mrs. Griswold, too. She advanced to within a few feet of the bed and then stepped back again. There was a moment of tension.

Dr. Huntziger, who hadn't forgotten the patient was his responsibility as long as she remained in the hospital, moved the side chair closer to the bed.

"Sit down, Mrs. Griswold," he said, "... please."

She continued to stand in the same spot.

"I don't think I care to come any closer to a murderess," she protested.

"Why don't you leave judgment to the courts?" Dr. Huntziger suggested. "Surely that isn't contrary to Dr. Whitehall's teaching."

His voice was soft; Naomi Griswold could find no fault with the words. Timidly, she accepted the chair, never taking her eyes from the bed. Anna Bardossy watched her and then looked at Douglas Marshall. The quick anger had gone from her eyes; a question remained.

"I've asked Mrs. Griswold to help us restore your memory, Miss Bardossy," Marshall explained. "She's going to tell what she knows of your actions yesterday. I want you to listen and try to remember if her statements are correct. You do remember Mrs. Griswold, don't you?"

There had been recognition the instant the woman entered the room. Anna Bardossy couldn't deny that.

"I know Mrs. Griswold," she affirmed. "She is—was a patient of Dr. Whitehall."

"And do you remember if she had an appointment with Dr. Whitehall yesterday morning?"

Anna Bardossy was no longer at the verge of hysteria, nor was she half lost in a state of shock. She could hear; she could reflect; she could remain noncommittal.

"I suppose she had. She was in and out of the house every day."

"That's not true," Mrs. Griswold protested. "You see, she is lying. It wasn't every day or even nearly every day—"

"But it was yesterday morning, wasn't it?"

"Yes, yesterday. I've been suffering from nervous spells—"

"You needn't explain the reason, Mrs. Griswold. Just tell Miss Bardossy what occurred when you reached the house. Begin with the time, please. This is the beginning of your day, Miss Bardossy. Try to remember."

Naomi Griswold sat on the edge of the straight-backed chair. She didn't look at the bed at all. She told her story to the gloved fingers working at the clasp of the fabric bag in her lap.

"My appointment was for ten o'clock," she said in a tight voice, "but I came early. Dr. Whitehall was always annoyed at tardiness. Not that she was ever unkind or cruel, but I did want to be prompt. It was—yes, it was just ten minutes until ten when I parked my car in the driveway. I remember looking at my watch. It was five minutes until ten and I always keep it five minutes fast so I'll never be late. I was ten minutes early, but I didn't go in until ten o'clock exactly. Being early isn't promptness any more than being late, you know. Promptness is being on time, not around it."

She pronounced the words as if she were an elderly child reciting a catechism. They were probably written in one of Dr. Whitehall's pamphlets.

"But I didn't stay in the car," she continued. "It was a lovely morning—not at all like today. There was no fog, the sun was shining, and the whole world seemed so fresh and pure. I decided to spend the time walking in Dr. Lillian's garden. It's such a quiet, secluded spot—so safe from the world. The camellias were blooming. Dr. Whitehall was so fond of the purity of the white camellia."

A melancholy smile touched Naomi Griswold's thin lips. Her eyes were beginning to moisten.

"I was under the impression that they pollinate," Dr. Huntziger remarked.

The interruption was just in time. Naomi Griswold didn't seem to understand the words, but she disapproved of the tone. Disapproval had a drying effect on her eyes.

"The garden leads directly to Dr. Whitehall's study," she added in a firmer voice, "and there are lovely French doors opening out on the patio. One, of the doors was partly open. I couldn't avoid overhearing the voices inside. Loud, quarreling voices coming from the study."

"Did you recognize the voices?" Marshall asked.

"Oh, yes indeed! The loud voice was Miss Bardossy's. I knew it at once by the accent and the language."

"What do you mean by language, Mrs. Griswold?"

"Profanity. She often uses profanity. That's blasphemous, you know."

"A great many things are blasphemous in this world," Dr. Huntziger observed. "Language is the mildest form of profanity, and under certain circumstances it has more therapeutical value than a laxative."

Naomi Griswold did understand these words. Her glance severed the doctor from redeemed society, and then she continued.

"Vile language, Mr. Marshall. I've heard her swear at Dr. Whitehall—right at her!"

"Did she swear at her yesterday?"

The woman looked at the bed for the first time since beginning her recitation. She seemed to need reassurance that the subject of it was actually incapacitated. Anna Bardossy met her eyes with an unblinking stare, but she didn't speak. Naomi's eyes returned to her handbag.

"I didn't actually hear what was said yesterday, but I did hear quarreling. I mean, Miss Bardossy was quarreling. Dr. Whitehall never quarreled."

"Isn't it a bit difficult to quarrel with someone who never quarrels?" Marshall asked.

Naomi Griswold smiled knowingly. "A soft answer turneth away wrath," she said.

"But what were the nature of the quarrels you did hear on other occasions—that is," Marshall acknowledged Mrs. Griswold's smile with one of his own, "the nature of Miss Bardossy's irritation?"

Mrs. Griswold hesitated.

"There were different things," she said.

"Such as?"

Mrs. Griswold glanced nervously at the bed. Anna Bardossy still stared at her.

"She knows. She hasn't forgotten that much."

"Can you be more specific?"

"I don't like to talk about other people's private lives, Mr. Marshall, but *she* knows."

Marshall turned his attention to the woman on the bed, and it struck him then how very strong her face was, in spite of its delicacy. She had absorbed every word and said nothing: Her face was a mask without emotion.

"Do you remember having quarreled with Dr. Whitehall, Miss Bardossy?"

"I remember nothing," she said.

"I don't mean a specific quarrel yesterday morning. Do you remember having quarreled with Dr. Whitehall about anything at any time?"

Anna Bardossy hesitated. She didn't look at Mrs. Griswold, but he could sense her dislike at being questioned in the woman's presence.

"Yes," she said at last, "I have had words with her."

"On what subject?"

"Many subjects."

"Did you ever disagree with her on her manner of treating patients?"

Marshall hadn't meant to go into that subject so soon; it simply happened. Her eyes never faltered.

"At times, yes. She was careless."

"That's not true!" Naomi Griswold gasped. "Dr. Lillian was the most precise, the most absolute—"

"Dr. Whitehall," Anna Bardossy said, her voice rising above the interruption, "sometimes took cases she didn't understand. I've known her to make a diagnosis any student nurse could recognize as wrong."

The contradiction was more than Naomi Griswold could bear. Her waning timidity vanished in an angry outburst.

"Don't listen to her! She hated Dr. Lillian, can't you see? Killing her wasn't enough; she has to destroy her name as well!"

"I hated no one," Anna Bardossy answered, ignoring the accusation. "I merely tried to save her from killing someone, or from being killed herself."

Dr. Huntziger, who had remained silent but absorbed since his consignment to the lower regions, beat Marshall to the question.

"—from being killed herself?" he echoed.

"I told you she was careless. Several times she made dangerous mistakes. Some years ago there was a child, mentally retarded. I thought he might have been helped by expert treatment; but when I tried to speak to his mother about it, Dr. Whitehall ordered me off the case. God only knows what that child is now. And only a few months ago there was a tragic case—a man, prepsychotic, who needed expert attention. Dr. Whitehall put him on a diet and used the ray box."

"The what?" Huntziger demanded.

"A small box that plugs into the wall and releases a slight shock through the head clamps. She bought it from the inventor a year ago. He told her it would cure anything, even contagious diseases."

"I had no idea she was that kind of practitioner!" Huntziger said.

"She wasn't when I first came to her. She was sincerely trying to help people. But then she became confused. She imagined that she had some kind of power no one else had, and then she imagined that she was losing the power. That was when she began to acquire devices and formulas. They were harmless in themselves, but dangerous when a patient was really ill."

"And the prepsychotic man, Miss Bardossy. What happened to him?"

"I don't know. The treatment failed, of course. He finally stopped coming; but he might have become dangerous. I tried to warn Dr. Whitehall that she was endangering herself as well as others ..."

Naomi Griswold had followed the story with intense interest. She leaned forward on the chair, her eyes dark with trouble.

"I don't believe it," she said. "I don't believe a word of it! Can't you see what she's trying to do? She's trying to make you think some crazy person killed Dr. Whitehall so she can get off free!"

"It's a possibility the law will have to consider," Dr. Huntziger mused, looking at Marshall. "You did tell Sergeant Lansing that the front door was unlocked when you discovered the body."

"But it was always unlocked at that hour!"

"Exactly. If I were a defense attorney, I'd hit on that the first thing."

Anna Bardossy stirred against the pillow.

"Mrs. Griswold discovered the body?" she asked. "When ... ?"

"At seven-thirty last night," Marshall answered. "What is it, Miss Bardossy? Do you remember something?"

Her change of expression was almost imperceptible; but Marshall's eyes were sharp. This was what he was waiting for—a reaction. But Anna Bardossy kept her secret.

"No—nothing," she said.

"She's lying!" Mrs. Griswold cried. "That's how it is with these people— that's the gratitude they give us! We take them out of their wretched countries, feed them, give them good Christian homes—and it means nothing. They never change. Always plotting, always lying—"

"Mrs. Griswold," Marshall said sharply, "please confine your remarks to answering the questions. You've told us that you heard Miss Bardossy quarreling in the study when you were in the garden. Now, when you went into the house, did you see her there?"

"I certainly did! She almost knocked me down!"

"Deliberately?"

Mrs. Griswold hesitated. The emotional outburst had brought her even closer to the edge of the chair. She perched precariously—tense and still frightened.

"No, I don't think it was deliberate," she admitted. "As I reached the entry hall—the chimes were just striking ten—Miss Bardossy came out of Dr. Whitehall's study. She had on her hat and coat and was putting on her gloves. Her head was down and she walked very fast, as if she was angry. She didn't see me until we collided. She didn't so much as apologize—just stepped aside, rude as you please, and reached for the doorknob. I remember remarking to the effect that civilized people usually say 'pardon me' when they bump into someone. She stared at me—hard, the way she's staring now, and then she said—yes, I remember her exact words—she said, 'Be patient, Mrs. Griswold. You won't have to put up with a barbarian much longer!' Then she marched out and slammed the door behind her."

"What did she mean by that?"

"Why don't you ask her?"

"Miss Bardossy ..."

Mrs. Griswold was right—Anna Bardossy was staring at her—hard. For a moment she didn't seem to hear Marshall. Her mind was too intense on what she wouldn't say.

"I don't remember," she answered.

"She remembers!" Mrs. Griswold insisted. "She's lying. I know she's lying because she lied about the cause of her quarrels with Dr. Lillian. Make her tell the truth!"

The chair wouldn't hold Mrs. Griswold anymore. She was on her feet, trembling with anger.

"Make her tell," she repeated. "Dr. Lillian tried to keep it quiet, forgiving soul that she was. She even took her away on a lecture tour this summer to save her—to get her away from that man!"

The last word cut like a lash, and the lash stung. Anna Bardossy drew back sharply against the pillow, and then her careful control vanished.

"No!" she cried. "Don't listen to her. She hates me—can't you see that?"

"And why shouldn't I hate you—you murderess!" Mrs. Griswold forgot to be timid. She moved toward the bed. "No one was ever kinder to you than Dr. Lillian. I remember when she told me you were coming. 'She's to be my spiritual daughter,' she said. 'We must help her to forget the past and start a new life.' I warned her then not to trust a refugee. I warned her, Mr. Marshall. She's one of them, you know."

"Don't listen to her!" Anna protested.

"She's one of them. Make her tell the truth about what she is. Make her tell why she hated Dr. Lillian and threatened her life!"

"Because she wouldn't let me alone—"

"Because she wouldn't let you alone to do your wickedness!"

"To live my life—my own life! Doctor ..." Anna Bardossy's eyes were desperate now. She strained forward with all her strength, and then fell back against the pillows. "Take this woman away," she cried. "I won't listen to her any more. I won't listen—"

But she had to listen until Dr. Huntziger could pull the screaming accuser away from the bedside and urge her toward the door.

"Murderess! Vile, filthy, whoring murderess!" And then Mrs. Griswold stopped, shocked by the sound of her own words. One gloved hand flew to her mouth and she turned her face away. "Oh, I am so weak. Help me, God. Help me to forgive. Dr. Lillian—please help me!"

She was sobbing as she left the room.

CHAPTER FOUR

Decency demanded that Marshall leave Anna Bardossy alone now; the search for truth demanded that he stay. She had fallen back against the pillow, exhausted from her own outburst and from Mrs. Griswold's tongue lashing. Her face was marble-white again, her eyes were fixed on the ceiling.

"Miss Bardossy ..."

She didn't move her head or alter the direction of her gaze. "Is it true that you threatened Dr. Whitehall's life?"

He didn't expect a direct reply. She surprised him with her response.

"Yes," she said. "I did."

"Do you recall the occasion?"

"Yes."

"And the provocation?"

"I was angry. It meant nothing. That's why I denied it earlier."

"Were you angry because of her treatment of a patient?"

"No, not that. It was personal."

She still wouldn't look at him. There was a hardness about her mouth that gave warning the answers wouldn't come easy now; but the boxes of lingerie were still stacked on the chest at the foot of the bed, and her eyes betrayed her.

"Who is the man, Miss Bardossy?"

Silence. Only silence.

"I'm trying to help you, Miss Bardossy. If there was someone with whom you might have had contact yesterday, we may be able to avoid other distressing interviews. He might supply you with an alibi for the time of the murder. We know the time. She was killed by a blow from the crystal desk clock. It had stopped at five twenty-two."

"Five twenty-two ..."

She repeated the time slowly.

"Does that mean anything to you?"

"No ..."

"But the man."

"I don't remember anything."

"You're lying, Miss Bardossy."

The words brought her eyes to him; nothing more.

"You may not remember anything that happened yesterday, that remains to be seen; but there was a man and you know who he is."

Her jaw might have been cast of iron.

"I want you to thoroughly understand your position, Miss Bardossy. Dr. Whitehall has been murdered in a vicious manner, and her books and pamphlets ripped from the shelves and scattered about on the floor. You've just told me that you disagreed with her methods of healing and considered them dangerous, and three witnesses have given statements to the police to the effect that you frequently quarreled with your employer. That doesn't sound good for you, does it? But that isn't all. For several months my office has been investigating certain letters written to us concerning Dr. Whitehall's practices. I suppose it's a waste of time to ask if you remember writing them."

He waited, but her jaw was still set.

"And now you have just admitted threatening Dr. Whitehall's life, and given us the first hint of a valid motive. In addition, there is your attempted suicide."

The bandaged wrists—they were the silent witnesses. Silent and accusing. She looked at them and a sadness came into her eyes.

"Why, Anna Bardossy?"

She closed her eyes.

"Suicide isn't an act of impulse. You must know what brought you to that extreme."

It was useless; she would answer nothing now.

"As you wish," he said. "I merely wanted you to understand your situation. I could make an arrest now; but I won't. I think there's a way to make you remember what you want to forget—that's what it amounts to, isn't it, Dr. Bardossy?"

Her eyes opened in an instant of surprise. It must have been many years since she'd heard herself addressed in that manner. Douglas Marshall turned away from the bed. He took down the lingerie boxes from the chest of drawers and stacked them on his arm. When he turned around she was still staring at him.

"I'll be back," he said. "We're going to continue the search for your lost day. If you do remember anything, you might as well tell me. We'll dig it up one way or another."

"There's one thing—"

Just when he didn't expect an answer, she spoke.

"The French doors to the garden ..."

"Yes. What about them?"

"Mrs. Griswold couldn't have heard quarreling through the open doors, because the doors weren't open. They're always locked and sealed with weather stripping at the beginning of the rainy season. They haven't been open since early October."

Naomi Griswold had left the hospital by the time Marshall reached Dr. Huntziger's office. It wasn't too important. The condition of the French doors could be checked any time; but the doctor found Anna Bardossy's remarks interesting.

"Not because of the doors. Mrs. Griswold, now there's a patient for you! I'm really grateful that she dislikes doctors. Mrs. Griswold probably had her ear to the door and her eye to the keyhole, which would account for the collision in the hall, and went wandering off down the garden path in her story in order to cover up her un-Whitehallish behavior. The important thing is that Anna is fighting back. She doesn't like Mrs. Griswold. There's nothing like being denounced by someone we dislike to revitalize the will to live. Coffee, Mr. Marshall?"

The coffee was fresh and fragrant. Dr. Huntziger had many skills. Over the cup he accepted, Marshall eyed him carefully.

"You really are beginning to sound like counsel for the defense," he said.

"Oh, I'm more than that. I'm her doctor. It's my business to keep breathing things breathing, Mr. Marshall. We went into that this morning. The sentimentalists tell us it's love that makes the world go around; but from my observation I'd say most people are alive just to spite someone who wishes they weren't. If you can find any more callers who'll make my patient's blood pressure rise the way Mrs. Griswold did, bring them on."

There was only one caller Marshall really wanted to bring in. His eyes moved to the lingerie boxes which were now stacked on Dr. Huntziger's desk. He raised the lid from one and a sales slip fluttered to the floor. He retrieved it and frowned at the figure.

"One hundred and twenty-nine dollars and thirty-eight cents," he read aloud. "The Bardossy woman is right, you know. She couldn't afford this."

"Women do strange things," the doctor mused. "It might have been a repressed desire. After all, think of those grim years in a concentration camp."

"I'm not so certain the desire was repressed. I should have questioned Mrs. Griswold more about the man. If she hadn't gone off into hysterics—"

"Take my word for it, if that woman knew any more than she told us you would have heard it. Does Miss Bardossy admit there was a man?"

"She doesn't have to. You saw her, you heard her reaction. But she refuses to tell me his name. That makes the case more interesting, don't you think?'

"Oh, much more interesting. There's nothing like a juicy scandal to liven up a murder."

Huntziger dropped down into the chair behind his desk. Beneath his light manner was an unmistakable gravity.

"You really have her sewed up now, don't you? A crime of passion. Imagine that, passion in Dr. Whitehall's temple of purity. I wonder how the camellias stood it." Dr. Huntziger buried his face in the coffee cup for a moment and then looked up owlishly. "She's a very sick woman, you know."

"Naomi Griswold?"

"Yes. She doesn't know it yet. She has the horror of the murder to use as an anesthetic; when that wears off she'll have the funeral and the trial and then the emptiness will close in around her. She'll have to find somebody else to use for God. These poor protected women who never learn to think for themselves! But I suppose thinking would seem as sinful to Mrs. Griswold as a love affair."

"Could she be in the same class as Anna Bardossy's prepsychotic?" Marshall suggested.

Huntziger frowned over the thought. "That was an important point, wasn't it? Particularly with that front door unlocked. Of course, she could have made up the whole story as Mrs. Griswold claimed; but I'd like to know, out of professional curiosity, if nothing else, if there really was such a man and, if so, whatever became of him."

The telephone on the desk jangled Dr. Huntziger out of his musing. He put down the coffee cup and took up the phone. It was Sgt. Lansing calling from the Whitehall house where he was still busy with his research activities. But he was sending over a man who claimed to have a story to tell—the lawyer, Harold Elrod. There was no time then to continue with Huntziger's suggestion. It was time for the second caller.

Harold Elrod was a quiet man—in voice, manner, and dress. He was in his mid-forties, blond hair thinning toward the top, wearing neat, rimless eyeglasses. He sat straight in the chair at Anna Bardossy's bedside— straight and deep with his shoulders against the back of the chair and his feet flat on the floor so that the toes of his black Oxfords were exactly even and not one a fraction of an inch ahead of the other. He reminded Marshall of an earnest high-school valedictorian anxiously awaiting the moment of his address.

He turned his face toward the bed and smiled in a vague and embarrassed manner.

"Miss Bardossy," he said. His voice was steadier than might have been expected. "I hope you're feeling stronger now."

"I am, thank you," she answered.

"I understand you can't recall anything that happened yesterday."

"That's true, Mr. Elrod."

"I hope I may be able to help you. I called on Dr. Whitehall yesterday morning. You weren't in the house at the time. I recalled that it was your day off."

"At what time did you call on Dr. Whitehall?" Marshall asked.

"Time?" Elrod's head swung back as if pulled by a string. "Eleven—yes, eleven o'clock. I had an appointment."

"Eleven o'clock exactly, I suppose," Dr. Huntziger remarked. "Promptness is being on time, not around it."

The interpolation and its maker held Harold Elrod's attention for several seconds. If the phrase was familiar, he didn't remark on it.

"No, as a matter of fact I was a few minutes late—three minutes to be exact. I had difficulty starting my car. There seems to be something wrong with the fuel pump. I remember the exact time because I looked at my watch after colliding with Mrs. Griswold on the front steps."

"Mrs. Griswold again?" Dr. Huntziger smiled. "She seems to have had a day of collisions. Rather a flighty person, isn't she?"

"Yes, quite flighty. She's been taking treatments from Dr. Whitehall for several years—ever since she was widowed, I believe. Last night, when she came to fetch me at the lecture hall, she was almost incoherent. But I'm digressing. Let's see, it was eleven—three minutes past eleven—when I entered Dr. Whitehall's house. I went directly to her study. She was expecting me, of course. It was she who made the appointment."

Harold Elrod was a remarkable man. He had come to discuss the violent death of his employer, friend, and mentor; but his manner was as devoid of emotion as anything Marshall had seen outside an aquarium. He waited for the next question, the toes of his shoes still as even as if lined up against a straight edge.

"What was Dr. Whitehall's manner?" Marshall asked. "Did she seem disturbed or agitated?"

"Dr. Whitehall? Oh, no, she was never agitated. Firm, yes. A great disciplinarian, but always in a loving manner. Still, I did notice ..."

Elrod paused. His eyes were lost behind the glittering lenses of his glasses.

"What did you notice Mr. Elrod?"

"She did seem tired. That's an odd thing to say about Dr. Whitehall. You would have had to know her to understand. She had a tremendous vitality. A remarkable woman, really. Few people knew her exact age, but I being her lawyer, did. She was seventy-two years old. Just think of that! Seventy-two and she had more energy than I have at forty-seven. But yesterday ... well, I can't put my finger on any one thing. I merely had this sense of weariness. What was the word she used? Yes, disturbed."

"Or worried?" Marshall suggested.

"Why, yes. Possibly."

"As if she might be losing something—or someone—dear to her?"

Douglas Marshall's eyes were on Anna Bardossy. She met them without flinching.

"That's remarkable, Mr. Marshall. Yes, that's exactly the way she seemed. A part of her mind was somewhere else all through our conversation. And now you've reminded me of another thing. While we were talking, the telephone rang. She answered it eagerly as if she were expecting a call, and then, when she heard the voice, her face fell. 'Oh, it's you,' she said. I had the distinct impression of disappointment."

"Do you know who made the call?"

"No, I don't. She took it on the extension in a little room off the study. That was customary if a patient called during an interview."

Harold Elrod was a man without mannerisms. He straightened his glasses, but only because one side of the frame seemed loose. Then he waited.

"I don't suppose she mentioned having quarreled with Miss Bardossy."

"No. No, indeed. Dr. Whitehall never discussed her personal or domestic problems."

"And yet you did tell Sergeant Lansing last night that she didn't get along well with the nurse?"

A trace of embarrassment gave the lawyer pause. It was as close to outward emotion as he had come. He glanced at the woman on the bed and then back to Marshall.

"I had hoped that we might have this interview in private," he said.

"Because it concerns Miss Bardossy?"

"Yes."

"But wouldn't that be unfair, Mr. Elrod? She's in a desperate position. Her life depends on what she can remember of her actions yesterday. Something you may say—some trivial, incidental thing—may be the switch that starts the recall mechanism. Isn't that possible, Dr. Huntziger?"

"With a device as complicated as the mind, anything is possible," the doctor answered.

Elrod acquiesced.

"I see. Very well, then. The situation is this: Last night, when I was questioned by Sergeant Lansing, we were all in a state of tension. Mrs. Griswold, as you mentioned, is extremely nervous. My wife spent the night with her, incidentally. She was in no condition to be left alone. Our first thought, after the shock of discovery, was of the whereabouts of Miss Bardossy. That was natural, I believe."

"Quite natural," Marshall agreed.

"After all, she was a member of the household and she was missing."

The lawyer had met the distasteful necessity of telling his story in the subject's presence by ignoring her. He didn't look at the bed as he spoke. She watched him with eyes he didn't see.

"When the call came in from the Santa Monica police, and Sergeant Lansing informed us that Miss Bardossy had been found, and in what condition, I'm afraid we all leaped to the obvious conclusion. We agreed to cooperate with the police and not make statements to the press; but accusations were made."

"False accusations?"

Elrod hesitated.

"No," he said at last, "not false, although Mrs. Griswold was much too emotional. I'm afraid she never approved of Miss Bardossy. She has an almost primitive fear of anyone unlike herself."

"A foreigner, you mean," Dr. Huntziger suggested.

"Yes—a foreigner."

She's one of them. The phrase crossed Marshall's mind, but he had no time for it. Harold Elrod was the witness now.

"Did you approve of Miss Bardossy?" he asked.

"I was instrumental in arranging her entry—at the legal level, I mean."

"That's not what I asked, Mr. Elrod."

The eyeglasses had slipped loose again. Elrod set them firmly this time.

"Let's put it this way, I was happy that Dr. Whitehall had obtained an assistant of such ability. Miss Bardossy is a woman of unusual intelligence. But I was afraid Dr. Whitehall's interest in the nurse wasn't entirely professional."

Harold Elrod listened to the echo of his own words and flushed slightly.

"Please don't misunderstand," he said quickly. "Dr. Whitehall had a very sympathetic nature. Something about the plight of this young woman— she had heard of her through one of the rescue committees—appealed to her great heart. She was childless, you know."

"And a widow, I believe," Dr. Huntziger said.

"Oh, yes, for some twenty-odd years. In addition, at that time she was estranged from her brother."

"That's interesting," Marshall said. "How did that happen?"

"I was Dr. Whitehall's legal and financial adviser, Mr. Marshall. I didn't delve into her personal life, although I know she had suffered many trials. Her marriage wasn't a happy one; her brother was a problem."

"Davies," Dr. Huntziger mused. "Byron Davies—of course! He's managed to make the newspapers off and on over a period of years—usually on a drunken driving charge. I think there was even a paternity suit...."

Harold Elrod cleared his throat noisily, and shifted his position on the chair. When he was through shifting, the toes of his shoes were still exactly even.

"That's true, Dr. Huntziger. Mr. Davies has been a thorn in Dr. Whitehall's side for many years. There was a period when he seemed to delight in deliberately embarrassing her; but he's been more conservative for some time now."

Coming in at 3:30 A.M. sporting an aromatic breath and a plaid cummerbund? Lansing's description of Byron Davies didn't suggest any major reformation. Marshall glanced at Anna Bardossy and caught the remains of a disdainful smile. Then she noticed his eyes and her face became a mask again.

"So you see," Elrod continued, "Miss Bardossy became somewhat more than a nurse and an assistant to Dr. Whitehall."

"Mrs. Griswold referred to her as a spiritual daughter," Marshall said.

The light glinted on the lens of Elrod's glasses as his head came up. "Somewhat more than that, Mr. Marshall. Within a year after Miss Bardossy came to live with her, Dr. Whitehall instructed me to make a new will. Up until that time, she had bequeathed the bulk of her estate to the society with Mrs. Elrod and myself as joint trustees. The new will changed all that. Everything, except for a small bequest to her brother, was to go to Miss Bardossy and she was named as trustee of the society."

Elrod glanced at the woman on the bed again. His emotion drained face betrayed itself by a sudden hardness at the mouth.

"I don't know ..." Anna said softly.

Elrod looked away quickly.

"That's true, Mr. Marshall; Dr. Whitehall wanted her change of mind kept confidential and, to my knowledge, it was. Naturally, some of us who were close to her, who had been her earliest followers...."

The sentence was left dangling. Harold Elrod adjusted his glasses again.

"It did seem strange," he said.

"Dr. Whitehall was an elderly woman even then," Dr. Huntziger suggested. "Perhaps she wasn't in full possession of her faculties."

"Oh, no!" Elrod's head swung about and his eyes, visible behind the lens, seemed startled. "She never did that, Dr. Huntziger. She might have been under some influence for a time, but she never lost her reason. Miss Bardossy was Dr. Whitehall's heir for three years. She isn't now. Shortly after Dr. Whitehall returned from her lecture tour six weeks ago, she changed her will."

The stunned surprise with which Anna Bardossy had received the news that she was Dr. Whitehall's heir was only deepened by the added news that she was not. Marshall watched her face. She was oblivious to everyone but Harold Elrod.

"That's really the matter I wanted to discuss with you, Mr. Marshall," he added. "It completely slipped my mind last night."

"Who benefits by the new will?" Marshall asked.

"The brother—Byron Davies. There's a bequest for one thousand dollars in cash for Miss Bardossy; the rest of the estate—everything—went to him. I never really understood that. I suppose it's a matter of blood returning to blood."

A shadow of chagrin crossed Elrod's face, and then, as if sensing the self-betrayal, he straightened his tie in a first gesture of nervousness.

"What reason did Dr. Whitehall give for the change?" Marshall asked.

"Dr. Whitehall never gave reasons for her actions, Mr. Marshall, and I never asked for any. I trusted her judgment completely. But she did make one peculiar statement that sticks in my mind. When everything was done, signed, and witnessed to her satisfaction, she mentioned Miss Bardossy by name for the first time and then she said, 'It doesn't seem wisdom to place so much temptation in the hands of one so weak.'"

CHAPTER FIVE

A quiet man, an unemotional man. Cold, precise, correct. Harold Elrod made his damaging disclosure in the calm monotone of a real-estate lawyer reciting a list of holdings. The accusation was Dr. Whitehall's, not his own. He wasn't personally involved.

But the woman on the bed was. A flush of color returned to her face. Marshall used it as a signal for his next question. "Why, Mr. Elrod?"

The directness of it seemed to surprise him.

"What?" he asked.

"Why did Dr. Whitehall make such a drastic reappraisal of her nurse's character? Surely you must have some idea."

And now Harold Elrod would have to come down from his objective pedestal and commit himself. He glanced toward the bed. Anna Bardossy's eyes impaled him there.

"Go ahead, Mr. Elrod," she said. "Answer the question—if your piety will allow it."

Elrod seemed hurt.

"I'm sorry to have to give this testimony, Miss Bardossy. Surely you realize that I have no choice. Yes, Mr. Marshall—" he seemed relieved to escape Anna's eyes—"I do have an idea. I hope you won't think I was trying to withhold information. I hate to be placed in the position of a rumor monger."

"Dr. Whitehall's murder is considerably more than a rumor."

"Yes, that's true." A grayness came over Elrod's face, as if far under that cultivated repression he did remember that something once alive was gone. Then the grayness passed. "I can't name a name," he continued, "because I never knew it; but it's been common knowledge among those of us close to Dr. Whitehall that she was deeply distressed about Miss Bardossy's relationship with a man in this city. I don't know how long it had been going on—Dr. Whitehall was extremely reticent about her personal problems—but I believe that was the reason behind her lecture tour last summer. For two months she and Miss Bardossy were away from the city. Apparently she hoped the separation would end the affair."

"And it didn't?"

"Dr. Whitehall changed her will, Mr. Marshall."

Dr. Whitehall changed her will. The pieces were falling into place, and each piece made a picture darker for Anna Bardossy; and yet, one piece was still missing. One piece that could complete the story.

"And you have no idea who this man might be?"

"None, Mr. Marshall."

"But someone must have known. How did Dr. Whitehall learn of him? Did she follow the nurse—spy on her?"

"I hardly think that likely—or possible," Elrod answered. "Dr. Whitehall didn't drive—never owned an automobile. She was entirely dependent on her friends for transportation, except for the walks she took in the neighborhood—to the shops, bank, that sort of thing. I've really no idea how she learned of the affair—unless Miss Bardossy told her of it."

The indiscretion of his slight betrayal of human emotion had passed. Harold Elrod was himself again. He didn't seem to expect a response to his suggestion. He didn't look toward the bed for a sign of affirmation. He did look at his watch, frowning slightly.

"I really hadn't meant to spend so much time...."

"I suppose you're a busy man, Mr. Elrod."

"Yes, I am. Particularly today. The newspaper reporters have been quite a problem. After all, Dr. Whitehall was a woman of spiritual dignity. She should be treated with respect."

Marshall smiled wryly. "If you can convince them of that, you're a better man than I am—and a great many others. But I won't keep you. There's just one more thing—you told me that you went to see Dr. Whitehall yesterday because she had made the appointment. What was the nature of your business?"

Elrod had come to his feet. He stood stiffly in front of the chair.

"She requested a financial report," he said.

"A financial report—of her entire estate?"

"Yes, the property, the college, the publications—"

"Was this customary?"

"I make a full report once a year."

"At what time?"

Elrod hesitated. His right hand was fingering his wrist watch again.

"Usually in January, Mr. Marshall. Sometime in January. In any event, prior to April fifteenth."

"But this is ... what? December sixth. Didn't you consider the request unusual?"

"The property belonged to Dr. Whitehall. She had a right to request a statement at any time she so desired."

Elrod's words were just a bit too concise; a tinge of testiness came through.

"She gave no reason, then, why she wanted the report at this time?"

"None, Mr. Marshall."

And so here was another piece but it didn't fit. Marshall looked at the nurse. Her eyes were elsewhere—somewhere not in the room at all. Elrod's were still lost behind his glasses. Then he cleared his throat.

"If there's nothing else—"

"In a moment, in a moment," Marshall said. "I won't keep you much longer. Dr. Whitehall was disturbed, Dr. Whitehall had changed her will, Dr. Whitehall wanted a statement of her financial condition ..." Marshall was talking to himself. Suddenly he turned to Elrod. "Did you notice if the doors to the garden were open?"

"The doors ... garden?"

"The French doors—were they open?"

"Why, no—I don't think so. I didn't notice in particular, but it would have been chilly."

"Yes, that's right," Marshall said. "It's December. Just one thing more. At what time did you leave Dr. Whitehall's study?"

"It was just about noon, Mr. Marshall. I recall asking Dr. Whitehall to accompany me to lunch. Purely a formality—she lived on a strict diet of her own making. She smiled at that—more like her old self—and then she said—"

Elrod's words stopped abruptly.

"Yes, Mr. Elrod?"

"Strange, but I'd forgotten all about that until now. She said ..." Elrod spoke slowly, dredging up each word from memory ... "'I might surprise you, Harold, and accept your invitation, but I have to stay in this afternoon. It's Anna's day off, and I'm expecting a caller.'"

"That's all she said?"

"That's all, Mr. Marshall."

Elrod still stood stiffly before the chair. He waited. There were no more questions. He walked toward the door and then he turned.

"Mr. Marshall, I can assure you that Dr. Whitehall's finances are all in order. If you wish to have the books examined—"

"Thank you, Mr. Elrod. I don't think that will be necessary. But there is one thing."

"Yes?" Elrod responded.

"Did Dr. Whitehall, to your knowledge, keep a record of her patients? A permanent record, I mean."

Elrod appeared puzzled. "A permanent record?" he echoed.

"I understand she treated patients with various kinds of disturbances, some mental. With that front door unlocked all day—"

Now Elrod's puzzlement began to grow into a disturbance of another kind. "Oh, no!" he said quickly. "I'm sure it couldn't have been anything like that! Dr. Whitehall's pure thought could detect any undercurrent of violence—" And then he broke off deliberately because Harold Elrod, student, disciple and loyal friend, was as much aware as anyone in the room that one act of violence had occurred which Dr. Whitehall had not detected in time. Sobered, he added—"A permanent record. I can't say offhand, Mr. Marshall. I shall make a search, of course. But you must understand that Dr. Whitehall's work was of a highly confidential nature, much like that of the confessional at times."

"My office has wide experience in dealing with confidences," Marshall assured him. "We'll respect whatever you may find."

Harold Elrod left as quietly as Naomi Griswold had left noisily, and when he was gone the question still remained. Dr. Huntziger followed him out. He did have other patients; Douglas Marshall didn't. He had only the enigma of the woman on the bed.

"Well, Miss Bardossy, how does it feel to have been the heir of Dr. Whitehall?"

She came back slowly from the far place her eyes had gone. She looked at him, and some of the distance was still in them.

"I didn't know," she said quietly. "I didn't know she had ever thought of me in that way."

"Wasn't she good to you?"

"Yes, she was good—and kind."

"What happened, then?"

She looked at him again and this time there was no distance in her eyes.

"Is that enough, Mr. Marshall—to have found a friend who is good and kind?"

It was a question that needed no answer. He couldn't look at her eyes any more. He walked to the window and stood looking out at old yesterdays.

After a while he said, "Dr. Whitehall didn't want you to leave, did she?"

"No."

"Is that why you quarreled?"

When she didn't reply, he turned around. She sat up against the pillows, her head bowed slightly and her hands over her face. Her shoulders were trembling and her breathing labored. He'd seen this thing before in the drab dawn light as she fought back tears. Then her hands pulled away from her face, and she saw him watching her.

"Must you stand there looking like God?"

"Who is the man, Miss Bardossy?"

"I won't tell you! I won't let you destroy him, too!"

"But even now the newspapers are carrying stories of the murder which state that you're missing. Won't he come forward anyway?"

The thought seemed new to her. She held it in her eyes and began to turn to fear.

"Or is there a reason why he can't?"

It seemed a simple question—no reason for the fear to grow greater. And then she seemed to withdraw from him—to pull back within herself. Her shoulders trembled again and the color drained from her face.

"Miss Bardossy—what is it?"

"I don't know," she said. "I felt a chill...."

"I'll call Dr. Huntziger."

"No—I'm all right. I'm just tired."

"I'm sorry. I shouldn't have kept Mr. Elrod so long. I don't suppose you know who Dr. Whitehall's expected caller might have been?"

"No—I don't remember. Won't you believe me?"

"I only thought an appointment might have been made in advance."

"No—no!"

The fear in her eyes had spread to her voice. It was time to leave her to rest. Marshall was at the door when she called him back.

"If I confess, will you leave me alone?"

It was such a surprising thing for her to say that he could think of only one answer.

"Are you guilty?"

She hesitated. Her eyes had a searching look now, as if she were trying to penetrate some intangible barrier.

"I don't know," she said. "I think that I must be guilty; but if I am—if I did kill Dr. Whitehall—it wasn't because of the will. If I killed her it was because I hated her!"

CHAPTER SIX

It was almost noon. There were no visitors in the hospital at this hour. The corridors were bustling with nurses preparing to deliver the luncheon trays, and any outsider would have been in the way.

Dr. Huntziger wasn't in his office. Marshall considered waiting, but the activity in the corridor reminded him that he, too, was human and the human machine needed occasional fuel. He took the elevator down to the lobby, left the building, and started walking across the parking lot buttoning his topcoat as he walked. The sky was still overcast and the wind blowing in off the ocean had a gnawing chill. It occurred to him how cold it must have been on the beach last night when Anna Bardossy went down to the sea to die. He stopped and glanced back over his shoulder at the building behind him. Perhaps he shouldn't have left her alone in that strange mood—but that was nonsense. She was safe in the hospital, and she wouldn't be alone long. He walked on.

"Marshall! Hey, Mr. Marshall!"

He looked back once more. The blunt-faced man in the wrinkled raincoat was trotting toward him.

"Looks as if I got here just in time," Lansing said, reaching his side. "What happened with Elrod? Did he tell his story?"

"He told it," Marshall said.

"Adds fuel to the fire, doesn't it? Personally, I think the old lady was crazy."

"Why do you say that?"

"Well, aside from some of the stuff I've read in those pamphlets, there's the matter of that first will. I can't imagine Dr. Whitehall left much of real value—the house on Hillmont is badly run-down and the college, as Elrod insists on calling it, is nothing but a converted store building with a potted palm in the window. But people are peculiar about their property— particularly if it's something they've built up themselves. It becomes a kind of symbol, and when they leave it to someone it's as if they were passing on their own life."

"That's true," Marshall said.

"And yet Dr. Whitehall left hers to a woman she evidently disapproved of."

"But she changed the will."

"In favor of her brother—whom she disapproved of even more. Doesn't look as if she thought much of her friends, does it?"

The bite in the wind cut deeper the longer they stood in it. Farther down, where the cars were parked, it was more sheltered. Marshall led the way to his own sedan. Someone was tinkering on the motor of the car next to it, and the raised hood formed a shield.

"What about the nurse?" Lansing asked. "Did you get a reaction?"

"She didn't know about the wills—either one of them."

"Is she still faking a blackout?"

Douglas plunged his hands in his pockets and scowled at the asphalt.

"I don't think she's faking—but she offered to confess."

"She did? Then what are we still working for?"

"The same thing we were working for in the beginning—the motive. There's a man in the story, Sergeant. Mrs. Griswold told us, Elrod told us, and the nurse admits it but won't reveal his identity. We've got to find him. Anna Bardossy has been in this country for four years—she had to know someone outside the Whitehall house.... Did you find that appointment book?"

"No appointment book."

"But there must have been something."

"Nothing. Frankly, from the looks of the place, I don't think business was too good."

"But I know she was expecting at least one more caller. That's what she told Elrod before he left."

"Probably her brother. He did come around, you know. He's the one who said he saw the nurse drive past the house a little after two. Or it might have been the gasman."

Marshall had forgotten about the brother—he must have been the third caller. But then he heard Lansing's afterthought and looked at him for an explanation. The sergeant was fumbling through his coat pockets. He finally came up with a wrinkled slip of paper and handed it to Marshall.

"I found this in the wastebasket while I was looking for that appointment book. I thought it might interest you."

Unfolded and smoothed out the slip of paper became a sheet from a desk memo pad. On it, written in the graceful script of an unhurried age now past, was a brief message:

> Gasman:
> Please use the rear door to the service porch. It is un-
> locked. Have gone to the bank and will return shortly.
>   Dr. Lillian Whitehall

Lansing waited until Marshall had read the note and then added, "I checked the setup. There's a service porch just off the kitchen. It has three doors: a door to the furnace room downstairs—it's an old house with a par-

tial basement—a door to the kitchen, and the outside door. The kitchen
door can be locked by a bolt from the inside. With it locked, anyone could
have access to the service porch and furnace room without getting into the
rest of the house."

"Was it locked?" Marshall asked.

"No, it wasn't—but that doesn't mean anything. It could have been for
the time Dr. Whitehall was out of the house. As soon as I found the note,
I put in a call to the gas company. They checked their records and found
that a request for service had been telephoned in from the Whitehall residence a few minutes past nine yesterday morning. It was the third call in
the last two weeks—something wrong with the pilot light on the furnace.
Apparently the service man hadn't located the trouble on his other calls,
because there was a notation to make certain the job was done right and
that it was definitely done yesterday. They're looking up the job sheets now
to see who handled the call."

"That means there was a fourth caller," Marshall said. He glanced
down at the note again. "It's addressed only to the gasman—apparently
Dr. Whitehall had already seen her brother and was expecting no one else."

"At a little past two," Lansing added, "and the banks close at three on
Thursdays."

"That's true ..."

Sgt. Lansing had framed an interesting situation. The prompt and orderly
Dr. Whitehall must have made a last-minute call at her bank. It hardly
seemed in character.

"I wonder if you're thinking what I'm thinking," Lansing said. "Anna
Bardossy was cruising in the neighborhood. She probably came back—"

"To demand money?"

"She bought a lot of expensive lingerie."

"But that doesn't make sense. She'd quarreled with Dr. Whitehall before
she went out. Would she come back and ask for money—and get it? No,
Sergeant, it still comes back to the man. We've got to find him."

Marshall pocketed the note and turned about trying to locate his own
car. It was then that the hood came down on the sedan next to which he
and Lansing were standing. He found himself facing a conservatively-
dressed man whose hat was squared on his head and whose eyes were lost
behind the lenses of his rimless glasses. Harold Elrod smiled self-consciously
and came around the front end of the sedan wiping his hands on a handkerchief.

"I'm afraid I'll have to go to the garage with that fuel pump," he said.
He finished wiping his hands and pocketed the handkerchief. He looked
at Marshall and Lansing—then back to Marshall. The smile was still lin-
gering in the background. "I hope you gentlemen won't think I've been

eavesdropping," he added, "but I couldn't very well help hearing some of your conversation. It's very strange that Dr. Whitehall went to the bank on Thursday."

"Did she have a certain day for banking?" Marshall asked.

"Oh, yes, always Friday.... But that's not what I came over to discuss. There's one thing I didn't tell you, Mr. Marshall. You were speaking just now to Sergeant Lansing about learning who were Miss Bardossy's friends. That's a strange thing, but she never seemed to make any. She was a quiet, self-contained little thing."

"Except when she was fighting with Dr. Whitehall," Lansing interjected.

Elrod looked at him with a perfectly bland face. Then he continued as if there had been no interruption.

"But she did attend classes at the University—has been for ... oh, I should say about three years."

"What kind of classes?" Marshall asked.

"I don't know as I could tell you that—English, I believe, although she spoke quite good English when she arrived. History, literature—she wasn't communicative, but I think she was trying to adjust to her new surroundings in this way. It's terribly difficult to be uprooted and have one's entire way of life changed...."

Harold Elrod seemed to ruminate over his own words. It was the first time he'd spoken with a trace of emotion in his voice. Then he recovered himself and continued in his concise monotone.

"When Miss Bardossy first arrived, some of us attempted to make her welcome. We asked questions about her homeland, but she didn't seem to care to discuss it."

"I can understand that," Marshall said.

"Yes, I'm sure the memories were painful. Gradually, we ceased to discuss it or her. But I recall one Sunday afternoon in the library—Dr. Whitehall held open house once a month for those of us closest to her. We would have light refreshments and listen to some good music or watch a play on television. Occasionally Miss Bardossy joined us, and this day we were watching television. It was two years ago—during the Hungarian rebellion. A newsreel was on showing scenes of the fighting in Budapest. Ordinarily, Miss Bardossy was quite self-contained, but I noticed that she was becoming upset by the film and was about to turn to another station when there was one particularly horrible shot of a group of rebels displaying the bodies of some murdered Hungarian communist soldiers. I saw Miss Bardossy turn pale, and then she cried out—not loudly but distinctly—a name. A Hungarian name—Lazlo. She left the room immediately and never returned."

"And never explained, I suppose," Marshall said.

"Not to my knowledge."

"A communist soldier ..." Lansing echoed. "Maybe that's what Mrs. Griswold has been hinting at. She seems to think the nurse should have been deported."

One of them. The phrase came back to Marshall's mind, this time with new significance. But Harold Elrod was wearing his vague smile again.

"I don't think I'd depend much on anything Mrs. Griswold says at this time," he advised. "She's barely in command of her faculties. I don't think the incident had any significance except to indicate the emotional disturbance brewing underneath the surface." Elrod looked up at the hospital and the sun, peeking momentarily through a rift in the overcast, glinted off his glasses. "The things some people are forced to endure—it's small wonder their minds give way." Then his eyes came back—pale blue behind the lenses. "I must apologize for intruding, gentlemen, but I did think the information about the University might be helpful. If I can be of any service in any way just let me know."

Elrod got into his car and touched the starter. It sputtered once, then took hold. Seconds later, he was pulling out of the lot. Sgt. Lansing looked after him with disapproving eyes.

"If that's an example of Dr. Whitehall's handiwork, I'll take a zombie," he said.

"That's only his humility, Lansing."

"So that's what it is. Personally, I think humility is like underwear—essential, but indecent if it shows. We should have asked him which university."

"I know which university. What I should have asked him was which bank."

Marshall had the wrinkled piece of note paper in his hand again. He read the message over once more.

"I can tell you that," Lansing volunteered. "It's the California National at Vermont and Third. I found a checkbook in Dr. Whitehall's desk."

Marshall pocketed the note again, grinning.

"Nosy little fellow, aren't you? Shall we go?"

The bank manager was a friendly, middle-aged man named Corsi. He had read the morning papers and was deeply distressed at the news of Dr. Whitehall's death.

"I was fond of the old lady—all of us were," he said. "She had a kind of inner peace, Mr. Marshall, that could almost be felt whenever she walked into the bank. But lately it wasn't quite the same. I was worried about her. I suppose you'll think I'm peculiar, but I take an interest in our patrons. A bank is a little community in itself, and a banker gets a pretty close look at the problems of his customers."

"Did Dr. Whitehall have financial problems?" Marshall asked.

Corsi shook his head.

"No, her finances seemed to be normal, as far as I know. Mr. Elrod handles the estate proper, but Dr. Whitehall always took care of her own household account—she or Miss Bardossy." The banker's face darkened. "I noticed in the papers that Miss Bardossy is missing from the household. I hope that isn't significant."

"Do you think it could be?" Marshall asked.

Corsi was no fool; he had wit and imagination and what the reporters had pounced upon so gleefully was as obvious to him as to any reader. But because he was no fool, he understood the import of the question. He wasn't being asked for a personal opinion, but for something that might pass as evidence.

"When I read in the paper," he said slowly, "that Miss Bardossy was missing, I realized that she hadn't been in the bank yesterday. Thursday was her day off and she usually came in on Thursday."

"And Dr. Whitehall on Friday," Marshall said.

"Yes, that's correct—unless she had Miss Bardossy do her banking for her on the previous day. Yesterday the situation was reversed. Dr. Whitehall came in, and quite late in the day. The doors are locked at three to keep additional customers from coming in and I recall that the guard had to unlock the door to let her out when she left. She seemed distressed."

"In what way?"

Corsi fingered a slim, silver pen, turning it over and over lengthwise in his hands. A frown furrowed his forehead.

"I said that she *seemed* distressed, Mr. Marshall," he said at last. "I didn't have a chance to talk to her. I called to her as she left, but she didn't hear me. Usually we had a little chat. And then there's this—" Corsi put down the pen and opened the top drawer of his desk. "If you gentlemen hadn't stopped by today, I would have gone to the police. Here is Dr. Whitehall's bankbook—" He placed the small book on the desk. "She left it at the teller's window yesterday. In all the six years I've been managing this bank, I've never known Dr. Whitehall to forget anything before."

Marshall flicked open the bankbook. It was a savings account and the last withdrawal, made on the previous day, was for $1000. He stared at the figure again to make certain.

"Just a minute," he said. "Does this mean that Dr. Whitehall walked out of here yesterday afternoon with $1000 in cash?"

Sgt. Lansing edged closer to look at the book. Corsi nodded.

"As soon as I read of the murder," he explained, "I became curious about her unusual visit to the bank. I went to the teller who took care of her and that's when I learned that she'd forgotten her book." He paused and awareness came into his eyes. "I see what you mean," he said. "It's strange how easily we leap to conclusions. When I read in the papers that Miss Bardossy was missing, I naturally assumed— But there could have been another motive. All that money in the house—it might have been a prowler, or even someone who saw her in the bank and followed her home."

Corsi's eyes were busy, but no busier than Marshall's mind. It wasn't a new thought he was hearing; Dr. Huntziger had hit on the same idea early in the morning before anyone knew of money in the house. But Corsi had said more than he knew.

"Miss Bardossy," Marshall said, "did her banking here. I wonder what is the status of her finances."

"I could find out for you."

"Would you—please."

Corsi spoke to the attractive young woman behind the next desk and the wheels began to turn. In a short time she returned. They were in luck. The monthly statements were in the process of being prepared and Anna Bardossy's modest expenditures were laid out before him—a small check to a local garage, a premium payment to an insurance company, a check to a neighborhood dentist. It was amazing how the habits of a life could be constructed from a handful of canceled checks—a subscription to a literary magazine, a donation to a refugee rescue committee.

"Nothing to any of the shops or department stores," Marshall mused aloud.

"Not even Bannock's Westwood?" Lansing suggested.

Corsi looked up, puzzled, but didn't comment.

"Not even Bannock's Westwood," Marshall said. "Mr. Corsi, you told us when you came in that you took a personal interest in your patrons. What is your impression of Anna Bardossy?"

The banker wasn't an evasive man. He accepted the question as he accepted his responsibilities.

"She is a quiet, well-mannered, efficient young woman," he said. "I believe her income was small—after all, she received her room and board with Dr. Whitehall—but she lived within it. She has always been pleasant but not very communicative. I suppose that's because of her situation."

"Quiet, well mannered, efficient, pleasant," Marshall repeated, "and yet, a short while ago when you reflected that Dr. Whitehall had withdrawn a large sum of money yesterday—wasn't that rather unusual, by the way?"

"Extremely unusual, Mr. Marshall. I've never known her to withdraw such a sum of cash."

"When you reflected on the money," Marshall continued, "and the possibility that a prowler, or a robber, or even someone who had followed her home from the bank might have been responsible for her death, you made a peculiar statement. Your words were— 'But there could have been another motive.' That seems to indicate that you had established, in your subconscious at least, a motive for Miss Bardossy."

Corsi accepted the words with somber eyes. He'd taken to playing with the pen again. Now he laid it down on the desk.

"I suppose I had," he said.

"Could you explain?"

"It's not meant as evidence, Mr. Marshall—merely a snatch of conversation overheard by chance. It was about three months ago when Dr. Whitehall was preparing to go on a lecture tour. Miss Bardossy came into the bank one day to purchase traveler's checks. I had gone to the rear of the bank to consult with one of the employees and overheard her conversation with the teller. The girl had asked if she were planning a trip. Miss Bardossy's reply caught my attention. 'A trip is being planned for me,' she said. 'The omniscient Dr. Whitehall does all my planning now. It saves me the trouble of being human.' It was the first time I'd heard her refer to Dr. Whitehall in such a manner, and it occurred to me then what was wrong with their arrangement."

"Their arrangement," Marshall echoed. "What, exactly, do you mean?"

"It was somewhat more than employer and employee, Mr. Marshall; at least it was to Dr. Whitehall. I remember her attitude when she was making the arrangements to bring Miss Bardossy from Europe. She came to see me about arranging the bond—"

"Dr. Whitehall did? Why didn't Mr. Elrod handle that?"

Corsi shook his head.

"I can't answer that, Mr. Marshall. Perhaps it was something she wanted to do on her own. But she was so enthusiastic about it—so dedicated, as if this were some kind of mission she had to perform in bringing the young woman out of bondage. Dr. Whitehall was somewhat of a mystic, you know."

"She was also childless," Marshall recalled. "Her mission, as you call it, could have been nothing more than wish fulfillment."

"I suppose it was; but it was a very close attachment and close attachments between women seldom work out. The day I overheard that conversation with the teller, I realized why it couldn't last. Dr. Whitehall was a strong-minded woman, but she'd failed to take into account something much stronger. Anna Bardossy was too young and vital to live indefinitely in an unnatural world."

CHAPTER SEVEN

Corsi was right; she was young and much too vital—even in sleep. Douglas Marshall sat on the chair beside her bed and waited for Anna Bardossy to awaken, and the uneasy memories that had started with the predawn vigil returned. Much had developed since that time. It was now more than two hours since Harold Elrod sat in the same chair and told his quietly devastating story, and more than three hours since Naomi Griswold had rushed out of the room on the verge of hysteria. But it wasn't of evidence, or even of murder, that Marshall thought as he waited. The window shade was partially drawn—a stripe of sunlight fell across her mouth and chin. For such a mouth there had to be a man. An old anger, mingled with pain, stirred inside him.

But this wasn't Elsa. This was Anna Bardossy, and now her eyes were opening, still glazed with sleep. The room was too dim for instant recognition; but even in the twilight of awakening she seemed to sense that someone sat beside her. Her head turned and a sudden expectancy in her face gave it a childlike quality.

"Paul ... ?"

And then the word died and she was awake. She wasn't Elsa; he wasn't Paul. At least now he knew the man's name.

"Oh," she said, "it's you. Have you been there long?"

"A few minutes," Marshall answered. "Who is Paul?"

"Paul?"

"You spoke the name just now as you awakened."

"I did? I must have been dreaming."

She looked away from him. The ceiling was her favorite horizon and staring at it left him free to study the profile of her face. Strong. More and more the word for Anna Bardossy was strong. He found himself again pondering Dr. Huntziger's early morning puzzle—why anyone who had endured so much to find freedom would choose, once it was found, the long despised death?

"The triangle is the most familiar shape of murder," he said, "but this is a strange one to say the least. Dr. Whitehall, Anna Bardossy, and—Paul. What could have happened between them that made violence the only solution?"

When he talked to himself, she looked at him again.

"You don't believe that I can't remember, do you?" she asked. "You think it is something I pretend, and if you sit there long enough, or if you bring in enough people to talk, I'll forget myself and tell you what you want to know. Oh, I know how policemen think—"

"I'm not a policeman," Marshall said.

"You're the same thing—worse because you are more clever. I've been watched and questioned before, Mr. Marshall. I've been forced before to confess to crimes I knew nothing about by men even more clever than you. I know how you think."

"But I don't believe you do, Miss Bardossy. In the first place, you weren't forced to confess to anything—that was your own idea. And just now, as I sat here, I wasn't plotting anything. I wasn't even thinking of you at all."

She looked at him for a long while then. Her eyes were blue even in the shadows.

"Of what were you thinking, Mr. Marshall?" she asked.

"Of a woman," he said.

"A woman ... ?" She was puzzled, and surprised. The tightness at her mouth eased a little. "That is good" she said. "It is good to know a policeman who can think about a woman, but now—" She drew herself up against the pillows. The coarse cotton hospital gown rode up about her shoulders like a stiff cowl, and she had to pull it straight. Coarse, plain, not at all like the lingerie in the boxes. He saw her eyes wander to the top of the chest, but the boxes weren't there anymore. The puzzle lingered in her eyes for an instant and then she added, "—now we are back to me again. Who is going to denounce me next, Mr. Marshall?"

"I'm sorry you take that attitude," Marshall said, "but as long as you can't remember what happened yesterday, I'll have to keep digging away at the truth. There's one thing you may remember. Was Dr. Whitehall having trouble with her furnace?"

The question was unexpected. Then she remembered.

"Oh, you must mean the pilot light," she said. "I called the gas company—"

She stopped as suddenly as she had begun. Twin frown lines crept across her forehead and converged at her nose. When she continued speaking it was as if she were reaching for each word.

"Dr. Whitehall complained about the cold," she said slowly. "Yes, it was quite cold in the house. The pilot light had gone out in the night and the furnace was shut off because of the thermostat. So I called the gas company for the repair man to come again. He'd been at the house twice before—I told the girl at the office about that so he would be certain to call the same day."

She paused and looked directly at him. The frown lines were very deep.

"Yesterday," she said.

"Yes, Miss Bardossy, it was yesterday."

"I know. I remember." Her voice was almost a whisper. If he'd ever doubted the genuineness of her blackout, the doubt was gone now. The excitement of discovery was too real. "I telephoned from the study, I told them about the other times, and they promised the man would come even if it was late in the day. He'd gone out on the truck already, you see. Dr. Whitehall was annoyed. She said—"

She paused again. The memory seemed to be fading. Her eyes were troubled.

"Yes, Miss Bardossy, what did Dr. Whitehall say?" he asked softly.

"She said there was no excuse for such carelessness, and she intended to speak to the repair man about it. She could be very sharp about such things. I do hope she didn't get him into trouble. Did he come to the house yesterday? Have you talked to him?"

"Not yet," Marshall said. "He's out on the truck again. The gas company is trying to locate him."

"But can't you tell by the furnace? Is it working?"

The question elicited a blank stare and then a sheepish admission, "How do you like that? Nobody thought to look."

"You forget things, too, Mr. Marshall."

"It seems we all forget things, Miss Bardossy."

The policemen in Anna Bardossy's troubled life had never admitted an error—that was the flaw in the armor of the absolute and sooner or later they perished of it. But Douglas Marshall, who was more than a policeman, was less than absolute; and from that moment an undercurrent of tension that had been always between them began to wear away. When he showed her the note Lansing had found in Dr. Whitehall's wastebasket, she didn't draw away. She studied it, but she didn't remember it or what it might have meant.

"'Have gone to the bank ...'" she read aloud. "That was a strange thing for her to do, Mr. Marshall."

"That's what Mr. Corsi said."

"Mr. Corsi? You have talked to him?"

"Yes, I've talked to him. He said that it was you who usually came to the bank on Thursday, but yesterday you didn't come. Instead, just before closing time, Dr. Whitehall came in and drew out one thousand dollars."

"One thousand—!"

"A large sum, isn't it? The same amount, incidentally, as the bequest made to you in her will."

The frown lines creased her forehead again. Inadvertently, her eyes sought the chest at the foot of the bed once more, and then, as if suddenly aware that she was betraying her own fears, her gaze dropped to the bed. Now she could stare at her bandaged wrists—the greater betrayal.

"I don't understand," she said softly.

"Miss Bardossy," Marshall said, "a few moments ago you remembered calling for the repair man for the furnace. You said that Dr. Whitehall was annoyed. Was that a normal condition?"

"Normal, Mr. Marshall?"

"I mean, was she easily irritated?"

For a little while the nurse seemed too enthralled with her own thoughts to answer the question. When she did speak it was with deliberate slowness.

"Dr. Whitehall was a fine woman," she said, "and I'm sorry if I caused her grief; but she wasn't a healer, Mr. Marshall. Oh, there are healers. Anyone who has lived as I have lived knows this. I've seen them in the camps where there was no other help. I've seen them in the hospitals and asylums—and so has Dr. Huntziger if he will admit it. My own father was one of the finest surgeons in Budapest, and yet I've known him to pray for an hour before a delicate operation. Yes, there are healers, but Dr. Whitehall wasn't one of them. I wasn't with her very long before I knew that. The healers have different names for their faiths—or sometimes no name at all—but they have one thing in common. They have the kind of love Christ had when he hung on the cross and said, 'Father, forgive them; for they know not what they do.' Dr. Whitehall had no such love. She tried, but down underneath there was hatred."

"Hatred for whom?" Marshall asked.

"I don't know. I only know that it was there. I saw it in the way she sometimes spoke to people who were under her. Men—yes. It was always men that she hated."

It was a strange and interesting thing that Anna Bardossy was saying. Marshall listened and absorbed.

"And did she hate Paul, too?" he asked.

The question got him nowhere. She pulled herself up higher against the pillows and stared at him with unblinking eyes.

"Mr. Marshall," she said, "if you have another visitor for me, I think we'd better get on with it."

Byron Davies was the third caller. Sgt. Lansing's description was inadequate—any description would have been inadequate. To appreciate Byron Davies fully one had to see him, hear him, and smell him (he wore what the better shops called a masculine-scent perfume). He was tall and strikingly handsome in spite of his years. The photographs of Dr. Whitehall, now splashed across every front page on the newsstands, bore a remarkable similarity to his high forehead, straight nose, and forceful chin. With a flowing beard to match the satin-white of his deeply waved hair, he might have stood on Sinai and chiseled thunder onto stone. And yet he entered Anna Bardossy's room as timidly as a sightseer at the morgue.

"Sit down, Mr. Davies, please," Marshall said.

The straight-backed chair still stood beside the bed. He walked toward it, hesitated, and then sat down taking care for the creases in the trousers of his dark mourning suit as he crossed his legs. He straightened his narrow tie, touched the peaks of the handkerchief jutting up from his breast pocket and adjusted the black band on his coat sleeve; and then, because curiosity was stronger than discretion, he looked at Anna Bardossy.

He stared at Anna Bardossy. His eyes left her face and followed the contour of her body beneath the sheet until they reached her bandaged wrists. He stared at the bandages and then made the return trip to her face again. He said nothing and she said nothing; but Marshall was suddenly aware of a sense of hostility in the room—not the neurotic hostility of Naomi Griswold, but something almost electric. The defensive mask had frozen Anna's face again; the hostility was in her eyes.

Dr. Huntziger came into the room and went to the bed. He checked her pulse and then stepped back, nodding for Marshall to begin. The story of Byron Davies came slowly. He was a reluctant caller. He'd given his statement to Sgt. Lansing on the previous night—wasn't that enough?

"This is extremely unpleasant for me," he said. "My dear sister—"

Davies' voice broke dramatically. He restrained himself from looking at the bed again. The gesture, or lack of it, was more meaningful than his words.

"I'm sorry," Marshall said. "I didn't realize that you and your sister were so close."

The flatness of his words brought up Davies' head. The eyes never lied, and Davies' eyes were oddly empty of emotion.

"I didn't realize it myself," he admitted, "until she was gone. We're sometimes careless that way. But when I think of how she looked lying on the floor—"

"It might be easier for you if you tried not to think of that," Marshall suggested, "and tried, rather, to help us learn how and why she died."

"Help you learn—" Surprise leaped into Davies' eyes. He did look at the bed now, and then back to Marshall. "Oh," he added, "you mean because the nurse has lost her memory. Sergeant Lansing told me about that. I must say, Mr. Marshall, that I think it's a rather flimsy excuse for not making an arrest. I don't see what you hope to accomplish."

Davies, then, was another of the already convinced. Anna Bardossy was a murderer; his attitude left no doubt of his conviction. But was that enough to explain the tension between them? Two other persons had sat in that chair, apparently convinced of her guilt; but neither of them had held her attention so closely.

"I've already accomplished something," Marshall answered. "Just before you were called in, Miss Bardossy had her first recall of yesterday's events. She remembered telephoning for a service man to come and repair the furnace."

Huntziger was interested. "Is that true?" he asked.

Anna didn't seem to hear him; her eyes were only for Davies now. "It's true," Marshall said. "So you see, Mr. Davies, we are making progress. We've got a start on the day. We've checked with the gas company and the call Miss Bardossy made came in shortly after nine o'clock. At ten o'clock Naomi Griswold encountered Miss Bardossy in the hall as she left on her day off. The next caller to your sister's study was Harold Elrod. He was there until noon and Miss Bardossy hadn't returned by the time he left. Now you've told Sergeant Lansing that you reached the house shortly after two—is that correct?"

"About ten minutes after," Davies said. "My appointment was for two, but I was delayed at lunch with a ..." He paused long enough to straighten the handkerchief again ... "A business associate," he added.

"Did you always have an appointment when visiting your sister?"

"On weekdays, yes. I didn't want to intrude on her patients' time. I telephoned in the morning."

Dr. Whitehall's call. Elrod had mentioned it; Davies explained it. But one answer only gave rise to another question.

"And what was the purpose of your visit, Mr. Davies?"

Davies looked unhappy. "Purpose?" he echoed.

"Why did you make the appointment with your sister?"

"Oh, no particular reason. I made a practice of calling on Lillian whenever I happened to be in the neighborhood."

"It was just a brotherly call, then."

A shadow of a smile touched Anna's mouth—a bitter smile, enigmatic and interesting. Davies didn't notice it, but Marshall did.

"That's right," he said.

"And your sister was alone when you arrived?"

"Oh, yes. She never had callers between noon and two o'clock. That was her rest period."

"Then you were the next person to reach her after Elrod's departure."

Ten minutes past two. The missing day with its missing answer was just past the meridian. He glanced at Anna to see if the words had any effect; but her eyes were still fixed on Davies' profile—intense eyes that couldn't be diverted.

"Now, isn't it true, Mr. Davies," Marshall continued, "that you informed Sergeant Lansing last night—perhaps I should say this morning—that you had seen Miss Bardossy drive past your sister's house as you were arriving?"

"Definitely," Davies declared.

"You couldn't have been mistaken?"

"Hardly, Mr. Marshall. She drives one of those little foreign cars—the only one of its kind I've seen in that neighborhood. What's more, I got a good look at her. She slowed down as she came to the driveway, as if intending to turn in; then she saw me and drove on again. She probably doesn't remember that, either."

The disdain in Davies' voice had a cutting edge. He glanced at Anna, but only for an instant. Her stare wasn't easy to look down.

"Why do you suppose she drove away?" Marshall asked. "Why didn't she turn into the driveway, if that's what she'd meant to do?"

"Because she didn't like me," Davies answered. "She didn't like any of us; but I was held in particular contempt."

Anna stirred against the pillow. Her mouth was hard, but she didn't protest.

"Why do you say that?" Marshall asked. "Is there any specific instance?"

"Dozens of specific instances. Ask Elrod and Mrs. Griswold. Miss Bardossy is a strange sort of person. Cold ... distant."

Davies was losing his timidity. He spoke of the woman as if she weren't present. It was an insulting attitude, and Marshall found himself resenting it.

"Perhaps she felt strange being in a new country among people she didn't know," he suggested.

"People she didn't want to know! She didn't like us, I tell you! We tried to be friendly. Lillian, particularly. She did everything for the woman and look what she got for it! I warned her after she wrote that preposterous will—"

Byron Davies' voice stopped abruptly. The words had leaped off his tongue, but it was too late to retract them. He could only regret them. He stared up at Marshall with those pale, empty eyes slowly filling with the realization that he'd said too much.

"You talked to Elrod," he said weakly. "He must have told you about the will."

"He told me," Marshall admitted, "but he gave me to understand that your sister's business affairs were confidential."

"Oh, they were! Elrod's a good man—a loyal man. But this thing was so outrageous that he came to me about it. He was afraid Lillian wasn't— well, wasn't quite herself."

"Afraid she was incompetent to make a will?"

"Not exactly incompetent—influenced. Influenced by this woman."

Davies didn't even bother to use her name. Anna's face was flushed now and her eyes bright with anger; but before she could speak, Dr. Huntziger moved into the circle of conversation with a dry observation.

"In what way, Mr. Davies?" he asked. "A gypsy curse?"

His words took the edge off her anger for the moment and put Davies on the defensive.

"Nothing so romantic, Doctor," he assured. "My sister was a very good woman with the failing of reading more into people than was actually there. She sentimentalized Miss Bardossy. She imagined that all the privation and suffering she'd endured had somehow ennobled her character. Why is it that people think suffering improves character? It must be some old folk myth. All we have to do is look around with our eyes open to see that suffering can make people cruel, or scheming, or turn them into whimpering hypochondriacs; but the characters it's improved could be counted on the fingers of a man with no hands!"

"And what am I?" Anna demanded, "the scheming type?"

They were the first words she'd spoken to the man, and they were underlined with bitterness. Davies shifted his weight and tried not to look at those accusing eyes.

"It would appear that way," he said.

"But I didn't even know about the will!"

"That's what you say, Miss Bardossy, but it's still a good motive, isn't it? People have been murdered for much less. And if that isn't enough ..."

Davies was warming to his role. No longer timid, no longer the reluctant witness. He edged forward on the chair, eager for Marshall's attention.

"I'm a gentleman, Mr. Marshall," he insisted, "and I wouldn't say what I'm about to say if my poor sister weren't lying on a slab in the mortuary while her murderess hides behind a convenient loss of memory! This woman wasn't fit to live in my sister's house! She's been involved for more than two years in a scandalous affair with a man!"

If his voice were a little more falsetto, Byron Davies might have reached the accusative heights of Naomi Griswold. He must have thought the revelation hadn't been made before. He waited for the reaction and received only a blunt question.

"Who was the man?" Marshall demanded.

The question dulled Davies' enthusiasm.

"I don't know," he admitted.

"You don't know?" Marshall echoed. "You call yourself a gentleman, Mr. Davies, and yet you make such a statement without naming names? How can you be sure this man existed?"

"Because I saw him! I saw the two of them together!"

The interesting thing about tension was the way it could tear apart and leave bare facts and raw emotions where hidden hostility had been. Davies blurted out his words, and Anna Bardossy, a kind of choking anger in her throat, strained forward from the pillow.

"You!" she said. Barely a whisper, but cutting as a lash. "You were the one!"

Davies' forehead was beaded with perspiration. He faced her angrily.

"Yes, Miss Bardossy, I'm the one who found out about you and your innocent vacation," he said. "It was two years ago, Mr. Marshall—no, more than that. It was in June of 1956. My sister had given the nurse two weeks' leave, and she told us she was going to the beach at Carmel. She did go— even sent a post card of the hotel where she was staying. Brazen. Outright brazen. But then, I'm sure she didn't expect visitors. I was interested in a business proposition at the time—real estate in the Carmel valley. I had an occasion to drive up and look it over, and so I decided to stop by the hotel and surprise her. I surprised her all right! I got in late and went straight to the dining room, thinking I might find her there. I did, but she wasn't alone."

The words were all Davies', but it was Anna's face that Marshall watched. Bare facts and raw emotions. They were approaching truth, and the strain had made her face taut and her mouth a hard line drawn against the pallor of her skin.

"She was with a man," Davies continued. "They didn't see me. They couldn't see anyone but each other. I didn't want to barge in on them, so I went up to my room. The next morning when I stepped out into the hall, I saw them again. They were waiting for the elevator, arm in arm. I got a good look at the man then. A skinny fellow with no chest. Foreign looking. I can't imagine what a good-looking woman could see in him." A shadow of disgust crossed Byron Davies' aging but handsome face. "I was shocked, naturally," he added. "After they'd gone, I went down to the desk and made an inquiry. I learned they were registered as Mr. and Mrs. Smith—Paul Smith. Original, weren't they?"

"Some people are named Smith," Dr. Huntziger remarked.

"Not this man. I tried to trace him later and couldn't. But that day I checked out and drove back to the city. I went straight to Lillian. She simply wouldn't believe me until I drove her up to Carmel and let her see for herself."

"You did that?" Anna gasped.

Her words severed his story. He had to acknowledge her presence again—belligerently now.

"Yes, I did that," he said. "You weren't aware of it because Lillian didn't want to cause a scene at the hotel."

"You spied on us!"

"Call it spying if you wish. I was trying to protect my sister's reputation."

"*You*, Mr. Davies? A fine one you are to think of that! Are you sure that's what you were thinking about when you drove to Carmel the first time? Are you sure it was real estate that took you there?"

The scorn in Anna's voice had whipped Davies to the edge of his chair. Shaken, he said, "I don't know what you mean."

"Don't you?" she cried. "You, who wanted to be so friendly—and in your sister's house, too! Oh, I know what you thought! I had lived in the camps like an animal so I would be like an animal—an exciting animal! And you could do whatever you pleased with this animal because she was only a refugee. Do you know what it is to be a refugee, Mr. Marshall?"

She turned to him, eyes blazing. A few dry questions, a little friction, and the spark of that hidden hostility had flared into open conflict.

"Do you know what it is to be stared at as if you are an exhibition and talked about as if you aren't present? To be watched and suspected and accused of plotting? Plotting, yes! Plotting to take the inheritance, to take this, to take that—and not only in the house. Oh, no! I go to the shop to buy some little thing and I hear people talking about those terrible refugees who are trying to take over everything. Take over! What did I want? What did I ask but a chance to live ...?"

"Miss Bardossy," Dr. Huntziger cautioned, "don't get so excited."

She didn't hear him. Nothing could stop her now until her anger was spent.

"Since I was a child I have lived in and out of the camps," she cried. "In the camps I learned to steal food; I learned to covet freedom and bear false witness so I could get free. I learned to break most of the commandments just in order to keep alive, but I didn't learn to be an animal! I'm still a woman and a woman who loves—but for that I must break another commandment and be spied upon by this—this—!"

Tension had to break somewhere. Anna pulled herself upright. Her hands were struggling with the sheets, and her face was contorted with hatred. Davies had become the symbol of everything she'd suffered, and this symbol was only a few feet away. She had no weapon to hurl at him but herself. She lunged forward just as Dr. Huntziger stepped between them. A small table stood beside the bed holding a tray and a water carafe. It teetered wildly, toppled and fell. Davies leaped up from the chair to avoid the shower of water and falling glass, and Dr. Huntziger forced Anna back against the pillow.

"Miss Bardossy, that's enough!"

Huntziger's voice crackled with authority. It was unnecessary. The authority that quenched Anna's near hysteria was now spilled out on the floor. It was a small thing—a toppled table and a bit of broken glass; but it was a small thing that had killed Lillian Whitehall. She stared at it with suddenly-frightened eyes. Davies looked even more frightened. He edged toward the door but Marshall stopped him.

"I'm sorry to see you get so upset, Miss Bardossy," he said. "I asked Mr. Davies to come here, and if he can help us to find this man you refuse to name it may save your life."

Her head came up slowly.

"Save my life?" she repeated. "Is that what you're trying to do?" There was still a trace of leftover anger in her voice. "How noble of you, Mr. Prosecutor," she said, "but then, all Americans are noble, aren't they? Noble and heroic—but who can love a hero? I've known so many of them—the Nazis, the Communists, all the strong men in uniforms, and all alike. Sentimental and sadistic, the opposite faces of the same coin. They weep over traditions and rites and then walk past living tragedy and never see it, because no story is tragic until it's told and by that time it's only a notice in the obituaries...."

Her words ran out as if the supply were drained, her voice barely a whisper. She still sat upright—Huntziger hadn't forced her to lie down—and her eyes were fixed intently on some place beyond the foot of the bed.

"Miss Bardossy," Marshall prompted.

She didn't respond.

"What is it, Miss Bardossy?"

Something like this had happened before—a kind of time out of content, as if that emotional outburst had swept her to the brink of memory. She finally looked up at him and the familiar puzzlement was in her eyes.

"I don't know," she said.

Huntziger moved in again.

"I think you'd better lie back now—"

"No—" She shrugged loose from the hand placed on her shoulder. "No, I want to hear. Mr. Davies—"

Davies was a shaken man. His tie needed straightening and he'd mopped his forehead with the pocket handkerchief, leaving it wilted and awry. He started visibly at the sound of his name.

"—and you say that I drove past the house?"

"Yes," he said weakly.

"Did I come back?"

"I don't know, Miss Bardossy. I was with my sister only a short time—not twenty minutes."

"But I did drive past the house?"

"Yes. Yes, you did."

She hadn't looked at him all this time. Just the one puzzled stare and her gaze had wandered back to the nowhere at the foot of the bed. Now she lowered her eyes and brought up her hands, holding both bandaged wrists before her face. She studied them a long time and then asked a question nobody could answer.

"Where did I go?"

CHAPTER EIGHT

"I don't care what arguments you use," Dr. Huntziger insisted, "you're not going back into that room now. As long as Anna Bardossy is in this hospital, she's my patient. Make an arrest, move her to a police ward and take the responsibility yourself; but you don't run a risk like that again while I'm in charge."

They had returned to Dr. Huntziger's office—the exodus from the room, swift and compulsory. A doctor was still a doctor; a patient was still a patient. Murder could wait.

"But you saw how close she was to remembering," Marshall protested.

"I saw how close she was to relapse. Good Lord, man, do a little remembering yourself. Twelve hours ago we were battling to save the woman's life."

"And what do you think I'm doing?"

The challenge came as a surprise—even to Marshall. He saw the automatic response in Huntziger's eyes. Quickly, he added, "Or do you think she's right—we're like the others, the Nazis and the Communists?"

"That bothered you, didn't it?" Huntziger asked.

"Didn't it bother you?"

"No, I can't say that it did. The woman has a lot of bitterness in her." Dr. Huntziger raked through his pockets for the pack of cigarettes again. It was almost empty by this time. He offered it to Marshall, who shook his head. He offered it to Byron Davies, who accepted with a slightly trembling hand. "Bitterness," the doctor added, "that has to strike out at someone. The kind of adjustment she's been expected to make is never easy. It must have been far from easy in that household."

Dr. Huntziger held the lighter for Davies. Their eyes met over the flame—Davies pale and protesting. When he had his light, Davies took two nervous puffs from the cigarette and said, "My sister was very tolerant of that woman, Doctor. And I'm shocked, really shocked—" He'd taken the leather chair in front of the desk; he seemed to need it after the ordeal with Anna. He turned to look at Marshall who had moved toward the windows again and continued speaking— "To hear Mr. Marshall's statement, and to observe his attitude. Save Miss Bardossy's life, indeed! What about my sister's life—or isn't murder a crime any more, Mr. Marshall?"

Marshall had glanced out over the city. Not dawn any more—midafternoon, and still no answer. He couldn't hold out much longer. He turned to see Davies' face—not so handsome now, flushed, perspiring and indignant—thrust forward with that mock courage he summoned up between rounds of fear.

"If you don't think it is, the district attorney might," he added. "He's a friend of mine."

Marshall's tight smile held back his anger.

"Are you threatening me, Mr. Davies?" he asked.

"I'm questioning your judgment. Why haven't you made an arrest as the doctor suggested? Why isn't that woman behind bars? You don't even have a guard on her door."

"I don't believe she's in any condition to be going anywhere," Marshall said, "but I can make an arrest if what you want is to see your sister's death turned into a three-ring circus. A mystery makes for more headlines than a confession. Of course ..." Marshall paused, letting his words sink home ... "It might save me work, at that. The press is good at getting convictions—unless they decided to play it the other way. Miss Bardossy is an attractive woman with a wretched background. The public loves pathos."

The belligerence in Davies' eyes ebbed away. He became a tired old man puffing nervously on a cigarette. Marshall moved closer to him.

"How do you know your sister's nurse continued seeing this Paul 'Smith' if the last time you saw them together was more than two years ago?" he asked.

The question startled Davies.

"The last time? Did I say it was the last time?"

"Then you did see them again?"

"Not—not immediately. It was months later—several months. I had a dinner engagement with a—a business associate. I saw them together in the restaurant. It surprised me, because I assumed that Lillian had straightened her out."

"What restaurant?" Marshall asked.

"What restaurant? I don't remember ... someplace in Beverly Hills, I think."

"Did you tell your sister about it?"

"No, not then."

"Do you mean there were other times?"

Byron Davies had forgotten his cigarette. The ash lengthened and dropped unnoticed on the knee of his dark trousers.

"I wanted to make certain before I said anything to Lillian again. She was stubborn about some things. She wouldn't get rid of the nurse—she'd signed a bond and she felt morally obligated."

"And besides, she was a good nurse," Dr. Huntziger suggested.

Davies frowned. He was being questioned by Marshall, no one else.

"What did you do, Davies, follow her?"

"A few times—yes; but not until after a peculiar thing happened one Sunday afternoon when we were watching television. There was a newsreel—pictures of the fighting in Hungary—"

Marshall had heard the story before; Huntziger hadn't. He let Davies tell his version, and both were the same except that Byron Davies seemed to have greater imagination, or less discretion, than Harold Elrod.

"It got me to wondering," he concluded. "After all, we take these people on faith, but what do we really know of them? I thought this man—this Paul Smith—might possibly be a foreign agent."

"Why didn't you go to the F.B.I.?" Marshall asked.

"I thought of that—I really did; but I had to be careful of Lillian's reputation. Suppose it turned out there was something wrong with the woman? She might have been suspect for helping to get her into the country. I decided to play along on my own. Finally, even Lillian became aware that the affair was still going on. Last summer she went on a lecture tour—by that time we all knew the real purpose was to get the nurse away from a man. And she promised—Lillian confided that much to me. Miss Bardossy promised never to see him again. But she lied. Two weeks after they returned, Lillian called me to help locate the nurse. She was gone—just gone—for three whole days. Lillian told the others that she was sick, but I knew better."

"Did you find her?"

"No. She came back on her own. I don't know what was said. I wasn't there at the time, and Lillian didn't tell me. But I had a feeling afterward that something had changed. I don't think she could fool Lillian anymore."

Marshall was remembering. Shortly after the return from the lecture tour, Elrod said. Yes, something had changed. He watched Davies finish the cigarette in three quick puffs and then get out of the leather chair to snuff out the butt in an ash tray on the desk. He'd recovered most of his dignity after the ordeal with Anna Bardossy. Were her insinuations true? It wasn't a question Marshall could ask and expect an answer, but there was still one thing he had to do before Byron Davies departed.

"Mr. Davies ..."

He'd already found his hat. He didn't really want to stay.

"You told us a few minutes ago that Harold Elrod informed you of the existence of a will leaving your sister's estate to Miss Bardossy. Was that before you followed her to Carmel?"

Davies reddened.

"I didn't follow her, Mr. Marshall. I only stopped by—"

"I'm sorry, I didn't mean to imply anything else. But was it previous to that incident that you heard of the will?"

"I really don't remember. Perhaps it was."

"And the second will—did he tell you about it?"

The words Davies couldn't find to use for an answer were written on his bewildered face. He stared unbelievingly while Marshall explained.

"A second will, drawn up a few weeks ago, leaves a small cash settlement to Miss Bardossy—the rest of the estate goes to you, Mr. Davies."

He spoke clearly, but bewilderment only grew in Davies' eyes.

"To me?" he said, at last.

"It's natural enough, isn't it—her only blood kin?"

"To me," Davies repeated. He leaned back against the desk. His face was almost colorless. "Lillian did that—you're sure?"

"Mr. Elrod told us this morning. I don't think he'd lie about it."

"No—no, not old Elrod. Loyal man, Elrod."

Davies held his hat in his hand. He began to turn it about, fingering the brim. He didn't look at the hat or at anything else. This new turn of events seemed to have left him stunned.

"Poor old Lillian," he said. "I used to tease her about it. I thought it was a joke."

"You thought what was a joke, Mr. Davies?"

"Her work—her beliefs. They weren't a joke to her."

"I'm sure they weren't," Marshall said.

"They were everything to her.... Claude Whitehall was a son of a bitch, a real son of a bitch. Never a decent word to her, damn him. Maybe that's why a woman turns to something like that. A woman has to love something."

"You're right, Mr. Davies," Dr. Huntziger said. "We all have to love something—Anna Bardossy, too."

Davies didn't answer. There was no argument left in him. He looked at Marshall, almost pleading for dismissal. There was no reason to keep him any longer. He could be found at his apartment if he were needed again.

"Yes, certainly." Davies was at the door now. "I had an appointment with a—"

"—business associate," Marshall suggested.

"—with a business associate, but I've canceled it under the circumstances. I'll be there. Any time. Any time."

The door opened as Davies reached it. Sgt. Lansing entered as he left—unnoticed and unrecognized. The prophet had come down from the mountain, and there was no thunder carved on the stone.

Sgt. Lansing had been a busy man. To begin with, he was beginning to have trouble from the press. The initial stories were getting old; the newsmen wanted more. Where was the nurse, Anna Bardossy? Why hadn't she been found? What were the police holding back?

"I was almost afraid to drive down here in a police car," he admitted. "One of those smart cookies is apt to get the bright idea of following me. We can't keep the nurse under wraps much longer."

Lansing's words were but an echo of Marshall's thoughts. He glanced at Huntziger, his irritation over the forced interruption in the search for a woman's memory still showing; but Lansing had other troubles. The reporters had tired of the Whitehall house—there was nothing there for them now that all of the flower beds had been trampled. They had sampled other sources.

"They tried to get to Elrod," Lansing said, "but he froze them out, so they descended on Naomi Griswold. I got wind of it just in time and sent Elrod to shut her up, but not before she made a few choice remarks concerning Bardossy's behavior. This thing can't be bottled up, Marshall. It's only a matter of time."

"That's what I was trying to convey to Dr. Huntziger before you came in," Marshall observed. "He doesn't seem to understand."

"I understand anatomy," Dr. Huntziger answered. "A human being can stand only so much abuse before it breaks down."

"Maybe that's the answer—a breakdown."

Dr. Huntziger came slowly around his desk. The long strain was telling on them all, and he was an old man in spite of his vitality. But the vitality was still there deep behind his searching eyes.

"Mr. Marshall," he said, "what are you trying to do—in addition to getting a confession from Anna Bardossy?"

The question was a surprise, and it wasn't even wrapped with fancy paper. Dr. Huntziger waited for it to be absorbed, but he didn't wait for an answer.

"When you came down here last night—when you waited all those hours for the nurse to regain consciousness, I thought to myself, when I had time to think, here's an ambitious young investigator with his mind set on a political career. Later, in this office, you told me about the letters and we talked about motives. Then I thought, here's an ambitious young man who's also conscientious. He deserves a career."

Dr. Huntziger spoke slowly. His eyes never left Marshall's face. "But now I find myself wondering—what does this man really want? This man who probes and probes and probes—what is he looking for?"

"I don't understand you," Marshall said.

"I don't expect you to understand what I don't even understand myself. But I think it would be a good idea if you decided what you're looking for—it might be easier to find."

It was the wrong time for that kind of talk. It was too late in the day, Marshall was too edgy, and Sgt. Lansing was standing by looking much too interested.

"I'm looking for Paul Smith," Marshall said testily. "Paul Smith, or whatever his real name might be. Davies has seen him, Lansing. He does exist, and he's been a part of Anna Bardossy's life for more than two years in spite of Dr. Whitehall's determined opposition. It doesn't seem logical that a man who's been that devoted to a woman would disappear as soon as she's in danger."

"Maybe there's a reason," Sgt. Lansing suggested.

"That's what I've been thinking. Anna Bardossy refuses to give his name, insists she doesn't want him to be involved."

"What are you suggesting?' Dr. Huntziger asked.

"I'm not certain. But you saw how angry she was when Davies told his not-so-nice little story. She didn't like being spied on. I'm wondering how 'Paul Smith' felt about it. That's not his real name, of course. The Paul is genuine—I've learned that much from the nurse. Sergeant, this is ridiculous! This man is here, somewhere in the city. Anna Bardossy must have seen him yesterday. We know she left the house at ten o'clock; we know she returned a little past two, slowed down at the driveway, saw Davies and drove on. After that—"

"Dr. Whitehall went to the bank," Lansing said.

Marshall mulled over the thought. His mind was still disturbed by Huntziger's unexpected question. He pushed it back and concentrated on the sergeant's suggestion.

"There could be a connection," he admitted. "The nurse might have returned after Davies left. He was with his sister less than twenty minutes, by his own admission. That would bring us up to about two-thirty."

"And Dr. Whitehall reached the bank just before closing time at three o'-clock," Lansing added. "It's a slow ten-minute walk from her house. I checked it."

"Which means she could have had another caller."

"Or the nurse returned."

"Yes, or the nurse returned."

It wasn't easy to forget that last scene in the room down the hall—Anna Bardossy staring at her own bandaged wrists and pleading for an answer nobody had. He met Huntziger's eyes again; this time he didn't turn away.

"Between two-thirty and five twenty-two—less than three hours, Doctor—that's where our answer lies. That's all the farther we need to probe."

"But she doesn't remember those things," Huntziger protested.

"She's beginning to—surely you could see that. And she did remember calling the gas company. What about that repair man, Lansing? Why isn't he here?"

"He got lost," Lansing said.

"What?"

"I checked back with the company. They located him all right, but he was an hour off schedule. He got lost. As soon as he finishes the job he's on, he's coming here—if he doesn't get lost again."

"Is it habitual?"

"It seems to be from what they told me. He's a new man, only had the job a few months."

"Then go after him. He's our last chance. Obviously, he didn't get to the house until after Dr. Whitehall left for the bank. He fits in that crucial period. Anything he saw, anything he heard—just *anything* might give us the key."

And there had to be a key—never mind why. The urgency in Marshall's voice was as much for Dr. Huntziger as the sergeant; but the command was all Lansing's. He listened, he sighed, he started toward the door. There he hesitated, his hand on the knob.

"Oh, one other thing," he said. "The crime lab has made a report on what they could make out of that study. It was no good for fingerprints— anybody and everybody was in and out of the room all the time. The furniture, the books, the pamphlets—everything was loaded with all kinds of prints. But the clock was a different story—not for prints; it was smeared with them too—but it's a peculiar clock. It's a heavy chunk of glass fastened to a brass base. The base has an edge on it, and the lab found a couple of threads caught on the edge. Cotton. They think it might be threads from a glove."

"A glove?" Marshall repeated. "What color are the threads?"

"They're not certain. They have to make some more tests for the dyes. Some dark color, they said. Black or dark blue, maybe." Lansing smiled a tired smile. "Maybe dirty white for all I know. Anyway, you might check and see if the Bardossy woman was wearing gloves yesterday. If she was, and the threads match, who needs a memory?"

Lansing sighed again and went on his weary way. Marshall looked to Huntziger for the answer now. The doctor anticipated his request by buzzing for the nurse at the desk in the hall. Moments later, she arrived.

"Miss Kelly, the patient in room 402 has all of her personal belongings hanging in the closet. Will you see if they include a pair of gloves—and, if so, bring them to Mr. Marshall."

When the nurse left, Huntziger turned to Marshall.

"I'm sorry if I said too much," he declared. "I guess I'm getting a little tired."

"So am I," Marshall said. "If I weren't, I wouldn't have let Davies get out of here without explaining why he went to see his sister."

"But he did explain—he was worried about her."

"Or her money."

"Well, yes, if you want to be nasty about it—and why not be nasty? If I understood the previous conversation correctly, you've learned that Dr. Whitehall visited the bank immediately after seeing her brother. Why?"

"She withdrew one thousand dollars," Marshall said. "A thousand—Where is it now?"

Marshall stared at the doctor. It was several seconds before he could answer. It was just as Corsi said—how easily we leap to conclusions. Just because the amount withdrawn was the same as the amount left to the nurse in Dr. Whitehall's will, he'd gone hurtling toward a conclusion that didn't necessarily exist.

"How much did Miss Bardossy have on her when she was brought in?"

"I didn't look," Huntziger answered. "That's not really in my field."

"There was nothing in the car but the lingerie."

"One hundred and twenty-nine dollars and thirty-eight cents," Huntziger recalled. He shook his head sadly. "That still leaves quite a bit unaccounted for, doesn't it?"

"And her purse found beside her on the sand—I'd better have a look at that purse, Doctor."

Huntziger didn't have a chance to use the buzzer again. Miss Kelly returned promptly. She'd had no trouble finding what she'd been sent to find. There were gloves—black cloth gloves. Marshall barely glanced at them. He was more interested in the container they had arrived in—the purse. Miss Kelly didn't take things from patients' purses without a witness present, bless her, and that meant saving another trip to the closet. The purse was black, too—black cloth, long, narrow, overpacked with the many items of a woman's paraphernalia—a house key, a wallet, finally, well worn and thin. A few dollars inside. A coin purse containing perhaps another dollar in change. A zipper compartment containing—

"What is it?" Huntziger asked.

Marshall withdrew an envelope with familiar markings.

"It seems to be an airline ticket," he said, "no—" He opened the envelope and withdrew the contents—"Correction: two airline tickets. Two on a flight that left last night for Las Vegas."

CHAPTER NINE

It was such a simple case: a woman had been found murdered in her study; another woman, known to have quarreled bitterly with her, had subsequently attempted suicide. There were witnesses to the hostility between them, there were motives, there was opportunity. And yet, at three o'clock of the following afternoon—more than seventeen hours since a stranger had stumbled across a half-dead woman on the beach—Douglas Marshall, having ordered no arrest, left the hospital bound for an airline ticket office in Beverly Hills.

The wind off the ocean hadn't lost its bite. The sun, battling gamely for a breakthrough at noon, had given up the struggle and was now lost behind a threatening sky. Across the city, the pungent perfume of smoking exhausts mingled with the sea air, oil from the wells jutting up from the southern hills, and the occasional intense sweetness of the backyard narcissus. It was a gray day. The Santa Monicas were already swathed in early fog, and even the glitter of a glamorous shopping center couldn't rout the spell of melancholy."

"... what are you trying to do—in addition to getting a confession from Anna Bardossy?"

The thought was an irritation. Marshall swung the sedan into the hotel parking lot, determined to put it out of his mind. He was doing his job, that was all. He was a thorough man—that was his training. He'd learned to be thorough on a job where the slightest error could mean death for many—and Anna Bardossy's life was as important as Dr. Whitehall's death. Civilization—or whatever remained of it—rested on a premise as simple as that.

And now he had one definite lead: two tickets to Las Vegas. They hadn't been used, but they had been purchased. The place of purchase was stamped on the airline envelope. The ticket office was in a hotel lobby—warm, busy, oblivious of the outside gloom. It was an easy matter to check when the tickets were purchased. Each sale was recorded, and this particular sale had been made the previous day.

"I couldn't possibly remember the party. We do a tremendous volume of business in a hotel."

The efficient young lady behind the counter was pleasant but not very encouraging.

"If I describe someone," Marshall suggested, "you may remember. Was it a woman—"

"I couldn't possibly—"

"—dark, very attractive, in her early thirties? A small woman wearing—" He hesitated. He hadn't seen Anna Bardossy dressed, but her gloves and purse were black. It was worth a gamble—"Black," he said. "Smart but not expensive. She has blue eyes and speaks with an accent."

"An accent?"

"A slight accent—Hungarian."

"But so many people speak with an accent—particularly in a hotel. Wait a minute—" The ticket seller reflected, something kindling in her eyes. "There was a woman, small, dark, a soft accent—"

"When?" Marshal asked.

"In the afternoon, I think. Yes, right after my lunch hour—I go at twelve-thirty. There was a line because only one girl had been on duty, and I remember this woman because she was so nice about it—so patient and polite. You'd be amazed at how rude some people can be—and in a hotel like this one, too. Some people shouldn't be allowed to have money unless they can pass a mental maturity test."

"Did this woman seem to have money?" Marshall asked.

"I don't think so—no more than necessary. She counted out the bills carefully enough. All sales are cash, you know, unless they're purchased on a credit plan. I remember her very well now. She seemed so happy—but sad, too. That sounds peculiar, doesn't it?"

"It sounds possible,"

"I mean, she seemed as if she'd been sad or sick for a long time and now she wasn't. But that's probably all my imagination. Whenever people are polite, I think something's wrong with them."

"She bought two tickets," Marshall reminded. "Did she give two names for the passenger list?"

The woman had the order sheet in her hand. She ran down the list. "Bardossy," she read aloud, "Anna—"

"That's the one."

"And the adjoining seat—that must have been her second ticket—was reserved in the name of ... Sometimes I can't read my own writing. I think it's a K—yes, K-r-a-m-a-r. Kra-mar. Paul Kramar."

The man had a name at last. Marshall hardly dared to push his good fortune. He asked the next question anyway.

"Is there an address?"

"Yes. 1947 North Hillmont—"

"I mean for Kramar."

"I'm sorry. There's only one address listed."

Only one address, but at least he had a name. The woman behind the counter put away the order sheet and handed back the unused tickets. Then an awareness crept into her eyes.

"But she didn't make the flight."

"No, she didn't make it."

"Oh, I'm so sorry. She seemed so happy about it. I hope nothing happened."

Marshall didn't answer. He pocketed the tickets and went outside.

The sky was darker, and the smell of rain was in the air. He stood just beyond the wide, automatic glass doors and stared across the parking lot. The lights in a department-store window across the street showed brighter now, and he slowly realized that the colored bulbs, and the tinsel, and the silver trees meant that another holiday season was coming due. He'd thought of them in that way for a long time now—something that came due annually like a tax bill. It was a long time since that last Christmas in Berlin with the foot-high tree, a handful of candles, and Elsa trying to teach him to sing "O Tannenbaum" to the accompaniment of an old upright that had survived the blitz—but barely. The best times and the worst times always seemed tied together in some way, so that it wasn't possible to have one without the other.

He thought of Anna Bardossy coming out of the hotel the previous afternoon—happy. The old sadness underneath, but happy. And why? She'd quarreled with Dr. Whitehall in the morning. She'd left the house bitterly suggesting to Naomi Griswold that she might not have to put up with a "barbarian" much longer. She hadn't gone to her bank at any time during the day, but in the afternoon she'd purchased two airline tickets for a night flight to Las Vegas. What had she done then? Gone back to the house on Hillmont? The timetable would fit. Davies must have told the truth. But she'd driven on past the house.

"*Where did I go?*"

Where could she have gone? He stared at the department store across the way, and then walked back to his car. Lansing was probably waiting at the hospital with the wandering gas-company service man; but Westwood was on the way back.

The exclusiveness of a department store could be measured by the secrecy with which departmental information was kept from the public. Bannock's Westwood was a cut above middle class. It did have a directory—carefully hidden—and the directory did give information in an obscure manner. There was no lingerie department; but there was something designated "intimate apparel—Oval Room, upper level." Translated, this meant one escalator flight up and a sharp turn to the right.

Douglas Marshall came armed with a sales slip. The inscription thereon brought him eventually to a small, gray-haired saleslady with bright violet eyes and the eager expression of a good fairy in search of a tale. She listened to his as she studied the sales slip, and then she asked, "Do you have the merchandise with you?"

"No, I don't," Marshall admitted, "but it's soft and pink and lacy."

He'd said something wrong. He could tell by the tiny frown marks pricking at her nose.

"Cameo," she said.

"What?"

"Cameo pink—there, on the stand above your head."

Marshall looked up. A display platform rose up from the center of the long oval counter, and on it, draped over an angular wrought iron mannequin, was the same gown and negligee that had been found in Anna Bardossy's car. Even the slippers were there, side by side on the skirt of the negligee.

"She used to come in every Thursday and admire it—stand right where you're standing now and just admire it."

"You remember her, then?"

"Oh, yes, every Thursday for weeks and weeks. The first few times I went up to her and asked if I could be of assistance. Once she inquired about the price, but after that she thanked me and said she was just looking around."

"Did she come in alone?"

"Yesterday?"

"Any day."

The violet eyes had a way of wandering. Now they were focused somewhere beyond the back of Marshall's head.

"She always came in here alone," the saleslady answered, "but then she'd go out there, out by the escalator and meet him."

"Him?"

"Her young man. A nice looking chap, a little thin but nice looking. They met every Thursday, just about noon. I suppose they went to lunch somewhere together. Then yesterday she came back again later and bought the set. I was surprised. They usually don't buy, you know, when they're just looking around. It's a sweet little story, isn't it?"

Marshall showed his bewilderment.

The saleslady smiled knowingly.

"After all," she said, "it is trousseau lingerie."

It was trousseau lingerie. Marshall left the saleslady to glow over her departmental romance and returned to his car. Two tickets to Las Vegas and trousseau lingerie—yes, there was a reason now behind Anna Bardossy's defiance of Naomi Griswold when they passed in the hall. But what of the quarrel with Dr. Whitehall which had preceded that defiance? Had Anna told her dominating employer of her planned matrimony and met with opposition, a threat of deportation, perhaps? There were seeds of murder in what he'd learned on this small expedition; but it wasn't complete. He peered out through a windshield rapidly gathering mist. Just over the hill were the red-brick buildings of the University, and the University reminded him that it takes two to make a wedding. And it might even take two to make a corpse.

He drove directly to the administration building and made his inquiry. Everyone was pleasant and helpful—but did he realize how many adult education courses were being offered? If only he could designate a certain course. He couldn't. He wasn't even certain there was a course; this whole inquiry was based on a fragment of Elrod's testimony. But at least now he had a name: Paul Kramar.

"He's probably enrolled in a class which also includes a woman named Anna Bardossy," he added, "but it's Kramar I want. His address, telephone number, anything."

It was a simple request, but even simple requests consume time, and there was still the matter of the fourth caller to hurry him back to the hospital. Leaving the telephone number and Dr. Huntziger's extension, he returned to the sedan and headed back into the mist.

It was heavier as he neared the ocean, a low, dripping fog yellowed by the dim reminder of a declining sun. All cities were alike in the fog. The spires, the monuments, the mountains or the marquees that gave them identity were sponged away, and a wet street was a wet street in Santa Monica, or Berlin, or Budapest. And wet streets were dangerous. He drove slowly, searching the streets with tired eyes. The fog had brought a too early twilight, and shapes and forms and moving things could suddenly appear where they hadn't appeared before. At the entrance to the hospital parking lot he slowed gradually and then kicked on the brake. The shriek of it echoed from the car behind, a horn blasted and an angry face at the window shouted at him as the offended motorist veered sharply and went by. There was nothing in the driveway but an old newspaper blown by the wind. Not a body. Not a woman on the street, just a newspaper. He drove in and parked the car, and on the way to the building kicked the newspaper aside. The headline told of an unsolved murder. It was good to be reminded of what day it was, and what city.

It was more than an hour since he'd left Dr. Huntziger's office. He expected to find Sgt. Lansing and his wayfaring witness ready to resume the reconstruction of an almost finished day; but he was wrong. The vestibule outside Dr. Huntziger's office was empty; the nurse at the desk in the hall had seen nothing of the sergeant, and the doctor was in surgery. But Huntziger's office wasn't empty. Two tense, somber-eyed people were waiting for Marshall when he entered the room. Harold Elrod rose stiffly from his chair.

"Mr. Marshall," he said, "I've brought Mrs. Griswold to see you again. She wants to make a confession."

CHAPTER TEN

It was a startling statement. For a few seconds, Marshall couldn't get oriented—he'd heard too much, learned too much, and traveled too far within the hour. His mind was still crowded with airline tickets and trousseau lingerie and an old newspaper blowing in the wind. His face mirrored the confusion.

Naomi Griswold stirred uneasily on the leather chair.

"Please don't misunderstand," Elrod added quickly. "It's a small matter; but it may have some significance. Sergeant Lansing asked me to call on Mrs. Griswold—she had been having some difficulty with the press."

"They make people say things," Mrs. Griswold remarked. "They put words right into your mouth."

"Unfortunately," Elrod added, "she made several statements to the reporters that she hadn't made to me or to you, Mr. Marshall. We talked it over and decided it would be best to come here and straighten things out."

Dr. Huntziger had made fresh coffee. The pot was plugged in and the aroma inviting. There were cups on the desk. Marshall doffed his damp coat and hat and poured himself a cup. His unexpected guests declined. He warmed his hands on the steaming cup and studied Naomi Griswold's face. She didn't appear to have rested since the morning interview. Her skin was sallow and there were dark shadows under her eyes. Her gloved fingers still worked nervously at the latch of her purse.

"I'm afraid I didn't tell the truth this morning," she admitted—"the exact truth. I said that I'd heard Miss Bardossy quarreling with Dr. Lillian from the garden ..."

She hesitated and glanced up at Elrod as if there might be some last-minute reprieve. There was none. She continued.

"I really wasn't in the garden," she said.

"I know, Mrs. Griswold."

"You know?"

"The French doors were locked and weather-stripped early in October."

There was something like relief on Mrs. Griswold's troubled face. She sighed and her shoulders sagged a little.

"I should have realized you'd find out the lie. I knew it was wrong, but I hated to admit I'd been eavesdropping." And then her head raised quickly. "But only because of my concern for Dr. Lillian. You see, Mr. Marshall, I didn't go into the garden at all yesterday morning. The wind was chilly and I had been fighting off a cold all week. I went directly into the house and sat down on the settee in the hall because it wasn't quite ten. That was where I heard the quarreling. I couldn't help but hear it. Dr. Lillian's study is just off the hall."

Mrs. Griswold was having difficulty staying on the leather chair; she would have had much more difficulty staying on the settee.

"I imagine that accounts for your collision with Miss Bardossy," Marshall said.

"Oh, I didn't collide with her! She came out of the study in such a hurry I couldn't get back—" Mrs. Griswold tripped over her own words and then righted herself again. "The important thing," she said, in a louder voice, "is what I heard being said in that room. I thought this morning that everything was all settled—about the murder, I mean—and I wouldn't have to tell you. But now—"

"What did you hear, Mrs. Griswold?"

"She—that woman you're coddling—threatened. Dr. Lillian!"

"In what way?"

"Well, I didn't hear it all; but I did hear Dr. Whitehall say, 'You may be sorry if you go through with this,' and then the nurse said, 'I'm all through being sorry. I'm not afraid and you can't make me afraid anymore.'"

Mrs. Griswold spoke the words in a sharp, accusing manner. Her outrage was controlled but obvious.

"Anymore?" Marshall repeated. "What did she mean by that?"

"I don't know," the woman declared, "and she didn't either. She just has a wicked tongue on her! And then she said something terrible. She said, 'I couldn't work with you any longer if I did stay. I'm tired of trying to patch up your mistakes. I've even written letters to the authorities about the things you do.' Imagine that! Letters to the authorities!"

Mrs. Griswold's chin trembled with emotion. Her eyes were biting black. Marshall couldn't react with the shock she apparently expected. He hadn't brought up the matter of the letters to Anna Bardossy; he was waiting for the proper time. But the proper time to soothe Mrs. Griswold's indignation was immediate.

"I know about the letters," he said quietly. "I've read them."

"But they're lies! All lies!"

"Have you seen them, Mrs. Griswold?"

She couldn't answer. She looked up to Elrod for backing. He patted her shoulder with a reassuring hand.

"I don't know what Miss Bardossy wrote in the letters either," he said, "but I'm sure she was mistaken—"

"Why are you sure, Mr. Elrod?"

The question surprised Elrod. Before he could protest, Marshall asked another.

"Didn't you tell me yourself this morning that Dr. Whitehall seemed tired and disturbed? Isn't it possible that she was making mistakes—that she was getting careless? She wouldn't have noticed, but a younger woman would."

Now Elrod did protest.

"I don't think I like your line of reasoning," he began.

"But it is reasoning," Marshall said. "You must admit that. In addition, you told me of a financial statement Dr. Whitehall had requested. Didn't you wonder why, Mr. Elrod?"

Elrod glanced at Naomi Griswold. Her presence seemed to make him uncomfortable.

"I assumed she had a reason," he said.

"But you didn't wonder about it? Really, Mr. Elrod, I must congratulate you on your magnificent thought control. Had I been in your position, I would have wondered. One of the possibilities I would have considered was that she might be contemplating retirement."

Naomi Griswold smothered a protesting gasp with one gloved hand. Elrod's expression remained unchanged.

"I did think of it," he admitted, "but it really wasn't my affair."

"Your affair is handling the finances and legal aspects of the estate."

"Yes."

"And what would have happened to the society—the lecture hall and the publications—in the event of Dr. Whitehall's retirement?"

Elrod was a cool man. He wasn't a trial lawyer, but he parried the question artfully.

"The same thing that happens now that she's gone, Mr. Marshall. The society is self-supporting. We continue to operate as usual, at least for the present. The future is up to Mr. Davies."

"Davies?"

Marshall drained the coffee cup and put it back on the desk. It was an interesting thought—Byron Davies carrying on in his sister's practice. After all, those mail-order degrees were easy enough to come by, and the world never ran out of troubled people looking for someone to listen to their woes. Davies would be less sincere than Dr. Whitehall, but more colorful. Probably more successful.

"What does Byron Davies do for a living?"

This question caught Elrod by surprise.

"Do?" he echoed.

"He mentioned having business associates."

A fleeting smile curved Mrs. Griswold's tight lips; but Elrod's hand was still on her shoulder and sudden pressure tightened his knuckles.

"I believe he has some kind of investments."

"Did he ever borrow money to finance these investments from his sister?"

"From Dr. Whitehall? I—I really couldn't say."

"You handle her finances, don't you?"

"Well, it's possible that he did—some years back."

"But not recently? Not since she had a change of heart and rewrote her will?"

Elrod didn't answer. His resistance to questioning was hardening; it showed in the cords of his neck.

"Mr. Marshall," he said, "I didn't come here to discuss Mr. Davies or his finances. I've told you before, if you wish to have my books examined, they're at your disposal. Mrs. Griswold and I are doing everything possible to be of assistance in clearing up this terrible affair. We only came back here to help—"

"I appreciate that," Marshall said. "But it seems this case is a little more complicated than it appeared to be this morning. That's why I have to ask questions. Now Dr. Whitehall, if we can believe the smashed clock, was killed at five twenty-two P.M. I suppose you can account for your whereabouts at that time, Mr. Elrod."

"Account for *my* whereabouts—"

Marshall didn't expect wreaths of smiles at the suggestion. Elrod looked outraged; Mrs. Griswold, startled.

"I'm afraid you'll have to, sooner or later, Mr. Elrod," Marshall explained. "In the event Miss Bardossy doesn't regain her memory and is arrested without a confession, it will be my job to provide the district attorney with the evidence to prove she's guilty and the defense counsel's job to prove she isn't—"

"But she is guilty!" Naomi insisted.

"It still has to be proven, Mrs. Griswold. Well, Mr. Elrod?" Elrod was displeased at the turn of events, but he was also capable of facing facts. He frowned over the thought for a few seconds and then

"I was at my office in the college," he recalled. "Yes, at my office. That's where I went directly after lunch."

"Were you there alone?"

"No. Mrs. Elrod was with me until—"

Elrod paused, his face grave again.

"Until when, Mr. Elrod?"

"Until five o'clock. She drove the car home to prepare dinner. She came back and picked me up at six."

"But at the time of the murder you were alone, is that right? No other person on the premises? No janitor?"

"Mr. Marshall," Elrod answered, "we're a modest society. We keep down our overhead by doing such work in committees. To my knowledge, no other person was in the building between five and six o'clock."

"And you had no car," Marshall mused. "About how long do you think it would take to walk from the college to Dr. Whitehall's house?"

He expected another protest. Elrod's face was quite white, and his eyes behind the glasses were hard. But his voice was carefully controlled.

"Ten or fifteen minutes, I would say," he replied. "It's slightly uphill. I could have walked it, killed Dr. Whitehall, and been back to the college in plenty of time for my wife's return."

"Mr. Elrod!" Naomi gasped.

"I could have done so," Elrod added, "but I didn't. Does that answer your question, Mr. Marshall?"

"It does, thank you," Marshall said. "And you, Mrs. Griswold?"

Naomi Griswold, indignant at the questioning of Harold Elrod, now appeared at the verge of tears.

"I can't see why you insult us with such questions when you know the nurse is guilty. I just told you—"

"Five twenty-two, Mrs. Griswold," Marshall insisted.

"But how can I say where I was at that time? I don't know. I don't remember."

"Were you at home?"

"Yes, I think so."

"And your home is near Dr. Whitehall's?"

"It's a few blocks. Mr. Elrod—" Naomi turned toward her protector with pleading eyes. "I'm not feeling well, you know that. I didn't want to come down here at all. It was only because you said it was right to tell Mr. Marshall the threat I overheard!"

That was the nice thing about dealing with good citizens. They didn't have secrets, or, if they did, they repented and told them—accurately, word for word.

"I appreciate that, Mrs. Griswold," Marshall said, "but there's an odd thing about that threat. If you repeated it exactly as it was spoken, it wasn't Miss Bardossy who threatened Dr. Whitehall; it was the other way around."

Now he had spoken heresy. Mrs. Griswold's shocked face gave portent of argument, and Marshall, taking advantage of her indignant pause, returned to Elrod.

"What about that record of Dr. Whitehall's patients?" he queried. "Have you come up with anything yet?"

"Nothing," Elrod said, "except a few canceled checks in payment of treatments. I didn't think you'd want them—"

"But I do want them!" Marshall said. "I want anything you can find, anything at all! It does seem strange that a woman so meticulous in every other way would neglect to keep a file of her patients. I'll warrant she kept some record of successful treatments; but what about the failures? What about the incurables or the potentially dangerous abandoned to reenter and prey on society?"

Mrs. Griswold's face mirrored mounting dismay; but Elrod never lost his poise. "You're with the district attorney's office, Mr. Marshall," he said. "Do you keep a record of all your failures? Surely some citizens are falsely accused and even convicted on occasion, and we all know there are those who are falsely arrested. As for dangerous people, it seems to me that each time a terrible sex crime takes place the press reports that the police are rounding up 'known degenerates.' Why are they turned loose to prey upon society, Mr. Marshall? As for incurables of any kind, why do we have cemeteries?"

Harold Elrod's words were delivered with deadly calm. There was no rebuttal. Dr. Whitehall couldn't be blamed for not obeying laws nobody had bothered to enact, and the chances of learning anything from those canceled checks seemed remote. With the knowledge of what he'd just learned concerning two air tickets and an expensive set of lingerie all of these questions he'd been asking Elrod and Mrs. Griswold were probably unimportant anyway; but Marshall's mind still fought off accepting the obvious without proof. He let his volunteer informants go, but only at the arrival of Sgt. Lansing and a young man in need of a Whitehall lecture on promptness. The lost was found; the fourth caller had arrived.

His name was Timothy Waters. He stood six feet in his scuffed boots, weighed two hundred pounds in his black suede jacket with frayed, knitted cuffs, and was just old enough to have a soft fuzz where the beard would soon grow. He had a short crop of reddish hair, thick features and awkward hands that played with the soiled pigskin gloves in his lap. He sprawled on the chair, his legs wide apart and his round eyes busy with everything in the room.

Huntziger had relented. Anna Bardossy was allowed another visitor. She was calm now, not at all the woman who had lashed out at Byron Davies. She sat back against the pillows, not smiling and not sullen. This was just another ordeal to be endured. When Dr. Huntziger switched on the lights, Timothy Waters' eyes widened.

"Nice room," he said. "Nice hospital you got here."

"Thank you," Dr. Huntziger said, "but it's really not mine."

Waters grinned broadly.

"I bet you wish it was. Must be worth a lot of money—all the equipment, all the machines."

"Have you been here before?" Marshall asked.

"Here—no. Hospitals, yes. Not like this one, though. Army hospitals—you know. Syringe factories."

Waters dropped one of the pigskin gloves on the floor. He leaned down to retrieve it, and as he raised up again seemed to become aware for the first time of the woman in the bed. He stared at her, and then his expression changed from overdone nonchalance to startled surprise.

"Hey, that's the nurse! That's the woman the newspapers are looking for."

"Fine," Marshall said. "Let them look."

"But she's here!" Waters wasn't casual any more. He sat bolt upright in the chair, one foot drawn back ready to rise. "What is this? What are you trying to pull?"

"Why should we be trying to pull anything, Mr. Waters?"

"How should I know? I'm just out doing my job—trying to find an address up in them hills. Jesus, the streets in this town! All of a sudden this big cop is on my tail to come down to Santa Monica. Somebody from the D.A.'s office wants to talk to me."

"Weren't you notified by the gas company that you were wanted?"

"When I called in at noon, sure. But I wanted to finish up my work orders. The way they pile them on these days! I never get finished on time."

Waters couldn't keep his eyes on Marshall. His attention strayed back to the woman on the bed. He seemed afraid of her, and he was still poised as if ready to quit the chair on an instant's notice.

"What's she doing here?" he demanded. "She killed that old lady last night."

It wasn't the first accusation Anna had been forced to hear, but it was the most direct. She took it with unblinking eyes.

"Are you sure of that?" Marshall asked.

"That's what it says in the papers."

"It also says in the papers that the police are searching for her."

This thought sobered Timothy Waters completely. He stared at Anna Bardossy again, following the contour of her body underneath the sheet.

"What's the matter with her?" he asked.

"She's suffering from amnesia."

"What?"

"She can't remember what she did yesterday. That's why you were brought here, Waters. We need your help."

"My help?" The eyes were for Marshall again—startled eyes. "What do I know about it?"

"You went to the Whitehall house yesterday, didn't you?"

"To fix the furnace—sure. Those cheap furnaces. If people don't want trouble with their pilot lights, why do they buy cheap furnaces?" And then

Waters paused and studied Marshall's face with the same apprehension he'd shown for the woman on the bed. "How did you find out about that?" he asked.

"We found a note Dr. Whitehall had written and left on the door when she went out."

"There was no note! I didn't see no note! Anyway, the old lady was there. I talked to her myself."

And so they had another piece of the day. Marshall glanced at Anna Bardossy and their eyes met over the same thought. It wasn't ten minutes past two anymore. They had gone beyond the point where Byron Davies watched her slow down at the driveway and then go on down the street. He wished there had been time to talk to her about the airline ticket and the pink lingerie; but there hadn't. If she remembered them, the secret was hers.

Marshall turned back to the repair man.

"What time did you reach the house?" he asked.

Waters' attention had also strayed. His eyes were back on the bed again. "What's the matter with her hands?" he queried.

"Never mind that now. What time, Mr. Waters?"

"But her wrists are bandaged."

"What time?"

Reluctantly, Waters' attention returned to his questioner. He shifted his position on the chair.

"Nearly five, I think. I was late. I shouldn't of stopped at all so near quitting time, but my orders were to make the call no matter what time it was. Some customers get fussy."

"Five o'clock." The day was shortening rapidly. Only twenty-two minutes left to go. "And you talked to Dr. Whitehall?"

"The old lady, sure. Funny-talking woman."

"Funny?"

"You know, out of this world stuff. Preacher talk. People like that, how do they know how rough life is?"

A boy with peach fuzz on his face and a hardness around his mouth. Marshall studied him with calculating eyes.

"But you know, don't you?" he suggested.

"You bet I know! Korea, two years. They don't come no rougher than that!" And then Timothy Waters' eyes strayed back to the bed. The hardness went out of his mouth as he looked at Anna Bardossy. "The nurse, now," he added, "wasn't like the old lady. She was nice, always nice." There was unexpected gentleness in Waters' voice when he spoke of the woman on the bed, and an almost childlike expression on his face. "She showed me to the furnace room the other times I came," he explained. "I was out to that house twice before."

"So I've heard," Marshall said.

"Cheap furnace. I told the old lady ..." Waters didn't finish the statement; his eyes were still on Anna. "Hurt yourself?" he asked.

Anna was staring at him now. She started to reply; but Marshall interrupted.

"How long were you with Dr. Whitehall?" he asked.

Reluctantly, Waters' attention returned to his interrogator.

"Ten minutes," he said.

"You sound awfully certain."

"Why shouldn't I be certain? Don't you think I know how much I work overtime every day? And just for a little dust in the intake! The old lady could have fixed it herself if she hadn't been so lazy. That's the way with people like her. Always telling everybody else how to live and doing nothing themselves. Anyway, I know it was no more than ten minutes because I was at Sam's at five-fifteen."

"Sam's?" Marshall repeated.

"A service station down on Vermont. I noticed one of my wiper blades was falling apart, and this time of the year you can't count on the weather for anything but trouble. There was a clock in the window of Sam's station. Five fifteen, I noticed when I drove in."

Marshall continued to study the subject before him; a man's body, a child's face but what kind of mind? He glanced at Dr. Huntziger. The doctor seemed fascinated, too. Sgt. Lansing at the door wore only an expression of weariness.

"Doesn't your company take care of truck repairs?" Marshall suggested.

Waters was playing with his gloves again. His mouth twisted into a bitter smile.

"If a guy yells long enough. My supervisor, Christ, you'd think he had to pay for everything out of his pay! It's like pulling teeth to get anything out of him. I don't risk my neck in bad weather for a few lousy bucks!"

Timothy Waters' eyes strayed back to the bed again. The fact that he was being questioned about a murder didn't seem to interest him nearly so much as the reason he was being questioned.

"You really can't remember what happened yesterday?" he asked.

Anna stirred against the pillow. "No," she said. "I can't."

"Was Dr. Whitehall alone when you reached the house, Mr. Waters?" Marshall asked.

The interruption came as an annoyance. Waters turned toward him with a scowling face.

"The old lady? Sure, she was alone. She was sitting there behind her desk like a queen on her throne." And then the scowl slowly faded and a kind of puzzlement came into his eyes. He glanced at Anna Bardossy and then back at Marshall. "Say," he added, "if the nurse don't remember killing the old lady, how do you know she did it?"

"If she didn't, who did?" Marshall challenged.

Waters didn't seem to like the question. He shifted uneasily on the chair.

"I don't know," he said. "How should I know. Anybody, I guess. Sure, anybody could have walked into that house. It was wide open every time I been there. I walked in myself once. I rang the bell and nobody came so I just walked in. I walked down the hall to where the door was open, and there was the old lady sitting behind her desk as big as you please. She looks up. 'Oh, it's you,' she said. But it could have been anybody, don't you see? Just anybody."

The idea wasn't original; it had been cropping up again and again since dawn. Marshall glanced at the doctor again, but he was still too fascinated by the witness in the chair to have his attention distracted.

"That's a thought," Marshall admitted, "but why would just anybody kill Dr. Whitehall?"

This question didn't bother Waters at all.

"Why does anybody kill anybody?" he asked. "It happens all the time. You know what I figure? I figure, if ever we stop killing each other why we'll just all starve, or something. That's how people live—off each other."

"A philosopher," Dr. Huntziger remarked. "Exciting, these bright, fresh ideas of youth."

Waters looked up at the doctor. He seemed vaguely aware that something he'd said had met with disapproval, and was puzzled by it. But Marshall wasn't interested in his philosophy; only in his facts.

"During the time you were in the house, Mr. Waters," he said, "did anyone else come to see Dr. Whitehall?"

Waters' attention turned slowly from the doctor to his questioner.

"Anyone else?"

Ideas required time to travel through Timothy Waters' mind. A little directing might help.

"Please think carefully, Mr. Waters," Marshall said, "this is important. You're the fourth person to sit in that chair today. One by one, we've brought in each individual known to have been in the Whitehall house at any time yesterday. We know that the nurse, Miss Bardossy, left the house at ten o'clock in the morning—the first caller told us that. We know that at noon she hadn't returned—the second caller supplied that information. We know that a few minutes after two she drove past the house but didn't stop—a third caller saw her then. Now we've come to five o'clock—"

Timothy Waters seemed to absorb every word. His fingers fumbled at the frayed cuff on his left wrist, searching for his watch.

"I've got to get my truck back to the garage," he began. "My supervisor raises hell if I keep it out—"

"Yesterday," Marshall said quickly. "Five o'clock yesterday. At that time you were in the house with Dr. Whitehall. If you were there ten minutes, that bring us up to five-ten. The clock that crushed Dr. Whitehall's skull stopped at five twenty-two."

The missing time had dwindled to twelve minutes. Marshall's gaze strayed to Anna Bardossy on the bed. She seemed barely to breathe. He returned to Waters.

"To our knowledge, Mr. Waters, you're the last person to enter that house before Dr. Whitehall was killed."

To all appearances, Timothy Waters was hypnotized. He sat with his hands dangling between his knees, his face uplifted and his eyes riveted on Marshall's. His protest was slow but vehement.

"But that ain't so! The nurse—she did it! The papers all say—"

Moments ago he'd been unsure and offered a possible alternative; but now his concern for Anna Bardossy was superseded by concern for himself. Timothy Waters was a human being, nothing more. He raised one big hand and ran it over the stubble-field of hair. His eyes were busy and troubled. He seemed to be groping for something half remembered or hoped for.

"Did anyone else come?" he said in a low voice.

"What's that, Mr. Waters?"

"What you asked—did anyone else come to the house? That's a funny thing, now." The big hand dropped back between his knees. Some thought was kindling in his troubled eyes. "Yeah, that's a funny thing—your asking. You see, I forgot."

"What did you forget?"

"Well, I was down in the basement getting ready to fix the pilot, see. And I looked around and couldn't find my flashlight. So I went upstairs again, thinking I'd left it in the truck out front. But when I started through the kitchen, I seen the flashlight on the sink—you know, the sink top." It was a dark and perilous journey for a thought to find its way through Waters' mind. A slow journey. He frowned all the way. "So I picked up the flashlight," he added, "and started back to the basement when the doorbell rang. The old lady went to the door. I didn't see her, understand. I heard her. I heard the whole thing. I didn't see anybody."

"What did you hear?"

"Not very much—I guess that's why I forgot. It didn't seem important. But now you ask me, so I remember. When the old lady opened the door, she said something. She said—'Oh, it's you. I've been expecting you all day.'"

The dark journey was over. Waters looked up with relief and hesitant expectancy on his face, as if he were a schoolboy who had completed a recitation and wasn't sure how it would be received. He needn't worry. Marshall's attention was all for Anna Bardossy now. She had listened too. She was frowning, and her eyes were troubled.

"Do those words mean anything to you, Miss Bardossy?" he asked.

"The words—no," she answered, and the trouble wouldn't leave her eyes. "But, Mr. Marshall, the doorbell ... Don't you see? It couldn't have been me at the door. I never used the bell. If the door wasn't unlocked, I had a key!"

CHAPTER ELEVEN

A key. All day Marshall had been looking for a key to open the locked door of Anna Bardossy's memory—but not this key. This key opened nothing.

And now the day was almost gone. A white-uniformed nurse with a dinner tray took no heed of police investigations. A hospital must run on schedule, and not even Dr. Huntziger had the power to stop it. They left the room—Anna still frowning over the puzzle she'd uncovered—and went back to the doctor's office.

"That chow sure looked good," Waters remarked. "I don't suppose you got a mess hall anywhere."

Marshall glanced at the doctor, an unspoken signal in his eyes.

"There's a dining room for the staff," Huntziger said, "but I see no reason why we shouldn't have a little room service for this young man. Sergeant—" Lansing had come into the office with them. He waited near the door—"Why don't you take Mr. Waters out to Miss Kelly in the hall and see what can be done? He's gone to a lot of trouble to come down here and tell his story. The least we can do is give him a meal."

When Lansing and Waters were gone the doctor turned back to Marshall.

"You didn't want him to leave the building, did you?"

"Not after all the trouble we had getting him here," Marshall said. "You never know. If we give him enough time, something else may filter through that amazing mind of his."

"It is amazing, isn't it?"

Dr. Huntziger walked around behind his desk and lifted the coffee pot with a testing hand. It was empty again. He sighed and disconnected the plug. Then he sat down in his chair and leaned back, stretching his locked hands above his head.

"How did you like that little speech of his about people living off one another?" The hands slid down behind Huntziger's head. "The terrible thing about that kind of crude logic is that it's basically true," he added. "Today more than ever before."

"It's not the truth of his logic that concerns me," Marshall said. "It's the truth of his story."

Huntziger's eyes fastened on him—his face owlish and quizzical.

"Don't tell me you missed it, Doctor," Marshall said. "A slight touch of delusions of grandeur. Two years in Korea." He picked up a paperweight from the top of the desk. It was an old-fashioned glass ball with an artificial snow storm that descended on a miniature village when he turned it over in his hand. "The Korean War ended in 1953. I don't believe they had a Boy Scout division. Timothy Waters probably sees every war film made and plays the suffering hero in each one. Still, I doubt if he has the imagination to dream up his own dialogue. 'Oh, it's you. I've been expecting you all day.'"

Marshall scowled at the snowstorm and then placed the glass ball back on the desk. Huntziger read the scowl perfectly.

"The fifth caller," he said.

"I wonder. Was there actually a *fifth* caller, or did someone—someone who didn't have a key—come back?"

The thought was inescapable. Dr. Whitehall had been expecting someone—but who and for what purpose? The day began to unreel again in Marshall's mind, a day that was still a mystery in spite of all that had been told of it. Morning—a little past nine. Dr. Whitehall is annoyed because the pilot light in the furnace had gone out again. Anna Bardossy calls for a service man. This was the beginning of the day. And then a quarrel and a threat, overheard by a nervous listener in the hall. The nurse went out in anger, but she would come back—with a key. And then Naomi Griswold went in to see Dr. Whitehall.

"Naomi Griswold," Marshall said. "She would come back—it was Thursday."

Dr. Huntziger wasn't a mind reader, but he seemed aware of Marshall's pattern of thinking.

"In the evening," he reminded, "to drive Dr. Whitehall to the meeting."

"She would have had to do that in any event; it was expected of her. Even if she were the fifth caller, she would be forced to return at that time. Is she capable of it?"

"Killing Dr. Whitehall?"

"Returning to the house after she'd killed her."

Huntziger frowned over the suggestion. "Apparently you're assuming a pathological attachment between the women," he said. "Or, to be more exact, on the part of Mrs. Griswold. In the event the attachment was broken—"

"By Dr. Whitehall's retirement," Marshall suggested.

"By Dr. Whitehall's retirement, or by any other reason, she might react with violence."

"You said yourself that Griswold was a sick woman."

Huntziger's smile was slow and wry. "So I did," he said. "You tell me about a mutilated body, and I'll tell you, with scientific certainty, that it was put in that condition by a sick person. Beyond that, I refuse to commit myself. If I were with the district attorney's office, or the Police Department, and my job was investigating a murder, I think I'd stick to concrete reasoning rather than abstract conjecture. The question isn't whether Mrs. Griswold, or anyone else, was psychologically capable of murder; but whether she had the motive and opportunity."

"The motive we've just discussed," Marshall reflected. "The opportunity—that's the interesting thing about this case, Doctor. We have an open field. Do you realize that we've had the three people closest to Dr. Whitehall in this hospital today—each of whom spent some time yesterday in a house where murder was committed—and none of whom has volunteered an alibi, in spite of the fact that the exact time of the murder has been fixed by a smashed clock."

"Apparently none of them has anything to fear," Huntziger said.

"Of course not, Doctor, and why? Because Anna Bardossy went down to the beach last night and slashed her wrists. But what if she hadn't? Suppose she had come home some time after five twenty-two and found Dr. Whitehall's body in the study—would there have been anything for another murderer to fear then? She was the adversary in the house. She was the one who quarreled with Dr. Whitehall—three ready witnesses have told us that. Witnesses who knew Thursday was her day off, and who knew the front door was kept open ..."

Marshall paused, his mind caught on the edge of a random thought. He wanted to pursue it further, but Dr. Huntziger was listening and an audience was hard to come by.

"... and who knew she would be a natural suspect. If just one of them had said, 'I was at the market at five twenty-two. I talked to the butcher and the check-out man,' or, 'I was at Joe Smith's bar. Ask Joe.' But nobody is afraid. Is that a sign of innocence or of guilt?"

Marshall picked up the paperweight again, turned it over, righted it, and watched the snow fall. Paperweights were simple. There was no doubt about which way snow fell.

"Motive and opportunity," Huntziger reminded.

"Yes, motive and opportunity. So we come to Harold Elrod, the devoted legal and financial adviser. Mr. Elrod is sensitive about his books. What does that prove? Has he been dipping into the till and feared the accounting

Dr. Whitehall unexpectedly demanded, or is his sensitivity the natural reaction of an innately honest man outraged at a hint of suspicion against his character?"

Outrage seemed a strong word to use in connection with Harold Elrod, but feelings could be no less strong for being submerged. And then he thought of another kind of outrage. Dr. Whitehall had grown old and testy—possibly imperious, and she hated men. Others were paying for the sins of Claude Whitehall. Elrod's position wasn't enviable.

But he was straying from fact.

"If it was Elrod who returned to the house and rang the bell ..." Marshall paused again, that bothersome thought nagging at his mind ... "He had the advantage of knowing it was the nurse's day off and—unless she returned early—it would be Mrs. Griswold, her most vociferous critic, who would find the body when she made her weekly call."

"But he didn't know about the repair man," Huntziger said.

"No—only that Dr. Whitehall was expecting another caller. But, for that matter, it's not likely that either Naomi Griswold or Byron Davies knew of the repair man. Which brings us around to Byron's motive, the strongest motive of all."

"The will," Huntziger said.

"Exactly. Davies could be lying. Perhaps he did learn of the second will—he seems to have been rather adept at obtaining information. He'd gone to great lengths to discredit the nurse and wean his way back into his sister's confidence. He probably needed money. Men such as Byron Davies always do, and it seldom occurs to them to work for it.

"He went to see his sister at a little past two. He saw the nurse drive past the house. It could have reminded him of her day off. He knew she was seeing the man again and probably wouldn't be home until late." Marshall spoke slowly. He was telling this story to himself. Huntziger was just a follower now. "He left his sister within twenty minutes. After his visit, she walked to her bank and withdrew one thousand dollars."

"Which is still unaccounted for," Huntziger reminded.

"Which is still unaccounted for." Marshall put down the paperweight again. So many things were still unaccounted for: one thousand dollars in cash, a doorbell that rang, a pair of tickets to Las Vegas, twelve lost minutes of a day.... It was time to start balancing the books.

He went to the door, opened it and peered out. Timothy Waters was sitting alone in the waiting room happily devouring the food on a hospital tray. In the hall, Sgt. Lansing was happily devouring the conversation from the lips of Miss Kelly.

"Lansing—"

Wearily, the sergeant responded and came into the office.

"I want your men to make a check on Byron Davies," Marshall ordered. "Find out what he did after he left his sister yesterday afternoon. He must have gone somewhere, seen someone, spent money. You said that he came in early this morning reeking of whiskey. I doubt if he drank alone."

"Not while he was wearing a plaid cummerbund," Lansing agreed. "May I use your phone, Doctor?"

While Lansing made his call, there was more time to think. Thinking aloud was more productive.

"Assuming that Byron Davies asked his sister for money, in spite of his denial, why did he leave without it? Why didn't he take her to the bank?"

"Are you sure he didn't?" Huntziger asked.

"That's the devil of it—I'm not sure of anything. The houses in that area are old—they sit deep on wide lots, secluded from one another by foliage; not like the newer areas where everybody knows what everybody else is doing. What's more, the neighbors were accustomed to seeing people go in and out of the Whitehall house. They paid no attention. But we do know that Dr. Whitehall went to the bank at three and died at five twenty-two. It doesn't seem logical that Davies was there all that time."

"But was the one thousand dollars there all that time?" Dr. Huntziger asked.

If Huntziger ever retired from his profession, Marshall wanted him in the district attorney's office. He hadn't forgotten the missing money from the moment he'd heard of it. His question forced Marshall's mind in another direction.

"That brings up still another possible motive. This man in Anna Bardossy's life, why hasn't he come forward? Why is he so difficult to locate? There are two possible answers, either one of which could implicate him in Dr. Whitehall's death. She disapproved of him, even arranged her lecture tour, if we're to believe our witnesses, in an attempt to break up his affair with her nurse. How do you suppose he felt about that, Doctor?"

"Like murdering the old lady," Huntziger answered.

"Yes, that's a possibility I've considered, particularly in view of Miss Bardossy's stubborn refusal to give us any information about him. Even more particularly in view of the trousseau lingerie."

"Trousseau?"

Doctor Huntziger's face brightened expectantly, and Marshall responded by relating the results of his chat with the saleslady at Bannock's Westwood and with the ticket clerk at an airlines office in Beverly Hills. Through it all, the doctor listened attentively; but at the conclusion his face was no longer bright. The addition of Naomi Griswold's remembered threat made it positively grim.

"Marriage," he reflected. "Yes, that would mean a showdown."

"For everyone," Marshall added. "Remember that Anna Bardossy was essential for the continuance of Dr. Whitehall's practice. I'm sure the doctor knew this as well as Miss Bardossy. But what would she do about it? She could threaten deportation proceedings on the grounds of immoral conduct, or she might ..."

He paused, waiting for the idea to come clear in his mind. Huntziger's eyes urged him on.

"She might," he repeated, "have preferred to do business with Paul Kramar."

"The one thousand dollars," Huntziger said. "Do you think she could have bought him off for that? After all, if he wanted to marry the woman—"

"It would have been only car fare, money to get lost with," Marshall said. "The real price would have been Anna's freedom to remain in this country. Difficult as it was for her in the Whitehall household, it was better than returning to Hungary. As I said, it's only a possibility, and conjecture, as you pointed out, Doctor, isn't evidence."

Now Lansing was through with the telephone, Marshall turned to him. "When Anna Bardossy was found on the beach, her purse was beside her—is that right?"

"According to the report of the Santa Monica police—yes," Lansing replied.

"And this man who found her—"

"Oscar Dunlap?"

"Oscar Dunlap—is he an honest man?"

"I don't know how honest he is," Lansing said, "but I've heard how scared he was. I'd be willing to make a small bet he didn't think to rifle her purse—if that's what you mean."

"Then the nurse never had the money," Marshall said. "The lingerie and the airline tickets were purchased before it was withdrawn from the bank. Unless—" So many things to be accounted for; they continued to accumulate. He turned to Lansing again. "Sergeant, you must have handled hundreds of accident cases. Would you say that it's customary for a woman to carry a razor blade in her purse?"

Lansing seemed puzzled.

"What do you mean?" he asked.

"One razor blade," Marshall said. "Not a package she might have picked up at a drugstore on her way to the beach. They aren't sold singly."

Lansing scowled at his own feet.

"A woman's purse is apt to contain anything," he said, "and they use razor blades—I know that much. My wife uses them to sharpen pencils."

"But does she carry them in her purse?"

"I wouldn't dare to look. See here, Mr. Marshall—" Lansing's face came up, his tired eyes dark with disapproval—"I know you're a thorough man. I know you have a mechanical brain, an iron constitution, and an indomitable will. I told you this morning that we had enough evidence to arrest the nurse, and we have more now than we did then. But you don't want to arrest her. I don't know why not—maybe she reminds you of some little fräulein you knew overseas. But if you're going to go on splitting hairs, don't try to split them with a razor blade."

Lansing was right. No amount of talking could take them very far from the fact that Anna Bardossy still held the key to an answer locked in silence. Some of that answer he knew she was deliberately withholding; but how much? It might take hours to check on Davies—longer than that to locate Paul Kramar—but just a few steps down the hall they were exactly twelve minutes from the truth.

Sometimes a door had to be broken down.

"Dr. Huntziger," Marshall asked abruptly, "how strong is your patient?"

"Strong?" Huntziger repeated. "What's on your mind?"

"She still holds the key—and I don't mean the key to the front door. All day long I've watched her coming closer to the thing she doesn't want to remember. I think I know what part of it is—enough of it to force the rest, with your permission. How strong is she?"

Huntziger watched him with interested eyes. "Physically—strong enough to walk out of here, if she were free."

"And if I tell you that she just might do that—what do you say then?"

"What's your plan?"

It was the last plan. Marshall glanced at the windows—dark now. Twenty-four hours since someone had faced Dr. Whitehall across her study desk, picked up the heavy clock, and given vent to fury.

"Five callers came to Dr. Whitehall's house yesterday," he said. "Four of them have come to Anna Bardossy's room today. Now I want to bring the house—" Sgt. Lansing groaned—"by proxy," Marshall added. "I was in that house last night. It wasn't a pleasant sight. The crime lab must have taken some choice photos."

"Little beauties," Lansing said.

"I want blowups of those photos—the most graphic shots. Close-ups of the body, panoramic views of the havoc in the study—"

"It may not work," Huntziger warned. "You may force her mind in the opposite direction."

"That's a chance we'll have to take."

Lansing had his orders. The doctor made no attempt to countermand them. He started toward the door. And then Marshall had another idea— a remembrance of something almost forgotten that came like sunlight breaking through a fog.

"Lansing," he called, "wait. There's one more photo we'll need."

Anna Bardossy was interested but quiet. She sat up against the pillows and watched Sgt. Lansing adjust the stand at the foot of her bed. She watched Dr. Huntziger lower the blind at a window that was now completely black, and then watched Douglas Marshall focus the lamp so its beam would fall on the stand. He talked as he worked.

"You've had a rough day, Miss Bardossy," he said, "but I think we'll be able to leave you alone soon. I hope you're not too tired."

"I'm all right," she said quietly.

"You still don't remember returning to Dr. Whitehall's house yesterday, I suppose."

"No, I'm sorry, but I don't."

"Or buying the lingerie at Bannock's."

"No."

"Or driving past the house a little after two?"

She didn't answer immediately. He looked down at her. She was frowning studiously. She raised her head and met his eyes.

"Sometimes I almost remember," she said, "almost—"

Marshall smiled at her. "Don't worry about it," he said. "I think we can help you."

The lamp was adjusted now. Lansing, finished with the stand, turned off the wall switch. The white beam of the lamp fell across the bed, making a pale outline of Anna Bardossy's profile.

"I stopped by Bannock's this afternoon," Marshall added casually. "I talked to the saleslady in the intimate apparel—"

"Shame on you," Lansing said.

"—department," Marshall added. "She remembers the sale."

"I bought the lingerie, then?" Anna asked.

"You bought the lingerie. The saleslady says you seemed very happy, Sergeant—let's have the first photo."

As a warm-up, Lansing had chosen a view of the study, book-strewn and desecrated, with the body—the face half turned toward the camera—crumpled on the floor. The enlargement made the details vivid. There was the barely audible sound of a smothered gasp from the woman on the bed.

"I forgot to tell you," Marshall added, "that we found a pair of airline tickets in your purse, Miss Bardossy. Two for a flight to Las Vegas last night. I stopped by the ticket office where they were purchased, and the ticket seller remembered you very well. She was sorry that you missed the flight. She said you seemed so happy about it. Sergeant—"

On the second photo, the camera had moved in for a close-up of the body.

Now the details were more vivid and more horrible. Marshall saw the profile turn away, but horror had its fascination. The profile turned back, and she began to lean forward.

"Why were you going to Las Vegas, Miss Bardossy?" he asked.

She didn't answer. She continued to stare at the picture on the stand.

"Why were you so happy?"

He knew that she heard him. He could see her hands clenching at the sheet. Her back was like a ramrod.

"All right, Lansing."

The third enlargement Lansing pushed into the arc of light was a variation of the second—including a view of the bloodstained clock. The reaction was a continuation of past performance; but now she leaned forward until her shoulders cast a shadow on the stand.

"Don't you remember why you were so happy, Miss Bardossy?"

He didn't expect an explanation. All of her attention was focused on the stand at the foot of the bed.

"Did it concern Paul? Wasn't one of the tickets for him?"

The shadow trembled slightly, but that was all. He signaled Lansing to change the picture once more.

When the fourth photo slid into view the response was electric. The surprise and shock could be felt as well as seen; for this view wasn't of the study at all. It was even less attractive. The hurried enlargement had somewhat blurred the details of an old newsreel clip; but it was still clear enough to show the grotesque, dead face of a Communist soldier dangling from a lamppost somewhere in Budapest.

"No!" Anna cried. "No! What are you trying to do?"

Only Dr. Huntziger's hands on her shoulders restrained her to the bed. Her face, glaring up at Marshall, was stark white under the arc of the lamp.

"Who is Lazio?" he demanded.

"I don't know!"

"You're lying, Miss Bardossy. Why should you lie about a dead man? What can he do to you now?"

"I don't know what you mean!"

"I mean the man in that picture. You've seen the picture before, haven't you? Harold Elrod says you have, and so does Byron Davies. You cried the name 'Lazio' and ran from the room. Why, Miss Bardossy?"

She still glared up at him, breathing heavily, but she didn't answer.

"And why did you tell Dr. Whitehall this morning that you weren't afraid anymore? Why did you tell Mrs. Griswold that she wouldn't have to put up with you much longer? Why did you buy the expensive lingerie and the tickets to Las Vegas?"

He fed the questions with just enough time between for digestion. She listened and then something—some wide and terrible awakening—began to happen in her eyes.

"Miss Bardossy?"

Her shoulders pulled loose from the doctor's grasp. She sat upright staring into space.

"Miss Bardossy—"

There was a faint catch of fear in Marshall's voice. Lansing found the wall switch again and the room flooded with light. But the woman didn't seem to notice.

"I warned you this might happen," Huntziger said.

"But she remembers! I know she remembers! Miss Bardossy ..."

It was useless. She had withdrawn from them. She was mute, deaf and blind to everything but that which was happening in her eyes.

"You'll have to leave," Huntziger said.

"But I want to ask—"

"It won't do you any good! You'll have to leave!"

An order was an order. There was nothing to do but let the golden moment pass and make an anticlimactic exit into the hall.

Somewhere a telephone was ringing. Miss Kelly had left her desk to go into Anna Bardossy's room, and the hall was as empty as Marshall's last hope. Sgt. Lansing watched him with tired, reproachful eyes. They'd brought the house to Anna Bardossy, but there was still no confession.

"How much longer—" Lansing began.

The telephone had stopped ringing. The first Marshall realized that was when Timothy Waters slouched out of Huntziger's office with a sleepy expression on his face and asked, "Which one of you wants to talk to somebody at some kind of a school?"

CHAPTER TWELVE

It was the University; they had located Paul Kramar. His name was on the roster of an extension course in anthropology—one which also included the name of Anna Bardossy. Douglas Marshall jotted down the address and telephone number. As soon as the girl at the administration office was off the line, he dialed the number. There was no answer. That still left the address. With the room down the hall temporarily closed off from further communication, the time was right for action. He gave Lansing a quick explanation of the situation and his intentions.

"I'd better go along," Lansing said. "You don't know what you may be getting into. From the time the papers hit the newsstands this morning, the whole city's known the nurse was missing. You might think her boy friend would at least make an inquiry."

The sergeant was right. There was something strange about Paul Kramar. Two airline tickets in Anna Bardossy's purse meant that two passengers had missed the flight to Las Vegas; but only one had been found on the beach with slashed wrists. The most vital part of the nurse's forgotten day had to be tied in with this man; and if the truth was difficult to get from her, it might not be easy to get from him.

They left Timothy Waters deep in a chair in the waiting room—still sleepy-eyed and sullen—and headed back toward Westwood through a fog that had developed into a full-fledged drizzle. The address was in a neighborhood not far below the campus—one of the aging stucco apartment buildings that stood like faded but gracious reminders of something that had been substantial before the influx of barracks-style modern so popular with profit-minded builders. There was a small foyer with the manager's apartment at one side and on the other a wrought-iron railed staircase running up to the first landing. They took to the stairs. The first door had the right name plate. Marshall rang the bell twice before he began to knock.

"Kramar! Paul Kramar! Are you in there?"

He'd waited too long and traveled too far to run into another blind alley. He knocked again.

"Kramar! Paul Kramar!"

"Here, let me do this," Lansing said. "If anything's wrong you're likely to get hurt."

His hand was sliding toward the holster somewhere under the raincoat when a nervous cough behind them brought both men about sharply. A slight, gray-haired man was ascending the stairs. He wore a coat sweater pulled tightly about his stooped shoulders, suspender-hung trousers, house slippers, and an expression of troubled wonder. At the top of the stairs he coughed again and then paused long enough to swipe at his nose with a crumpled handkerchief.

"Damp weather," he explained. "Feels like I got the fog trapped right in here."

He thumped on his concave chest and promptly coughed again. When the demonstration was over, he peered at them with inquiring eyes.

"You gentlemen want to see Mr. Kramar?" he asked.

"Is he in?" Marshall asked.

"No—not now. He's gone."

Marshall glanced at Lansing. The gun could stay in the holster now. But the old man wasn't through answering questions.

"When did he go?" Marshall asked.

The old man swiped at his nose with the handkerchief again. His narrow face was deep-lined and it looked slightly gray in the none too bright light of the hall.

"Yesterday," he said. "About this time yesterday. No, earlier. Wasn't much past four when the lady came for him."

"Lady?" Marshall repeated. "Do you know who she was? Could you describe her?"

He was too anxious. The old man seemed confused as to how to answer. He seemed actually embarrassed, and then he said, "I suppose you might say she was Mr. Kramar's friend. A real good friend. She took care of him when he was sick."

"When was that?"

The old man frowned. "A few weeks ago—months, maybe. I'm not real sure of the time. I've got eight units here to look after, and I'm not as well as I should be myself. But Mr. Kramar was bad sick. I don't think he'd have pulled through if the lady hadn't come and stayed with him day and night."

A few weeks ago—months, maybe. At the time Dr. Whitehall changed her will? Shortly after a lecture tour that failed its purpose? Some of the pieces were dropping into place. If the old man talked long enough he might at least have the background of a missing day.

"Was that the first time the lady had come here?" Marshall asked.

"The first time?" The old man shook his head. "Oh no, she and Mr. Kramar were friends a long time—two, three years, maybe. I was thinking about that just today. Running a place like mine, you get all kinds of people. I don't let just anything go on; but the very first time she came here I knew she was a lady. And Mr. Kramar, he was a gentleman, too. What kind of world is it, I was thinking today, when a real lady and a real gentleman have to live like that, and people who can hardly read or write, and don't care, live like kings and queens? I tell you, mister, something's wrong with this world. Something's real wrong."

He was a sad old man. His face, when he stopped talking, had the kind of loneliness in it that can look forward to only one home. He stood with the faded handkerchief in his hand, and his eyes cast down at the worn carpet.

"A little past four," he mused aloud, "yes—that was the time. I was watering the plants outside the door when she came up the walk. 'Good afternoon, Mr. Granger,' she said. 'Isn't it a beautiful afternoon?' I hadn't noticed until she said so. The beauty was in her voice, I think."

"She was happy," Marshall suggested.

The old man's eyes came up to meet his own. "Yes happy," he said. "Happier than I'd ever seen her. I came inside and watched her go up the stairs—almost running. She knocked on the door and called out his name, and then she got the key out of her purse." His eyes faltered again. "I knew she had the key," he admitted. "The way the world is, why shouldn't she?"

"That's all right," Marshall said. "What happened after she took the key out of her purse?"

"She went inside. It was a minute, less maybe, before she screamed."

"Screamed?" Lansing echoed.

The old man didn't seem to hear the interruption. "I ran up the stairs as fast as I could," he continued. "I don't get around so fast anymore. The door was open and she was standing over Mr. Kramar. He was lying on the floor. There was a suitcase beside him—all packed. I guess he must have been going away somewhere."

"But what happened?" Marshall persisted. "What was wrong?"

The old man stared at him with tired eyes.

"Same thing as before," he said, "—heart attack. This time it killed him. If you gentlemen want to see Mr. Kramar, you'll have to go to the undertaker."

Why does a lovely thing who has survived hell to attain freedom decide death is a better way? A riddle posed by Dr. Huntziger at dawn was answered by an old man in a coat sweater twenty-four hours later. Paul Kramar was dead. The answer was as simple as true answers usually were. Paul Kramar couldn't come to Anna's assistance—he was dead. Paul Kramar couldn't make the flight to Las Vegas—he was dead. And Paul Kramar was the man Anna loved. A chill seemed to come over the hall—damp as the night fog creeping over a beach where a woman had gone to die.

"I suppose it was the excitement that killed him," Marshall mused aloud. "The happiest day of his life—"

This was no place to explain to himself what Marshall felt had to be true. There was still work to do. Anna Bardossy had come to Kramar's apartment at four, but she hadn't been found on the beach until after nine-thirty. That left five and a half hours to account for—hours which included a murder that had taken place in a house not half an hour's drive away.

"When was Kramar's body removed from the apartment?" Marshall demanded.

The old man frowned. "I wasn't watching the time," he said, "not with so much to do. The lady was upset and crying. I had to call the police myself."

"The police—"

Marshall turned to Lansing, and the sergeant anticipated his request.

"Is there a phone inside?" he asked.

The old man fumbled through his pockets for a passkey and opened the door. It was a small apartment—a studio bedroom, a small kitchen and a bath. The packed suitcase—open—still stood at the foot of the sleeping couch. While Lansing made the call, Marshall stooped down and examined the contents. A zippered shaving bag caught his eye. The zipper was open, as if Kramar might have been in the act of filling it when he died, and some of its contents were spilled across the clothing.

"He was laying about here," the old man said. "Been dead about half an hour the fireman said."

"Fireman?" Marshall queried. "Was the Pulmotor squad here?"

"Everybody was here—firemen, policemen, the coroner, and the lady sitting there on the bed with her face as gray as Mr. Kramar's. Sometimes they go all gray when they die of a heart attack, you know. All gray."

Granger's graphic description was brought to a halt when Lansing returned from the telephone. There was irony in his story. All day long they had been prying away at Anna Bardossy's secret, and all day long Paul Kramar had been lying in a mortuary across the street from the Hollywood Cemetery.

"The coroner records the death officially at four-forty—that was when they gave up with the Pulmotor. The ambulance was already here. They took him straight to the mortuary."

"What about Miss Bardossy?" Marshall asked. "Did she go along?"

Lansing shook his head. "I don't know. All I got was the official report—no mention of a woman at all."

"She walked out," Granger said.

"What do you mean?"

"Just what I said. I saw her. Nobody else did, but I saw her. She waited until the coroner said Mr. Kramar was dead. She told one of the police officers where to take the body, and then she stooped down beside him, right about where you're kneeling, mister, and after a few seconds she just got up and walked out. Nobody noticed her but me, and I didn't say anything. After all, she was a lady."

"Did she take anything out of the suitcase?" Marshall asked.

The old man looked puzzled.

"The suitcase? I don't know. Is something missing?"

"Not anymore."

Marshall stood up and turned to Lansing. He held out his hand to show what he'd found beside the shaving kit. Not a thousand dollars. Nothing to indicate Paul Kramar hadn't meant to make his flight to Las Vegas. Only a razor blade—single edged.

"What do you think, Sergeant," he asked, "will it split a hair?"

They took the long way back to the hospital, going first to the mortuary. A quiet young man in a dark suit showed them into the room where Paul Kramar's body awaited final rites. It was the slender body of a man about forty years old, dark hair graying at the temples, sensitive features—not handsome, but with a certain fineness in his face. This was the man Anna Bardossy loved. Marshall looked at the face a long time, trying to give it life in his mind. Kramar. The name took on meaning. He raised one arm and pulled back the coat and shirt sleeve. The number was there—that indelible humiliation that would follow its bearer to the grave. There was a common bond, then. It might have reached into the past, or it might have begun one night in an extension course classroom.

"We've been wondering what arrangements to make," the quiet young man in the dark suit remarked. "The lady said she would come back, but she hasn't."

"The lady?" Marshall asked.

"Mr. Kramar's ..." The young man hesitated. "Well, actually I don't know what the relationship was," he said. "His wife, I thought, or sister. She was terribly upset—almost in a dazed condition. She didn't even leave her name."

"Small, dark, attractive—"

"Why, yes. That sounds like her."

"How long was she here?"

"I really couldn't say. Only a few minutes, I believe. We'd barely started to discuss the arrangements when she broke down."

"But the time—don't you remember the time at all?"

The urgency in Marshall's voice brought a frown to the young man's forehead, then he brightened.

"A little past five," he said. "Five minutes past, possibly. That's when she left. I remember hearing one of the employees mention that it was five o'-clock just after the body arrived. The lady came at the same time. If you know where she can be contacted—"

"I know," Marshall said. "Don't worry about it. I'll contact her myself. One more thing. Did the lady leave money to pay for a funeral?"

The young man in the dark suit shook his head.

"No," he said. "She had no cash with her. She offered to write a check as a deposit, but I assured her that we could take care of everything when she returned. She was in no condition to talk business. I do hope the shock wasn't too much for her."

"So do I," Marshall said.

The drive to the hospital was a grim journey. One answer had been found; but the big answer still eluded them like the shadowy figures moving through the fog ... sometimes almost clear, then suddenly lost again. Anna Bardossy hadn't gone directly to the beach from Kramar's apartment; she'd gone to the mortuary and left there in time, in bare time, to drive to the house on Hillmont on a mission of vengeance. As a murderess, she could have but one motive. The lingerie was for a trousseau, the plane tickets were for Las Vegas, and Anna Bardossy had been happy. There was only one conclusion to draw from these things; but no one takes orange blossoms to a funeral.

"If Dr. Whitehall stood in the nurse's way until it was too late ..." Lansing mused.

There was no need to finish the sentence. Grief could derange a mind already tortured by life. If someone beloved died, why shouldn't someone hated? Marshall's fingers clenched white on the steering wheel.

"I wanted to murder someone once," he said. "I drove all over Berlin for hours trying to talk myself out of it."

"I hope you succeeded," Lansing said.

"I succeeded," Marshall answered. "The question is—did Anna Bardossy?"

She would answer that question now. He remembered the expression in her eyes as she stared at the blowup of an old newsreel clip. He'd known then what it meant—some mental wall was crumbling, some light was breaking through. Huntziger would have to let him talk to her now. No one could stop him this close to the truth.

But he was wrong. The hospital corridor was empty. Miss Kelly was gone from her desk. The waiting room was empty—he glanced at it, scowling, on the way to Huntziger's office. Dr. Huntziger was working over some reports on his desk. He accepted the interruption with a good-natured smile, and then sobered as he studied Marshall's face.

"Where's Waters?" Marshall asked.

"Waters? Oh, you mean the charming repair man," Huntziger answered. "Isn't he outside?"

"No, he isn't. Neither is Miss Kelly."

"That much I know—her relief is late. What's the matter, Mr. Marshall? You look as if you'd come from a wake."

"I have. I've got to see Miss Bardossy again."

Dr. Huntziger hesitated. He glanced at Lansing and then back at Marshall. The faces of both men told him something was important.

"I've got to see her," Marshall insisted. "I know everything that happened yesterday except for a few vital minutes. I know why she tried to kill herself."

Huntziger got up from his chair.

"Not because of Dr. Whitehall's murder?"

"No. If she killed Dr. Whitehall, it was after she decided to kill herself."

Marshall took one hand out of his pocket. Between his fingers he held the razor blade—cold and blue under the light. Dr. Huntziger's eyes demanded an explanation, but he could get it better in a room down the hall.

"I'm not sure if she'll talk to you," the doctor remarked as they left the office together. "She wouldn't talk to me. I tried after you left the room, but she wouldn't speak a word. I don't think it's shock—"

Dr. Huntziger rapped his knuckles on the door in a preliminary gesture and then turned the knob. The door opened. One light had been left on at the side of the bed; it was enough to spill over the wrinkled sheets, the deserted pillow, and the hospital gown crumpled in a small heap on the floor. The closet door stood ajar—it was empty. Anna Bardossy was gone.

CHAPTER THIRTEEN

A driver waiting in his cab outside the hospital had some information. He'd seen a young, attractive woman wearing a black coat and no hat come out of the hospital about fifteen minutes earlier. She'd seemed anxious, but he thought it was because of the drizzle and the fact that she wore no hat. She'd driven off in the cab that had been parked just ahead of him.

"Did you hear her say where she wanted to go?" Marshall asked.

"With my windows closed? I've got to keep 'em closed in this weather. It gets cold in here, chum."

Fifteen minutes was a long time when it was the wrong fifteen minutes. Every street ran in two directions; but there was the smell of sea in the fog and the memory of a woman's eyes when an old newsreel enlargement forced upon her the horror she'd wanted to forget. Suddenly Marshall was afraid. He turned to Lansing.

"What part of the beach was she found on last night?" he demanded.

"Do you think she's gone back to try suicide again?"

"I don't know what to think, but I know what to do. Get out an all-points alert on this woman. Check the beach—"

"—and the mortuary," Lansing suggested. "She told them she'd call back."

"Yes, that's what she told them; but I don't think she meant it—not with the razor blade she'd picked up at Kramar's apartment in her purse." Marshall's face was grim. He glanced back at the hospital doors standing bright against the darkness, and then he added, "And nothing else. Doesn't that tell you anything, Sergeant?"

"What do you mean?" Lansing asked.

"A razor blade, two airline tickets, a few dollars, a house key and nothing else in her purse. It's beginning to tell me everything—that and the ringing doorbell. I almost forgot about that when we saw Kramar's body. All I could think of was how Anna Bardossy must have felt when she found him dead; but she told us how she felt by what she tried out on the beach last night. Don't you see? Huntziger was right this morning when he said the suicide attempt might have nothing to do with the murder—"

Marshall fell silent, listening to the echo of his own words.

"What have you found on Davies' activities?" he asked.

"Not much yet," Lansing admitted. "I sent a man to his address and he talked to the switchboard operator. Davies wasn't in his apartment all afternoon. He received a call a little past three—"

"A call?" Marshall interrupted. "From whom?"

"His sister. She left word for him to call back, but the operator went off duty before Davies returned and he never got the message."

Davies hadn't, but Marshall was getting it now. "Of course he didn't," he mused, "the doorbell rang." He left Lansing to puzzle over the statement and turned back to the driver. He might remember the number of the cab the woman had taken. He didn't, but he could check with the dispatcher. By this time the other driver must have radioed in.

"Do it," Marshall ordered. "We've got to find that woman!"

Anna Bardossy didn't go back to the beach, and she didn't return to the mortuary. There was only one place she had in mind to go, and she planned her escape carefully. It wasn't difficult. They were all so sure of themselves, these people who had forced her memory. They were so confident and naïve. They knew that she had almost died on the beach, and so they assumed it was safe to leave her room unguarded. Life was too easy for them. They didn't know what strength can be left when all strength should be gone. They hadn't lived in the camps and learned.

She knew that her clothes were in the closet. She'd seen a nurse take her purse and then return it later, leaving the door ajar. She awaited her chance and then dressed as quickly as possible. She was weak, but she could manage. She heard the nurse in the hall complain to Dr. Huntziger that her relief was late, and then she heard the doctor tell the nurse to go along home. It meant she would have to move quickly before the relief did come. She watched through a crack in the door until the hall was empty. The repair man, Waters, still sat in a chair in the waiting room; but he appeared to be asleep, and she had to take the risk. She made it to the elevator without mishap. It was an automatic, fortunately, and no other passengers were inside. The foyer was empty except for a receptionist who paid no attention to her as she passed. She was fully dressed, and with great effort she could walk almost as steadily as if she were a visitor instead of a patient.

Outside the doors, she met the drizzle. She raised up her face and let the wetness help revive her from the strain of her long walk—but she couldn't wait long. Douglas Marshall might return at any moment, and she had no time for his tricks now. She saw a cab at the curb and hurried forward. The driver saw her coming and opened the door. She made it as far as the back seat, and then sank back against the cushions with just enough strength to give the driver an address.

She'd made it. For a time, the urgency to get away had forced everything else from her mind; now it flooded back again. Paul was dead. Time had stopped for her more than twenty-four hours ago. She remembered the apartment and Paul on the floor; she remembered the razor blade— Her eyes sought her bandaged wrists, and then she concealed them under her sleeves so the cab driver wouldn't notice. His face had been in the rearview mirror, but only for an instant. Now it was blotted out by the glare of head-lights behind. He adjusted the mirror and then his face disappeared from view. It was raining harder now; he needed his eyes for driving.

The razor blade— But there was something more. She huddled in the darkness of the swaying back seat and tried to remember the rest. The mor-tuary—yes. First the landlord coming into the apartment; then the firemen and the police; finally, the ambulance and the mortuary. Five o'clock. She inadvertently felt her wrist for the watch that was no longer there. She re-membered looking at it at the mortuary—as if time could be of importance any more. Someone had asked—that was it. Someone in another room had asked the time just as she came into the mortician's office. She'd glanced at her wrist out of force of habit.

But she hadn't stayed long. The stimulus in the shock of finding Paul's body had been wearing off. She'd had to leave quickly, and then the dark-ness moved in.

The cab was on the boulevard now, moving swiftly through another kind of darkness; but a fragment of the old darkness remained. She could re-member as far as leaving the mortician's office—no further. One thing she couldn't remember, no matter how hard she tried....

The house on Hillmont was barely visible from the street. There was no fog this far inland; but the corner lamp cut only a small circle out of the streaming darkness, and deep foliage banked off the building. Anna had just enough money to pay the driver and send him on his way. Her keys—yes, they were still in the purse. Her hand found them as she hurried toward the house. She didn't really look up until she'd mounted the steps and stood un-der the shelter of the porch roof ... there she paused and searched her mind for that missing fragment of time. Had she done this last night? Stood here, hesitated sick with dread and then gone in to commit murder? Had she hated Dr. Whitehall that much? The fragment wasn't to be found outside the door. She reached forward, the key in her hand, and then drew back the hand in puzzlement. The door wasn't locked; it has swung inward at her touch.

It was a huge house—a monster of a house, and it had the smell of age in it that a day in the hospital made more pronounced. She hesitated at the threshold, listening for some sound of life within. She couldn't understand about the door, unless the police had left someone inside. But there was no light showing. The only light was what little reached this far from the street and the night reflection against a cloudy sky—enough to give form to the heavy newel post at the foot of the stairs, and enough to reflect faintly on the glass face of the tall clock in the hall. Farther down the hall, a pale shadow on the carpet marked out the entrance to the study. When she was quite certain there was no sound, she walked slowly toward that patch.

This was the way to a murder. There was no other approach; she would have had to come just this way. She would have had to stop at the doorway and turn in, hesitating, probably, as she hesitated now. The patch of pale light on the carpet came from the French windows on the near side of the wall. In that long rectangle of half-light her eyes automatically sought the place on the floor where she'd seen Dr. Whitehall's body in the photograph. It was gone, of course. Everything was gone, everything clean except for what might have been a stain near the corner of the desk. She walked forward until she bumped against the desk. Her eyes were becoming accustomed to the darkness now. She looked down at the place where the crystal clock had always stood. Was this the way it had been? Had she stood here, her hand reaching down for the clock and her eyes raising up to the austere, aging face of the woman who always sat in the high-backed swivel chair behind the desk? Her eyes followed her thoughts and then reason fled. The chair wasn't empty. It was turned toward the windows, and in it, eyes closed and hands clasped tightly on the arms, sat a woman with an austere, aging face.

When Anna cried out, the chair turned toward her. In that dim light seconds passed before mutual recognition.

"You—" Naomi Griswold said. "What are you doing here?"

She leaned forward in the chair, and a little more of the window light fell on her face. It was a strange face. It seemed almost to have a glow of its own.

"Why haven't you been arrested?" she demanded. "Did you make that foolish Mr. Marshall believe your wicked lies?"

It was the accusation that gave Anna a voice.

"I didn't lie to Mr. Marshall," she said.

Naomi's chin lifted. How like Dr. Whitehall she was!

"You lied," she declared.

"I did not lie! I never lied to anyone!"

"You lied to Dr. Whitehall—I heard you lie! You made her lose faith in herself and in her work. You're the one who broke her. I stood out in the hall yesterday morning and heard you. After you left I pleaded with her not to let you hurt her; but you already had. She told me then what she was going to do."

Now that the shock of finding Naomi in the study had been absorbed, Anna could begin to think. Naomi shouldn't have been there. The police must have left the house locked.

"How did you get in?" she asked.

Naomi's mouth twisted toward a crooked smile.

"I have a way," she said.

"How? How did you get in?"

"I always had a way before you came. I could come and go whenever I felt the need of help. Dr. Lillian was kind to me then. I was closer to her than you once. She used to talk to me after Mr. Griswold died. When I couldn't sleep at night and would have terrible dreams, she used to let me come to her at any time—any time at all. You see—" Naomi loosed one hand from the arm of the chair and took something from her pocket. It glistened in the pale light—"I had my own key the same as you. I didn't dare to use it after you came. You would have run me off. I know what you thought of me. You told Dr. Lillian I was crazy—"

"No, Mrs. Griswold, I never—"

"You told her I should go to another doctor—that's what she told me yesterday. She said that she'd decided the work was too much for one person, and, since you were leaving to go off with that man—"

"We were getting married, Mrs. Griswold."

The words meant nothing to the woman. She didn't seem to hear them.

"—she was going to retire. I begged her not to do it. I tried to make her understand how much she was needed. She wouldn't listen to me. Now she's dead."

Naomi's voice dropped. She leaned back in the chair, her face half hidden in shadow.

"Mrs. Griswold," Anna said, "why are you here?"

"I want to be near her," she answered.

"But Dr. Whitehall isn't here, Mrs. Griswold. You shouldn't be here either."

"Then who should be here—you? You who killed her?"

Naomi's face came out of the shadows again. Now it was twisted and bitter.

"You did kill her. You may be able to fool Mr. Marshall and that doctor; but you can't fool me. I'm not a silly man to be taken in by a pretty face. I know."

Anna steadied herself against the desk. The weakness was coming over her again; but she had to keep her feet.

"What do you know, Mrs. Griswold?" she asked.

"What you did here yesterday. I came back—don't you remember that either?"

"You came back?"

"It was late in the afternoon, but I couldn't stand it any longer. I had to talk to Dr. Lillian again. I had to try once more to make her see what you had done to her; but I was too late. I couldn't get in. The door was locked— even the bolt."

This was important. Anna forgot her weakness. At first, finding Naomi in the study, she'd had a twinge of hope; but if the door was locked—

"I knew something was wrong," Naomi declared. "It was only five o'clock and the door shouldn't have been locked. I rattled and pounded and rang the bell, but nobody answered. And then I saw a shadow on the glass. I was frightened and ran away; but afterward I knew whose shadow I'd seen. You were standing inside the door waiting for me to leave so you could come back in here and finish—"

"Mrs. Griswold!" Anna said sharply.

It wasn't so easy to stop her. She'd risen up out of the chair, a small woman towering in her anger.

"—murdering Dr. Lillian and desecrating the temple. You hated everything she did, didn't you? You had to destroy everything!"

"Mrs. Griswold, sit down!"

Anna Bardossy had suddenly become a nurse again. Her words were a command, and her command was obeyed. Naomi sank back into the chair, fear tightening her face.

"You don't know what you're saying," Anna told her. "You haven't even listened to your own words. I don't believe you came back to this house at all."

"But I did! I did!"

"And found the door locked?"

"Locked and bolted. I couldn't use my key."

"And you rang the bell?"

"Yes. Yes, I rang …"

Yes, somebody had rung the bell. Anna was beginning to understand. She grasped the edge of the desk with both hands, oblivious of the pain in her wrists.

"At *five o'clock?*"

Naomi Griswold sat upright in the chair, her face chalklike in the pale light. She stared at Anna Bardossy for several seconds, and then her lower lip began to tremble. She was thinking now.

"I checked my watch," she said. "I always check my watch before I come in. It was five minutes past five, and I keep it five minutes fast."

"And where was my car?" Anna demanded.

The question surprised Naomi.

"Your car?" she echoed.

"It wasn't parked in the driveway, was it?"

"I don't remember."

"*You* don't remember, Mrs. Griswold? Are you having my trouble now? I'm the one who doesn't remember. That's why I came back here. I thought if I returned to this house and tried to live it all over again ..." Anna was trembling. She'd come back to the house looking for truth, and it was truth that she'd found. "But I can't live it over because it never happened. At five o'clock I was in a mortuary on Santa Monica Boulevard. I can prove that. It wasn't my shadow you saw on the door, Mrs. Griswold. I didn't kill Dr. Whitehall!"

The truth. It was raining harder now. The rain lashed against the French doors and streamed down the glass panes; and for a few seconds the sound of the rain was all the sound in the room. Naomi looked shrunken in her chair. She turned it a little sideways, never taking her eyes from Anna's face.

"I don't believe you," she said. "I don't believe anything you say."

But it didn't matter what Naomi Griswold believed. Anna barely heard the words. Such a long time she'd searched and pried for the answer, and now it came—all of it, washing away the dimness as the rain washed at the window panes.

"I didn't kill her," she said softly. "I didn't come here at all. Paul was dead and I didn't want to live anymore. I left the mortuary and got into my car. I drove ..."

She was telling the story to herself. She didn't have to tell anything to Naomi now.

"I drove a long time. I had the razor blade in my purse—I knew what I was going to do; but I wanted to go back to Carmel. Back to the beach where we'd been so happy once. But I forgot about the fuel tank. I looked down and it was almost empty. I didn't care to drive anymore. I stopped and got out of my car and then I walked down to the beach."

The lashing of the rain had subsided into a steady flow. Anna's words were slow—almost whispered. And they were true. She hadn't come back to this house after Paul's death. It wasn't her shadow on the locked door. But if there really had been a shadow ...

For a few seconds she'd forgotten all about Naomi. Now she turned back to the chair behind the desk. It was empty.

"Mrs. Griswold!"

The woman was gone. Anna spun about. Her eyes were accustomed to the darkness now—but there was no one in the room. She went to the hall door.

"Mrs. Griswold ..."

There was a coldness in the hall. She stepped out into it. The front door stood open, the rain falling steadily beyond the curtain of the porch. Naomi

Griswold was gone—for the police, probably. The house was empty then; she was alone. She hesitated in the study doorway, uncertain for the moment as to what she should do. Mr. Marshall? Yes, that was the best way. Go back to the hospital and tell Mr. Marshall what Naomi had told her.

She took one step into the hall and then stopped. The front door that had been standing open since Naomi's flight was closing slowly from within.

CHAPTER FOURTEEN

The first she saw of him was the shadow against the glass pane in the door—the same shadow Naomi had seen yesterday at five o'clock from the other side of the glass. The latch clicked. The bolt slid home. The shadow moved toward her.

Anna stepped back into the study. By the time his heavy footsteps had reached the doorway, she was on the far side of Dr. Whitehall's desk. She groped at the darkness until her hand found the switch of the desk lamp, and then waited until he came into the cast of the window light to snap the switch. The light fell on his face. He stopped, blinking at it—an overgrown child with a sullen face.

"You ran away from the hospital," Timothy Waters said.

Anna watched his eyes. They were bland, expressionless and deadly.

"You shouldn't have run away from the hospital. They want you back there."

Anna tried to keep her voice steady.

"I was just going back," she said.

Timothy Waters stood with his big hands dangling at his sides. He wore the soiled pigskin gloves, and the frayed cuffs of his jacket sleeves crowded up on them at the wrists. Anna had difficulty remembering to watch his eyes with those hands so close to her.

"You shouldn't have run away," Waters repeated. "Everything was working out fine."

"How," Anna said, "how did you know where to find me?"

A vague smile crossed Waters' face. "I followed you," he said. "I saw you sneak out of your room. You didn't see me, but I saw you. I took the other elevator down and saw you heading for the front door. I took a short-cut to the parking lot through the ambulance entrance. You didn't have a car, I knew that. You'd have to take a cab or walk where you was going. I was sitting in my truck with the motor running when you drove off in that cab. Cabs are easy to follow. But you shouldn't have left the hospital. They want you for killing that old lady."

He could have reached out with one of those hands and taken her by the throat, or bashed in her head with a clock, had there still been a clock on the desk; and if he had, his facial expression wouldn't have changed or his eyes lost their childlike stare.

"But I didn't murder her," Anna said.

"That don't matter," he answered. "You don't have to be afraid. They won't do nothing to you. Not a beautiful lady like you. What did you do to your hands?"

The blandness of his eyes was a mask. They were as watchful as her own. She drew back her hand from the lamp.

"I tried to kill myself," she said.

"You did? Why?"

"I loved someone very much, and he—"

"Turned you down? I saw a movie like that once. But I can't imagine any man turning you down. You were always nice, not like that old bitch. 'I've been expecting you all day,' she said. Sassy, like that. All day, as if I had nothing else to do but chase out here and fix her damn pilot light! Why didn't she spend some of that money for a decent furnace? I asked her."

"Money?" Anna echoed.

"A whole stack of bills piled up on her desk. A thousand bucks! Who ever saw so much money all at once? 'What's that for?' I asked her. 'Never you mind!' she said. 'You do your work right and you'll have money of your own someday!' Bossy old bitch. I told her off and then she started preaching at me. I never could stand her preaching at me."

"You *never* could stand ...?"

Anna was too fascinated by Timothy Waters' story to miss so much as a word of it; and the word she hadn't missed was important. She stared at his face, trying to find something there to remember. He noticed the change of expression and smiled again.

"You never recognized me, did you? I knew that. The first time I was here and the second time, too, and even today in the hospital. You never recognized me at all. Nobody looks at a repair man as if he was even human."

"That's not true," Anna protested.

"But you were nice to me before when my old lady used to make me come to Dr. Whitehall. You used to smile at me, you even gave me candy once."

"Timothy," Anna said, trying the name on her memory. And then the memory came. "The child—the boy!"

"I was a punk then," Waters said. "Fourteen years old and just a little punk. I grew a whole foot in one year, what do you think of that? Then I began to fill out. I ain't a punk no more, and I don't take preaching from nobody! When the old lady said I should straighten out my thinking and handed me one of her books, I threw it at her. Then I just started throw-

ing everything. I hated her. I hated her all these years. That's why I always
left the furnace so I'd have to come back. I kept hoping I'd see her again
and show her I wasn't a punk kid she could preach at. I showed her." Waters' large eyes slowly swept the study. "I showed her what I thought of
her damn books."

"You killed her," Anna said.

"Sure, I killed her. I couldn't stop once I'd started, not until she was dead."

It was a confession of a horrible crime, but Timothy Waters didn't seem
to notice. His hands were clutched into tight fists, but that was his only
show of emotion. Anna wanted to keep him talking. She forced back the
fear and heard a quiet voice that was, unbelievably, her own ask a question.

"When did you lock the front door?"

He seemed to have forgotten. "The door?" he repeated.

"The door was locked and bolted when Mrs. Griswold came back. She
rang the bell, but nobody let her in."

Now he remembered. "That was afterward," he said. "I had to fix that
pilot light, didn't I? I had to check out the call or the supervisor would raise
hell. I didn't want nobody walking in here while I finished my work." Then,
for the first time, a brightness came into his eyes. "I changed the hands on
that clock, too. That's another thing I saw once in a movie. I gave myself
enough time to get down to that gas station on Vermont and get those
wiper blades so I'd have an alibi if anybody asked questions. Maybe I
should have kept going right on down to Mexico, you can live high for a
thousand bucks in Mexico. But this morning I read in the papers where
the police thought the killer was the old lady's nurse, so I figured there was
nothing to worry about. And there wouldn't have been if you hadn't left
the hospital. I'm sorry you did that. Now I have to kill you, too."

There was no passion in his words. He might have said that he had to
turn off a dripping faucet or plug up a hole in the roof. It was just a job
that had to be done. And Anna's tone had to match his. That was vital.

"That won't help you, Timothy," she said softly. "The police will know
I'm innocent if you do that. They don't know it now."

"They won't know," he said.

"But when they find my body."

"They won't know," he repeated. The wide-eyed stare dropped to her
wrists. "What did you use, a razor blade? It seems a woman always uses
a razor blade. I've read about it lots of times in the papers."

Anna pulled her hands back out of the light.

"The police might just figure that you came back here to do it again,"
he added, "because you felt so bad about killing the old lady. This here
ought to be as good as any razor blade."

Anna saw the silver letter opener on the desk at the same time as Waters; but he knew the dark thought in his mind before his words gave warning, and one of his big hands closed over the handle of the instrument even as she reached for it. The conversation was over. No soft words would dissuade Timothy Waters now. Anna stepped back quickly, colliding with the swivel chair behind her. The misstep threw her off balance long enough for Waters to clear the corner of the desk. She grabbed the chair and shoved it between them; but the chair was a toy in his hands. He tossed it aside, barely noticing the slight interruption in his plans. His free hand grabbed her shoulder and pulled her toward him; the hand with the letter opener jabbed wildly at one bandaged wrist. Anna twisted her body away from the slashing blade, and then, getting one foot behind one of his, shifted her weight suddenly. The camps had taught her many tricks.

When Timothy Waters' heavy body lunged backward, there was nothing to stop him until he crashed against the French doors. They sprang apart, locks, bolts and hinges torn by the clumsy, hurtling weight. The room was suddenly filled with cold air and a rush of rain, and there was the smell of freedom in it. No time now to calculate chances; Anna ran. She felt a hand grab at her skirts as she passed through the doors; she pulled loose and stumbled out onto the patio. The cement was slick from the rain, but she had to run again because Waters was hard behind her. She reached the driveway. It was like a long, narrow carpet suspended in space, waving, rolling, and at the end of it, between her and the street light, the blunt nose of Timothy Waters' truck. She reached it—if only the keys were inside! She grabbed at the door. One wrist was bleeding again, she could feel the blood streaming down her arm. The door was jammed, and before she could get it open heavy hands were clawing at her shoulders. She turned on him, flailing with both fists, helpless and hopeless until the bright beam of headlights swung suddenly into the driveway and a man's voice shouted, "Waters! Timothy Waters!"

His hands fell away from her body. Suddenly, he was gone. She caught a glimpse of a man in a raincoat racing after him, gun in hand, and then she caught a glimpse of another man, Douglas Marshall, hurrying toward her as she sank slowly to the grass....

It was a long time before Anna learned everything that happened after she sank down into the grass and dark oblivion; time to rest, time to stop trembling at every sound that came into the room, and time for Douglas Marshall to assemble the facts. And then they were all back where they had started nearly twenty-four hours earlier: Anna Bardossy small and hopeless in the hospital bed, and Dr. Huntziger and Douglas Marshall at her bedside. They watched her with eyes more tired but less strained. She looked first at the doctor and then at Marshall, and then she asked, "Did you catch him?"

"Timothy Waters? Yes," Marshall answered, "we caught him."

"He killed Dr. Whitehall."

"We know. He told us everything. He's rather enjoying himself, in fact."

"Rather?" Dr. Huntziger repeated. "I'd say he's enjoying himself immensely. His photo will be on every front page within a few hours. This is much more exciting than an imaginary two years in Korea."

Timothy Waters, half-boy, half-man, half-mad, needing only a touch to send him all the way.

"I'm so sorry," Anna said. "I sensed there was something wrong with him when he made those other calls; but we never had time to talk, and I didn't recognize him. It was only when he began to tell me about himself that I could see that child, that poor retarded child hiding behind the bravado and anger."

"Apparently Dr. Whitehall had time to talk to him," Marshall said, "too much time. She must have said all the wrong things."

"She always did, that was her worst trait. She was so opinionated, and if one didn't submit completely to her viewpoint she became abusive."

"Out of love, of course," Dr. Huntziger remarked.

Anna smiled. "Of course," she said. "That's the authoritarian way. Don't you remember how Hitler wept at the ruins of Warsaw because the wicked Poles had resisted the blitz and forced him to destroy them? And the Communists, they liberate us from our freedom out of pure love." And then Anna's eyes found Marshall's, and a tinge of guilt crept into them. "I owe you an apology, Mr. Marshall," she said. "You aren't like the other policemen at all. You've given me every chance."

She remembered. In spite of the horror of a night that was rapidly passing into another day, she remembered the angry words that had rankled at his mind, and that made everything easier.

"You needn't apologize," Marshall said. "I thought you were guilty. Dr. Huntziger was the one who had doubts from the beginning. He told me it wasn't a woman's crime."

"Professional loyalty," the doctor remarked—"and a little wishful thinking."

"He even suggested the solution," Marshall added, "although neither of us was aware of Waters' existence at the time; but I was only after a confession. It was only later—" His mind went back to those few moments of near intimacy shared with Anna as she came out of her sleep with a dead man's name on her lips. "Paul ..." she had said, and turned toward him, incredibly lovely and helpless. But the mind needed reasons, not emotions. "—I think it was when I heard of Dr. Whitehall's thousand-dollar bank withdrawal that I began to suspect a possible alternative. The money wasn't found in her house, it wasn't in your purse, and the expenditures traced to you were all made prior to the withdrawal. Unless a caller we knew nothing about had come to the house sometime between three and Waters' arrival at five, it was obvious the killer had taken the money. And that's what happened, of course. Such an amount was a fortune to Timothy Waters. He probably had murder in the back of his mind the moment he saw the money on Dr. Whitehall's desk."

"But why was it there?" Anna asked. "It wasn't like her to withdraw such sums."

"No, it wasn't. Byron Davies can vouch for that. We've questioned him again, and, now that he has nothing to fear, he admits to having asked his sister for that sum when he called on her Thursday. He'd lost the money gambling, and when she refused the loan, he went out searching for other sources. Dr. Whitehall relented after he left. Apparently she was doing a great many things out of form that day. In any event, she was preoccupied enough to leave her bank book at the teller's window—something the bank manager told me had never happened before."

Anna's eyes were troubled.

"I think I was responsible for that," she said. "Mrs. Griswold told you the truth—we did quarrel, and I did say I was leaving her. She couldn't continue without me—I knew that; but I couldn't help it. I had to have a life of my own."

And then the trouble in her eyes deepened, because behind all of the words and explanations the inescapable fact remained that what was to have been Anna Bardossy's life was now contained on a narrow slab in a mortuary on Santa Monica Boulevard.

Douglas Marshall continued quickly, "Yes, Mrs. Griswold told the truth; but not all the truth, and what she did tell came in installments. She didn't tell us about that five o'clock call at the house because, after discovering the body later, she felt guilty for not having reported the locked door."

"Mrs. Griswold will always feel guilty for something," Dr. Huntziger remarked. "She wouldn't be happy if she couldn't."

"I'm afraid you're right," Marshall said. "A little while ago she told me that she thought at the time it was Dr. Whitehall she saw behind the glass, and that the doctor wouldn't let her in because she'd protested so vigorously against her announced retirement at her morning call. She felt guilty about that, too. But at least she did tell the truth, which is more than I can say for Davies and Elrod.

"That bothered me," he added, "particularly Elrod's lie about not having disclosed to anyone the existence of another will when we know that he did tell Byron Davies. A man like Elrod doesn't lie easily. I even found myself considering, after Waters' testimony, the possibility of Harold Elrod being our fifth caller. He's spent many years working for something he believed in—it must have been a blow to realize Dr. Whitehall was planning to retire. But he would have been even worse off with her dead. The estate goes to Davies now, and it doesn't require much imagination to realize what he'll do with it. If Byron Davies had been found dead in that study, I would have been inclined to suspect Elrod. As it was, I had to go along with the obvious until I found the real reason why you tried to commit suicide, Miss Bardossy, and why Timothy Waters heard the doorbell ring. It all came back to the doorbell. The doorbell that rang when it should have remained silent. It was nothing less than a confession of murder that had been intended as an alibi.

"You see," Marshall explained, "four people came into this room today." He glanced at the window which was beginning to pale again. "Or was it yesterday? Four callers to Dr. Whitehall's house, and one of them confessed to murder without realizing it. I knew Waters was lying about his hitch in Korea, and could have been lying about the fifth caller in order to establish an alibi, the only alibi I'd heard all day. But I didn't think he had the imagination to make up the story out of whole cloth, and he didn't. Do you remember his exact words? 'Oh, it's you. I've been expecting you all day.' He didn't imagine those words; he heard them. That was the way Dr. Whitehall addressed him when he let himself in through the unlocked front door. He told us about that, too. 'One time,' he said, but that time had to be yesterday because he'd already testified that the nurse had let him in on the two previous trips. If I'd known then that Paul Kramar was dead, I'd have realized that I had my killer. But I didn't know, and when Waters, frightened by my statement that he'd been the last person to see Dr. Whitehall alive, applied the words she'd spoken to him to a mythical fifth caller, I was thrown completely off the track. And the fifth caller wasn't entirely mythical as we now know."

"She was providential," Dr. Huntziger suggested.

"But not providential enough. As Miss Bardossy pointed out to us at the time, she wouldn't have used the doorbell because she had a key. But who would have used the doorbell? Not Elrod or Mrs. Griswold or Byron Davies, each of whom knew the door was kept open all day and would have walked right in as they did on their previous calls. A stranger? That didn't tie in with the words Dr. Whitehall was quoted as having used in greeting. But what about Paul Kramar? I had the man on my mind. I'd been trying to ferret out his identity and whereabouts all day, and when Waters told that story it seemed to me he was the only logical suspect who might have come, probably in response to a call from Dr. Whitehall, and used the doorbell. You see, Miss Bardossy, at that point I wasn't beyond suspecting that your friend might have been persuaded to cancel your wedding plans under pressure or for a cash consideration."

Anna Bardossy's eyes protested. "No, not Paul," she said.

"No," Marshall agreed, "not Paul. I realized that later. But at the time of Waters' testimony there were only three possibilities: Paul Kramar, an outright lie on the part of Waters, or the possibility that the door had been locked because of the amount of cash Dr. Whitehall had brought home from the bank. And that brought me right back to the question I couldn't avoid, what had happened to the money?

"When Lansing and I returned to the hospital after finally locating Paul Kramar, I had a pretty fair idea what had happened to it. Then, when we found you were gone, Miss Bardossy, and that Waters was gone, too, I was really frightened. Fortunately, a cab driver out in front had seen you drive off in another cab. We learned its destination through the dispatcher. The rest you know."

The rest. Anna closed her eyes as if to shut out still another nightmare; but there was no shutting out anything anymore, no convenient escape from memory. She opened her eyes again. Douglas Marshall was looking at her with an expression that was both tired and relieved.

"We could have spared you that last shock if you had told us the name of your friend," he said.

A little color had begun to come back into her face. She could talk about it now.

"I didn't remember that Paul was dead," she said softly, "not until that terrible picture of Lazlo. I didn't want him hurt. He'd been hurt enough."

"Who was Lazlo?" Paul asked.

"My husband," she said. "We met at the University in Budapest right after the war. My family had all been killed by the Nazis—so had his. We were lonely and we thought it was love. It didn't work out. He dropped out of school and went into the Party—he was ambitious, or maybe just afraid. Sometimes it's the same thing. We separated finally, but were never divorced. After I escaped from Hungary, divorce was impossible. I was afraid to let him know where I was. That's why I couldn't marry Paul."

"But when you knew Lazlo was dead—"

"I had no proof, Mr. Marshall. Just a momentary glimpse of a face on a film. I told Paul about it, of course. We even went to the television studio and studied the film again, and then I started writing letters of inquiry. It takes a very long time—too long."

Anna's voice faded to a whisper. For a moment she was lost in a silence no one dared disturb, and then she continued.

"It was only a week ago that I finally received legal documentation of his death. We made our plans then. Paul was a chemist—he'd been an instructor in Vienna. We met in one of the night classes at the University. We were both refugees—from different countries, it's true; but it gave us something in common. We liked the same things and we remembered the same places and we were good for each other. It was hard all those years having to hide out like criminals. This summer I had to promise Dr. Whitehall never to see him again. It looked then as if I would never get the proof of Lazlo's death, and I meant to keep the promise; but then Paul became ill, and I knew no one could keep us apart."

No one—not even Dr. Whitehall. Now Douglas Marshall understood all there was to know about the quarrel Mrs. Griswold had overheard in the hall. Anna Bardossy wasn't afraid any more. She was free.

"I met Paul for lunch at Bannock's—we always lunched there on my day off. It was near the University, where he worked as an assistant professor. I had admired the lingerie for several weeks. At lunch he said, 'Buy it.' 'But it is so expensive!' I told him. 'Buy it,' he said, 'and buy two plane tickets for Las Vegas.' Then he gave me some money—quite a lot of money. I asked him if he'd robbed a bank, and he laughed and said it was better than that. He'd just received clearance for an important job in an industrial laboratory, and we could be married immediately. I was so happy...."

Only a few hours ago, and now that happiness was as far away as eternity. She was too exhausted to weep and too tired to feel more than the dull edge of grief—that would come later. Now she talked because talking was a necessity.

"I remember now buying those things after Paul returned to the campus, and then I drove back to the house intending to pack a small bag. When I saw Mr. Davies in the driveway, I changed my mind. I knew there would be another argument if I went in. He never forgave me for not groveling at his feet simply because I was a refugee." A tinge of bitterness came into her eyes, a smoldering spark that would have delighted the doctor's heart if he'd caught it. Anything that could fight could live. "I drove on," she added. "I remember going to a small place for tea, and then I just counted the hours until it was time for Paul to return to his apartment."

There was no more to say. At least she was free. Timothy Waters had taken the heavy clock in his hands, caught a thread of his knitted jacket cuff on the frame, and vented his fury on a woman whose tongue was quicker than her wisdom. Timothy Waters—not a woman who'd gone down to the dark beach in search of oblivion.

They had come a long way together in a few hours. Douglas Marshall looked down at her, and again that awareness of strength—of the incredible durability of life, and the incredible fragility. He looked down and remembered.

"Who can love a hero?" he said.

The words had been Anna's. She recognized them and smiled softly.

"I gave you a hard time," she said. "I'm sorry."

"I'm not, Miss Bardossy. You've helped me to understand something I couldn't see before. Gratitude and love aren't the same thing at all. They can even become enemies."

"The woman?" she asked.

"My wife," he said. "She was killed one night in Berlin—riding in a jeep with a drunken soldier. But that was a long time ago. Dr. Huntziger—" Marshall was a man with a watch on his wrist again, and work to do— "I'm going to do a little extracurricular investigation in the field of expatriated professionals. It seems to me that we have enough killers in this country. I think we could make room for another healer."

"Now you're beginning to speak my language, Mr. Marshall," Huntziger said.

"Good—we'll talk it out together over a thick steak as soon as your patient has decided to live a while longer. You may learn, Dr. Bardossy, that having the same things to forget can give people as much in common as having the same things to remember."

And then he went out of the room, and left her to watch the gray window light lengthening across the ceiling. It was just before dawn, that time when life reached its lowest ebb ... and then began again.

THE END